REA

COMING THROUGH

COMING THROUGH

Three Novellas

DAVID HELWIG

With a Foreword by Noah Richler

B&B
Bunim & Bannigan
New York Charlottetown

Published in the United States by
Bunim & Bannigan, Ltd.
PMB 157 111 East 14th Street New York, NY 10003-4103
Bunim & Bannigan, Ltd.
Box 636 Charlottetown, PEI C1A 7L3 Canada

www.bunimandbannigan.com

Manufactured in the United States of America

Design by Jean Carbain

The Music of No Mind first appeared in
New Quarterly

Grateful acknowledgment is given to
Porcupine's Quill for permission to reprint in this volume:
The Music of No Mind
A Prayer to the Absent

Library of Congress Cataloging-in-Publication Data

Helwig, David, 1938–
Coming through : three novellas / David Helwig ; with a foreword by Noah Richler. — 1st ed.
p. cm.
ISBN-13: 978-1-933480-16-9 (trade hardcover : alk. paper)
ISBN-10: 1-933480-16-5 (trade hardcover : alk. paper)
I. Title.

PR9199.3.H445C66 2007
813'.54—dc22

2007012810

ISBN: 978-1-933480-16-9
ISBN-10: 1-933480-16-5

1 3 5 7 9 8 6 4 2

First edition

Contents

Foreword

ix

The Man Who Finished Edwin Drood

1

The Music of No Mind

69

A Prayer to the Absent

131

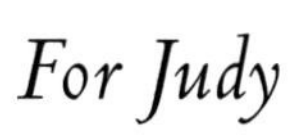

For Judy

FOREWORD

NOVEMBER is David Helwig's month. In *The Year One,* a book-length poem, he writes:

> the leaves of the wild roses are yellowing,
> the nights growing colder, soon the garden
> will be stripped.

November is when the wise take cognizance of their days and grasp those diminishing flashes of beauty the dying month offers with tempered enlightenment. It is the month when time seems at its most extended, the full and spent fury of the summer behind us, but still vivid, and the frozen white of winter stretching long months away. We become, in the face of it, either patient, or slightly mad, poised as we are on the cusp of some inevitable reckoning when order, meaning, and a tidy resolution matter less in the inconclusive story of which we have become a part.

I'd hazard that Canadians, Helwig's people, feel this November chill most acutely. Here, Northern winds augur that winter will be long (it always is) and cold (it always is), so that Canadians learn to face the winter as animals do—wondering, at some behavioral level, who among their number will "come through" to see the spring. November is a creed inscribed on the land—Helwig one of its subtle, lyrical interpreters.

The obdurate, rocky terrain north of the city of Kingston, where Helwig lived for almost two decades, the countryside where his novella, *A Prayer to the Absent,* is set—is terrain that one of his late contemporaries, the poet Al Purdy, once famously described as "the country of our defeat." Helwig, more generous in spirit, was nevertheless profoundly influenced by it, the land there and on Prince Edward Island fundamental to the atmosphere of his stories.

Born in 1938, Helwig was raised in Ontario in Toronto and in Niagara-on-the-Lake, not far from Buffalo, NY. He won a scholarship from General Motors, one of several car manufacturers with assembly plants in southern Ontario, which allowed him to study English at the University of Toronto. After graduating, he moved to England, where he received his M.A. from Liverpool in 1962. He then returned to Canada, having accepted a position at Queen's University in Kingston, Ontario. Helwig taught there until 1974. Then for two years, he commuted to Toronto to work for CBC TV Drama. From 1980 on, Helwig lived in Kingston as a freelance writer with very occasional teaching assignments at Queens. He moved to Montreal in 1992, and finally settled, in 1996, in the Canadian maritime province of Prince Edward Island, rehabilitating an old farmhouse there.

The years in which Helwig started writing were heady ones for Canada. During the nineteen sixties and seventies, the country was forming its present identity—through the nascent separatist politics of Québec and, in Ottawa, the urbane and sophisticated nationalism of Pierre Elliot Trudeau's Liberal Party. The country was discovering itself through argument, and much of this reconnoitering took place in books from small independent publishers: Les Editions du Boréal in Québec; The House of Anansi and Coach House Press in Toronto; and—occasionally from abroad—the ten books that Helwig published during that time with Oberon, a publisher based in Ottawa. This singular, exhilarating moment of Canada's cultural realization (when the sheer paucity of working artists meant that the stage was freely shared by those hoisting themselves onto it) was reflected, too, in the sexual liberation of the day, when "Kingston being Kingston," wrote Helwig in his later memoir, *The Names of Things* "what began with two people became a triangle, a rectangle, a many-sided polygon." There were casualties—Helwig's first marriage among them. It was, Helwig wrote in *The Year One:*

> the decade when everybody's life was
> broken, remade.

By then, ensconced by the Prince Edward Island hearth that he had built himself, Helwig understood—remembering a line that Margaret Atwood, another of his contemporaries, had written—that

> *There is only one of everything,*
> she wrote, meaning love, meaning joy
> when, stricken, you can't count beyond the first sound,
> the outcry. And yet the mornings and the nights
> return, and we breathe, breathe, breathe.

The years in Kingston were Helwig's summer, though it is the author's November that has become him most—that age of late assessment when wit is also possible. In November we learn to consider life at a distance because to do otherwise would be to invite weariness and the possibility of an earlier death. Of course Helwig had been doing that already—we're brought up doing so in Canada, where the effects of living away from where so much of the discussed action is, and of being Nature's tolerated guests (we do not forget this fact easily), accrue to our circumstance a curious equanimity.

So, in *The Man Who Finished Edwin Drood,* an affecting story of unfinished lovers' business explicitly tinged by Helwig's affinity for the Victorian literature he taught (until, understanding the course of a life, he noticed that a former student's class was more popular than his and, choosing not to compete with her "spring," he quit), the narrator—the Wicked Uncle—observes, or even disdainfully *admires* the way life, inchoate life, can whip back at you in ways that would be outrageous to anticipate. Helwig's shadowy, hearthside gothic tale ("fun to write," the author has said) is about a mortifying turn of events all conscientious lovers have dreaded at some point in their lives: a cuckolded husband, gravely ill, is invited back into the house, where he dies. And yet the Wicked Uncle, instigator of the wife's deceit, finds a measure of reward—late happiness even.

Wicked Uncle is, in fact, a perspicacious man, who is only superficially unlike another of Helwig's men of November, the narrator of *The Music of No Mind,* the second of Helwig's novellas collected here (the novella is a form the author has always liked). An unnamed professor replaces the late Denman Tarrington in a lecture series at a provincial Canadian university. He rails, he offends, he confesses. His meandering soliloquies seem extemporaneous and invoke, among other things, the life of a Canadian painter, the use of mirrors in art, the lessons of a bygone badminton game, and of musicology too. (Helwig has appeared as bass soloist in Handel's *Messiah,* Bach's *St. Matthew Passion* and Mozart's *Requiem*—he once wanted to sing professionally.) His digressions are the author's frequently hilarious game. His Professor, strutting and fretting his late hour upon the stage, is illustrating, before he is heard no more, the point that Helwig makes in *The Year One,* where he writes that

> There is nothing to understand. Consider
> Beethoven and his art of fragments which contain
> themselves and their consequences, falling to bits
> to prove that design is whole because it is partial;
> as every poem is a syllabary captured
> by an illusion, syntax.

We choose, in time, the landscape that suits. In *A Prayer to the Absent,* Helwig portrays a retired policeman, Carman Deshane, and the proprietress of an old curio and antique store, Norma, achieving a certain harmony between themselves and with the rocky terrain to which Al Purdy was referring in his poem, "The Country North of Belleville," though it would best be described in Helwig's story as the "the country of our making."

The one time we met (in Kentville, Nova Scotia, in 2004), Helwig told me these two characters belonged to novels that he had abandoned, but they would not go away, and so he threw them into this story together. Life is like that. We stumble towards each other and into stories started a long time prior, the endings of which we only rarely recognize in real time. Carman and Norma speak to Helwig's fascination with characters as stories in themselves, to his early love of the stage, and to his particular penchant—unmistakable in these three novellas—for *situations* that are placid but volatile and frequently comic for that reason: the ex-husband invited back to the hearthside by a wife who, for some absurd reason, has not stopped loving him; a slightly deranged professor admonishing *life,* trying against better knowledge to make some kind of story of it before it's too late—and, in the last, a tender story of reconciliation with November's situation that is really quite profound.

"We get one life, we do what we can, we go," says Helwig in *The Names of Things.* It's that one of everything again—coming through the point and simple truth of it.

—Noah Richler
Toronto, March 2007

COMING THROUGH

THE MAN WHO FINISHED EDWIN DROOD

I SPAKE unto the Dutchess, and she said, "You wouldn't dare."

"Dutchess . . ."

"No," she said.

Back to staring at the fire, the tongues of yellow flame reaching up from the bright red embers of the logs as I stroked my little beard, and neither of us broke the silence. However, the Dutchess knows me for what I am. Recalcitrant is a word she has used, a word among many. Pig-headed. Two words among many. The Dutchess knows me for what I am, since what I am has been her fellow for years now. Ever since. Yes, ever since. So, knowing me for what I am, the Dutchess knows that I will do as I please. She will state, or even more likely overstate, her opinion, and I, when the fit is on me, will ignore it. That is what we were both thinking as we sat in comfortable chairs, the doors of the airtight open so we could see the flames, a cold rain falling outside, wind howling in the chimney. Gather round children, gather close to the hearth, and Wicked Uncle will tell you things, such things. Tell us what? Of girls born out of their time, a face like Leonardo's "Girl with an Ermine," body by Cranach perhaps, the tiny waist and florid curve of arse below. In fact, I had forgotten about her since I saw her in the Registry Office yesterday, but the sweet thought of wickedness brought her back. Most lawyers send a clerk or a title searcher to the Registry Office, but I go myself. The phone never rings there. You hear a quiet bustle of pages turning and pencils scratching, and you save the money paid to the clerk or title searcher. Yesterday I was rewarded for my industry by the sight of this exotic thing, a face and body from another time, something from old paintings in old books, and Wicked Uncle looked upon her with the eyes of desire. I told the Dutchess about her, the Dutchess being tolerant of Wicked Uncle's eye. Without it she would not be here, would not be the Dutchess, would have another name altogether.

I have been reading, secretly. Grewgious defines true love. Chapter Eleven. Hush, the Dutchess will hear your thoughts. She stirred in her chair, knowing, and I quickly turned my mind to something innocent, the swelling behind of the Renaissance Girl, and the Dutchess was still again. It is the nature of Wicked Uncles to feel such stirrings of fancy, and the Dutchess ignores them. She was wicked enough once. Is still, perhaps. Tonight, I can tell, she will leave me limp and panting and sated, and she feels she has nothing to fear from my concupiscence, whereas what I had just proposed to her was a trespass.

No Trespassing. Trespassers Will Be Prosecuted To The Full Extent Of The Law. I did that once, prosecuted a trespasser, who just happened to be the brother of a previous wife of the trespassed upon, and somehow the case got laughed out of court. Not the only time. It is a good thing I don't take the law too seriously. It has a certain baroque splendor from time to time, and I enjoy the ingenuity of legal argument, have some bent for it, this verbal logic run wild, but mostly the process of law is a matter of bullying, conniving, and the not quite illicit use of influence. Still, every process must be lubricated somehow. Note to self: look up meaning of *lubricious.*

There can be no coolness, no lassitude, no doubt, no indifference, no half fire and half smoke state of mind in a real lover. Grewgious again. The Dutchess stirred and I stood and left the fire, made my way to the kitchen window and observed how the wind and the rain beat on those tall sentinels, the sunflowers. They would soon be killed by frost and stand like dead soldiers of some vanished war. *Dark intangible presentiments of evil.* The wind shook the flowers and the rain poured down, and the chill sent me back to the fire where the Dutchess sat straight in her chair, an old fashioned college clipboard on her knees as she studied the flames and now and then made a note. She was at work on another article, prelude to an edition.

"The cheaper sort of red herrings are always too salt," she said, reading to me from one of her old books. I made an agreeing noise. Red herrings, yes, yes, of course. In the last few years, the Dutchess has come into her own, her studies of the history of domestic life just sharp enough to please a feminist audience while curious enough in their detail to intrigue the rest. At first I was dismayed at her success—it was bright eyes and smooth skin and lubricious afternoons that I had bargained for. One evening, as I sat at the large antique desk in my office, irritable and lonely (the Dutchess away at a conference on the Invention of the Mangle or some such thing) I wrote a title, *The Boy Who Got Everything Wrong,* and after the title I began to tell the little children one of Wicked Uncle's stories. After a secret pursuit of some months, I was able to announce to the Dutchess that I had written a story for children, and that it would appear. When she read the book, she said I had stolen the whole thing from her anecdotes about a hopeless little gaffer she had met earlier in her professional life, when she was doing gigs as a substitute teacher. Very sniffy she was, and told me not to steal from her again, and I claimed it was all invented from my own rich imagination, and we didn't speak for three days. Ever since she has been ready for war on the subject. Note: *lubricious,* also *lubricous* and (archaic) *lubric,* means just what Wicked Uncle thought it meant.

Autumn. It is the time of year for it. *A fire shines out upon the fast-darkening scene, involving in shadow the pendent masses of ivy and creeper covering the building's front. As the deep Cathedral-bell strikes the hour, a ripple of wind goes through these at their distance, like a ripple of the solemn sound . . .* I could hear from the other room the Dutchess bubbling like a boiling pot, aware of my thoughts, my trespass on her territory, but there was no stopping the thing now. I would ride it into the winter, and she would perhaps retaliate, and on we would go. The sunflowers held up their heads under the cold rain, and the Dutchess made notes, and the wood in the stove burned. The season moved on; the color of the leaves had begun to change, showing flashes of red on the rolling hills. A fox crossed the road on dainty feet. The Dutchess does not forgive, but she lets things pass and gets on with what must be.

The wind outside was loud and the rain beat against the window of the little back room where I sat on a straight chair, shivering but not unhappy to be there in the dark. The night was full of voices. This was once the Doctor's House, and these small rooms at the back, probably built for servants, now served as a home for shelves of books never consulted and occasionally as guest rooms if both the little Dutchesses arrived at once with children in tow. The little Dutchesses are Orland's daughters. After they were born and before I met her, the Dutchess had been fixed, although she was still a young woman.

Here once upon a time, servants lay still in their beds, muddled girls who hoped to find a farmer or fisherman as tall and straight as the sunflowers. One stood outside the door, listening. The doctor dreamed of new refinements of disease. Rooms away, the Dutchess was snoring quietly. I had lain awake for a while, and then I had got out of bed without disturbing her and wandered down the hall to the small back rooms where one might wait for ghosts to come. Orland collected ghosts. His book was on the shelf near where I sat. Orland was a good bit older than the Dutchess, but she and I are of an age.

It was when the world was young, and I was breathing my few months of Irish air, that the Dutchess was born of respectable Dutch parents in the Netherlands and was named Marijke Van Zuylen. At the time the family emigrated, she was three years old. I had come ashore a couple of years earlier. When I first learned all this, I started to call her Dutch, which evolved to Dutchess. She calls herself Mary Van Zuylen these days, but at the time I met her, she was Meg Fothergill, so renamed in and by marriage to Orland Fothergill, famous folklorist and cuckold. She was also called—by me but not out loud—the Dairy Queen. Young Meg, child bride, though already mother of two, had perfect creamy skin, breasts that watched serenely from low cut dresses; she gave the wonderful impression of being made of the finest quality dairy products. All butter and eggs. And I so lean and hungry. The Dutchess has blossomed a little since, developed an aristocratic scope, and I have kept in step.

Just how miffed would she be if I went ahead? It had been a long wait since my one thin book, and now this idea had arrived, prompted by what she told me about her work, (as had the last—I'd have to admit that). Well then, she was an inspiration. Why was she so possessive? Did she have to keep it all to herself? I could have ideas too, with a little stirring about. The further history of that evil man John Jasper was much to my taste. Let the Wicked Uncle enquire into the possibilities of his wickedness. *I love you . . . I would pursue you to the death.* There had been a time when I was determined to make the Dutchess leave her husband, but she wished to stay, and I had pursued her to the death. The wind shook the window and told old stories. She had no right to prevent me.

Farewell, my sweet, I'm on my way. The morning was foggy, and in the dim early light, only the few trees close to the road were visible. Beyond, hills and the salt sea. Two large black crows rose from the side of the highway where they had found roadkill to feed upon, and they flew blackly off into the mist. *Oh Billy Magee Magar.* Orland taught me that song about crows pecking the eye of a dead horse, same tune as all those other fierce songs, the folk not having a wide range but a good ear for a note or two. Orland teaching old songs and his wife waving her milky things.

The Dutchess teaches Life Skills three days a week, but this wasn't one of her days. On her teaching days, we sometimes drive the long road to town together, but this morning I had left her all loose and soft in a pink dressing gown, surrounded by Victorian recipes, the bag of flour ready to be thrown all over self and kitchen. Not a tidy cook, the Dutchess; we are not a tidy pair, things fall into disorder about us. Deep in her researches, she produced more food than even two well-grown adults could eat, and I found myself taking this and that—Lardy Cakes, Devonshire Splits, Corn Chowder, Lancashire Hot Pot, Skirlie, Leek Pie—off to town to be distributed.

Another crow in the mist. *Oh Billy Magee Magar.* Note to self: try to find the words for the song. A truck with Nova Scotia plates raced past, in a hurry to be somewhere. Life Skills. How to go out for milk. Reading the label on the aspirin bottle before feeding them all to the baby. How to write a check, but not if you don't have a bank account. She does a brisk business with criminals, the thought being that if they knew how to get along better they would stop their criminal behavior. Judging by criminals I have represented in court, this might have something to it, for they are, most of them, tediously foolish and fucked up. Defending these people is always tricky; they don't like you telling the court they're stupid. Often Dwayne or Kevin Thief will have ideas about his own defense, and a good deal of time is spent explaining that he shouldn't say he was far off in another city, since a constable grabbed him ten minutes after the theft, two blocks away, with the loot in his possession. Send him to the Dutchess to learn Life Skills.

More crows in more mist. *Oh Billy Magee Magar.* A few days back, the Dutchess came upon a farmer cutting cabbages and got a box of them at a good price, and we spent last night cutting them up and laying them down in a crock for sauerkraut. And yesterday afternoon, stirred by the sight of machines in the fields, I took my yearly look at Sir Charles God Damn sonneteering in 1886 on the potato harvest. *A clamour of crows that fly in from the wide flats where the spent tides mourn.* Same crows fly still over the fields. *Oh Billy Magee Magar.* Now downhill to the bridge over the river, line of cars, fog thickens, cormorants on the abutments, birds of ill omen, murderous sailors out there invisible in their dories, the oars splashing as they come toward you to do you to death. The old seas were full of wooden ships instead of debris. *In memory of HECTOR CAMPBELL Master Mariner who was lost with all his crew whilst in command of the ship Aeternia of St John N.B. on a voyage from Rangoon to Liverpool in Nov. 1872 Aged 33 years.* The Dutchess found that in the graveyard up the road. She is fond of death, the Dutchess is, reminded by it that she is so largely and voluminously alive and has years of trouble yet to make for me. Now and then I wondered if she had always, always, always been faithful, if she didn't just once find a lad whose need for Life Skills included warming between the white cheeks of his instructor. She had deceived Orland so easily, but then he was older and suffered from one of those tedious things, what do they call them? Dysfunctions. He could breed but not please, and the Dairy Queen, in all her creamy whiteness, insisted on being pleased. I (she being permanently plugged) could please but not breed.

Into the city, a church spire appearing out of the fog. Dickensian. Fateful word.

The Wicked Uncle would, must, evoke the Wicked Uncle. Later in the day

I would go to the university library and look at some things. The Dutchess had arranged her schedule so that she gave her weekly class there—History 387, as adjunct lecturer—in the morning of one of her Life Skills days. They continued to have her, but as money grew ever tighter, there would be more pressure to send her away. Who was interested in the History of Domestic Life, when it was possible to study Computer Science and Entrepreneurial Development? Life Skills, Parts 2 and 3. Still, her course was part of Women's Studies, and that was still a good racket. *There were three crows sat on a tree, oh Billy Magee Magar.* I parked the car and stopped on the way to the office to buy a package of cigars for Elaine, my secretary. It was her birthday and I was one of the few who knew of her secret vice.

I spake unto the Dutchess, and here is what I said.

"Wouldn't it be a grand thing, Dutchess, if your chap was known as the Man Who Finished *Edwin Drood*?"

"You wouldn't dare."

"Dutchess . . ."

"No," said the Dutchess.

Chaps do not encroach on the territory. Rule One.

How is the territory to be delimited? Question One apropos Rule One.

In the course of her rummagings a while back, the Dutchess came upon a book called *What Shall We Have For Dinner? Satisfactorily Answered by Numerous Bills of Fare for from Two to Eighteen Persons,* a Victorian curiosity published as the work of Lady Maria Clutterbuck. We discovered it in a bookstore in Moncton, while we were on our way back from Montreal. Just her line of country, of course, made more piquant by the fact that Lady Maria Clutterbuck was in fact Catherine Dickens, wife of the Inimitable, as he liked, grandiloquently but fairly enough—there was no other like him, god knows—to call himself. She has been looking into Dickens while doing an article on the book and planning to do a new edition of it. By the rules of East and West Dutchessville, that means that I should keep my hands off him. I will admit that the idea of the unfinished novel came to mind because the Dutchess left various biographies of the Inimitable lying around, and doing a little rummaging of my own, I was reminded that Dickens had died in the midst of darkish Drood. I discovered that the book had been finished by others, and yet the thing gnawed, nagged, picked at my eyes, and so, on a cool and rainy afternoon as we sat by the fire, the picture of domestic bliss, I got up my courage and spoke. John Jasper, Wicked Uncle, demanded it of me.

A play, I thought. Time to go back to the theatre perhaps. The theatre is where I had met the Dutchess, far off in Upper Canada, when she was quiet, blue-eyed Meg. Butter wouldn't melt in her mouth, I thought, though there were rumors. I was a student at law and bored senseless. When I saw an advertisement, auditions for *The School for Scandal,* I went along. I had displayed myself in high school and once or twice as an undergraduate, to notable effect I always thought, and my lovely mother did too. I fancied myself as the hypocrite Joseph Surface and was non-plussed all to hell to find myself cast as his honest brother, Charles. The hero. I never wanted to be the hero but was set to it by the hand of Fate, old busybody, old pimp, and I found myself playing scenes with a demure young woman, modest as could be, who, I was astonished to learn, was married and the mother of children. Though she seldom spoke except to read her lines, she looked at me from time to time, and her eyes were so very blue that I looked back and looked back. I met her ancient husband (younger then than I am now) who was good and true and adoring. When the little imp playing Sir Peter hinted that she could be had, I was immensely displeased. That he might know, or think he knew. By then, I was in a lather about her. I wanted to be with her in the paradise garden. The night she first appeared in costume, her white breasts scandalously, sumptuously, maddeningly on display in a naughty eighteenth-century décolletage, I felt a bit dizzy and thought I might faint. Just as we were about to make an entrance that night, she turned to me, plumped up her titties and said, "Don't you think I should be playing Lady Teazle?" Lady Teazle, who'll tease and perhaps do a good deal more, the misbehaving wife of an older husband. Two lines into the rehearsal of the scene I dried, and no amount of prompting would bring the lines back. Later, off-stage, and passing through the dark wings of the little theatre toward the dressing rooms, she so close in front of me, I put my hand on her bare shoulder, and she stopped, and I drew her to me, put my arm around her neck and pressed my hardening thing against her sweet Dutch arse and bent to kiss her skin. She gave a soft sigh, and that night we consummated the affair behind a bush in a back lane.

I am touched still by the memory of how she began to come to my little apartment up a flight of stairs in a gray stone house, but the question is, when did she begin to have firm opinions, when did Rule One come into effect, and Rule Two and so on? I approve, on the whole and of necessity. Dairymaids must grow up and become Dutchesses, who cause a very different brand of trouble, but I can't perfectly tell just when it happened. I suppose she always got her own way. She had decided to have me, I am told, and did, got herself into my bed in spite of the difficulties of family life, but I was meant to be a passing fancy, and I refused to pass. Perhaps the flood of tears when she got on the train with me, leaving Orland and the little Dutchesses behind, washed away some kind of innocence.

A play about the Drood case. Would that bring it all back? We have escaped. We are two settled bodies somewhere *nel mezzo del cammin di nostra vita,* and neither much wants to venture into any dark woods nor trail about the underworld following ghosts, not even the wiser ones. Besides, Drood has been made into a Broadway Musical. Still it lies there, always unfinished, as provoking in its way as was the sweet young arse of Orland's wife.

"No," said the Dutchess. "No, no, no."

Late afternoon, and Wicked Uncle sat in the chair behind his office desk and looked out the back window at the rare autumn sunlight on a brick wall, light the rich color of a fine pilsener in a tall glass, falling into an alley where cats were known to roam.

> *Down in the street cries the cat's meat man,*
> *Fango dango with his barrow and can.*

One of the comic ditties that the Inimitable performed with his sister, when his father was trotting him about showing everyone that the little bugger was smart as a tick, stood up on tables to perform, clever boy, clever boy, and learning that he was somehow to be famous. Like the little Mozart, though without the same divine skills. Still, brother and sister performing together, it all comes out in the wash. Wicked Uncle was paging through two volumes of biography when he should have been dealing with a zoning dispute as described in the file on his table. Swot up details, then go to see the town clerk to enquire what can be done to allow said restaurant to build said deck in said alley, tastefully screened from what went on round about. Tomorrow. I am on good terms with the town clerk most of the time but mustn't be seen to push. The actual zoning bylaw and appended survey not perhaps relevant, but must be committed to memory. In the outer office, Elaine is scanning something we have on CD-ROM that might be of use, but we both know that what will be of most use is flattery: tickling the clerk who will tickle the council.

The days grow short, the sunlight precious to us here in the north end of the continent. In a bit, Wicked Uncle is meeting the Dutchess for a meal, and I am very tempted to drink more than my share of the wine and to eat to excess and later to sit by the fire sipping Jameson's and bring on bad dreams anent the lost body of Edwin Drood. Murder most foul, a delicious thing. Of course we don't know that he has been murdered, not for certain, though young Charley Dickens says he asked and was told. Poor dead Drood, poor dead Ed. And John Jasper, Wicked Uncle, a black figure in deep mourning, leaning on the sundial waiting for the girl who is frightened of him, of his menace and adoration, who shrinks from his touch even as he claims her, claims even her anger and scorn. Delicious. Perhaps it should be a movie. Narrated in the third person by an educated, musical voice At the end, we see a man in a cell, and as the camera moves in, we are aware that he is speaking, and that the voice is that same one we have been listening to, that the story we have been told is his own.

The door opened, and Elaine came in and caught Wicked Uncle staring out into Cat's Alley at the last of the late sun.

"Jane the Carpenter phoned," Elaine said. "When you were at the Registry Office."

Elaine doesn't like Jane the Carpenter and disapproves of our friendship with her, jealous because Jane comes to the house, although Elaine has been invited the house and has declined. Elaine is, in her spirit, a creature of the marshes, at ease only among the dank places and foul vapours. She reads a lot of magazines—always a sign of rancour and disappointment. Though she is efficient and polite to clients, her belief that life has failed her goes deep. This dates from her husband's absconding with a cocktail waitress. It was then she taught herself to smoke cigars.

"Have you ever read a book called *The Mystery of Edwin Drood,* Elaine?"

"I don't read books," she said. "You know that. Except romances."

"You like those?"

"No, not especially, but they pass the time."

"And magazines."

"If my stupid reading habits are all we have to talk about, can I go home?"

"What will you do when you get home?"

"Mother's coming for dinner."

"What will you feed her?"

"TV dinners. It's all she'll eat."

"And then you settle back with brandy and a good cigar."

"She doesn't drink, and I don't smoke when she's there."

"I'll see you in the morning Elaine."

Note to self: look up those old pictures to see if the girl in the registry office really does look like them. Don't faces change from generation to generation? Or is the change in what we choose to see?

Come close to the fire, children, and Wicked Uncle will remember things from oh so long ago. Jackdaws, Harlech, being left in the rain, hiking along the road. All of that, and more. It was today's crows started it, at their business of scavenging in the cold morning, the crows leading me on to the rooks of Cloisterham, and those leading to the jackdaws on the broken stones of Harlech castle, black birds, gray ruins, and in the distance the gray sea.

When Meg and I ran away, that was where we went, to England and then to North Wales. Once she had decided to go, she wanted to go very far, spent a little legacy from a grandmother to get us there. There was a plan somewhere, if only in my mind, that we might get as far as Belfast, my birthplace, but we never did, a result of poverty, grief, and the inability to stop screwing long enough to make a plan. We were scared of what we had done, of what might come of it, and half strangers to each other, but in the darkness there was no place for thought.

I looked out the window and saw the reflection of fire on the glass, our seasonal burning, wood fires as the days get shorter. In the cities, where I grew up, the steam pipes heat the malls and office buildings and apartments, heat by numbers. I turned away from the coming night full of other worlds, wandering planets, and I stared into the flame of the wood fire and tried to remember what it was we fought about at Harlech, standing in the ruins of the ancient castle, looking over the field of sheep toward the sea, but I can't, and I won't go out to the kitchen to ask the Dutchess as she stands on a floor covered with debris making a milk punch from the Clutterbuck book. Her cheeks will be a little red from working over the heat of the stove, her face intent. I can't bring myself to enquire what we broke our hearts about that day. She walked away from me as I stood by the gray castle wall, and when I turned to look for her among the ruins, there was no-one. The gray day dissolved into rain. I waited for a bit, and then I went back to where we had left a rented car, expecting to find her sitting in it, perhaps still angry. It was gone. For the last two days I had been driving, wrong side of the road, wrong side of the car, always in danger of sideswiping an oncoming lorry or a stone wall. She had never once taken the wheel or wanted to, and now she had driven away. I was as bare as the stone and as old, frightened in an empty place, unable for a moment even to be angry, but as absolutely alone as a man dying. I walked back into the castle and looked down the hill at the dirty-colored sheep grazing in the rain, and I couldn't tell whether the wetness on my face was rain or tears.

I walked into the town, rain wetting my hair and clothes, and saw the car in front of a stone cottage, and thinking she must be in there, I knocked, and a short woman with bright red cheeks, rivers of broken veins, an apron over a housedress, looked at me and said in her beautiful Welsh lilt, "Oh yes, your wife has said you would be along," and when I was in the house, she told me which room and that tea would be ready in a few minutes. Meg was waiting for me in the bed, her back to me, and she said nothing as I undressed and climbed in and lay behind her, never seeing her face until we were done, and by then it was dark, and we went down the stairs for fried eggs and bread and butter and strong tea in front of a coal fire.

I put another log in the stove, and as I sat down in the rocking chair, the Dutchess came in with mugs of punch. Settled in her place, she took up a book.

"It does sometimes happen" she read aloud, "that when you are living in the country, in the neighborhood of considerate gentlefolks who possess game preserves, that they now and then make presents of a hare and a few rabbits to the poor cottagers in their vicinity."

"No-one has ever brought us a rabbit," I said. I warmed my hands around the cup of hot spicy punch. Dickensian punch on this dark and droodly afternoon.

Late at night, a celebratory glass of Jameson's in hand, Wicked Uncle stood by the back window and looked out across the lawn to the patch of overgrown woodland behind, celebrating another day of living, another night, the brightness of the moonlight on the lawn and on the leaves, leaves which were now beginning to fall. The owners of the property behind live far away. When we came here, the owner was an old woman somewhere in New Jersey, but she died and her nephews have inherited, and they are letting the house fall down and the land grow up in weeds and brush and trees. The apple trees have been untended and unpruned for generations. They produce small bitter pulpy apples that catch the light on sunny fall days, a parody of harvest.

We came to this house loaded with debt, half frozen between the futile wheezing of the old furnace and the gaping holes to the outdoors. I knew nothing about country life, how to chop wood or build walls. Trapped in a crawl space trying to insulate, my face covered with mud, panting with fear, I knew I would never survive. The trees in the woods behind were black and dead, covered with moss and lichen, drowned in brush, and at the edge of the lawn an old shed looked as if it might contain bones of murder victims, tools of torture, the impedimenta of witchcraft. It stands there still. Though the house is beautiful now, and warm, and the Dutchess has made gardens and lawns, we have never touched the shed. It is built across the property line, and some superstition has kept me from tearing it down or even hiring someone to tear it down. Just once in a brave moment of that first month—the house a ruin, too old, too broken, and we too poor—I went into the shed, and there I saw the remains of other lives. Such things. A basket full of the heads of dolls. Broken dishes. An inexplicable piece of fur that might have been the skin of a dead cat. Old iron and tin, three windows with broken glass. An enamel chamber pot with a rusted hole in the bottom. I looked quickly and went away, closed the door behind me, and left the place to the spiders and mice and skunks. Do so still, the gray rotting wood a reminder of the cold days when some dark thing waited in the woods to take our heads, when we were still trying to learn to be together, in hell and paradise once an hour, organizing the little Dutchesses to come for part of the summer, counting the change in our pockets.

I stare into the world painted with moonlight, looking for the answer to the mystery of how to finish the unfinished. If I were writing another book for children, it would be simple. Wicked Uncle would smile mysteriously upon the boy hero, and suddenly everything would change. Time would fold, and the two of them would be sitting in a Victorian drawing room, heavy drapes, much furniture softly upholstered, a coal fire burning, fog outside, and a bright-eyed figure with curly brown hair would burst into the room and begin doing imitations. There he would be, Dickens himself, and the young hero would contrive to ask him just what he meant to do about Drood and be entertained by his mime of the imp Deputy stoning Durdles home through the drunken night.

By the time of Drood, of course, he wasn't a bright-eyed creature but a man prematurely aged, deep wrinkles, one lame foot, priming himself with oysters and champagne in order to get up in front of the audience and kill Nancy one more time, and if he were to appear in front of me, I would have nothing to say except to warn him that he was exhausting himself. During his last appearances in London, on the first night he read the Sikes and Nancy scenes, his pulse went from 80 to 112, and on the second night to 118. His body was giving out.

We cannot have ghosts for the wishing though Wicked Uncle invoke them with Jameson's. The Dutchess lay loose and white and happy in our bed, and Wicked Uncle stumbled about the cold house with a glass of whiskey in his hand and a black toque on his head for warmth, seeking visions when he ought to sleep and dream. I turned from the moonlit lawn and the old shed to one of the bookshelves Jane the Carpenter had built there. I found Orland's book of ghost stories, and opened it though I didn't know what I was looking for. Orland's name had come up in conversation twice recently, and I was suspicious. I read a few lines about horses that would not cross a bridge, knowing, as horses do, that an evil creature lurked on or near it, and as I read the lines, I was shocked to hear them in Orland's voice, as if he might be beside me reading aloud. Not the ghost I wanted, no ghost at all, for Orland was alive back there somewhere. The girls visited him, and he and the Dutchess wrote letters. I didn't know what they said, didn't wish to know, it would make the small hairs bristle. Monsters. The other people. Best keep them on television where they belong.

These thoughts stoned me home to bed, the glass left half full on a table behind me, lights out, time for sweet oblivion, dreams.

"Where were you?" the Dutchess said, as I climbed back into bed.

"Looking for ghosts."

"Danger of finding them," she mumbled sleepily.

"Know it too well."

She rolled over and cuddled herself against me, all hot and soft.

"Orland," I said. "It was Orland's ghost."

"Yes," she said, "I suppose so."

Then, instantly, she was asleep.

Fire burning, rain falling.

THE MYSTERY OF EDWIN DROOD COMPLETE. *Part the Second. "By the Spirit Pen of Charles Dickens, through a Medium." Published in Brattleborough, Vermont, U.S.A. 1873.*

Dickens comes back from the dead, as Drood, perhaps, came back from the dead to confront his murderer. The medium sits up late at night in a dark room with a single candle, listening to the wind, waiting, saying magic words, until at last the pen begins to move on its own and the Inimitable gives dictation, sitting in the other world with his toasted cheese, laughing and crying at the antics of his own creations. Inventions in the mind of a ghost. How far from where I am, seeing the green of winter wheat on the reseeded potato fields, the black silhouettes of ducks and geese moving across the sky, a bull standing in a paddock in the autumn rain. The Dutchess is silent these days, and I suspect her of plotting something.

At the university library I found an old book on Drood, 1912, dated from Bay Tree Lodge, Hampstead. All those English houses with their cozy names. Note to self: get a sign, Wicked Uncle's Lodge, formerly The Doctor's House. Everyone would take it for a bed and breakfast. I learned from the old book that there were a number of Drood plays, one of them, never produced, by Charles Dickens the Younger with someone named Joseph Hatton. Charles Dickens the Younger. Wicked Uncle the Younger, no such critter. Come, my son, and I will tell you the story of my long and happy life, and you can tell it to the little ones.

Fire burning, rain falling. It was Donald Gillis who got us here. There we were in London, in a small residential hotel in South Ken, eating an English breakfast, porridge, boiled egg and two rashers, nearly out of money, making it last, and no idea where we would go, I with a law degree of sorts, the Dutchess—but I didn't call her that, not yet—with nothing. Sometimes I thought that after the holiday was over, she would return home to Orland, who would forgive, and it would be a tall story to tell someday on the other side of the moon. Sitting over breakfast, I saw the keen eye of a long man with gray hair and a gray, considering face watching the pretty Dutch girl sip her tea. I knew he watched her as I had, helpless, stricken, and I was afraid that she would notice and run away with him.

Not quite what happened. I never had the illusion that Donald had any interest in me or my obvious cleverness. It was the lovely skin and bright eyes he adored. That's what made him set out to save us. The next morning he was at breakfast again, and he engaged us in conversation—we were Canadian, he was Canadian—and that day we went together, to the British Museum, which we had missed, incompetent travelers always. There among the plunder of the ages our stories got told, and he affected to find ours romantic, and I was invited to return to Canada to become his junior, to be called to the bar here. He fell in love with the Dairy Queen, frightened for a girl who had fallen into the arms of a lustful lout without the brains to support her. That's how he saw me then. True enough, maybe. I proved competent at the practice of law, and I let him educate me. Though I was from away, as his junior I was accepted as having my wits about me, and I learned to interpret the quack and croon and chortle of the local accent.

I have thought sometimes that my lover loved another. They shared an interest in history, and Donald lent her books and insisted that she complete the degree she had abandoned to marry Orland. He was a kind man, perhaps even a wise one, and I, callow and hungry, couldn't be like that. I would say bitter things under my breath as I drove past the wet red fields of spring, the white hills of winter overlooked by the dark spruce. And then he grew thinner and grayer and died, and I took over the practice, paying something to his wife over the years.

Now we have been here forever. I have lunch with Fred the stockbroker and Mike the government man, and I hear what the boys in the backroom are saying. I know all the current lies and how to listen to them retold. I am worldly in a small way. I know which cabinet minister is on the booze and who can be bought and sold. I know people, meet people. I know a man, a retired policeman, who is preparing a landing field for UFOs. Today I stood in a government office and looked down into the street and suddenly, for a moment, eternally loved a pretty, anonymous young woman going by, swinging her way along through the autumn sun in a pale dress, a slit in the skirt showing the movement of her young and shapely legs. I watched from above, through glass, and knew we have one life each, that this was heaven, then turned and began to negotiate with the environment people on behalf of a client with effluent problems.

The book on Drood tells me that the mysterious figure of Datchery, the white haired "old buffer" who comes to Cloisterham and begins secretly investigating the probable murder must be Helena Landless in disguise, Helena Landless, *an unusually handsome lithe girl . . . very dark and very rich in color . . . almost of the gipsy type.* Imagine the dark, lithe girl dressing herself in a man's clothing, undressing secretly by candlelight in her little bedroom near the old cathedral. *A white-haired person with black eyebrows.* Dickens gave her a name a little like that of his mistress, the beautiful, cold goddess of the later books.

The Dutchess announced last week that of all the unpleasant things Dickens did to his wife, the worst was inventing the name Lady Maria Clutterbuck for the author of her cookery book. Clutterbuck. Wife as dunce. He liked to joke about her awkwardness. Why did the Dutchess mention Dickens? Watching to see my response? She must know by now that I have invaded Dutchessville, in my thoughts at least. It takes nothing from her. I have no interest in Victorian domestic life, rather the dark business of murder and obsession.

Fire burning, rain falling.

"You're being silent," the Dutchess said from the kitchen where she was making a medieval stew from meat I would have called inedible.

"No, love," I said, "I'm not being silent. I'm just not saying anything."

A chill autumn night, and the two of us sat on the back porch in wicker chairs, bundled up in winter clothes, long scarves and funny hats, to watch an eclipse of the moon. The next one wouldn't happen until after the beginning of the new millennium, and so we paid tribute to its rarity by staying up late while inside the fire died, and the slow wheeling of the planets brought earth and sun and moon into alignment. The shining sphere of the moon, floating mirror where once, they say, men walked, moved slowly into the shadow of the earth. Such things. We all live in the shadow of the earth.

The Dutchess was whistling under her breath. It had been a quiet day. Neither of us went to town, and in the afternoon, we took a long walk on the road that starts at the sawmill and leads on for miles into the woods, first along the millpond and then uphill and down through thick woodland, the air damp and fresh as you travel along the narrow road, wondering who is ahead, who is leading you forward, waiting, wondering where the road will end and whether you want to get lost and sleep cold and helpless in a wet corner of the woods. You hear the soft wind, occasionally the rustle of feet, a squirrel running away over the leaves, a sudden explosion of wings, and silence, you hear silence.

A pile of wood, thin sticks, abandoned on the path ahead, like an altar to the woodland god, the Dutchess said. We walked past and onward to the place where the road ends in a clearing, trees surprisingly large to have escaped logging, thick yellow birch, white birch, spruce, hemlock. We stood there in the clearing, had a piss, turned back and followed the road to the sawmill, past the metallic glow of the pond, the little waterfall that perhaps once drove the mill, past the old blue truck sinking into the earth, and back home to sit here in the night.

The moon was half covered, and we could feel but not quite see each moment's gradual expansion of the shadow over the shining surface.

"I had a letter from Susan," the Dutchess said. One of the little Dutchesses.

"What did she say?"

"Orland's dying."

"He isn't that old. He's probably just making it up."

"No."

She was silent again.

"I want him to come here," she said.

"Why?"

"So I can be with him."

"You left him."

The shadow was further over the moon, and at the edge of the shadow a pale perfect ring of green light.

"I didn't want to leave him."

"It's what you decided."

"You bullied me."

"You agreed."

"Sometimes I thought it would kill me," she said.

"You screwed around. You sneaked out to come to me."

"That's not the same. I loved him. You never understood that."

Around the vanishing moon, stars and planets, multiple, bright, nameless.

"I want him to come here to die," she said.

"And what do I want?"

"Whatever it is, you'll do it."

"Will I?"

"Aren't you already writing that Drood thing?"

"Only in my head."

"In your head."

I couldn't quite make out the tone of that last remark and wasn't sure I wanted to. I shivered from sitting out in this cold darkness. We waited, and gradually the moon disappeared.

A Monday morning, gray and grim. I wonder, does the Dutchess believe I should have left her there, with Orland? Fucked her and moved on? *Oh Billy Magee Magar.* I could do no such thing. She must know that. Young Meg picked the wrong man for that. It was Monday morning, and I looked at the picture on my desk as I waited for Elaine to come and tell me what to do.

Bobby Shafto's gone to sea. The gray boats out there in the fog on their way to war, steel against ice and torpedoes. He'll come back and marry me. No, he won't, he won't. Bobby Shafto's getten a bairn. Has indeed getten a bairn and then vanished with the gray ships into the noise of war. I looked at the picture on the desk in front of me as the dim light of the window fell on it, a picture of my pretty mother at nineteen, just before Bobby Shafto came along on a Canadian merchant ship put in at Belfast for repairs, and with whatever lies and charm and force got her up the stump in no time at all. He went off promising to come back but was never heard of again. So I was born and she was shamed, and over the years she would claim to be the widow of a heroic sailor who went down with the ship, and maybe so, how else not to have found him later on unless, like some country maid in a folk song, she never asked his name, but only laid her white flesh beneath him in a green field on a bright spring day as girls have gone to boys forever amen. She was RC, her family from County Wicklow in the south, and the priests were at her to give up the child, but she escaped from the home they put her in and got herself to England and then somehow to Canada, and by then she was, in her own mind, a war widow. She rented a little frame house on Nairn Avenue in Toronto and left me with neighbors while she got on the Rogers Road streetcar and then the St Clair car and down Bay to where she was a clerk at Eaton's.

We were deeply in love, my mother and I, and only in later years did I discover that the headshrinkers called this wrong. She kissed me goodnight and woke me with a kiss in the morning, and every day, before she left for work, she would stand in front of me and spin round, and I would tell her that she looked beautiful. Sometimes when she was away I would play with her makeup, try on her high heels. I loved her so much I wanted to be her. When she came back from work, the same streetcars in reverse order, she would fetch me from the neighbor's. We would come home for tea, and in the evening, we would listen to *Lux Radio Theatre or Amos 'n Andy,* and she would explain it all to me. I would go to bed, and she would read *Ladies Home Journal*—Mrs. Elva Burge at work brought it for my mother when she was done with it—and I might wake in the dark and smell the cold cream she put on her face at night and hear her getting into her bed across the room. She called herself Mrs. and said that her Canadian sailor husband had gone down with his ship. She loved me best of all, and so far as I was concerned, this was perfect happiness. I liked Mrs. Hamp, the neighbor who minded me during the day, but mostly I waited for my mother to come home.

There is always an end to Eden. She married Ray, who had asthma and a hardware store, and there was more money but less love. He was slow and decent, and in spite of his wheezing, he outlived her. I grew hardened to her abandonment of me and of that perfect love and happiness we shared, but I couldn't forget that something had been lost, and when I was grown and found myself among women, I was always searching for the vanished perfection. The doctors would say that I must have been ruined, but the doctors are wrong, only I always expected a return to paradise. There were girls who wanted friendship or a little fun, but I wanted a straight train to heaven. I was always disappointed until the adventure of my first adultery, insatiable upon the rich flesh of Orland's naughty wife. It was forbidden, and it was perfect. I swore I couldn't live without her, made her leave him, and now here we were, facing the dark days of the year, and she said she wanted to bring him back. Time foreshortened, and the years that had gone by, second by second, had turned themselves into bits of memory that could be canvassed between sleep and waking, between thought and thought.

Elaine stood by the door looking at me, as if she might have been there unnoticed for a long time.

"Bobby Shafto's gone to sea," I said.

Sometimes she is more tolerant when she thinks me mad.

"Wants to see you," she said. "If you can spare the time." Elaine knows I have been in the company of the absent, led astray by phantasms.

"Who is it?"

"Maude McIsaac."

"Again?"

She nodded.

Maude is a pleasant and well spoken woman who is a kleptomaniac. The doctors can't do much, it seems, and the courts are losing patience.

"Send her in," I said and prepared to be censorious, though I know it would do no good. We would offer to make restitution. What else is there?

I was walking through the fallen leaves under the bare trees with Jane the Carpenter. The sun was not far above the horizon, and light fell in little patterns of brightness on the forest floor among the underwater greens of spruce and hemlock and fern. The vertical trunks of the trees, gray columns standing apart in the filtered woodland light, led us onward into some ancient story. Jane was telling me about the beauty of wood, how she had laid hands on an old apple tree, milled it herself, and was making small boxes out of the hard, fragrant wood. I had contracted to buy one of her boxes as a present for the Dutchess. Today's outing was planned for all three of us, but the Dutchess had come down with something and lay abed in our room amid the clutter of books and newspapers and clean laundry and dirty laundry, suffering from fever and chills. We had forgotten our plan to walk in the woods with Jane the Carpenter until she arrived at the door, so I made the Dutchess a hot toddy, and she sent the two of us out for our hike. Now Jane and I walked, like Hansel and Gretel, hearing the soft whistle of the wind that moved through bare trees and over fallen leaves, and now and then the rustle of a squirrel or the screech of a jay. See the two figures far off there in the cool golden light. We see them, but we can't quite remember who they are.

"This morning ," I said, "I was sitting out in the sun on the porch with a book. I heard a great clattering in the sky. A helicopter flew by, and I was sure it would come back and land, and a man in uniform would tell me that they had come for the Dutchess, to take her away."

With her short brown hair, pale face and gray eyes, Jane the Carpenter looked boyish and very young. Wicked Uncle takes the innocent lad into the woods and murders him, under some mysterious compulsion, but the lad comes back to life and returns in the night to haunt the bad man. The days pass by like years, the years like days, and everything is possible. John Jasper, we must assume, killed his nephew.

"You have such ideas," Jane said.

"Yes," I said.

We walked on, our shoes scuffing the leaves.

"What shall we have for dinner?" I said.

"I won't stay. Mary's too sick to cook."

"I'll make Winter Soup and Roast Something for us all. She'll get up to eat."

Jane said nothing. I took that for agreement, and we followed the old road-further into the woods.

"Have you ever read *The Mystery of Edwin Drood*?" I said.

"Who wrote that?"

"Charles Dickens."

"We read something by him in school."

"The Drood book was never finished. He died with half of it written."

She stared at the sky again.

"So you're going to finish it?"

"I wouldn't be the first. Still, it's a temptation."

"What's the story about?"

"A murder. Or at least we assume it's murder. The body isn't found."

We walked on as a cloud blew over the sun. The woods were different, colder.

Jane put her hand, long, shapely, hardened and capable, up to her neck as if to protect herself.

"Maybe it's time to turn back," I said.

"Always never walk forever, "she said.

Jane the Carpenter is a mystery. I met her when I defended her on a charge of theft, money missing from a house where she had been building a set of kitchen cupboards. I got the charge dropped at the preliminary hearing. There was, in fact, no real evidence, though it was clear that there was more to the story than had been told by the couple who had laid the charge or by Jane herself. After the case, I hired her to do some carpentry around our house, and both the Dutchess and I found that we liked having her there, quietly working away, pretty in her boyish way. We kept finding new jobs for her to do, adopted her for a bit, though she would disappear for days and then turn up again without explanation. Sometimes she answers her phone, sometimes she doesn't. I tell the Dutchess that Jane the Carpenter has another existence somewhere else in the universe and needs to go there from time to time, and I almost believe it.

The sun was far down the sky by now and casting long shadows across every open space in the woods. The wind blew in gusts among the tall spruces or shook the branches; a solitary brown leaf came loose and fell. The empty spaces between the trunks were full of golden light, but there was an edge of darkness, and everything was growing cold. At the end of the road, the car waited to take us back to a house and a warm fire. The Dutchess would be curled up in bed, waiting for us. Unless the helicopter had come for her. Or perhaps it was waiting to take Jane the Carpenter off to her other life and the Dutchess with her.

Come close to the fire, children, and Wicked Uncle will stroke his goatish little beard and summon up ghosts. The divine music chases its soft echoes through the spaces of the cathedral, the voice of the lay precentor leading the chanting of the psalms, his voice strong and pure. Yet to the precentor himself, it all sounds diabolical. *The echoes of my own voice seem to mock me with my daily drudging round.* He is driven by some longing for something more, and the longing has turned murderous. Dickens had lived for years on his own huge reserves of vitality, the certainty that he was right, the energy that was like a kind of possession; he had been in and out of a hundred lives. Bernard Shaw said that *Drood* was the work of a man already three-quarters dead, and there is a mortal intensity about Jasper, a confusion of love and hate.

I stroked my beard (grown when I first came here as a deliberate eccentricity, a defense—look, Mephisto come from away—and by now something I keep because I am used to it), stroked it as I always do in certain moods, as if drawing the hairs to a point would bring concentration to a point as well. I looked into the fire. The flame was calming, as for a hundred generations before me, though fire was a luxury now, inefficient, out of date as a way of heating. I grew up with a furnace turned low. My first fire, the first I remember, was in high school, the graduating class at a final get-together on a beach with a great pile of burning driftwood. Across the fire the faces of the girls were masks of unbearable beauty. Now, like some primordial groaner in his cave, I drew close to the flames, touched the hair on my face to feel myself alive.

The air in the house smelled of the mussels we had eaten for supper, greedily scooping them from their shells. On the way home from work, I picked them up at a mussel farm in a cove near here, driving down the gentle hills between the fields and then looking over the tidal flats to the water. *The nets are unwound; they hang from the rafters over the fresh stowed hay in upland barns.* In the bright summer we dig clams at low tide and taste the salt in their flesh. We live a small, provincial life at the edge of the great sea.

The wind was blowing in vicious gusts as I stood on the pavement outside the bus terminal and watched the men and women get out of the bus, bending themselves away from the rain and sleet, scurrying toward the terminal or gathering in a little hunched group waiting for the driver to pull the cases out from underneath. The lights of the terminal shone on the wet pavement, and the headlights of the bus stared madly into darkness. Winter was upon us, that dire Fate. Gather in the longhouse, bodies close together in the fug of smoke and breath, clothed in the skins of animals, eating flesh. Rain blurred my vision as I waited for the man whose wife I had taken away, tried to remember his face.

In front of me, a stocky young woman took off her glasses and rubbed them with her fingers, put them back on and stared about, looking for love. The bus has come from far. In winter. Lovers nested tight together. Lonely night travelers seeking rest. No sign of Orland. The driver threw more suitcases to the wet pavement. Cars passed, lights across the long strings of icy rain. Skins wet, we all watched the world go past. This is the end of the day, so long now. A tall Chinese boy lifted his backpack and walked away into the darkness. Stoics, we endured, waiting. Ice. An old man on crutches was trying to go by me, and I knew he would fall, but he stopped, breathless, and looked at me and spoke my name.

Orland. Pale and wild-eyed. One-legged. The Dutchess didn't tell me that he had only one leg, and I was furious. It made all the difference. What were we to do with a gimp? Dying, she said he was dying, fine, she is a notorious liar when it suits her purpose, and her purpose was to have her old man in the house after twenty years, and the story that he was dying was as good as any. Dying men can't get on the bus. Well known. He was here and struggling to get his breath, and I wanted to kick the crutches out from under him and watch him go down. He closed his eyes. Dying. Bring the old man here to expire. Bury him in a field or feed him to the crows. *Oh Billy Magee Magar.*

"Orland."

He nodded, eyes still closed, breathing heavily. Stertorous, the word for such heaving breath, pant, wheeze.

"Do you have a bag?"

"I lost it somewhere."

No wonder he couldn't keep his wife. Incompetent even in his dying. Now he opened his eyes, and they were watery and red. Was he crying with joy to see the Samaritan who would take him home safe and tuck him up with a white warm belly to comfort him? More likely the rain, sleet, hail, whatever it was coming down on us.

"You've only got one leg," I said.

"Lost it," he said.

Leg, luggage, bits and pieces dropping away into the garbage can, a shedding, ceremonial divestiture by the wise elder before he walks naked into the storm. We have much to learn from the other tribes, and none of it will improve us. A woman was staring at me, murderous. Long nose with a drop of water at the end of it. Tall. I had represented her husband in a rancorous divorce proceeding. An ugly business. No wonder she wanted to kill me. I should have been a priest and grown wise. Orland was staring at me.

"You're fat," he said.

"No," I said, "I'm not."

Get him to the car. That was the next thing to be done, and the heater turned on, two chaps to thaw and hit the road. The Dutchess awaited us, dressed in all her splendor. A woman was tapping on my arm, then tugging.

"Are you from the tourist bureau?" she said.

There was a growth on her chin, and she wore a purple rain suit.

"There is no tourist bureau," I said. "It's closed for the winter. No one comes here in the winter. You should get back on the bus."

She turned, and a young women with a big smile received her into the faith. The freezing rain came down harder, a cold immensity falling upon us from the poisoned skies, and I could feel my trousers growing sodden with it. Orland had closed his eyes again.

"To the car," I said into the wind.

"You don't need to shout. I'm not deaf."

"Wonderful thing, a man of your age. Don't slip on the ice."

I led the way across the parking lot and got him stowed, the crutches in the back seat with the two bottles of Jameson's I'd picked up earlier. Word from home. Note to self: do a little research into the history of Irish whiskey. Once I was myself aboard, I started the engine, turned the heat as high as it would go, and drove out of the parking lot, back ending swinging wildly on the ice, not quite killing new arrivals, and off we went toward the end of the world.

That night we lay in bed after Orland was stowed in one of the other bedrooms wearing the Dutchess's nightgown since, bag lost, he had no nightclothes of his own. His heavy breathing was audible through the closed door. The crutches were close to the bed in case he needed to rise in the night, the little case of diabetic equipment which had emerged from the pocket of his coat, saved when all else was lost, on the table beside him. After dinner, he had taken the thick socks and boot off his one remaining foot which was misshapen, toes missing. The other leg gone altogether. They were cutting him to pieces, starting with the toes. Soon he would be nothing but a talking head. The foot was swollen, and had a nasty red spot on his heel, and we soaked it in hot water and Epsom salts, which the Dutchess had on hand, having been warned.

"Well then, "I said to the Dutchess, "he's here."

"Do you hate it so very much?"

"Is he really dying?"

"Can't you tell?"

"He could go on like this. Keep trimming away a few bits."

"He has congestive heart failure," she said. "He always had an enlarged heart."

An enlarged heart: Orland had a big heart, true enough. There was the way he welcomed me to their house when the cast had a party while we were rehearsing *The School for Scandal.* Curator of the university museum and art gallery, collector of the folklore of back-country Ontario, amateur musician, lovely man whose wife I would steal away. He sat on a straight chair, an old guitar in his hands, and his elegant fingers plucked at the strings and made soft chords while his clear baritone voice sang old songs and taught them to us who sat at his feet. *There were three crows sat on a tree. Oh Billy Magee Magar.* Later in the evening, several beers to the better, we stood in the kitchen, a narrow room with children's bright crayon pictures on the walls, and I was telling him how I'd been born in Belfast and found that I was ready to tell about a poor girl betrayed by a sailor as if it were one more folk song. In the doorway, I saw the young Meg, her hair fastened up on her head in combs, the smooth skin of her neck, a black dress. I made myself look away from her, and I met the gentle brown eyes of her husband, who smiled at me as if he understood how I must be struck by her beauty. I stopped in confusion, said only that I'd come to Canada very young. Orland's big heart. I took the pretty Dutch girl away from a man who was in every way my moral superior. Am I to make it up now, as witness to his deterioration? Wicked Uncle learns nursing.

Rain and sleet blew against the window on a gust of wind.

"It's cold out there, Dutchess," I said.

She reached over and put her arms around me, and the two of us clung together for warmth.

"I need to have him here," she said. "I never stopped thinking about him. He was so good with the girls, all those years."

Other lives sat in the darkness watching us.

"There are no other lives," I said to keep them off.

Outside, a few thin flakes of snow were dropping through the empty air, the first of the year, the effect tentative, a hint of what was to come, no wind, only the small white flakes, and in front of the fire Orland lay watching Oprah Winfrey. The television is seldom off since his arrival. He claims that TV is the new folklore, that and tabloids like *The National Enquirer,* and with them he spends his time. No longer driving down back roads asking frisky old fellows what they remember, the stories they heard as children.

That's all gone, he says, and what the people are expressing, the new magic stories, are told on *Oprah* or picked up at the supermarket. It's possible that Orland is right. It's also possible that he's dropped one of his oars and the dory is drifting.

This morning when I got up, a heavy dew lay on the grass and fog in the hollows, but as the day went on, the air grew sharper, and now these flakes of snow. A Life Skills day, and I had arrived home before the Dutchess. I had made Orland a cup of tea and brought in more sticks, built up the fire when I saw him shiver.

"I think I could write a chapter about the taboo of embarrassment," Orland said as he watched.

Wicked Uncle did not want to discuss deep matters with this dying man. We should be hauling out the hot water and Epsom salts to soak the remaining foot, which swells alarmingly. The Dutchess will do that and feed him his antibiotics when she comes in. I took some chicken stock out of the refrigerator to make Winter Soup, famous for its curative powers. On the way home tonight, the Dutchess plans to stop and buy a portable TV for Orland to have in his room, so he can watch from the bed. In the evening, she goes up and sits there with him, and I don't know what they do or what they talk about, death perhaps, or what it was like when they were together long ago. Perhaps he strokes her round belly with his delicate white hands. I know not.

At the registry office today, I spoke to the Renaissance Girl. She is much the age of her avatar, seventeen or so, but the ermine girl had already been seduced by a Sforza prince and borne a child, (her eyes attentive as she holds the ermine in her long fingers, the sharp, dangerous snout of the animal close to her delicate throat, their faces bent the same way). The girl in the Registry Office is dim and polite, yet she will have a history, which is all still to come; the brightness of possibility shines on her exotic face. All future time will one day be a few past facts. She will never know her own beauty. She would have been confused and offended if I had said her face and body were archetypal, her back and arse like stem and flower. So instead I told her about my friend who has the landing field for UFOs—I'd seen him at lunch and asked if he'd found any traces of unobserved use. None, but he lives in hope. The Renaissance Girl was made uneasy by all this, and I forbore. Am not Leonardo, cannot express my hunger for the mystery of her untouched youth. Will smile and pass by from now on. Perhaps I have never grown beyond my young days, when every attractive girl was a promise of the paradise garden, when I expected so much, gladdened by an eyebrow, a nose, a hank of hair, a breast, falling in love twice a day, never satisfied. Only pain could make it right, an obsession with the impossible, tantrums to make it happen, and here we are, the Dutchess knitting up the fallen stitches, comforting her husband's last days.

The television made its noises, and I heard Orland shift on the couch. His body is white, the skin smooth and mostly hairless. The shape of muscles is visible under the skin of shoulders and arms, but the muscles are betrayed by the useless, flopping heart, and any amount of activity exhausts him. Sometimes he watched me intently, and I wondered if he thought we should talk about the past. There was no peace to be made, and when he watched me like that, I wanted to put a pillow over his face and finish him.

John Jasper, if we are to trust the clues, choked his nephew to death with a long black scarf, a detail of clothing that Dickens added in revision. From the beginning, Dickens loved his murderers. The irremediable Sikes. Old Orlick. There is some indication that Jasper was connected to the Thugs, those philosophic killers, adepts of the goddess of destruction. *All creation is the sport of my mad mother, Kali.* To see that a thing exists is to will its destruction. To know is to annihilate. Orland's flirtation with death provokes a more focussed rage. The Dutchess leaves us alone here to tempt me. Even when the three of us are locked in the house, gathered at the fire, it is too silent, too bare to bear.

Wicked Uncle seeks his whimsies. The Renaissance Girl is dim-witted, will not know her secret face. I never met my father, never sired a child—a state of winter, even with the sweat of the Dutchess's great things damp on my chest.

The goddess Oprah spoke, her followers roared, and Orland, her student, mumbled something. The dory gone adrift on the great waters.

The storm surrounded the house, and the snow came from all directions, sweeping across the hills and spinning through the empty trees, shaping itself with the pattern of the whirling wind, millions of flakes thick in the air. The light was almost gone. I crouched by the fire and remembered the panting white figure upstairs and wished the Dutchess would return. The way the eyes looked at me from some other world was too difficult, and the growth of whiskers around the mouth, the lips as red as if thickly coated with lipstick, wet as blood.

There was a loud knock on the door. As I went to answer it, I knew that it was someone come for him, someone in authority, men in uniforms who would take him away to die in a sanitary place where no one need observe. When I opened the door, a man stood there, younger and shorter and thinner than I am, straight blonde hair, features that looked as if they might have been carved from wood, a wide smile, his clothes covered with snow as if he had walked a long way through the blizzard. Hanging from his shoulder a small knapsack.

"Dropped me off at the corner," he said. "It's a good long walk in this kind of a storm."

He was smiling, showing his hard wooden teeth.

"Still, I made it," he said. "I made it."

"Who are you?"

"I'm here to see Orland. I heard he was going soon. I spent what I had on the bus fare and hitched from town, but he left me at the corner and I walked from there. A convivial sort but had to get home to the kiddies."

"But who are you?"

"Jackie," he said. "He was everything to me. I was just a boy."

The wooden features had settled in an expression of senseless happiness. Beyond him, the snow swirled and the night came on. I held the door for him to come in, and he brushed off the snow before stepping over the threshold. Once inside, he took off his shoes, black running shoes with holes in them, holes also in the white socks he wore underneath. A bony toe protruded.

"Would you have a slice of bread and jam that isn't urgently needed by anyone else? I haven't been eating, except someone gave me a sandwich on the bus and a couple of candies. I kept one for later, but it didn't last. You tell yourself that you're not going to chew it, but then you do."

He had taken off the windbreaker he'd been wearing, something with a crest on it, and hung it up on the rack by the door, and now he turned, grinning, and met my eyes.

One of his eyes, which were dark green, had an odd mark in the middle of the iris, what looked like a jagged black line extending out from the pupil. It gave his face a tilted, one-sided look. He was cheerful and plausible and I didn't believe anything he said. He had come out of the woods where he had been hiding for a hundred years, waiting to appear in the dark and storm. As we stood there in the hall, the phone rang, but when I answered, there was no one. I heard Orland's voice calling thinly from upstairs. Jackie's head gave a sudden abrupt turn, and he stood perfectly still for a second, then picked up his knapsack and ran up the stairs, taking them two at a time.

I went to the kitchen and put on the kettle to make tea, got out a slice of bread and covered it with butter and dark red raspberry jam. While I waited for the water to boil, I poured a glass of Jameson's and took a little for warmth. The wind sang its plangent ballad in the old kitchen chimney, and the kettle groaned. I thought of the Dutchess driving from town in the snow, the road vanishing in blowing whiteness, and half expected her to call and say she'd stay, get a hotel room for the night. To leave me alone with a dying man and this new creature who had come to him. The Dutchess must have invited him. There was no end to what went on without my knowledge. I sipped whiskey and the kettle boiled, and I heated the pot, made tea and poured two cups—sometimes Orland would have a little. It took me a while to find the tray to carry all this upstairs, and when it finally came to light behind the refrigerator, I loaded up and carried it to Orland's room. Jackie was seated on the edge of the bed, holding Orland's hand, while his other hand combed the long thin hair with a small black comb. In the corner of the room, the little TV that the Dutchess had bought for him was playing, something with a black family and a lot of audience laughter.

"Bread and jam," I said. "And some tea."

"We're getting him all cleaned up," Jackie said. "After tea, I'll get out the razor and give him a bit of a shave."

Orland's eyes were fixed on the TV.

"Families," Orland said. "Families for the orphaned." Then he stopped to get his breath.

"Seesaw Margery Daw," Jackie said, then bent and kissed Orland on the cheek.

"Jackie shall have a new master." Orland's mouth was hanging open a little. The window shook in the wind that was filling the woods with snow, birds and rabbits in hiding as we all waited for news from outer space. The room was hot, as if Jackie had brought with him some fiery warmth, and there was a flush on

Orland's pale cheek. I put the tray on the table beside the bed, and Jackie picked up the bread and jam and ate it with the swift bites of a hungry dog, then drank half the cup of tea. He put down the mug and passed the other one to Orland, placing it gently in his fingers and helping him to lift it to his lips.

I went downstairs. The wind was rising to a howl. Then footsteps on the porch, and the Dutchess came in the kitchen door, and with her, like good news, was Jane the Carpenter. The Dutchess hung up her coat, and I put my arms around her.

"I was frightened for you," I said. "All that wind and snow."

"Jane was watching out for me."

"It's good to see you here," I said to Jane. I hugged her too though it's not my habit, and I noticed as I let her go the darkness under her eyes and how beautiful she is.

"Jane's here to measure Orland," the Dutchess said.

"Measure him? What for?"

"The coffin," Jane said. "I have to order the wood."

She and the Dutchess were smiling at each other as if this was a lovely joke. I put my hand to the glass of Jameson's.

"There's someone here with him," I said.

"Jackie."

"Yes. Do you know him?"

"I knew he was coming. Orland took him in after I'd left. Helped to educate him."

"Where did he find him?"

"The theatre. He's an actor."

"Chicken pie," Jane said.

"Chicken and leek pie," the Dutchess answered.

"We talked all the way out about what we were going to eat when we got here," Jane said.

"Chicken and leek pie," the Dutchess said.

While they cooked, I opened a tin of smoked oysters and sliced up some Cheshire cheese and crushed garlic for dressing. When the pie was almost done, I went back up to Orland's room. Jackie had shaved him and changed him into clean clothes, one of the new outfits the Dutchess had bought him, and he was sitting up in bed as the two of them held hands and stared at the TV. The sound was turned off.

I put a little tray of oysters and cheese and crackers on the table. Frost and snow had gathered in the corners of the window.

"We have chicken pie," I said. "Will you come down?"

Jackie looked at Orland as if he were to decide, but Orland continued to stare at the TV.

"Would it be possible to have a tray?" Jackie said. "The children will eat in their room tonight." He smiled his wooden smile.

"I suppose so," I said.

Jane was the one who took the tray up, and she was a long time coming back down. Hungry, I waited impatiently. The Dutchess stoked the fire and glanced at her mail. Jane was bright-eyed when she returned.

"What a pretty boy," she said. Wicked Uncle was jealous.

"Is he?" the Dutchess said. "I'll have a look after dinner."

We ate heartily, and the Dutchess and I drank wine. Jane is a teetotaler. When we had eaten, and while I was doing away with the last of the bottle of wine, Jane and the Dutchess vanished upstairs and came back with empty dishes.

"I got his measurements," Jane said.

"You got him to lie down with his hands crossed on his chest and you pulled out your ruler?"

"I have a good eye. Won't be above an inch off either way. I'll leave a bit of extra space."

"Does Orland know about these plans you've got?"

"We've talked about it," the Dutchess said.

Nights when she sat with him, they discussed the making of his coffin.

"What about the girls?"

"They saw him off when he came here. They know."

I sat in a rocking chair and stared into the fire. Outside the house there was a blizzard, and inside we were preparing for death. They were. Myself, I could not approach it with such calm. The deterioration of Orland's body horrified me, and I would have preferred him taken away. Jackie's arrival, his cheerfulness, appalled me. I wondered if he had been Orland's lover. The others were gathered in strange couples. Jackie and Orland, the Dutchess and Jane, and I was left out. I wanted to run away into the snow, but I knew that if I did, I would be lost and not come back, that I would walk among the trees until I found a place to lie down and never get up.

Turning the pages of a book, but unable to take it in, I listened while all the arrangements were made. Jackie would stay with Orland, Jane would take the little back room. The fire burned down.

In the night, I woke from a dream about a difficult court case in which I was defending a man charged with plagiarizing from Charles Dickens, who appeared in the court covered by a sheet and intoning the words of the stolen novel. Myself, I was naked under my lawyer's gown and had some difficulty keeping it over my dick, which rose energetically. When I wakened, I heard the wind still blowing. I remembered all the strangers who were in the house, and I was frightened, convinced that a figure was waiting in the dark to do some terrible thing, that Jackie was in Orland's room with a knife. The Dutchess didn't stir as I got up and put on my dressing gown. I stood by the door or Orland's room, listening to his breathing. It was regular enough.

Further along the hall, there was a little light coming from the back room I wondered if Jane might be awake and reading, and I went down the narrow hall and round the corner. There was a candle on the table by the bed, burnt down almost to the end, and the flame waved and guttered, ready to go out. Fast asleep, cuddled close together in the bed, Jane and Jackie. Her face was younger asleep, but his looked older. They were like two children in a cabin in the woods by candlelight, a bare shoulder, a hand clenched, a breast, nipple like a raspberry for jam, arms twined, their breath so quiet as to be unheard. The candle guttered and went out, and in the dark I made my way back to bed. The Dutchess turned to me in her sleep and mumbled something.

"Wicked Uncle has no more stories," I said.

She mumbled and put her arms around me.

In the morning, the wind had gone down, and everything was white or outlined in white. Bits of snow fell from the twigs and and left marks like mysterious tracks going nowhere on the snow beneath. The first up, I watched the sun rise and the snow begin to glitter, and as I put on the kettle for coffee and squeezed oranges for juice, Jane the Carpenter walked into the kitchen, came to me and kissed me on the cheek. Wicked Uncle could smell sex, turned to her, and she met my gaze with her accurate shadowed eyes. I thought that she had seen me looking down at the two of them naked in each other's arms.

"Jackie says he heard voices in the house last night," she said.

"Me and the Dutchess?"

"No. Other voices."

"It's an old house, full of old lives."

"I suppose they never leave."

"What were they saying?"

"He couldn't quite make out. The usual story, he said."

"What's that?"

"You'd have to ask him."

I gave her a glass of juice, and she drank it down as I squeezed one for myself.

Two lost children stood looking in the window, envious of our warmth and food. The usual story. There were footsteps on the back stairs, and the Dutchess came into the kitchen, looked at Jane as if she couldn't remember who she was.

"Eggs," I said. "Will we have eggs?"

"The egg of the universe hatches the world."

It was Jackie speaking from the other doorway of the kitchen. Now we were all in place, but I couldn't tell why we were here. The electric kettle was boiling.

"I'll make coffee," Jane said.

"I'll slice some bread."

"And I'll scramble eggs," the Dutchess said, and opened the refrigerator door.

"Scramble the egg of the universe," I said, "and we'll all shout, 'Chaos is come.'"

Everyone laughed as if I had told a fine joke.

"Is there juice for Orland?" Jackie said. I began to squeeze some, and he wandered to the back window of the kitchen and looked out over the snow.

"Two naked-arse babies run to the woods," he said.

"What?" I said. "Did you see something?"

"Nonsense rhyme."

"Seesaw Margery Daw . . ." I began.

"Sold her bed and lay upon straw," said Jane the Carpenter, in a voice unlike her own. "Was not she a dirty slut, to sell her bed and lie in the dirt?"

"Never heard that one," the Dutchess said.

"That shed," Jackie said. "I saw it last night at the edge of the trees. Watching us."

"I should have knocked it down before now," I said. "Though it's over the property line."

"Leave it to Jackie. Demolition expert. Penny a day to earn my keep."

The Dutchess was cracking brown eggs into a white bowl. She began to whip them, her hand moving in rapid circles. Jackie took the glass of juice I held out to him and disappeared. Jane the Carpenter sat at a chair by the table and watched.

"Is anybody going to town?" she said.

"Both of us, I expect. Work to do even after the blizzard."

"If the roads are ploughed," the Dutchess said. "Will you come or stay here?"

I couldn't help watching Jane's face as she prepared to answer. She saw me watching. Everyone knows everything. I turned away and began cutting bread from a sourdough loaf the Dutchess had baked, beginning it with starter from the pot of fermentation she kept in the basement. Yeast found in Egyptian tombs will still cause dough to rise.

"Stay here," Jane said. "I think there's some wood in the basement I can use for framing. I'll order the rest. They might deliver it by this afternoon."

When Orland tired of TV, she and Jackie could perform for him in ancient postures, the wisdom of the folk embodied in the eternal act. The Dutchess patted my bum as she went to get the frying pan. Outside a jay landed on a branch, and the snow dropped off it. Looking out the window, I had seen this and no one else had except God. Suppose God had not seen it, and I fell dead. It would vanish into eternal night. *Drood* would lie unfinished.

Jackie came back with the empty glass, on his face a wide smile as if he had made a great discovery, won the raffle.

"He drank up manfully," he said. Jane was watching him.

"You heard voices in the night," I said.

"I told him," Jane said.

"Couldn't make it out," he said. "But I thought I must know."

"It used to be the doctor's house," I said.

"A repository of old ills. Where else to take your sorrows?"

"It's there or the priest," Jane said. "And the priest will blame you up and down."

"The doctor will nod sagely and give you the mixture as before."

"A World of Old Houses," the Dutchess said. It's the title of a book she's planning.

"I'll drive you to town," I said, "when the eggs are done."

Though it's a Life Skills day, I was afraid that she would invoke the weather, refuse my offer, and say that she would stay with the others to dance around Orland's bier.

"Yes," she said. "I'll get ready after we eat."

Perhaps while all these voices were about I would tell Elaine to report to the world that I was not to be disturbed, and I would invoke the Inimitable there at my office desk. Drood's body was never to be found, only the ring which survived the action of the quicklime. Outside the house, I heard the loud grinding of a snowplough going past. The roads would be open, but I might have to dig out the car. When I looked to see, the sun was shining across the snow with a blinding brightness that hurt my eyes. I must remember to take dark glasses for driving.

The wind was blowing sleet against the window. I couldn't be sure how it had come about, but here we were, gathered in Orland's room, Jane the Carpenter and Jackie, the Dutchess and I, Orland propped up in his bed in some cushions, his eyes damp and bright, his mouth composed in a smile. I had somehow confessed or boasted to all assembled late at night, in my cups, wanting attention, that I had plans for fragmentary *Drood,* and now, for Orland's entertainment, Jackie and the Dutchess were about to perform a scene that I had extracted from the book, a scene between John Jasper and the pretty young thing, Rosa Bud. Ages were reversed, the Dutchess far too old for her part, but Jackie, who was responsible for all this, cared not.

The storm had gone on for days, and Jane had never gone back to town, though the Dutchess and I had been in and out. When I let out the idea of a Drood play, Jackie leapt on it and insisted there would be a reading. First he said that he and Orland would do a performance together, but Orland would have none of that. His breath was short, his voice thin. It would not do. In fact, I had done nothing about this play I boasted of except brood on it, but challenged, I produced a scene, easily enough stolen from the book. Now Jackie and the Dutchess had pages in their hands, and Jane and I were seated in straight chairs at the end of Orland's bed, under the slope of one of the gables, while across the room a chest of drawers served as the sundial against which Jasper leaned, waiting for the sweet young thing to come to him, and another straight chair was the bench where Rosa would take her place. On the wall behind hung an old print of William Lyon Mackenzie King, celebrating his first run as prime minister in the twenties, a print I'd found in a junk shop and brought home. All I knew about King was that he was sly as a fox and trafficked with spirits, but he seemed a proper domestic god for at least one room of the house.

I looked toward Orland. The smile was beginning to fade as he grew tired. Jane's face was in profile against the light from the lamp beside his bed, and I could see the tiniest blonde hairs on her upper lip.

"Are we ready?" Jackie said.

The Dutchess, who stood by the door, nodded.

"I think the audience is prepared," I said. "Aren't we, Jane?"

She nodded. She was watching intently, as if the action had already begun. Jackie turned toward the Dutchess, and as he fixed his concentration on her, he appeared to grow taller and heavier, and the wooden features changed. The Dutchess caught his look and shrunk into herself, then walked to the chair and sat down, Rosa Bud waiting for the feared John Jasper to address her.

"I have been waiting for some time to be summoned back to my duty near you," Jackie said, and his voice as Jasper was different, softer, and yet with a hard edge of insinuation.

"Duty, sir?" The Dutchess was too smart to do too much, to fake the voice and presence of a girl, yet one felt her fear.

"The duty of teaching you, serving you as your faithful music-master."

"I have left off that study."

"Not left off, I think. Discontinued. I was told by your guardian that you discontinued it under the shock that we have all felt so acutely. When will you resume?"

"Never, sir."

"Never? You could have done no more if you had loved my dear boy."

"I did love him."

"Yes; but not quite—not quite in the right way, shall I say? Not in the intended and expected way."

The Dutchess, almost without moving, shrank into herself, leaned just an inch away from him, her eyes focussed on some distant thing that might give her strength. The two of them were all too good at this. Jackie was a very fine actor. I had not, since *The School for Scandal,* observed the Dutchess's capacities in this line of work.

"Then to be told," Jackie went on, "that you discontinued your study with me was to be politely told that you abandoned it altogether?"

"Yes. The politeness was my guardian's, not mine. I told him that I was resolved to leave off, and that I was determined to stand by my resolution."

"And you still are?" The eyes of the Dutchess had taken on a strange light. It frightened me. She could be anyone.

"I still am, sir. And I beg not to be questioned any more about it. At all events, I will not answer any more; I have that in my power."

"I will not question you any more, since you object to it so much; I will confess—"

"I do not wish to hear you, sir."

In her anger, she stood up and began to move one foot as if to escape, and as she did, Jasper's hand—Jackie's hand was Jasper's hand by now—reached out to touch her, and as she shrank from the touch, the recoil pulled her back into her seat.

"We must sometimes act in opposition to our wishes. You must do so now, or do more harm to others than can ever be set right."

"What harm?"

"Presently, presently. You question me, you see, and surely that's not fair when you forbid me to question you. Nevertheless I will answer the question presently. Dearest Rosa. Charming Rosa."

Again she rose from her chair, and this time he did touch her, on the shoulder, and a shock went through my nerves. I felt Jane reach out and put her hand on mine, then take it away.

"I do not forget," the man said, "how many windows command a view of us. I will not touch you again; I will come no nearer to you than I am. Sit down, and there will be no mighty wonder in your music-master's leaning idly against a pedestal and speaking with you, remembering all that has happened, and our shares in it. Sit down, my beloved."

He looked at her, and bravely she tried to meet his eyes, but she could not endure the intensity of his glance, the gleam of madness, and she sat. Jasper's obsession drank all the air from the room.

"Rosa, even when my dear boy was affianced to you, I loved you madly; even when I strove to make him more ardently devoted to you, I loved you madly; even when he gave me the picture of your lovely face so carelessly traduced by him, which I feigned to hang always in my sight for his sake, but worshipped in torment for years, I loved you madly; in the distasteful work of the day, in the wakeful misery of the night, girded by sordid realities, or wandering through Paradises and Hells of vision into which I rushed, carrying your image in my arms, I loved you madly. I endured it all in silence. So long as you were his, or so long as I supposed you to be his, I hid my secret loyally. Did I not?"

As he spoke, I could see some kind of strength growing in her, this new young Dutchess, an angry determination.

"You were as false throughout, sir, as you are now. You were false to him daily and hourly. You know that you made my life unhappy by your pursuit of me. You know that you made me afraid to open his generous eyes, and that you forced me, for his own trusting, good, good sake, to keep the truth from him, that you were a bad, bad man."

"How beautiful you are. You are more beautiful in anger than in repose. I don't ask you for your love; give me yourself and your hatred; give me yourself and that pretty rage; give me yourself and that enchanting scorn; it will be enough for me."

The two of them had sheets of paper in their hands and were reading the lines. The lines themselves had something of the vaporizing of Victorian melodrama. They had no light or set, only the pudgy face of tricky Willie King above them, yet I was unsurprised by the tears that ran down the Dutchess's face, the low sobbing that began, the struggle to rise and run.

"I told you, you rare charmer, you sweet witch, that you must stay and hear me, or do more harm than can ever be undone. Stay, and I will tell you. Go, and I will do it!"

She stood by her chair, one hand on the back, as if she feared to faint or fall.

"I have made my confession that my love is mad. It is so mad that had the ties between me and my dear lost boy been one silken thread less strong, I might have swept even him from your side when you favored him."

Her grip on the chair tightened, the grip of the other hand on the pages of script.

The low sobbing went on.

"Even him," he repeats. "Yes, even him! Rosa, you see me and you hear me. Judge for yourself whether any other admirer shall love you and live, whose life is in my hand."

"What do you mean, sir?"

I had tried to speed up the next few lines, the plot material about Neville Landless and whether he might be guilty of Drood's death, and I was aware as they spoke that there was something awkward about what I'd done. They seemed almost to lose their way, but then we got back to Jasper's obsession, and Jackie's voice strengthened. Outside the window, the wind grew louder, as if in sympathy with his passion. I thought I must find some similar effect to use on-stage, though the scene took place at the height of an English summer.

"I am going to show you how madly I love you. More madly now than ever, for I am willing to renounce the second object that has arisen in my life to divide it with you; and henceforth to have no object in existence but you only. Miss Landless has become your bosom friend. You care for her peace of mind?"

"I love her dearly."

"You care for her good name?"

"I have said, sir, I love her dearly."

"I am unconsciously giving offense by questioning again. I simply make statements, therefore, and not put questions. You do care for your bosom friend's good name, and you do care for her peace of mind. Then remove the shadow of the gallows from her, dear one!"

"You dare propose to me to—"

"Darling, I dare propose to you. Stop there. If it be bad to idolize you, I am the worst of men; if it be good, I am the best. My love for you is above all other love, and my truth to you is above all other truth. Let me have hope and favor, and I am a forsworn man for your sake."

The sobbing had thrown Rosa into disorder, and she pushed at her hair with an uncontrolled gesture which was familiar, not Rosa Bud, but the Dutchess in some terrible moment that I had seen and forgotten.

"Reckon up nothing at this moment, angel, but the sacrifice that I lay at those dear feet, which I could fall down among the vilest ashes and kiss, and put upon my head as a poor savage might. There is my fidelity to my dear boy after death. Tread upon it! There is the inexpiable offense against my adoration of you. Spurn it! There are my labors in the cause of a just vengeance for six toiling months. Crush them! There is my past and my present wasted life. There is the desolation of my heart and soul. There is my peace; there is my despair. Stamp them into the dust; so that you take me, were it even mortally hating me."

From the other side of the room, I heard a soft moan, and when I looked toward it, I saw Orland with his hands over his mouth like the speak-no-evil monkey, and tears running down his face and into his fingers. On our little stage, Rosa began to move away, and Jasper followed.

"Rosa, I am self-repressed again. I am walking calmly beside you to the house. I shall wait for some encouragement and hope. I shall not strike too soon. Give me a sign that you attend to me."

She moved her hand.

"Not a word of this to anyone, or it will bring down the blow, as certainly as night follows day. Another sign that you attend to me."

The same small, desperate movement.

"I love you, love you, love you. If you were to cast me off now—but you will not—you would never be rid of me. No one should come between us. I would pursue you to the death."

With that speech, the thing was over. Jackie was grinning toward us like a puppet, and Jane began to clap her hands. I looked toward Orland, and he was wiping his face with the small towel he kept by his bed. The tears gone, he gave a couple of little claps.

"What I need to write next," I said, "is the appearance of the ghost of Dickens at the end of the scene. But I'm not sure if he should be the sick old man who wrote that, or if he should, in his ghosthood, have gone back to his bright-eyed youth."

"Why does the ghost of Dickens appear?" Jane said.

"I don't know," I said. "That's just what happens. I can feel him offstage, the Inimitable, a little bored with ghostly life and ready for a performance, a celebration, walking about the room, getting himself ready, taking a glass of champagne, breathing deeply, barely able to wait. After all, he's the only one who knows for sure how it all works out."

"He may not want to tell," the Dutchess said. I was surprised at her voice, her own now, different from the voice that had spoken those lines.

"I'd forgotten," I said, "what an actress you are."

"I suppose I had too."

"I'd like to turn on the television set," Orland said. "I have to make some notes."

"An't I a clever boy, Orland?" Jackie said. "Aren't you proud of how you trained me up?"

Orland nodded, and we turned on the TV and left him there. Downstairs we had tea by the fire, not saying much, and then found our way back up, Jackie and Jane turning one way, the Dutchess and I the other, to the bedroom we had shared for so long. It all went on well, our life, and yet at times I had the sense that the two of us had betrayed each other—I would never have children, and she would never have peace. Wicked Uncle watched lasciviously as she undressed in the half-light of the bedroom, lit by one small lamp with a red shade. Her skin was still perfect, a creamy white, one small mole near the soft indentation of the navel, and though the breasts were heavier now, hung lower, they were shapely, and rich as butter. As I looked at her, I could imagine the voices of children downstairs, her children who were playing some kind of game, while I prepared to have their mother in her marital bed. It was the end of something when I began to come to her door in mid-afternoon to take her away from her domestic duties, lead her up to the room she shared with Orland and close the door. I had power over her, I knew, the power of her desire for me, her need for my absurd wild hungers. There were times when I wasn't sure she even liked me. I recognized that I was callow, shallow, hollow, but I was possessed by a pure fierce lust, and that she couldn't help responding when I told her she was everything I could ever want. She would lock the door of the bedroom, and we would conjugate the verb in all its tenses, and when she was roused and hungry, I would threaten to get up and leave if she wouldn't promise to come away with me. Sometimes a little girl would come to the door, and Meg would steady her voice to say we were having a grownup talk and tell them to eat cookies until she returned to them, soon, soon. But I wouldn't let her come and then go. I tormented her.

Now, in another bedroom, we prepared to be naked together. The endless storm went on over the roof, beating against the walls. Jane the Carpenter was joining her strong slender body to the clever puppet, a whim it might be, or perhaps she was in his power. I imagined that I could hear her bright cries. The nineteenth-century prints of Punch and Judy enacted their ancient violence on the wall beside our bed. We had bought them years ago on a trip to England, after we'd seen a puppet show, the old story, one beating the other with a stick,

Judy dead, the devil coming for Mr. Punch. They lacked Life Skills, Punch and Judy. We saw them somewhere in a park near a zoo, the giraffe watching with us, philosophical and dim.

I went to the Dutchess and put my arms around her, and our heavy flesh was pressed together. We didn't beat each other with sticks.

"My maid Mary she minds her dairy," I said, "while I go a-hoeing and mowing each morn."

She gave me a little nip on the shoulder.

"You make a fine rosebud," I said.

She drew back from me and looked down at herself.

"Rosebud? Full blown and then some."

"We do eat well."

We tumbled each other into bed and round about the sheets. Slept, and in the darkness I woke and found myself alone in the bed, waited a bit, and no one came. The wind was quiet, but there were a few noises from the furnace. As a way of not thinking about my solitude, I reflected on the long chemical history that made its way here for our comfort, but when my nerves grew imperative, I rose and put on a warm dressing gown and went down the hall. The door of Orland's room was partly open, and I could hear the Dutchess's voice coming from the far corner where he lay in his bed. I couldn't see, but I knew somehow that she was lying there beside him. Her soft voice sounded as if it might be praying or telling some long and intricate tale that wound its way round the facts like a vine round a tree. Turn and turn about: once I had her in Orland's bed, and now he had her in mine.

Along the hall, Jane the Carpenter mumbled in her sleep. I went back to the bedroom, opened the curtains, and saw that the moon had come out between clouds and was shining over the snowy fields.

I woke in the morning to the scream of a skillsaw ripping through wood. The Dutchess was back in bed beside me, awake, her bright blue eyes staring at the ceiling.

"Jane's hard at work," she said.

"Took a look at Orland and decided she'd better have the coffin ready."

"Yes."

"You don't think he should be in a hospital?" I said.

"He wants to die here."

"Why here? Why not in the house where he lived all those years?"

"He sold that long ago, once the girls were grown up. He's been living in an apartment. A cold sort of place."

"Why?"

"It was all he could afford. They closed the museum and gave him some pitiful pension."

"I thought universities were generous."

"Not if they can avoid it."

I climbed from the warm bed, put on some clothes and went toward the stairs, observed Jackie sitting in a chair beside Orland's bed, holding his hand and talking to him. The old fellow was certainly getting all the attention a dying man could want. What did a dying man want? Not to be dying best of all, to be dead next best. Not that I knew. Wicked Uncle was only aware of death as a rhetorical device. It is a far far better thing I do etcetera.

From the kitchen window, I could see Jane the Carpenter at work, pieces of wood leaning against the wall of the house, others lying on a pair of sawhorses painted pale blue. A noble animal, the sawhorse, infinitely patient, infinitely kind, worthy partner in the dignity of work. It was cold out there. I could see Jane's breath as she worked, wearing an old jacket of mine that usually hung by the back door. It pleased me that she had taken it to guard her against the winter. Adopted daughter, Dickensian sister-in-law, whatever she was, it was good to have her at work out there, and I was pleased to take her a cup of strong coffee when it was made.

Her face had a blank, irritable look when she turned to take the cup. The wind ruffled her hair as I felt it blowing mine.

"You've started early."

"As well start as not. Lying there alone."

I didn't ask the question, only looked it.

"Jackie heard voices in the night and decided that it was his duty to be with Orland from now on."

A maiden betrayed, bereft, and mightily pissed off by the looks of her. I put my arm around her shoulder, but she wasn't having any.

"Not your fault," she said, took a long drink of the hot coffee, put the cup down on the edge of the porch and turned to her work. When I went back in the house, Jackie was standing by the refrigerator door.

"Something for Orland and his little boy," he said.

"Take what you please."

"I met someone in the hall last night, in the dark."

"Not me," I said, "perhaps the Dutchess."

"No," he said. "Someone else. One of the others."

"The others?"

"The old ones."

"John Jasper, I suppose," I said.

"The man who made him be the man. That's what I thought."

"You met Charles Dickens in the back hall."

"That came to mind."

"What did he look like?"

"Hard to see in the dark. He was there as I went to my place at Orland's bed. He had something to say for himself, but I couldn't quite hear."

"The ghost of the Inimitable."

"Who's that?"

"What he called himself sometimes."

"Inimitable."

As he talked, Jackie was pulling things out of the fridge and setting them on the counter, butter, jam, oranges, a lemon, a blue bowl containing the last of a sherry trifle.

Outside the skillsaw screamed through wood. Jackie looked toward the noise.

"Last things," he said.

The Dutchess arrived in long skirt and boots with heels, her coat already on, briefcase hanging from her shoulder, hair in a rage.

"I promised to meet with a student before my lecture. Only just remembered."

She was pouring coffee into a plastic device used to infuse the drink while she drove the car. When it was full, she turned, waved, and made for the door.

"What do you lecture on today?" I said.

"Piss and shit. Development of the water closet. Next week it's sewers."

She slammed the door behind her. Jackie was piling things on a tray to take upstairs. I poured myself coffee and sliced sourdough bread and sat alone at the table preparing for the day, while outside the house Jane drove nails into wood. Upstairs Orland spun out the threads of his mortality.

Once in town, I closed two property sales, deliberated with a civil servant on the financial consequences of his adulterous fondlings, dictated a letter proposing a settlement for a blind woman who fell in a hole, and, having checked my calendar and found it empty for the afternoon, went and bought Elaine two expensive cigars and left the office in her hands. It was a clear, still day as I drove out from town, a break after the days of storm, and I had an idea.

As I drove up to the house, I saw the half-built coffin leaning against the side wall. It had the old-fashioned shape, narrow at the ends, angling out from head to shoulders and then back in at the feet. Wicked Uncle was aware, looking at that old-fashioned shape, how long men and women had been dying in this world, how many had been planted in the soil. Inside the house, I found Jane curled up asleep on the couch, under a blanket and looking like a child. Phantom daughter, unborn sister, untouched lover. I hesitated to wake her, but as I stood looking down, her eyes opened, blinked, and she moved her shoulders to wake herself.

"I hardly slept last night," she said.

"An outing," I said. "I have something to show you."

"I'll be ready in five minutes."

I'd brought mail in from the box when I came. It all seemed to be for the Dutchess, from various magazines and universities. Her field, as a collateral branch of Women's Studies, is a lively one. At the bottom of the pile there was a letter for me, but I looked at the return address and didn't open it. A royalty statement for *The Boy Who Got Everything Wrong,* which still sold an occasional copy but not enough to buy much more than a bottle or two of Jameson's. Note to self: record all the rude verses I recite while driving and make a book of them. Wicked Uncle's Rude Rhymes and Polysyllabic Skullduggeries.

A brute I am, I know I am.
I squashed my sister into jam.
I browned my brother into toast.
I frizzled auntie into roast.
I cooked the cat and called it ham.
A brute I am, I know I am.

Jane appeared, her hair damp at the edges. Water splashed on her face and getting all around.

"Where are we going?" she said.

"You'll see when we get there," I said.

She was wearing her own jacket now, but she helped herself to a large scarf from the rack by the door. It was one of those striped English university affairs; we have never known who left it, but it remains there in case the loser returns to claim it. Jane wrapped it twice round her neck and tucked in the ends, and the two of us set off. The farm fields showed traces of ploughed earth through the drifted snow. Like raked light on a painting, the drifting revealed the uneven pattern of the surface, a texture of dark and light. Sun shone from the west across the tall spruces, which were striped with white. Smoke rose from the chimneys.

We were mostly silent as we drove across the countryside. Once Jane the Carpenter spoke.

"Pounding the peg into the hole," she said. "A children's game."

I could think of nothing acceptable to say in response to that, drove on up and down hills, the evergreens dark against the sweep of snow-covered fields, the brief sun going away from us, and then we came up the final hill and I pulled the car to the side of the road.

"Is this it?"

"Get out and I'll show you."

We walked to the edge of the field. It was broad and flat, and it had been kept mowed so that the grasses and weeds were low bits of stubble penetrating the snow. At each corner of the field was a thick post painted silver, the top shaved to a point.

"What is it?" Jane said.

"A landing place," I said. "For UFOs."

She watched me, not sure whether to laugh.

"He says they're going to come, or have already come, and he wants a place ready for them to show them that we're friendly."

"Is he serious?"

"There are people with the gift of faith. Millions of Christians are waiting for the Second Coming, and some of them know the exact date."

"Silver rockets at the corners."

"So they know it's for them. In the exact centre of the square made by those silver rockets he's buried a powerful magnet. From far out in the darkness of space, they'll understand that this is a signal, that one man at least is ready to accept them and their holy message."

Jane looked across the field, her head lifted a little, as if the small straight nose searched for some exotic scent coming off the snow and stubble, or as if her eyes held at a slight angle, could see into the darkness of the woods behind. Now that we have conquered the green world, we no longer fear the darkness of the woods. We look outward into space, inward to the electronic ruins of madness and disease, for the fears that keep us sane. Sex with aliens kills us. If AIDS did not exist, we would have to invent it.

A wind was coming up, and the chill made me shiver. Wicked Uncle thought the spacemen wouldn't come for him tonight, turned back toward the car, and on the next hilltop saw the lights of a house where they were not thinking about the silver ships imminent in black distance, only stumbled from pleasure to heartbreak as everyone did in every house. I thought of Orland making dinner in the dark winter evening for two motherless girls. That was one story, among all the stories.

A brute I am, I know I am
I never gave a tinker's dam.

I cut the tails off all the dogs
and fed a kitten to the hogs.
I sent the baby to Siam.
A brute I am, I know I am.

Wicked Uncle stood by the car door, looked back at Jane the Carpenter, who was staring over the empty field that was an altar to the hope of help. I could almost feel the rise and fall of her breath, and I remembered the naked arm and breast and nipple I had seen in the bed. Coming here was what I could give her, someone else's act of faith. On the way back in the car, we would sing old songs, "My Grandfather's Clock" and other classic tunes, and if she didn't know them, I would teach them to her.

She didn't know them, and when Wicked Uncle taught them to her, it emerged that she didn't quite sing notes, but she learned the words and followed my lead. The dusk was translated into night, and we followed the track of the headlights over the hills as the wind blew a little snow through the air. Just as we turned the corner that led us slowly up hill to the Doctor's House, I saw a dangerous light in the sky, then the orange dance of flame in the dark air and reflected on the snow. I held hard to the wheel, stepped down on the gas, racing to see my home destroyed, frightened and yet for a moment excited too by the power of fate taking charge.

"The house is on fire," I said.

"No," Jane said, "it's not the house. Look, it's back by the edge of the woods."

We were closer now, and as I drove toward the flames, I could see a figure watching them, moving up and down, arms waving.

"The shed," Jane said. "Jackie's burning down the shed."

I braked the car, and it slid over the snow and gravel at the edge of the road. The two of us scrambled out, tangled in belts, seats, doorways, all the bits of farce that come with rushing, and then I was running across the lawn. Jackie, his face full of laughter in the glow of firelight, was looking toward an upper window of the house and waving to someone. He was so close to the fire that I was surprised his clothes didn't begin to burn, or the wooden limbs under his clothes.

"What are you doing?" I shouted.

"I promised you I'd get rid of the old shed. Remember? Earn my keep. Penny a day. Fireworks for Orland too. We've got him in his chair in front of the window. Look at the pretty fire, Orland," he shouted. "All for you."

The skin on my face was stinging. I moved away from the fire, which crackled and roared as it ate through the dry old wood.

"You'll set the trees on fire," I said. "The whole woods will go."

"That would be pretty," he said. "Orland would love that. Forest fire, Orland," he shouted.

I didn't see Jane in the leaping firelight, and I couldn't think where she could be.

One side of the shed was beginning to collapse, but the back end, closest to the trees, was only just beginning to catch. Then it started to roar.

"I put a bit of gas on it," Jackie said. "Gas front and back, to make sure it got a good start."

There was a scrabbling at the end of the shed and in the grass as some animal saved itself. I looked at how close the leaping flames were to the trees, and I knew that the old expression about your heart sinking was no metaphor. I could feel mine dropping away, the strange hollowness that was absolute terror. Jane, her face deep-eyed in the firelight, was standing beside me and holding something out to me. It was the garden hose.

"Use it a minute at a time," she said. "Don't lose the prime on the pump."

She must have gone into the basement to turn on the outside tap and bring the hose. It didn't seem there was time for all that. How long had I been standing here watching? I turned to the fire and pulled the trigger on the nozzle. A fine spray came out and blew back into my face, and I tried again, inept with my growing panic, until I got a long stream of water and directed it at the back of the shed and on the ground and trees nearby.

"Are you putting it out?" Jackie sounded surprised and yet agreeable, ready to change the rules of the game if that's what was required.

"We have to keep it out of the trees," I said. "If the woods go, everything will."

Jane appeared with a garden rake in her hand and went toward the fire.

"Don't go too close."

She ignored me and walked up so close her skin must have been seared. She pushed at the frame of the shed and it bent a little, then she pushed harder and the front of it went down, a shower of sparks rising into the night toward the trees like evil thoughts. I tried to play the hose on the branches where I thought they might land. I saw Jane turn her head to get her face out of the smoke that had already blackened her skin. She was beginning to cough, and I shouted at her to come away. She moved away from the fire, and Jackie took the rake from her and took her place, walking over embers as if he couldn't be hurt, knocking down the burnt frame, swinging the rake in great arcs. I had stopped spraying to let the pump build up pressure. The parts of the shed that lay on the ground burned more slowly, and I walked closer, my hand over my mouth and nose, and soaked the pieces of framing and the remaining fragments of shingled wall. The back corner was still burning in a high sheet of flame, the gas that Jackie had poured onto it not yet burnt off. I went closer now and poured a spray of water over a wild rose bush that had begun to catch fire. Near me Jane was beating her feet up and down on the burning grass. The dance of the end of fire. Jackie worked now to put out the fire with the same enthusiasm with which he'd set it going. He was as frantic as a fly on glass. Wicked Uncle coughed and felt mortality rack his bones. Nearby, Jane was coughing. Jackie swung the rake. The back of the shed broke. When he swung again, it came down, and he jumped back as piece of the roof slid toward him, the shingles spitting. I went as close to the heat as I dared and poured water over the ruins. Sizzling and steam. The flame receded a little. When the heat became too painful and I turned away, I saw a figure standing between the fire and the house. It was the Dutchess, and she moved no closer, stood silent on the snow as if to observe some lesser species struggle, ants whose hill had been dug up and who scurried in their quaint insect way to save the queen. Above, by the light of a table lamp, I could see a shape that must be Orland propped up in his chair by the window. Close to the fire, my skin was seared, but when I stepped back, I felt that my clothes and feet were wet, and my whole body began to shake with the cold. We are such small things in the face of fire and ice. Wicked Uncle heard himself singing "My Grandfather's Clock" in a loud and unmusical voice, in a rage with the Dutchess because she stood far off like an interested tourist. I had waited for a minute to let the water pressure build up, and now I walked back to the fire and soaked it wherever it still burned. It was small patches burning now, like bonfires, neighborly and usual, and I thought it might soon be under control, though the heat still came off it fiercely. Jane had found a shovel and was turning over the piles of rubble to reveal the fire beneath, and I turned the hose on the embers, which sent steam into the darkness. There was less flame, and it was growing hard to see what we were doing until suddenly, there was brightness all around us. The Dutchess had driven her car over the lawn to play the headlights on the place where the shed had stood. The powerful side lighting made it all stagy, a poorly rehearsed ballet, the three dancers stumbling and bumping against each other. I set down the hose and walked past the burning scraps of wood until I reached the trees, illuminated by the headlights, snow outlining the branches, and I looked for any sign of fire. When I came back, the Dutchess was standing there in one of my old coats with the hose in her hand.

"The worst is over," she said. "You three go in and get warm. I'll watch this. Then we'd better take turns."

At first we all stood dumb and useless, then I turned toward the house and the others followed. Once inside, we looked at each other, blackened skin, eyes reddened from the smoke.

"I'll go up and see Orland," Jackie said. "See if he liked his fireworks."

There was a slash of red across the back of his hand where he'd been burned. I was furious, but I couldn't quite think of what to say. I was beyond speech.

"Do something about your hand," I said.

"Presently," he said and vanished.

"I have no clothes," Jane said.

"I'll get you a dressing gown, and you can wash and dry them." I took off my wet shoes and socks and followed my bare white feet upstairs to find the dressing gown, and when I had given it to Jane, I sent her off to clean herself up and wash her clothes. Wicked Uncle poured himself the fireman's medicinal size dram of Jameson's and looked out the window to where the Dutchess stood guard over the remains.

In the morning, the weather had turned warmer. The snow had melted a little and fog stood over the fields and wrapped the trees. Where the shed had been, a pile of blackened boards, a few bits of metal bed frame, an old aluminum pot in the charred ruins. Jackie had promised to haul it all to the road, and the

Dutchess would phone Don Maclean, the trucker, to come and take it to the dump. It would vanish, all its old fearful power gone with it. The dolls' heads with their blank smiles melted into flame.

The Dutchess had risen early and made flaky biscuits for breakfast, and now she was in the shower, all hot and soapy, while I poured a cup of coffee and spread rhubarb and strawberry jam. As I turned to the table, I saw Jane the Carpenter in the doorway, dressed in the clothes that she had washed and dried last night while we all sat and waited for the last embers of the fire to go out. Her face was pale and her expression distant. I was sure that while I had slept like the dead, Jackie had come to her bed again, excited by his fire. Pounding the peg into the hole. Or not. We had arranged that I would go to town with the Dutchess, and when Jane was finished the coffin, she would drive my car to town and park it in my space near the office.

I put the biscuit I had prepared for myself on a small plate and handed it to her, poured her a mug of coffee. She sat down at the table. I didn't want her to tell me about the ghosts that Jackie encountered in the darkness, and she was obligingly silent. I jammed a biscuit, poured a mug.

"Charles Dickens could do conjuring tricks," I said.

She met my eyes. Then the Dutchess was in the kitchen, sizzling like a frying pan, warming the air, stirring us up like a bowl of ingredients. She was all dressed in black, pants, boots, blouse, jacket, with a long red bandana around her neck. It was an outrageous outfit, and I was charmed. Tumbling on the menu for later. Wicked Uncle was tweedy, looked not a bit wicked. Note to self: buy a funny hat. Who did look wicked was Jackie as he danced down the back stairs, the black slash in his eye wider and deeper, wooden teeth rapacious, a bandage on his hand. Jane was not looking at him. Outside the window, dead sailors waited in the mist. If I sat down at the desk in my office and told John Jasper to speak to me, would he do it?

Note to self: try.

A quiet evening by the fireside. Jane was gone now, and Jackie was upstairs watching television with Orland and writing down the occasional words that Orland mumbled from time to time. The domestic fire burned comfortably, and the aliens were still far off in another universe preparing new diseases. They were the angels who came to earth and tempted the men of Sodom to apocalyptic buggery. Sent out the women first, but the men wouldn't have them; the hole of an angel shines like silver and will teach wisdom to your stiff little putz, and we all long for wisdom. Or do we? Across from me in a rocking chair, the Dutchess turned the pages of her book.

"An old cure for bedbugs," she said. "Beaten egg whites put onto the bed with a feather."

This afternoon, I had sat at a desk with a blank sheet in front of me, and waiting for the ghost of Dickens to speak, imagined that he might materialize through the window beyond which the air was again turning to ice. The handsome figure would walk from one end of the room to the other, the arms striking out with large, theatrical gestures, the eyes flashing.

"It is a perfect mystery," he would say. "There is no solution. Did you think I didn't know that? It was all part of my plan. That's why I left so many and such contradictory clues. Those who think they can find the answer are the greatest fools. The Inimitable hides himself better than that."

It was the wrong ghost. Wicked Uncle was not wicked enough to go further. The man who finished Edwin Drood was John Jasper. The other Wicked Uncle. Finished him with a black scarf. *Basta.* So I stood up from my desk, packed my briefcase, and went to the registry office to check title on two properties for clients who wished to buy. A good lawyer always suspects the worst and attends to the unlikeliest of bad possibilities. Hope is for the client alone. In my bag was a color photocopy of the Leonardo painting. In the middle of my work, I carried it to the Renaissance Girl and put it in her hand, and strange to behold, her face was still and then she smiled. She could see herself there. Wicked Uncle left it at that.

When I had finished up my work, I went along the streets toward the desk and the blank sheet of paper. As I walked in the front door of the office, I saw red. A great splash of roses on Elaine's desk with that self-satisfied air that florist's roses always have, cosmetic abundance, the cryogenic look of a movie star after a successful facelift. Behind them, Elaine, smug.

"Well!" I said.

Elaine looked toward me. Cat, canary etcetera. Said nothing.

"Well?" I said.

"He says he wants to move back in."

"Keith?" Keith was the husband who'd scarpered. "What happened to the cocktail waitress?"

"Moved on to the next table, I suppose. He says he's arriving on Saturday to discuss the situation."

"What are you going to do?"

"We'll go out to dinner, somewhere nice, and we'll have a glass or two of wine and a nice meal, and he'll look at me with that cute boyish smile, and I'll light up a cigar and tell him to go fuck himself."

I looked at Elaine's dark eyes glittering from behind the roses, and I knew she meant it. I left her planning the details of her revenge and went back to the sheet of paper on my desk, thought of a few empty words to get me started. The wrong ghost hovered, saying that beyond death there was no imagining the end of the tale. I sat there until it was time to come home. The cupboard was bare and the poor dog had none.

Across the room the Dutchess was watching me.

"It's all right," she said.

I wondered if she had read my mind.

"What's all right?"

"The Dickens thing that you want to write. Go ahead. You know I just like a fight now and then."

"You brought Orland. To get your own back."

"That was an excuse. I would have brought him anyway."

"Couldn't you have left him with the girls?"

"It would be too hard for them. They have little children."

"So you brought him here by the night bus, like a parcel."

"I had to."

"Yes," I said. "You did."

She looked back to her book.

"I can't write it anyway," I said. "I don't believe in it."

The Dutchess was silent.

"Remember, I told you about a girl in the Registry Office who looked like a Leonardo painting. I took her a copy of it today, and she recognized herself."

"Did you tell her you admired her big bum?"

"No, I didn't," I said. "I'm a respectable man."

She smiled at me with a hint of condescension, and I wanted to pull her hair. In the airtight, a log fell and sparks went up the chimney. Pounding the peg into the hole. Yes, we'd have some of that. I have my dignity to consider.

The house was very quiet as the afternoon wound down. It was snowing again, but the flakes were falling straight to earth and there was no sound. No cars passed. No jays cried out in the woods. Jackie had gone to town with the Dutchess, saying he must get Orland some new tabloids. I felt the house crowded with his abandoned ghosts, the voices he heard, the figures he kept meeting in the night, the old doctor, or the Inimitable himself. This morning Jackie announced to me that they were my ghosts, that I was the one who invoked them, though it was to him they appeared. I wouldn't have any of that, Orland's puppet perceiving what I invoked. He saw them, they were his ghosts. Wicked Uncle is a sceptic and knows the silence of silence. When he was a clever boy and perfectly adored in that small house, his sharp sayings noted, smart as Jesus among the doctors, his mother told him that there were no spirits in the air. We had no need of fathers above, of holy ghosts, for we had each other. When she was away, I crawled into the closet among her clothes, eager for the smell of her. Even though later she, lapsed Catholic, unrepentant atheist, went off to Bible Holiness with Ray to keep peace in the house, we had a wink between us to acknowledge our shared disbelief.

The house was too quiet, and I wished for a little wind, traffic, sleet against the window glass. I knew that I should go up and see how Orland was faring, but I didn't want to. The one-legged shape in the bed disturbed me. He made me think of his empty years and how the Dutchess had missed him, the husband of her youth, and had perhaps lain awake night after night when I was deep in the privacy of my dreams and thought about her old man far off. Do you love me? I said to her as we lay in Orland's bed, do you love me? Because if you love me, you must leave him and come away with me. All she wanted was a little innocent adultery, poor thing, a kiss or two, a little wet joy, and now she had this madman on her hands. Come, I said, and come again, and then come away and at last she did.

I delayed going to Orland as long as I could. I looked in the mirror and thought that I looked more than usual like a goat, long nose, big staring eyes, little beard. Shave. Grow it full. I put on a Wicked Uncle look, but it didn't make anyone tremble. I didn't suppose the arse of the Renaissance Girl would loosen at the glance of those glaucous eyes, though I cried love me, love me; the Dutchess would respond, but she saw me plain, a dreadful thing. I might soon have to abandon all dignity and start investing in property development, schemes to grow rich. When the sperm grew thinner one must have silver and gold to spend. Dear old puns. The Dutchess and I would have beautiful young people to look after us, breakfast in bed, massages, and the like. I turned from the mirror and made my way to the stairs.

Orland lay back against a pillow, his eyes closed, and at first I thought he was gone, but then a breath heaved the chest up. The red lips wavered as if struggling to shape a word, or perhaps it was only an involuntary shudder. On the bed beside him was a syringe, an empty insulin vial. I stood in the doorway, and his eyes opened for long enough to see me there and then closed again. They had left me here alone with him on purpose. Jackie had gone to find Jane the Carpenter, where she hid from him in her small apartment, to bend her to his will. Or he and the Dutchess had gone off to a dirty motel.

They abandoned me with this sick old man, and what was I to do about it, admit that he was a good man and didn't deserve his hard life, crave forgiveness?

The question marks accumulate until the full stop puts an end to syntax.

Wicked Uncle showed his teeth, but the figure in the bed was immersed in the events that shook his flesh. I walked across the room, took a straight chair, and set it beside the bed. Was not Jackie, wouldn't climb in with him.

"Anything you want, Orland?" I said. It was unconvincing, and he didn't open his eyes. His slender, bony hand twitched a little now and then. In the basement, the coffin that Jane had built waited on sawhorses. The snow fell softly and greenhouse gases ate away at the sky. Orland took another great breath that looked as if it would burst his lungs then sputtered it out again. Jackie hadn't shaved him today, and bristles stood out from the skin. He still had a full head of hair, and the gray stiffness of it was unnatural against the pale skin. I could see a pulse in his temple, rapid, uneven.

"Would you like tea?" I said. "A glass of ice water?" I knew he wanted nothing, but I couldn't just sit there much longer. I would run away and leave him.

"There were three crows sat on a tree, Oh Billy Magee Magar," I sang quietly. "Do you remember that one, Orland? You taught it to me, but I find I can't remember all the words. When you have a good day, you could tell me, if you remember them. You taught me that during the play. You had your guitar, and you were sitting in the living room of your house, and everyone was listening, and we sang along with the Billy Magee Magar lines. The Dutchess was called Meg then, wasn't she? That was what you called her." I stopped talking and listened to the silence of the house, hoping that I would hear a door open, that someone would arrive. The only sound was the knocking of the furnace.

"There were three crows sat on a tree, and they were black as black could be. I see crows when I drive into work in the morning, scavenging by the roads. Crows and rats and raccoons and cockroaches. They'll survive the greenhouse effect, won't they, Orland? Did you make that up to call her, Meg, or was that her idea? I never asked about that. I just assumed you made it up. I'm babbling, Orland, and maybe you'd like it better if I'd just be quiet. Tell you what, I'll read to you. I'll read to you from your book, all those old stories."

I went down the hall to the back room to find the book. The mattress was bare; after Jane had gone back to town, I stripped the bed, and the sheets were downstairs waiting for someone to have the idea of washing them. Perhaps I'd have that idea later, but one should never do today anything that can be put off till tomorrow. The small book came to hand, and I took it back to Orland's room and began to read. Fill the time until Jackie and the Dutchess got back from town and I could stop being Wicked Uncle the nurse and find a new hobby. Time passed and I uttered the words, and no one came. Once he turned his head to me as if he might be about to say something, ask something, but then he turned away and closed his eyes. It was in the middle of the second story that he turned to me again, and now the eyes were unfocussed and his hand reached out a little as if it could help get life and breath into him, and I knew that Jackie and the Dutchess wouldn't be in time, that he was going to go as I sat here beside him, the last man he would care to have with him at the moment of death. I stopped reading and put down the book. Dying, I knew nothing about dying. I missed my mother's death, the only one that that counted. It happened while I was arriving on the airplane. Otherwise, death was what you heard about, and you sent flowers. Orland's hand shook a little, and I took hold of it. It was warm, and I pressed my Judas flesh on his, the only human thing available. He was making sounds, and I thought there should be old words. He had been kind to me, the fool, when I invaded his sanctuary. There must be something. Anything, not to go in silence. A doctor told me once that right to the last they can still hear. Make a noise, any noise, and now I was singing, "Bobby Shafto" of all things, and out loud, whether for Orland or to shut out the sounds of his dying I couldn't say.

I sang, not looking, and then I realized that the grip of his hand was loose, and when I dared to see him, the face was empty. The UFO had come silently, perfectly down into the snowy field and had taken him on board. I put his hand on the bed, and not knowing what to do next, did what I'd seen in the old movies. I pulled the sheet over his face. That looked ridiculous, a final indignity, so I folded it back again. I could go to the basement and get the coffin and have him set up in it before they got back, but I didn't think I would.

Come close to the fire, little children, and Wicked Uncle will tell you things. Such things. I was walking through the autumn woods with Jane the Carpenter. The leaves were falling from a big maple, and as they fell, they rattled against the still-hanging yellow leaves below them, loud in the quiet of the woods. Earlier we had heard geese overhead. The sky over the tops of the trees was clear, with only an occasional streak of cloud. The air was damp and the light clear and the edges of everything sharp, and we had walked a long way into the woods and now were almost back to the mill where we'd left the car. On the lawns of the houses, there were circles of leaves under all the trees, a carpet of yellow or brown that would later be raked up or blown away, but now they made a perfect pattern. A jay cried out and we emerged from the woods, got into the car without speaking, and drove back to the house.

The Dutchess was sitting at the kitchen table. She appeared to have been ripping the weekend paper apart, and pieces of it lay on the floor all around her. There was flour on her face. Jane looked toward her with some anxiety; we'd been gone longer than planned.

"He just woke up," the Dutchess said. "But I thought I'd wait and see if he went off again."

He. Jane's baby son. It was Wicked Uncle she first told about her state, came to the office one chill day last March, long after Orland had been washed and wrapped and shipped to the bonfire place and the long winter had turned us white and stilled the water.

She came in and found me studying how to respond on behalf of a client being sued for damages after his goat had bitten someone, sat herself down in the client's chair and announced that she was in the family way. Not that phrase, surely, though that's how I've chosen to remember it. Wicked Uncle, I'm in the family way. Bobby Shafto's getten a bairn. I wondered for a moment if she wanted me to commence legal action against the putative *père*, but that was a professional deformation, of course, she only wanted to talk. To Wicked Uncle. I was as flattered as could be and tried to be sensitive and understanding, though that's against the grain and gives me a toothache. Gave it up soon enough and asked who'd put the bun in the oven, as if I couldn't guess, and it was as you'd expect. As I listened to her, a few words, long pauses, it became clear she was planning to keep the little thing. That she had no intention of chasing down Bobby Shafto and putting the bairn in his arms, was prepared to be what's now called a single mother. It isn't all to the bad, the way the world has changed so that Jane wouldn't ever be shamed by it all. Take the bun into the business. Jane and Family, Carpenters. As I listened, I thought this was the time for it and told her the story of my mother and the dead sailor, and we both had a tear in the corner of the eye; old tales retold will do that.

Over dinner at a local eatery we told the Dutchess who was eager to exhibit her Life Skills in finding out young Jackie, but Jane said nix, better he didn't know. Bobby Shafto's gone to sea, so long Bobby. It was over dinner that Jane announced she wanted Wicked Uncle to be the Godfather. Just like Marlon Brando in the movies, I thought: such things. It then appeared that Jane was known to slip off to evensong at Saint Whatsits from time to time, and she meant the real show, in church, the bun properly baked and basted while Wicked Uncle stood by and made wild promises. Nothing for it but to agree. After all, my lovely mother had gone off to Bible Holiness to give Ray a little peace, had a Bible Holiness funeral, a bit long on noise and sincerity for my taste, but what's to be done? And the promises would never stand up in a court of law.

And so, in the fullness of time, a boy child was born, Wicked Uncle hanging about the hospital until the sharp-eyed nurses were convinced that I had sown the seed. Though it was a long business, it all came to an end with a few stitches, and the Dutchess swept the whole boiling off to our house for the first couple of weeks. The thing was small and red and pooped satisfactorily, a fine thing in babies, I'm told, and I was being taught how to keep its head from falling off when carrying it about. Knowing the world for what it is, I had started a trust fund.

I'd noticed as we came into the house after our walk in the woods that the sun was sinking and the air getting a nip, so I lit a fire while Jane went off to get the bun and attend to his diaper. The fire was just beginning to roar when she brought him back in, sat herself down on the couch and hauled out a once-small breast with a nipple like a ripe raspberry, and the baby flailed an arm and twitched and gaped and got the raspberry in his mouth and contentedly stoked up on raspberry jam. I put the screen in front of the fire and went out to the kitchen where the Dutchess was throwing flour and pounding things until they gave in, and out the side window, I saw the golden glitter of late sunlight falling through leaves and branches. Soon the snow would come again. We waited for Orland's ghost, but it did not arrive, unless to her while I slept.

"Dutchess," I said. "There were three crows sat on a tree."

"Oh Billy Magee Magar," she said.

THE MUSIC OF NO MIND

1

It is death brought me here, ladies and gentlemen. I am not the man you wanted, but Denman Tarrington, who had been invited to deliver this first set of Jakeson lectures, is no longer with us. A week ago he was found dead on a green tile floor in front of a mirror covered with steam in a hotel near Lincoln Centre. As a result of that—misadventure let us call it—your committee had to find a replacement with words at the ready and prepared to come to a small Canadian campus in the depth of winter. I am told that a Famous Feminist declined. A Great Scholar pleaded illness. And so it went, until I walked into my apartment in Montreal one evening, after an absence of a few days, and the telephone rang. A proposal was made to me. As a retired professor who taught for many years at this institution, I could be assumed to be prepared for the weather, and so yesterday afternoon, a small plane dropped out of the clouds into a snow squall, and I was driven through the white sweep of empty land and delivered to you as a last desperate gesture to avoid annulment.

We don't care what you say as long as you fill three hours. That is what I have been told. In words almost that blunt. Since I delivered lectures here for nearly forty years, it was felt I could be counted on. Yes, and when I left, I mentioned to one or two colleagues research subjects I intended to pursue in my retirement, a gesture conventional enough, but remembered by someone, I suppose.

Your president, when he introduced me, gave a brief and kind though somewhat inaccurate account of my career, but it is perhaps as well to let it stand. You will not remember corrections if I offer them, though I am compelled to say that I was not a championship badminton player, even when I was a hard-muscled and competitive young man. I will admit to a fondness for the game, but Denman Tarrington, who had long arms and a quick way of slicing the bird into a difficult corner, often defeated me, though in doubles my wife and I could drive him and his tall consort into the floor of the court. The late Denman Tarrington, as we must now refer to him. For most of you he is only a name, a celebrated, semi-divine figure who left this university before you arrived, before some of you were born.

I remember once meeting him in the corridor of Arminian Hall on his way to teach a class, when he stopped to explain to me how much he liked going in to lecture with the musk of a female student fresh in his beard. That was many years ago, of course, when teachers were allowed to treat their classes as a harem, although I'm not sure the Baptist elders on the Board of Governors ever gave their explicit approval. Still it was the way of the times and Tarrington was quick to sense possibilities. I imagine he was also quick to sense that the world had changed and he might have to stop.

Though he garbled a few things in his introduction, your president—and I am grateful to you, sir—got the title of my lecture series correct. "The Music of No Mind." Appropriate perhaps to mention at this point that I believe the title is a quotation, though I have been unable to locate the source. Yesterday evening, I spent an hour at the university library trying to run it down, but I failed, though I did overhear a conversation, which was not without interest, on the subject of tattoos and where on her perfect body a young woman might have one inscribed. The students who were discussing the matter were disgusted by nose rings. As I am myself. Some of you may be aware of Tarrington's little book, *Body Piercing and Theories of Transcendence.* The picture on the back cover shows Tarrington with a ring in his nose. Old bull that he was.

The Music of No Mind. What that means will become clear, I trust, as the series of lectures goes on, but it strikes me now that the errors in your president's introduction of me are indeed germane. I have corrected one, but will not correct them all, and from this day the errors will take on the nature of fact. What is spoken must be, in some sense, true. Did you know that the finest artist this country has produced was listed in an important exhibition catalogue as deceased several months before his death, and that even years later, many argued for the catalogue's veracity?

Beside me, on the table that holds my glass of water, you will see a book which is that artist's biography. The liquid in the glass, let me say, is water, though had Denman Tarrington survived his last hot wash to stand here, it would no doubt have been gin or vodka. After one or two youthful adventures, I made the decision to abstain from alcohol, and in earlier years this was held against me. I must be a sissy, since I didn't get drunk with the boys. When Tarrington, in his days on this campus, wasn't tampering with his female students, he was often to be found carrying on an uproarious and wide-reaching unofficial seminar in a local dive. Occasionally I would drop in—we were friends, at least of a sort—and now and then I would make my small contribution to the discussion. Once or twice, I believe, Tarrington or one of his students arranged to have my soft drink spiked. I hope I survived the evenings with my dignity intact. Memory is vague, but I believe on those nights there were more than the usual number of jokes in questionable taste. The world has grown more abstemious now. Once, drink was everyone's muse. No more. Now they are all dead or on the wagon.

The history of history: look here, inside the cover of my copy of this biography, a number of abrupt communications which have been placed there with a rubber stamp. In an assertive red we are told that the book is *Property of Maritime Air Command.* At some point in its history—letters also in red but in a different typeface tell us—it belonged to the *Maritime Air Command Station Library, Gorsebrook.* Just below these two messages are those saddest, saddest words of all, rubber-stamped twice in a sort of rusty orange, LIBRARY DISCARD, and below, again, yet paler, LIBRARY DISCARD. So it came into my hands in a second-hand bookshop in Halifax, though there is a name in greasy blue ballpoint ink which suggests I was not the first owner after the Maritime Air Command had abandoned it.

Of course we ask ourselves questions about the book, who it was in Maritime Air Command who read it, and whether—it was published in 1936—it might have been the favored reading of a young pilot who hoped to become a painter but later went down over the Atlantic or in Germany. In the lower corner of the blank page before the half-title, there is one more imprint of a rubber stamp, in purple this time. *With the Compliments of the Canadian Committee, 56 Sparks Street, Ottawa.* So this, we must guess, is how the book came into the Station Library at Gorsebrook. A few patriots in Ottawa, determined that men in the armed forces should be made aware of the art of their country, sent it off.

The cast of characters in Ottawa: in a good but slightly worn suit, a man of middle age who until recently had difficulty finding work, but has now got a place with the Canadian Committee and who reads through the publishers' lists in search of books that might be sent out to sailors, soldiers and airmen. Giving this man his marching orders, the chairman of the organization, a short broad person who has made his living as a lawyer, one with many political connections and a surprising streak of idealism as well as a powerful dislike of the United States. He is reputed to be the slave of his shrewish wife, but that is a misunderstanding of their relationship, for in fact they are fond of each other, and if he listens to her opinions, it is because he respects them. There were, of course, others involved in the committee, but they are no business of ours. One of the men we have met was aware of the work of James Wilson Morrice and felt that copies of the first biography should be bought and distributed.

All this is less than perfectly certain, you will say, but the imprints of those stamps are there in the front of the book. Here, if I hold it up, you can see them. There, you see, LIBRARY DISCARD, LIBRARY DISCARD, stamped twice with the energy of some inchoate anger by one of those librarians whose most urgent desire is to throw things out. The unofficial editor set loose in the book of life. Here in the corner is the stamp of the Canadian Committee, those two men in Ottawa.

This biography I hold in my hand comes from the days when it was still possible to write a life without a thousand footnotes. Such a book would now be twice as long, swollen with attributions. Here we have only a prefatory note explaining who it was the author spoke with when he set out to tell his tale. He was, of course, writing when those who had known his subject were still alive, including Somerset Maugham, whose work I admired in the days before he was consigned to the junk heap. Hard to believe now, but I met Maugham once, in a restaurant near Menton, though I spoke only a few words, and he was silent, a wrinkled, stone-eyed old creature with the face of a snapping turtle, basking in the sun of the Riviera, hating the world. Memory and hate: the two are twins.

Let us look at two moments, many years apart, each of them, perhaps, indicative. In 1905, Maugham was in France, and he got to know Morrice as one of the artists who dined in a restaurant in Montparnasse called Le Chat Blanc, in an upstairs room where a number of artists and literary figures gathered. This was La Belle Époque, when Paris was the centre of the world. In one of his novels, Maugham described the painter, a man with a shining bald pate, pointed beard, bright exophthalmic eyes, drunk. Maugham would have it, in his portrait of Morrice under another name, that he was frequently so shaky from drink that his hand could hardly hold a brush. The biographer tells us that while Maugham perhaps exaggerates the painter's alcoholism, he was known to sit in the cafés with his little box of paints, drinking absinthe, doing those small rapid brilliant oil sketches—on thin pieces of wood—of whatever he saw in front of his chair at the café, perhaps close by his apartment on the Quai des Grands Augustins, only a few steps from where Picasso, who had arrived in Paris months before, set up a studio some years later.

So there we have Morrice, as portrayed by Maugham, inebriated, popular, a man of whom no one had a bad word to say.

Well then, we move forward to 1961. Just like that. One quick cut. We all live in the movies now. Morrice is long dead. The clothes the actors wear are different, of course, the furnishings, the quality of the light. We are at Maugham's villa, not very far from the restaurant where I saw the ancient reptile. He is well on in years, and on this evening, he has grown weary and abandoned his company, including his daughter, and retired to his room where he has fallen into a state of agitation. The old brain is failing, and a primitive rage is set loose. "I will show them," he shouts, or so we are told. "I'll put them back into the gutter where they belong. I'll get even with them. Sons of bitches!" The man who was his secretary and lover gave him a sedative and he lapsed into sleep and silence.

I will have more to say about silence. The phone rings. No one there.

Biography is a curious discipline. No secret that the selection of incidents allows the story to be told in any number of ways. If the subject wrote or spoke, the bias of his own statements will create the framework which is filled in by the later babblers. Of course, in nearly every case, the subject of a biography is celebrated. It is clear that fame has its own narrative, and the public achievements must be the justification of any life's telling.

Say that I was to write a biography of our colleague, Denman Tarrington. That phrase—our colleague—is merely conventional, of course, since few of you knew him. I do see Frank Puncheon and Annabelle Disney among you. Yes, Belle, I noticed your presence and those perfect new teeth. Did you notice mine? *Où sont les dents d'antan?* You of course knew Denman when I did. I remember things he said about you, though I won't repeat them right now. We can meet later.

Perhaps I am out of the habit of giving lectures. I notice—as I shouldn't—the faces in front of me, Annabelle of the Perfect Teeth, your ruddy president, several with their eyes closed who may be contemplating my words or, more likely, have simply dozed off. There are three men with striped neckties. Now the necktie is growing more unusual everywhere, even in the academic world, and to see three striped ones in this audience is odd almost to the point that one might consider it ominous. Old school ties. Three members of a Certain Department. Three strips of stripes from the drunken brush of God.

To return: say I was to set out to biographize D.T. The justification would not be that my wife and I trounced him and Madeleine on the badminton court. Who would wish to know such a thing, or any of the other events of our young lives that were shared here on nights when snow howled round the house, except that *our* Denman went on to become *their* Denman, the public intellectual, coming forth from his small New England college to define the symbols of contemporary life in those famous, and if I may say so, incoherent essays like "Happy Electron Bombardment" and "The Suicide Note as a Rhetoric of Desire?" I would be compelled to search for the roots of his informing ideas on the badminton court or in the dark nights of snowbound endurance or to tell shaggy anecdotes of what came later, how his wife vanished, how my wife became his.

Every generation has its own language. To catch Tarrington's essence, one would have had to catch the tone, half learned, half vulgar, of his speech. Maugham's biographer, if I may make a quick step back for a flick-of-the-wrist drop shot, points out that he was in his manner of speech essentially an Edwardian, a fusty old party who habitually used the phrase "sexual congress" for an activity he was fond of. With both sorts, it appears, but mostly with chaps. Morrice had a pretty French mistress. That was how things were then.

I may say, Mr. President, that it had been my hope to illustrate this lecture with slides, but in my race to the airport in Montreal, I left the box of slides in a taxicab, and though I will attempt to trace them, it is possible that I will never see them again, and I must create the required images by means of words. I would not disparage the power of language, but have you ever tried to find words for color, green, let us say? We have that one word, and so we are driven to likenesses, metaphors. There are all the vegetable greens, the green of a stick of celery, the green of a pepper squash, the green, not very different perhaps, of spinach, the green of the avocado, unknown in Canada in my youth but now so common, the green of unripe pears, unripe apples, leaves in bud and the mosses and fungi, all the greens of green. My daughter married a man named Green, and I have Green grandchildren. There was too the hint of green in the skin of the great D.T. as he lay dead on the floor of that New York hotel, blood no longer circulating, the skin first pale, then growing discolored and under the fluorescent lights showing that slightest tendency to the pallor verdurous.

Then there are Morrice's greens and hints of green. I was speaking of Maugham, who as a young man couldn't see the point of the Impressionists. Though he collected paintings later on, some of them valuable, we can't take him seriously as an art critic, but it's worth noting that he says of his fictionalized Morrice that he has the most fascinating sense of color in the world. If one were to examine the small painting of a juggler entertaining a crowd on a street by the Seine, one would say that the predominant colors are black and certain tones of ochre, the juggled balls highlights of red, and yet there is everywhere a feeling of green or blue or conversation between the two. I revived my memory of all these things in your library just this morning. The river is brown but not quite brown, for like the Seine itself, it has a dim green transparency. In an earlier, smaller, quicker oil sketch, a Paris street with a kiosk, there is a sense of the light of evening, and in the darkening background, against a sky that is mauve with touches of yellow ochre, once again, hints of some odd green. If one examined his work side by side with the Impressionists who were still painting around him, or even the *intimistes* like Bonnard and Vuillard, one might say that he was the prince of greens. The manner of his famous painting looking outward from a café in Cuba is in ways parallel to that of his friend Matisse, but the colors, green orchestrated against yellow and blue, would have been alien to Matisse.

You take my point, patient while I sip my water, and of course some of you will wonder whether I told the truth, whether there may not be a little vodka or a touch of gin. No, of course not, though we all know that while speech and truth may sleep in the same bed, they never marry.

Madeleine drank vodka. If we went to their house after a badminton game, she would sometimes take a bottle of vodka out of the freezer, pour some, put a little pepper on top and drink it down. In an emergency—and there were emergencies, but that was in another age—she drank it warm. After three drinks she became vague and slack and easy. It was a kind of happiness, I suppose.

Battledore and shuttlecock, that's what the game was called originally, or perhaps that was the name of the children's sport that was the origin of badminton, named, we are told, for the country estate of the duke of Beaufort where it is supposed to have originated around 1873. J. W. Morrice, our prince of all the greens, was then eight years old, a schoolboy in Montreal, attending school in a building which is now the site of the Ritz Carlton, where I eat from time to time.

Badminton was the favorite form of exercise of another of the great Edwardians, H. G. Wells. Some of you will have heard the story of the pleasant odor of Wells's skin, how he smelt like honey and though odd-looking, was irresistible to women. There are men like that, blessed by the gods, while the rest of us are judged by our behavior. Madeleine told me that Tarrington's skin smelled like fresh-cut hay.

They were an oddly assorted lot, the Edwardians, Wells, with his honey skin, Maugham trying to hide his inversion, Bennett, like Maugham a stammerer, making himself a writer out of sheer vulgar determination. They were between two worlds. Propriety made its demands, but certain kinds of freedom called out. There is the story of how Bennett, settled in Paris to write *The Old Wives Tale,* offered to share his mistress with Maugham. She had two evenings a week free, and she liked writers, he said. The new bohemians, struggling to break free from the rigid proprieties of Victorian England, went to France where sexual release was more easily available. It was the city of *maisons de tolérance,* the place where certain celebrated courtesans were known as *les grandes horizontales,* where Degas returned obsessively to the brothels to draw his lean, accurate sketches of the women at leisure between customers.

A kind of freedom, freedom for men, and for some few women, those who could turn the conventions of the time to their own advantage. Once when I met Tarrington in Paris—we were both there doing research and met in a little café on the Quai des Grands Augustins, in the green light under the plane trees where he drank wine while I consoled myself with a café-crème—he spoke as if such a city still existed. Perhaps for him it did. He had left Madeleine behind in Canada, and he had two regular lovers, an American who was at the Sorbonne, and a young Frenchwoman he had picked up somewhere.

Madeleine was slow to suspect what he was up to. I found this out when I arrived back. She told me about it. That summer. She told me many things, some that I kept to myself for years after. That was the last summer that Tarrington lived among us here. Belle will remember the farewell parties as he prepared to go off into the great world. A last blow-out in their small bungalow, a corn roast on the beach. And the rest of it. The end of it all. Yes, Belle, we both remember.

I have seen you, Mr. President, glancing at your watch, but you know my assignment. Fill the time. I am doing it. If you think my course as indirect as that of the river Meander, I will admit you are right, but it is surely no more roundabout than, let us say, the memoir by Clive Bell which is one of the sources of information about our artist. He wrote it many years after his first days in Paris, and he had reached the age when there are no straight lines in the tale of human experience.

Bell writes of Morrice's flute playing, beautiful until he grew short of breath. He remembers Morrice telling him that he played in the Hallé orchestra—which is almost certainly untrue, but then it is a story and as good as any story. I might tell you that I taught introductory physics at Harvard and met my wife there, a story no more unlikely. Both tales may be true. They ought to be. I must have met my wife somewhere, just as I lost her somewhere, and the scenes that are observed beyond the window, in the far distance, down the long vistas of perspective, are always unclear: tiny figures performing unidentified acts, the tiny dabs of black in the rich color of a Paris evening. It was a conversation we had about just such things that led Tarrington to the writing of one of his first famous essays, "The Triumph of the Background." In those days the two of us were teaching sections of An Introduction to Civilization, the course which attempted to bring our students into a little intimacy with art, music, literature and philosophy through the ages. An Introduction to Glibness, the head of the French department called it.

I was speaking about the color green. Morrice's Canadian paintings don't use it as one of their keynotes. There are lovely pink and purple shadows on the snow, and the light is usually the light of winter, gray and blue—though the original of his famous picture of the Quebec ferry, if examined carefully, has strokes of green in the ice, though they are almost impossible to see in small reproductions. There is so much we never see. Morrice chose not to see the greens of the green season in the Quebec countryside, because of its rapidity perhaps, the way the golden green of spring vanishes, is touched by darkness so soon and then gone, or because he was artistically blind to them. Part of the genius of any artist is his blindness. What he cannot see makes possible what he can. The long slow greens of rainy Paris hang in the air like the scent of smoke.

I've always enjoyed fine phrases. My record of publication is scant partly because ideas come to me in a likely phrase, a short paragraph, and the struggle to move from that to a coherently argued essay has been inordinately difficult. In youth, I was full of ambition, but the silences between the words conquered. In front of students, I was able to summarize and quote and add my own little insights. The repeated pattern from year to year, new faces in the same old seats, made it seem sufficiently commonplace that I didn't listen to my words. Here in front of you, it is something else, but I came knowing it was an emergency, inspired, perhaps, by the thought of that body lying dead on the tiles, and I will do my duty, after my fashion. I have often thought to write about Morrice, and I make regular trips to the Musée des Beaux Arts in Montreal to look at the collection of sketches on wood.

I can now count only two striped ties in the audience in front of me. Two ties in two seats of Madden Hall, where once there were three, and yet I was unaware of a departure. Perhaps my mind was on other things, as it should be, on history, art and badminton. Perhaps the man wearing the third striped tie did not in fact leave but slipped it quickly off. It might even be one of those ties that clips onto the collar, though I haven't seen one of those for years, but with such a tie, it would be the work of a second to remove it. In a moment of self-consciousness or cunning after I was bold enough to mention the presence of these three men with the strip of stripes that would identify them to each other. Now one has abandoned his team, his tie hidden in his pocket. Take that, cravat. Or perhaps he only got bored and angry and slipped out when I was staring up to the ceiling for energy and inspiration.

Bored and angry: Tarrington's rage, *La Furia di Tarrington,* that remarkable piece of baroque nonsense for the keyboard.

Biography, you will have noticed in your past reading, and I'm certain you are one of those who has, Mr. President, is often an invitation to bad writing, what is thought to evoke the times and places of the past, usually with the direst consequences.

You know the sort of thing. *In old Quebec Morrice would see the happy peasants tramping in from the countryside with their baskets of fresh farm produce, charming and colorful personages in brightest homespun. Then he came to Paris, the streets of the yellow fiacres, with his most magic flute, his passion for the pigments, and his great and high purpose.* An attempt to make the *mélange* of fact and opinion and rumor that is the source of biography into a story, usually the imitation of tawdry fictions already existing, whereas life, as we all know, is not a story at all. It is the music of no mind.

The shuttlecock summer. Back and forth. You will excuse my pun. Those of you who play badminton, will know the excitement of the slow rise and soft fall of the shuttlecock. It has about it a rare beauty, lovelier than the meaningless bouncing of balls in tennis and squash. It is a quiet game, only the sudden soft exhalations of breath as the player runs into position and lifts the bird high over the court or niftily slices it into the corner by the net. As I have explained, my wife Anne and I could usually defeat Denman and Madeleine. We were never so close as with rackets in our hands, had the unspoken ability to share the court even in the quickest passages of the game, whereas Madeleine's long elegant legs were, in the stress of competition, a little ungainly, and her husband tried to play the whole game himself, pushing her out of the way now and then to get at the bird, preventing her from making shots that she could have returned if left to herself. After every loss, we were treated to *La Furia di Tarrington,* and one sometimes wondered what Madeleine had to endure once he got her home. Anne, though she had shorter legs, pink and soft-thighed, breasts that slithered and bounced, was very quick on her feet and had an intuitive sense of where the opponent would move next so that the shuttlecock dropped just where the enemy used to be. It was my duty to drive Denman to the back of the court with long lobs and smashes while Anne finished the point with finesse.

After the game, we would recover our baby daughter from the sitter, and we might go to their house, or sometimes Denman and Madeleine would come round for an Ovaltine against the cold winter night. In the hour we spent together, as Denman and I bragged about the clever things we had said in lectures and set out our plans for the books we were to write, *La Furia di Tarrington* would, I hoped, calm itself so that Madeleine would have less to endure when they got home.

To move on, move on. I have a story about Picasso, which I recall from Clive Bell's book of memories. I have said that one of Bell's subjects was J. W. Morrice, whose friend he became on his first trip to Paris. Like all personal accounts of the painter, it is affectionate and favorable. He seems to have maintained his charm even when far gone in drink, an unusual enough characteristic, as we all know, who have been among the bores and vulgarians of late-night gatherings. In a journal, Arnold Bennett remarked of Morrice that he had the joy of life in a high degree, and he gave this characteristic, the delight in every detail of existence observed, to the character he based on his friend. Clive Bell claimed that it was from Morrice that he learned to enjoy Paris. That faculty of enjoyment was surely linked to the speed and small size of his oil sketches.

But Picasso. Picasso and the bath: in a discussion of miracles, the great Pablo said that he thought it a miracle that he didn't melt in his morning bath. This was during the days of his first marriage and rich respectability, and someone who heard him remarked that a few years before, one wouldn't have believed he knew what a bath was for.

In those days, in France, it was possible to have a bath sent in. A team of men carried in the tub and hot water and disposed of it when you were done. Bell knew a man who knew an actress who had one sent in to her top floor flat once a week. Women bathing, it has been a subject from Degas and Bonnard to the TV commercial. The peeper's delight. The long slender body in subtle tones of iridescent milky white, with touches of mauve and perhaps a little hint of green reflected from the leaves outside the window. She is bent to dry herself with the blue towel, and that too casts a little reflection on the hospitable skin. Outside the open window, a chirping of sparrows and the sound of a car driving by. Didn't know whose car, wondered.

I am not aware that our man Morrice ever painted a woman bathing. There are a few finely done nudes, and one astonishing portrait, now in the possession of the National Gallery in Ottawa, which is as sexual as any nude, though in fact only the head and bare shoulders of the model are seen, as she looks toward us from the top right corner of the painting, while most of the canvas is the remarkably delicate and sensual painting of the bed sheets. Though the model is unidentified, the name Jane is painted into the texture in large pale letters, and the small canvas evokes the greatest possible intimacy. The woman naked beneath the covers. The commonplace miracle.

Tarrington lying naked on the tiles after his last ecstasy.

This is not easy to believe, and I am myself astonished, but now suddenly I see only one striped tie among you. Is this a game? My eyes, at least with the aid of these spectacles, are accurate enough, and I know what I see. Three striped appendages. Then only one. Certainly I have noticed one or two people departing from the dim back corner, but the striped ties were, each one of them, buried among you, well forward in the light.

Wake up, Frank Puncheon. I see you there with your eyes closed. I know, as an astronomer emeritus you are compelled to be up half the night staring at stars, but it's only proper to pinch yourself and pay attention. In front of you, the three short-haired young female lecturers are doing me the courtesy of smiling and nodding even though I am a Dead White Male. You can do as much. You know badminton yourself. We used to play from time to time. I remember a particularly vicious slashing game just after we both had proposals for conference papers turned down. Tarrington, then creeping toward fame, was on my committee, though I fail to remember who was on yours.

One of the errors in your introduction, Mr. President, was in the matter of my involvement with the local naturalists' society. I was not merely one of those involved in bringing the annual bird count to the district, I was in fact the first of those to bring the bird count to this part of the country, and my birding columns were not merely published in the local press but were syndicated throughout eastern Canada and certain of the New England States. Credit where credit is due. Though I never became a celebrity, I played my part in life. An attendant lord? One would hope not just that. You will be able to place the quotation, Mr. President, from your memories of Introductory Civilization. You were, of course, in Tarrington's section, and I remember he said you were not much inclined to work but didn't need to as you would inherit a thriving chain of stores. It has been observed often enough that you have been good about passing on some of your profits to this institution and bringing your moneyed friends into the fold. Thus the Jakeson lectures, funded by your in-laws, Jakeson and Jakeson. So, as I acknowledge your good works, you will allow me the cavils of an old scholar.

Now in all this, we have forgotten someone. We have forgotten that man in a small office in Ottawa, an upstairs office on Sparks Street. It was a street in those days, a dim street of heavy buildings, though it is now a pedestrian mall where buskers come out to amuse the tourists who are in town to see the Parliament Buildings all sharp and Gothic on their hill above the wide river. I often take an early morning bus from Montreal to Ottawa and go to the National Gallery to see the Morrices, some other things by his friend Cullen, and a few other favorites. There is a charming painting by a certain W. Blair Bruce, an artist contemporary with Morrice and Cullen. It's called *Joy of the Nereids* and is a bubbling waterfall of nudes, a big painting, perhaps eight feet square, and in splendidly garish colors. It brings a smile to my face when all else fails. I recommend it. A sovereign cure for melancholy, and a splendid spread of naked belles.

Belles with an "e." An old-fashioned term, but appropriate enough to the period. Belle as in Annabelle, and you were, weren't you? *Nous n'irons plus au bois.* The man in the office, we are forgetting him again. He thinks, sometimes, that he was born to be forgotten. A few years before, he was a manager for a large firm selling office supplies, but the business failed in the Depression, and he was thrown on the street. For a short while he was reduced to selling insurance, but a friend who felt sorry for him told the Canadian Committee that he was the perfect man to manage their office. Until then he had thought very little about his patriotic duties, and early in life had considered moving to Chicago, but he was willing enough to become a patriot if there was a job in it. His children are beginning to be grown, and in fact his son, a feckless boy who quit school last year and delivers groceries on his bicycle, spending his pocket money on smokes, will come of age just in time to join the army for the war which is now imminent. He will die on the beach at Dieppe, and his father will wonder forever afterward if they might have been friends some day. Our man keeps very busy during the war, for the Canadian Committee takes on a number of contributions to the war effort, some of them in collaboration with the YMCA, and at the end of the war he will find a job running the Ottawa branch of the Y, and he will stay there until retirement. He has two daughters, but we will not enquire as to what destiny intends for them.

Earlier in my lecture, when I mentioned the inaccurate rumor of Morrice's death, I failed to mention the odd fact that this is an echo of a book, Arnold Bennett's *Buried Alive,* a book in which the character of the hero, Priam Farll, is derived in some small ways from Morrice. In that story, an artist still alive is believed to be dead. It is all a shade farcical. The incorrect reports about Morrice's death were spread partly because of his vanishing acts. Especially later in life, his friends often had no idea where he was. He would pack up and go at the slightest provocation. Léa Cadoret, his mistress, was accustomed to receiving a card mailed from a railway station announcing that he was off to Cuba or Morocco or Canada. He must have known that his health was failing near the end, for he bought her a house in the south of France. Not many years later he died in Tunis, alone.

We prefer, of course, to remember him in Paris, in his chair at a café, his paints in a little box in his pocket, to be taken out for one of those sudden tiny oils, the work punctuated by absinthe or whisky. Sometimes, when he needed a figure in one of the sketches, just there, a punctuation, he would send Léa over to stand in the right spot, and she obliged. She was clearly devoted to this curious lovable man, and he treated her well in his absent-minded, occasional, evanescent way. She had first come to him as a model, and it was easy enough to stand on the cobbled street, the kiosk in the background, the evening life of Paris going on around them, sudden dabs of black in the picture. A love story of a sort. There are so many. I called Morrice the prince of all the greens, but he was also king of the blacks. Never such speed and suddenness as the picture of figures and pigeons in the Piazza San Marco. Everything is there and flying. Black figures, black feathers, in one of the golden cities.

Once such things were in private collections, hidden on the walls of great houses and high apartments, and some are even yet, but more and more, they are in museums. If you own an important painting, you are caught between the thieves and the company that insures you against their depredations. Maugham, in his later days, growing anxious and irritable as old men do, was at last so terrified that his paintings might be stolen that he sold them all, even those he had given to his daughter. Ashes, ashes, we all fall down. Denman Tarrington fell down in that small bathroom. It might have been the subject of one last essay. "Dying in the Steam: A Mist that Never Rises."

The café where we met: I had walked along the Seine on my way and I had puzzled over his appetites and the ease with which he satisfied them. That summer, his first essay had appeared in *Partisan Review,* and he had been invited to New York to meet Philip Rahv. At least half of that essay was derived from conversation between the two of us, and I no longer knew which ideas were mine, but some of them were. He took them without so much as a by-your-leave, as he would always take what he wanted. If I had written the essay, it would have been more coherent and less successful. I looked down at a barge passing along the Seine, laundry hung across the deck behind the cabin, and I half imagined the life lived on the boat, a boat just like one of those passing by the Quai des Grands Augustins in the Morrice paintings I loved even then, though I had seen fewer of them.

As I walked toward the café, I saw Tarrington seated at one of the tables, making notes in a small book. When he saw me, he put it away. At the end of the summer, he would be leaving us for a more prestigious university, and there would be no more badminton games. No more Ovaltine on wintry nights, no more feeling sorry for Madeleine. Much more than that to be lost, though I couldn't know it then. As we met in Paris, Madeleine was back in their little house organizing the move, beautiful, awkward, unhappy. Anne was away, visiting her aunt, but I expected to find her at home when I got off the plane a few days later, though when I got there the house was empty; she had extended her visit. I sat down at the table with Tarrington and ordered, and it was only a few minutes before he was telling me about the pubic bouquet—both senses—of his American girl, and the cleverness of the French one. It was a mystery to me then and is now how Tarrington gained the belief that everyone loved him, and that he was excused in advance for all the wanton acts he might care to commit, that women would adore him in spite of his faithlessness, that the world would open its doors at his approach, that his lies would become truth once they were spoken, or if not become truth be found necessary and right in some other way. The blood that was shed was never his responsibility. Could I, one day, learn to shed blood?

I told you about the conversation I overheard about tattoos. One of the young women reported to the other that her boyfriend wanted her to put roses on her butt, as she phrased it. Tarrington would have made that sort of demand, and possibly some woman would have acceded, would have been willing to be branded for him. The secrecy of secret marks, a part of intimacy. Perhaps after the lecture, the clever young women academics in the second row will discuss this with me, and I can pass on their wisdom in the next lecture.

Astonishing. The last striped tie is gone. I wonder if their departures are carefully timed, and with an obscure significance that I have been unable to work out. There are those who believe that everything in the world is significant, that a pattern exists, whether or not we can perceive it. My wife Anne was known to read the horoscopes. She suspected that forces were moving outside the bounds of our awareness. As if the three men in old school ties might be gathered somewhere in the dark corner of the physics lab, listening to the humming of the cyclotron and comparing notes on my lecture, to make sure that between the three of them they have an accurate record of what I said.

Anne had a secret mark on her lower back. Sometimes I would stare at it, and try to describe it to her. It is like an Egyptian hieroglyph of a bird, I would say. It is like a tarragon leaf. It is like a like a dark and slender insect, perfectly still, waiting for its prey. It is the precise shape of your immortal soul. She flushed easily, blood mantling her skin. When we played badminton, her face grew pink and damp, and she had a way of pushing her hair back with her left hand.

That is what I recall. Once I thought of writing a work of fiction about the early years here. A question, of course, as to how a work of fiction can be about a real time and place. The reading of literary biography is unsettling in the way it shows us how writers mix experience, gossip and lies and call the whole gallimaufry a novel. Arnold Bennett's *Buried Alive,* as I have said, tells a long and unlikely story about an artist who is alive though believed dead. A note on influences: the painter's wife in that book strikes me as quite possibly the source for Joyce Cary's Sara Monday. Books are made from other books, as a critic observes. And paintings from other paintings. Lectures from other lectures. Of course both Bennett and Cary are out of style, and no one is likely to care how one book was made out of another book, one wife out of another wife. Late on in Bennett's novel, when his hero has gone back to painting, Bennett attributes to him a painting which is exactly an oil done by his friend J. W. Morrice—though he says it is a painting of London, when in fact it is Paris. The painting is now in Ottawa in the National Gallery. On the very next page, whether as a joke or an apology, Bennett mentions Morrice, side by side with his contemporary Bonnard. This is not imagination so much as a set of gossipy games. Everything is connected, but not by the force of the stars.

My copy of this Bennett novel, now long out of print, came from a second-hand bookstore like so many of my books. I have fewer now, of course, having left many of them with your library when I moved to Montreal. I hope the library has not tossed them all out. Library Discard. Library Discard. I didn't check when I was there, though I did pick up a copy of the recent library newsletter with its story about the early manuscripts given to the institution last summer by Denman Tarrington, probably when he was asked to inaugurate the Jakeson lectures. I asked to see them, but they are not yet catalogued, and so are inaccessible. I don't know how much of a saver he was, our D.T.—I used to refer to him as Professor Delirium Tremens—but if he was a saver of everything that touched his important life, as I suspect he was, there are letters of mine in the hoard. Letters from long ago, threats and explanations. Perhaps he never opened them.

Arnold Bennett, Somerset Maugham, Clive Bell, the three literary blokes who moved through the bohemian world of Paris and met the charming, brilliant, alcoholic Canadian painter, and then of course went on to other lives. Maugham became, among other things, a spy, married in odd circumstances and later complained to Glenway Westcott that his wife's physical demands were intolerable, inexcusable. The myth of nymphomania, a word that was current in my youth, though I think it is now gone out of common usage. Later on, intemperate desire was advertised as both common and exemplary. Witness Denman Tarrington's fame. Then came disease and a return to prudence.

More often than uncontrollable female appetite, a joint madness, nymph and nympholept in a state of demoniac possession for reasons beyond our power to express. The one tireless, the other insatiable. Nothing to do with love, but many have known what it was like, a woman possessed and needing to be possessed endlessly, for beyond was a vacuum, merest nothingness. Maugham's wife knew she could not have him, a cold man and a homosexual, so she would have his services, would insist on being filled. That he was horrified was only partly his misogyny. It was a terror of what lay beyond, the emptiness that could not be filled. Yes, it was like that.

I am stopping too frequently now for these sips of water. My throat grows dry, and my legs are aching from the time spent here at this lectern. I am coming toward the end of my allotted time. The three striped ties have vanished, and that is a signal. It is regrettable, perhaps, that the slides were left in that taxi, for those of you who haven't seen Morrice's paintings will be left with only my verbal evocations of them. There are books available in your library. I checked, when I was not listening to an essay on tattoos, and those of you who are interested may go there and see the only barely adequate reproductions. Or you may also get yourselves to the collections in Montreal and Ottawa. I recommend it.

I was a young man when I first became aware of some of those paintings. I was a young man. That in itself is a surprising thing, for I am now as you observe me, but once I was lean and quick on my feet, racing backward and forward on the badminton court, wrist and arm tireless, sweating only a little from the exertion as I dodged about, Anne's figure, sturdy and pink, as quick as my own. On the other side of the net, Denman Tarrington's sharp-featured, bearded face—I wonder how often the beard smelled of a recent student—Madeleine's tall, somehow helpless body reaching out, and sometimes, with her long reach, she would catch one of our shots, against all likelihood of its being caught, and lift it over the net, and I was aware of a kind of shudder of relief going through her body. Outside, always, the snow.

Apparently Morrice's winter scenes were mostly painted in his studio in Paris from pencil sketches and oil *pochades* done on the spot. His back turned to the window over the Seine, he studied the Canadian landscape in his mind and gradually, each morning adding a few more strokes, he made it real on canvas.

I will keep you from the important duties of your lives only a moment more. Indulge me just a little. You remember our friend in Ottawa, working for the Canadian Committee, filling out order forms for copies of the biography of J. W. Morrice, though in fact he has never seen the painter's work but has read a review of the book and believes that it is important, and it is among those he will see distributed to the army, navy and air force, a testimony to the importance of the country they serve. Then as he sits at his table in the small office, doing the work for which he is paid very little—though it is better than the hopeless idleness that came before it—he thinks of his wife, at home, waiting for him in the dim November afternoon, and he tries to imagine her as she was before he met her, tries to reach that ghost of the future, and is aware that he cannot.

Tomorrow afternoon, I will offer the second lecture in the series. I trust you will all be here once again.

2

It was kind of you to offer that little reception for me after yesterday's lecture, even though a number of those invited took flight after five minutes, and I did overhear one or two remarks that were characterized more by irony than comprehension. *We know what he means by no mind, don't we*? That sort of thing, tossed off by those who have learned all too well that worst academic habit, sly condescension. Even as an undergraduate, I was aware that a certain kind of thing that passed for wit was the anxious cruelty of the uncertain.

Your president, who has bravely come back for my second performance, was generous in the face of my caviling at his introduction and its inaccuracies. Little enough time for research, as he observed. We were both forced to speak on little notice. I had three days to prepare, he little more than three hours, he told me. So we have agreed that we both did our best in the circumstances. I do confess that it was dim-witted of me to lose the box of slides, though I had only a limited number prepared which were appropriate to my subjects. I hope they turn up. Most were slides I had used in my undergraduate lectures at this very institution.

One of the brisk and skull-shaven young women in row two—and I notice you have all come back, very good of you—said that she felt wholly unable to predict what I would choose to talk about in my second lecture but there you are, back for more. I could have claimed to have no idea myself of what I would say next, but you will see that there is a pad of notes and sketches here, places to start, *obiter dicta* that may be offered and glossed. Here, for example is a note that says: *The homogeneity of time, the condition of waiting.* I'm not sure we'll get to that one. I'm certain that when I scratched it down, I had something in mind. Is time homogeneous? Perhaps some physicist in the audience will let me know.

Our last lecture got us to Paris, and another of the quotations in front of me is about Paris, written by Walter Benjamin, about the city's mirrors, the immaterial element of the city, he calls them, and you will recall how often in a small café or restaurant you look up from the table, and a mirror will show you those who stand by the bar, and behind them, the buildings on the street outside. You may be familiar with the photographs of Brassai, how we catch the sense of ongoing life in the mirrors of the bars where he took pictures, two lovers, his face in one mirror, hers in another at right angles to the first. Love is this and this, but also this and this, and the mirror holds it without comment.

After the reception yesterday, I walked back to my room in a pleasant motel just down the road, and as soon as I was inside, one of the mirrors caught me and showed me myself. As I looked, I thought about that old trick of exposition, found in bad fiction, where the main character looks in the mirror and the author is able to describe the long pale face, the white hair combed straight across, the pattern of wrinkles beside the eyes, the thin mouth that might be about to smile. A face that a woman, in the grip of whatever madness, once called beautiful. You know the sort of thing. The mirror gives us an author's-eye-view of ourselves. When I walked into the bathroom, there was yet another, larger mirror, as there was in that hotel room in New York where Denman Tarrington could admire his naked body before stepping into the shower.

No one who wasn't a thoroughgoing narcissist could have lived his life. Each morning, he stood there, a little heavier, the face giving the impression of solid slabs of flesh with slight declivities where the slabs met, the long arms hanging from the sturdy body, a little ape-like perhaps, but effective for seizing the ripe fruit of life. Once he had those arms round a woman's body, there was no escape. Still pretty well hung, he would think to himself, as he observed the thing in repose.

I reflected as I stood in the bathroom of that motel, that if he had survived to come here and speak, he would have looked in the same mirror, stood where I was now standing. The two of us were there for a moment, side by side, as if washing up after a brisk hour on the badminton court. Then I turned my back, sent him once again to the underworld.

We are accustomed to mirrors by now, but once they were rare and expensive. The first mirrors were polished metal discs, hand mirrors that showed only the face. Before those metal discs, men and women had only the surface of the still pool, but that was enough for Narcissus. Fell in love with himself and that was the end of him. Perhaps the mirror changed history. Brunelleschi began his studies of perspective by drawing what he saw in a mirror, and it was only in twentieth-century art that his mirror was shattered.

For now I see through a glass, darkly, Paul says, in a passage we all know, and I suppose the reference is to an early mirror of poor quality, glass of limited transparency, full of flaws, backed unevenly with silver, but now the mirrors are perfect and the flaws are in the face observed.

I was in the middle of these reflections last night when the telephone rang, and I picked it up, for once unthinking, wondering if perhaps it was someone who had been assigned to take me out for dinner at the Boat Shed, always my favorite restaurant, but the instant I lifted the phone, I could hear the silence, and I said Hello, and Hello and Hello, and there was nothing, and I hung up. Beyond the motel window it was snowing. The calls had stopped, or so I believed. One or two after I moved to Montreal. Now another. Looking into the audience I search among your faces for the half-forgotten face, come here to watch me, to listen and then late at night to make a call, but there is nothing to be found. Are you there? No.

When the phone rang again, later on, I found it hard to answer, but I did and it was my daughter Sylvia calling from Victoria to ask how the lecture had gone. Now that we are back in touch, she tries to be good to me. I described the lecture to her, but of course she thought I was joking. Perhaps I was.

I see you, Belle, slipping in the back door. Hello. A little late. Well, I was afraid you had abandoned me. Tomorrow after the last lecture we must get together and bring back old times over dinner. I have been speaking, while you were struggling here through the snow, of the mirrors of Paris, the mind of the city which watches, unmoved, the little adventures of life. The mirrors on the walls of the brothel where the act is seen and then the empty room is unseen. As if the rooms might expect our coming, that room in the motel anticipating my return, my apartment in Montreal full of familiar shapes and smells although I am not there. The mirrors on the brothel wall offer a doubling or, with facing mirrors, a tripling and then a projection of the act to infinity, a hint that we can know the unknowable. He knew her and she was with child, as the Bible would have it, but of course he knew nothing. He stirred the nerves.

One of my favorite of Brassai's photos is of two women in a bar, the bartender seen in the mirror at an odd angle, and for me, it evokes Manet's great painting of the bar of the Folies-Bergère, a painting which is now in the Courtauld Institute. One can read essays about Manet's painting, and what we can or can't see in the mirror behind the lovely-looking young woman who is tending bar. The reason he is a great painter is that the questions he asks are not the same as the questions he answers. The portrait of the barmaid was the first in which he used a mirror, though Ingres and Degas had used the device earlier. Here the observer is struck by the oddity of the reflection which appears to be an angled view though seen in a straight mirror. You will all have seen prints of the painting, and I will not tell you what you already know, except to say that if he had used the mirror in a mechanical way, what we would see is the artist at his easel, but in this case the painter has disappeared, and his absence is as powerful as the unspeaking voice at the other end of my phone call.

I will come back to a painting where the artist is seen in the mirror. Perhaps you can guess what I'm referring to. We are all, of course, thrown back on memory by my absent-minded loss of the slides, and while some have a capacious and accurate visual memory—I have tried to train my own—others have only a few vague impressions, and those who have never seen copies of the pictures I refer to can only take my word for what is there. As easy as to imagine Tarrington's sturdy body lying dead in the steam. As easy as to imagine Madeleine standing beside me on the shore in the dark as the soft lap of the rising tide moved over our bare feet. As easy . . . well, you take my point.

Until I came to this university as a young man, recently married and a father, I had never lived near salt water. I was raised among long streets and flat country, bicycle rides and baseball, slow dusty summer evenings. From the window of the house we rented when we came here, a house we purchased two years later, you could see a narrow stretch of water some distance off over the marshes.

It is still there, that big frame house. Some of you will know it. It was too big for the three of us, but when we arrived, it was for rent, and Anne wanted it. When we first examined it, she stared out the window at the water, which was blue that day, reflecting a blue sky, and the marsh the drying green of late summer, and when she turned from the window, I could read the expression on her face and see that she wanted to live here. I was not always able to read that face.

Difficult to read the face of Manet's woman, the one behind the bar, in front of the long, deceptive mirror. As a model he used, not a professional, but a woman who actually worked at that bar, though who is to say why? He had a complicated way of confronting reality, not quite one thing or the other. If you study the original, you will find that the painting moves in receding levels. The effect is lost in reproductions. Manet asked, as I have said, one question and answered a different one. The music of no mind.

One of the women who came to last night's reception enquired if, given my title, I would be making reference to the history of music in these lectures, and I explained that although I mentioned music in the title, I would not. I understand the sound of music only when it is overheard, in fragments, perhaps from another room or from a passing car. That is music, the momentary haunting of the air by fascinating sounds, but the continuous scratching of fiddles is meaningless. Words too are best when overheard. Behind my back, just at that moment, as I was discussing music, a voice was saying, *She was never seen again.* My ears are not what they once were, all the senses growing dull, but I did hear that, a sentence summing up a life. She was never seen again.

The window of our house looked over the salt marsh toward that tongue of sea, and I kept binoculars hung close by so that I could watch the birds that appeared there. Birds to come in my third lecture. Below the window was the lawn where Anne and I would sometimes play a sort of badminton with no net. Yes, I know what Robert Frost said about free verse, though I'm not sure of its application to marital badminton. Our daughter Sylvia was only a little thing in those days, and while she was a charming child, she was a child, and Anne was alone with her for long hours while I prepared classes and marked assignments and attempted to finish my doctoral thesis. Never did. Tarrington, of course, had completed his before arriving, a year after we came here. Years later he referred to my difficulties in another of his early essays, "Night Baseball: Rules of the Academic Game."

Young, we all were, and recently married. Wedding photographs on the bedroom dresser. The long article on the symbolism of wedding photographs is one of the pieces of writing I did finish, as your president told you when he introduced me yesterday. Got that one right, rushed as you were, Mr. President.

In fact that essay was meant to be the start of a book. I had in mind a companion piece about the most famous of all wedding portraits, the van Eyck oil usually called the Arnolfini Wedding, which always made me think of my own wedding photograph. If you look in the indexes, you will find a long list of articles on van Eyck's picture, but for our purposes, the matter at issue is one small section in the upper half. The convex mirror. A favorite device in the Flemish artists of the period, Campin (or whoever it was painted what is attributed to him), Petrus Christus, Memling, Quentin Matsys, they all show their skill by rendering the glossy surface of the mirror and the odd corner of reality it catches. Of course we know little about those old Flemish masters, and among scholars there is a rage to name artists who might better be left anonymous so that we are invigorated by our ignorance, rather than stifled by what we believe we know.

Was she pregnant? A great belly brought into being by that long-faced expressionless man beside her. It's easily enough done, or was in the days before the pill. I gather, of course, that we are now in the days after the pill. Dangers to health of one sort or another. My friends in the second row will enlighten me later on. If I were as prolific as the lamented Tarrington, I would write an essay on the shaved head and new standards of female beauty. Yes, my dear, I have a shrewd suspicion that you are differently inclined, but the shape of your scalp is very appealing, and though not a professional lecher like D.T., I have never been able to keep my eyes off certain women.

And that is how my wife became my wife, quite against her better judgment. She didn't wish to marry me, but she did.

The convex mirror in the wedding portrait: look closely, though of course you can't because I-the-dolt lost the slides, but look closely at your memory, walk up close to it in a certain room in that building on Trafalgar Square, while outside, your friend who hates art is waiting impatiently to go for a cream tea, and what you see in that reflecting fish eye is the backs of the happy couple and two other more distant figures, behind the plane of the painting, invisible except in the mirror, and one of them is the artist himself. *Johannes de Eyck fuit hic.* Kilroy was here, that ubiquitous phrase from the days after the Second War, originally a soldier's joke perhaps. The painting is the world's fanciest marriage certificate, some would tell us, but of course it is not evidence as a photograph might be, for it would have taken months to paint, and the details are all thought to be symbolic—imagine a dog as the symbol of sexual fidelity all you who have found one humping your knee—but like the tourist's photograph of himself standing in front of the Pietà, the painting is offered as proof that the event took place, all of this in the face of the multiplicity and evanescence of what occurs. Bang, zip, gone. We hear a voice singing as we walk away down the street. The semen spurts and nine times out of ten the whole thing is lost in the next thing to happen. Now and then, the belly swells.

Giovanna Cenami might not have been pregnant. It may be the fashion of the dress, the long train that she holds against her front. The orange on the table symbol of something. The fruit of marriage. The vegetable of adultery—that is a whimsical, if private reference to the occasion when a woman handed me a carrot whittled into the shape of an erect penis. Never offer to help in the kitchen.

The other convex mirrors in paintings of the period are more indirect in their reference. The primary reason for their use in the painting was, I imagine, to show off the painter's skill, like all those empty wineglasses, brass vessels, the sort of gear that allowed the exploitation of illusion. Look what I can do in showing the gleaming surface of the world. Look how I can paint a mirror.

Max Beerbohm possessed a convex mirror. His father bought it at the Paris International Exhibition of 1867, and it was in the young Max's nursery, then stayed with him all his life. There is always a fascination with such things, the way they reach out and bring the whole room to a focus in the watcher's eye. It was suggested that Beerbohm intended to write an autobiographical novel about that mirror, but it never happened. The idea is an intriguing one but misses the point of course. The mirror reflects everything and sees nothing. It has no mind. *We know what he means by no mind, don't we?* I will remember that wisecrack.

Beerbohm's convex mirror showing the curve of life, the man in old age, dry and astute. One of the other essays I once planned was to be about artists in their last days. Matisse still drawing when he couldn't rise from bed. Saying he wasn't sick, he was injured, and calling himself *un grand mutilé.* Monet's colors getting brighter as his vision went until he was making neon scribbles of the Japanese bridge. In my first lecture, I told you a story about Maugham's senile rage. Perhaps I am ready to write that essay now.

Artists growing older, and I am at the age when, inevitably, one looks back. I still have a copy of the wedding photo that sat on the dresser of our rented house, and when I look at it, I think that we were young and knew nothing—which means, of course, we knew the insistent truths of eager selfishness and animal appetite. I had a smuggled copy of *Lady Chatterley's Lover*—it was legal a few years afterward—and we read it aloud to each other with the predictable effect. We slapped the little feathered shuttlecock across the lawn at each other in the summer evening while a hawk hunted over the marsh and our daughter slept in her bedroom upstairs, and as the sun went down, it flashed in my eyes until I couldn't see to play the game.

When we decided to buy that house, I did some research on its history. The documentary material I came up with is in the archives of the local historical society, and Janice Baglioni will make it available to you if you are interested. The builder was William Smithson, who is recorded to have built a number of houses here in the period from 1890 to 1905. He had an interest in Doggett's mill, and the wood for the houses was milled there. He seems to have worked from a pattern book he got hold of somewhere in New England, and the houses often look as if they belong in Massachusetts or Connecticut. Isabel Smithson, his daughter, was still alive when I was doing my research, and though she had a reputation for being strange, perhaps even mad, she knew things, and if you had the patience, information could be obtained. I spent some hours sitting at her kitchen table with a cold cup of tea, running my fingers over the checked oilcloth while I waited for her to remember, or perhaps only to agree to tell me what she remembered. She lived, as we say, in another world, and talking to her, you went back in time into the previous century. When I told Denman Tarrington about her, he was convinced that she had been sexually misused by her father in the years when the two of them lived alone together, and that was why she could not get past the year 1900, but I was not convinced. Another of Tarrington's vulgarities. Not everything can be explained by what's between the legs, I said to him, and he laughed, but I am here and laughing last.

The wood was hauled from the mill by a horse and wagon, and as the men unloaded it, Smithson would scribble patterns in the dirt, imagining the shapes that were to be built, and then he would give orders to the other carpenter who worked with him and to the apprentices, and they would set the wood on saw-horses and begin to cut the framing members. Behind the hole in the ground where the foundation was to be built, the red-winged blackbirds were loud at the edge of the marsh. I can't explain why, but I always thought of that big frame place as the Summer House, even when January blizzards were swirling past the windows. It held summer in its memory, and I could never bear to leave it until I retired and decided to go away altogether. Peaceful out there by the salt marshes, in the empty house, and it was not easy to grow used to the noise of life, all the radios and television sets and babbling newspapers and signals arriving from all over the planet. The gibbering of the eternal spaces frightens me, to abuse a familiar quotation. You will allow me my little games.

Petrus Christus, he of the odd name, is the next on our list. Peter Christ. Another craftsman going carefully about his work. Scholars battle about dates and influences, though the facts are few and all awash in suppositions. The painting we're concerned with is dated, so we can be certain that it was done fifteen years after the van Eyck wedding picture, and can perhaps assume that he got the idea of using a convex mirror from van Eyck's work, though there is no proof he ever saw it. Perhaps he received a suggestion from a gossipy visitor.

The subject of our painting is another couple, lovers, perhaps about to be married since they are visiting the jeweler, to get a ring we may suppose, though in this case the jeweler has a halo, picked out in delicate pale lines about his head as he weighs up a bit of gold on a balance in his hand and looks upward. That makes him St. Eligius, the patron saint of gold and silversmiths. Not easy to tell whether he is looking beyond the lovers to some heavenly wisdom or whether the painter's draftsmanship was faulty. Certainly, as I recall the painting, the eyes of the lovers are fixed on the gold.

The climax of courtship, the moment when the ring is chosen: not perhaps a scene to be found in every wedding album today, but interesting enough, and in this case its importance is guaranteed by the sainthood of our jeweler. A marriage made in heaven and at the bank, just as it should be, and documented by an expensive painting done by one of the best in Bruges.

Our point here is the mirror, and when the young couple saw the image, one wonders that they didn't send the painting back, for what is reflected there, by the magic of optics and the curvature of the device, is a street scene somewhere outside the jeweler's shop, quite possibly a cheat on the optical inevitabilities since it's not clear whether we are looking through a door or a window—a large doorway perhaps—in order to see the houses across the way. In front of those houses are two other figures, tiny commentators visible only in the upper body, the one, who seems to hold a large bird, perhaps a bird of prey, turned to the other with the sly vile expression of a malicious gossip. *He's only marrying her for the money, you know. That baker's girl in the square is with child and he's the one who set the loaf to rising. I've heard the things he says about her, what he will do with her money, and how he will keep her silent and obedient. She's got a bad one in him.* Perhaps I misread the painting, and if we had the slide, you might form your own opinion, but as it is, you are left with mine. Perhaps some of you know the painting. It is in the Met in New York and not out of reach. I looked at it on a recent visit.

The irony of van Eyck is gentle, a whimsical joke by which he places himself in the painting and shows himself as witness to the important ceremony, which, even if the bride is up the stump, is treated in a serious way. He loved painting the texture of the clothes, of course, and the symbolism may be taken as a pedestrian labeling, but still the technique is perfect, and the event is placed in time as a crystal wineglass might be placed on velvet.

Mr. Christ, however, had none of this delicacy. No doubt he was paid a goodly sum to show the two lovers just when they should be seen, as good Protestants, guaranteeing the union with an investment in gold, but I have always wondered what he told the purchasers of the painting they were seeing in the mirror. Maybe it was other members of the family. The two mothers-in-law, the price of the painting adjusted upward for each extra figure included. They have the look of the conventional mother-in-law, snide and disapproving.

Myself, I never had a mother-in-law, for Anne had been orphaned—an accident, then a heart attack, the two perhaps related—before I met her. She had a kindly aunt who came to the wedding and smiled, though she can't have been entirely pleased with the situation. It had not been easy to convince Anne to give in to necessity and accept me, but I insisted. I wanted her quietness, her lovely skin. She never put her reservations in words. Perhaps the figure in our convex mirror was Anne's other face, as sly and disapproving as those two gossips.

We could, while on the subject of mirrors, take a step to one side and lob the bird, look, there it goes, a little white object against the summer sky, into the territory of literature. There's the Lady of Shallott, virgin evader, and some nice lines of Auden's about Ferdinand and Miranda in his poems from *The Tempest*. "*My dear one is mine as mirrors are lonely*." Very pretty, though I'm not sure I could explain what it means. Virginity again, that white thing that we no longer understand. A strange obsession to make virginity sacred. Prudence on the subject, well yes, whether at the level of health, self-respect or commerce, none of them a romantic or holy matter, we can be sure, and I wouldn't knock anyone's choice of prudence even if it means keeping your legs crossed for a long time, but the sacredness of the hymen is another matter altogether. I suppose Freud got it right. Sex had become undervalued in the Roman empire and the pendulum swung the other way. Asceticism made it a Big Thing. The metaphors are having their way with me.

That was another of the essays that Tarrington stole from our conversations; "The Virgin's Breast and Other Dirty Movies." We had been discussing Mediterranean culture one night after we saw *La Dolce Vita* at a film society screening. We had both told our first year classes to attend, an assignment that was thought *infra dig* and a little scandalous by some of the others. After a number of drinks, Tarrington announced that he was going to create a giant sculpture called "The Great Tits of Ekberg," but instead he wrote the essay. Five years later, when he was able to forget how much of what he was writing came from me.

Two evenings later we played badminton, the four of us, and I noticed bruises on Madeleine's pale thigh and wondered how he had done it and whether he was prompted by Fellini's disorderly world. *Tarrington's Lust,* a sprightly Elizabethan number for the virginals.

Belle, where are you going? Don't leave. I find it reassuring to see a familiar face. Is it something I said? Unrespectful to our old pal D.T., I suppose, didn't observe the old saw, *de mortuis, nil nisi bonum.* I have a brain full of Latin tags, but I can't put them all into effect. It's not to be expected. Well there, she's gone, and I regret it. It was a long long time ago that we met, when she arrived as assistant to the Dean of Arts and soon enough, because she was quick-witted and wise, became the effective Dean of Arts and stayed that until retirement, and while of course she was never paid a salary to compare to the Dean's salary, she was the brains of the office no matter which academic butterfly wore the title. When the Boat Shed opened, run by that rather sweet couple who divorced and sold it after five years, Annabelle and I were among its first customers, but now I have spoken unkindly of old Delirium Tremens, and she has remained faithful to his memory and departed. *Tarrington's Lust*: perhaps he left a bruise or two on Annabelle's firm flesh as well and she is loyal to those old wounds.

No striped ties in Madden Hall today, not one to be seen as I cast my eyes over the attentive group, smaller than yesterday's of course, but listening politely, no heckling, only Annabelle Disney's abrupt departure. Faced with the choice between me and Tarrington, she chose him, but she would always have made that choice. I wonder whether those ties belonged to the very busy or whether I am no longer under their scrutiny, having revealed myself as harmless, unlikely to call into question any matters of importance. I would like to call into question the accepted wisdom, but there is so much of it, ponderous, immoveable. I can only mark a detail here or there. I don't possess Tarrington's gift of the apparently significant phrase, the grabby oxymoron.

Moron and oxymoron. My brother was a moron—I know we don't use that word—but he had been put away and I never saw him, though I know that as a small child I was eagerly watched for signs of mental decay, but I have lasted all these years with my wits about me. I remember the occasion of his death when I was fourteen. Once, after my parents died, I thought of him, Joseph was his name, and he was long gone, and on a certain afternoon as I stood by the back window with binoculars watching an osprey hunting beyond the marsh, I thought that only I in the world was aware that Joseph had existed, that he was as close to oblivion as could be, but now I have mentioned him to all of you, though I had no such intention, and now he exists for you, and some of you are still young and sixty years from now, may recall this set of lectures—I flatter myself that such a thing is possible—and when you do you will remember Joseph and he will have as much existence as any other remembered soul. For how many years, he babbled there. No mind. Well, yes and no.

Perhaps Annabelle left us to take a windblown walk to the library and once there to use her influence and get a first peek at the Tarrington papers, to have a look at the letters I wrote to him those many years ago.

Petrus Christus. We had finished with him, I suppose. The painting is a puzzle, but so are many paintings. So in its way is the Manet I mentioned earlier. There is an odd idea abroad that art is related to beauty, and that was one of the things I liked to dispose of early in the Introduction to Civilization course. Tarrington and I would compete to see who could denounce the belief most fervently, most wickedly, and we would meet afterward for badminton and quote our good lines aloud. You see we were friends at that time. We were friends when we met on the Quai des Grands Augustins. Yes, I think we were, and the light from the river glittered among the trees, and at the back was a mirror that caught fragments of it all. That night, through some strange misapprehension, I got into a metro station after the last train and suddenly found that the lights had gone out, and I thought it too dangerous to find my way out in the dark, so I endured the night there, the odd winds and sounds, and the terrible thoughts of life ending and nothing achieved. A week later I returned to summer here and what ensued.

The van Eyck wedding picture which we have already discussed appears to be the earliest of those I plan to mention, and scholars who have chosen to comment on the use of convex mirrors in other paintings of this time and place usually describe them as something derived from van Eyck, and probably they are right, but each painter uses them in his own way. The most obscure of them is Robert Campin. Who may not be himself at all—that is, he may not be the man who painted the paintings known by his name. The wonders of scholarship. I will skip some of the historical problems as to whether Campin and the Master of Flémalle are the same man. Call him what name you wish. I have a greater problem in the fact that I have never seen the original, and can only deal with it through inadequate reproductions. It is dated just four years after the van Eyck paintings and appears to be the most directly derived from it. Campin, one would say, was no ironist, and what the convex mirror sums up is what would be expected, a back view of John the Baptist and a kneeling donor, the same scene which the painting portrays from the front, though there may be other details. Hard to make out from reproduction, a small figure perhaps, who could be the artist, an open door.

Mirror, mirror on the wall. That's the other great Disney, of course. I say that although Annabelle is not here to enjoy the reference. Mirror, mirror on the wall. I remember one night coming in late from a public lecture, and finding my wife Anne sitting naked on the bedroom floor in front of a mirror with a pencil and paper, attempting to draw herself. When I appeared in the bedroom door, she crumpled the pictures and would not show them to me, and she pulled on a dressing gown and carried them off and burned them. She wanted to see herself and couldn't, she said when she came back, and I said there was no need, for I could see her, and I drew back the fabric of the dressing gown and described what I could see, the pink, soft body, and perhaps she was pleased. I don't know whether she ever tried to draw herself again.

The donors in those early religious paintings had found a way to see themselves as part of a holy story, to combine vanity and piety. *Look at me on my knees with the saint just behind my back, the two of us reflected in the same mirror. I have paid a good sum to a master painter in order to have this done. It will hang in my house. All the things I own return me to myself, show who I am, but this more than any. John the Baptist with his beard and curls and little lamb, bare-legged, in a loose cloak, holds a book which must be a book of truth and on my knees I am attentive to that truth. You can see my seriousness in my face.* A pause for a glass of water also gives me a moment to catch my breath, stretch, perhaps assemble my thoughts. As I draw toward the end of this second talk, I confess that I understand those who need a little Dutch courage mixed with their water, something to propel them the last few steps up the hill. There is no hilltop, of course, for the landscape of these lectures is discontinuous. Even the capacity of the convex mirror to catch events over a wide angle is insufficient, and of course the things captured are distorted. Welcome to the funhouse. It is some years since I have gone to a midway, so perhaps the innocent charms of the house of mirrors where you giggled at yourself stretched or compacted, where you kept discovering a new angle of the reflecting maze, are all gone by. I have seen a Ferris wheel on a distant horizon, and I'm sure that somewhere the rollercoaster still makes the timid shriek, so perhaps the house of mirrors is to be found. If so, I should take my grandchildren, but they live a long way off, and we meet only occasionally, although more often now than in the past. It was at the Canadian National Exhibition in Toronto that I saw my first house of mirrors, and I remember a moment of terror when I thought I would never escape, but would be trapped there forever watching my own small frightened face coming at me wherever I looked. I wonder if children are still scared by such things.

More water. The memory of that old terror dries the mouth. In my first year lecturing here, I carried a glass of water with me to every class because I was nervous about standing in front of all those students and thought my mouth might dry to the point where I would be left mute. I got over that soon enough and developed a glib fluency. *De mortuis nil nisi bonum.* And of those who vanish, like Madeleine, what are we to say? *She was never seen again.* That is what we can say and no more. I do wish that Belle had not flown the coop. Frank Puncheon reached the end of his patience and has not appeared today, and besides we knew each other very little. Occasional badminton. A moment's chat in the coffee shop. Annabelle remembers it all, I'm sure, and that is reassuring in some ways, though she holds her own opinions, and there are many things we chose not to mention over all those years, and after her marriage to a respectable widower, we met only occasionally and in public.

Denman Tarrington is gone, and the past with him. He lies there on the tiles, and in the room beside his, a man sits waiting for a phone call and listening to the shower pouring down endlessly in the cubicle beyond the wall. The water was left running, did I mention that? It was what caused the other man to phone the front desk. Earlier, he thought he heard voices, but now the sound of the water goes on and on, and it begins to work on his nerves, which are a little rattled already. He is in New York for a job interview. The man is an accountant with a somewhat checkered past. When very young, he was arrested for possession of marijuana—he was in fact selling it, but the quantity he had on him was small enough that though he was convicted, he served only a comparatively short sentence in a prison in Washington State. When he got out of prison, he began to study accountancy, and he is quick with figures and has had some success. He has a small office in a suburb of St. Louis called University City, and he lives on a pleasant street with tall trees and little traffic, but recently his wife told him she wants a divorce, and that she plans to take the two children and move to Palo Alto. She is love with someone. Everyone is in love with someone. On the day in question, our man is in New York because he has applied for a job with a firm of forensic accountants, and yesterday he went through an interview with them. He feels that the interview went well, and he is waiting impatiently for the phone call that will summon him back for a second and decisive interview, and in his state of impatience and apprehension, the continual running of water in the room next door makes him want to scream. Repeated noises will do that.

When he planned the trip to New York, he wondered about staying at the YMCA to save a few dollars. He makes money, but there's never enough, and the YMCA is connected in his mind with his Canadian grandfather who worked for the institution. In childhood, he met this grandfather at his home in Ottawa. He was a kindly man, and the memory of him is a good one. Still, our accountant decided that it wouldn't look right if he had to have messages left at the desk of the Y, not when he was trying for a New York job. Look successful. Always look successful. So he is paying for the hotel room, and the water is running endlessly just behind his head as he lies on the bed trying to be patient, and just before the phone rings, he calls down to the desk to complain. Because of his complaint, a bellman will come to the room, open it with a pass key and find the late Denman Tarrington, that prominent thinker and essayist, lying in the steam. So long D.T.

Mirror, mirror on the wall. The doges tried to keep secret the technology of the wonderful Venetian mirrors with their astonishing beveled edges, but the trick escaped and went north. The mirror was the first great advance in the technology of the self, the dominant instrument of our vanity until the camera came along. Explorers carried mirrors into those societies we no longer call primitive and created astonishment. The word mirror is related to the word mirage.

Yes, I stop more often to drink. You can tell that we are once again close to the day's conclusion. Your president waits patiently, having learned in his years of public life how not to fidget in his chair. Today's lecture will soon be done. We mark out the ends of things, the punctuations that offer relief from incoherence. We find words. *She was never seen again.* We were each trying to be Tarrington's equal in carelessness. There was a fire burning across the night. The tide was rising. Annabelle, who was there, has abandoned me on this bare gibbet.

As I totter about here, guzzling my water, there is a look of concern on the face of one of my young friends in the second row. I hope you will not take it badly that I refer to you in that way. As friends. Certain that you will tolerate my little jokes, I have adopted you, all three, and as I mentioned Annabelle and those past things, I reflected that you are now the age we were in those days, and you are living out the savage intensities of those years. Two of you are perhaps a couple, and the other is the observer or is waiting for the cure of a vanished madness. It is possible that the three of you share intricate delights and jealousies or that I misread the fashions of the time, and one of you awaits a soldier home from the wars. Forgive my intrusion. There are those who say that passion is no longer fashionable among the young, that they do it and forget. Like the province of Quebec, *je me souviens.*

The bird is about the fall to the court, but I make a long step and with a sweeping forehand swat it down the sideline.

Campin, van Eyck, Petrus Christus, and let me see who is left. Memlinc, yes, a nice artist's joke, for we are looking at a diptych, Virgin and Child in one wing, in the other the young donor, in his twenty-third year, it says. Anne was in her twenty-third year when we married. Where and how the two sections of the diptych were to be hung we can only guess, but behind the Virgin and Child is another of those convex mirrors, van Eyck's legacy, summing things up, joining, and in it we can see the Virgin's back and the donor kneeling in front of her, the figures from both panels brought together in one. A trick, a joke, call it what you will, but it bridges the contradiction of space and picture planes, and as the young donor got older, he must have been pleased to show the trick to his friends, look at me *there* and yet also *there*, like one of those movies in which an actor gets to play both twins. The painting is in Bruges. Those of you who plan to summer in Europe can go and take a look at it, and you will have your own opinions, of course, and while you are there in that part of Europe, you can take a look at our next work, in that great maze of heaped-up masterpieces, the Louvre. Anne and I went to the Louvre just after we were married, but she tired easily in those days, her feet would swell, and she found it all overwhelming and went to sit outside while I wandered down the endless corridors, making notes. Long before the days of the glass pyramid, that was, before the hotels had been Americanized, when a toilet was still a hole in the floor somewhere down the hall. Anne didn't like Paris, and the next time I went, she spent the two weeks visiting her aunt. When I returned, the house was empty. I called, and she said she had decided to stay longer, so I was alone with my thoughts, as I had been that night in Paris.

My head is spinning, and I can't remember what I have said and not said. Lost in the hall of mirrors, I see my own distorted face, and try not to cry, to believe that I will find my way out, that my parents will be there, that all will be well. I will gather my forces for a race to the end. Tarrington lies in the steam while the man next door is picking up the phone, and we turn to Quentin Matsys. Gold again here, and no saints, though one would say that the painting must have been done under the influence of that other, for the mirror is once again set on a table so that it shows a view of what is outside.

A memory: I am in the lobby of a New York hotel, and I am surrounded by men and women from some sort of convention, all of them with those cheerful name tags, and close to me is a man whose tag reads, Hi, my name is Legion. Chances are I made that up, whether waking or sleeping. There was that business of the striped ties. I saw them, then didn't. *Ubi sunt qui apud nos fuerunt?* Where indeed. Perhaps my phone is ringing. Perhaps the ties are concealed under high-necked sweaters worn against the cold and snow that we know waits for us beyond the walls of Madden Hall.

Denman Tarrington got his name in the newspapers one last time. The badminton bird lay in the long grass, its feathers damp with dew. Feathers on a summer lawn where a neighbor's cat has torn apart a song-sparrow, the lovely long call vanished. I pick up the feathers and hide them from Anne. The dead bird lies in the grass. I will drive to the hill above the beach and with the binoculars, try for a sighting of the piping plover. Not easy to distinguish from the more common semipalmated plover or even the least plover, but with my powerful opera glasses, I can make such fine distinctions. The tides are high at this phase of the moon, and everything is flooded with the moaning salt. There is a wind in the hollow of the dunes and we feel it on our bare skin. Her skin is very pale.

Perhaps as I stand here lecturing, the phone in my hotel room is ringing over and over again. I must finish up here and go to answer it.

Quentin Matsys: *The Banker and His Wife.* This banker, we assume, will not find that his records are being sifted by forensic accountants. Double entry bookkeeping has just been invented in Italy, and it is possible that this banker possesses the two books, journal and ledger, that allow a systematic assessment of profit and loss. In our day, of course, there is something called a spreadsheet that is produced by a computer and creates the illusion of knowledge. In fact, this particular banker may only keep a pile of gold in a locked chest and judge his riches by the weight of the chest. Notional money, a trust in paper, has yet to come, and so he and his wife sit at a table while he examines the coins in front of him, weight and texture, congratulating himself on their value. There are, as you will remember, pearls on the table, and they allow the painter to show his skill in rendering shape and iridescence. The portrait of the banker, who paid for the work to be done, is an excuse for the painting of a still life. His wife, as all commentators note, has in front of her an illuminated book of prayers, but her eyes are on the pearls. That was her reason, surely, for marrying a banker. But that woman in University City is about to leave a successful accountant for the love of some adventurer in California. Love, love, love.

I am forgetting the mirror. Once again, almost a century after van Eyck's wedding portrait, there is a small convex mirror, and once again it allows the artist to show his consummate technical mastery, a perfect slice off the side of a sphere, the gleam of the texture of what is seen, the view of a window, its lines slightly distorted by the curvature of the mirror and beyond the window a corner of a building against the brightness of the sky, and below all this, in the corner of the mirror, the head of the other woman.

The Other Woman. Oh goodly melodrama of domestic life. Sacred adultery, the holy act of modern times. The shuttlecock husband, the shuttlecock wife. Of course in this painting, we only know that it is *some* other woman, and it is impossible to comprehend the meaning of this face. As with the two reflected women of Peter Christ, the meaning is for us to add. Perhaps this face is a maid, a mother-in-law, or perhaps it is another view of the banker's wife in a different hat. She couldn't make up her mind which hat to wear in the picture, so he offered, for a couple more gold coins from the pile on the table, to include her in the picture wearing both hats. Artists are ingenious and inventive creatures, and they can be tempted by gold.

The badminton bird floats down. The real bird soars. The piping plover is an endangered species, more and more rare as its breeding grounds vanish. Their nests can be swept away by storms. The tide is always rising somewhere. Brassai's Parisian mirrors always offer another angle, the face of a detached observer. The accountant from St Louis hears the phone ring and leaps up to answer it, hoping that it will give him the news he seeks. Just as he picks up the phone, he is aware that the water has been turned off in the room next door to his. Though he doesn't know it, he has been responsible for the official discovery of Denman Tarrington's body. Nor does he know that only a week later, I will be here, in Tarrington's place, offering you a few thoughts under a title which you may have found obscure at first, but are by now surely coming to understand.

3

As I look down from this bare platform at the little loyal group of you gathered for the last of my lectures, I wonder whether there is among you the person who phoned me last night. A cruel prank. I was asleep, exhausted after a long day, dinner at the Boat Shed with your President—and thank you sir, it was a great kindness—and I was roused from sleep by the telephone ringing. Not the first time of course, and I stumbled from bed, my pajamas tangled, and lifted the phone, though perhaps I should have known enough not to, but I did it, I lifted the phone and spoke, and there was that long painful resonant silence, and then something. I can't say exactly what it was, a voice, I suppose, but it seemed far off and blurred, the voice itself cracked and uncomfortable, as if speech was a great effort. It's true that I am growing a little deaf, that it is more difficult to separate voices from the surrounding noise and I'm sure that the highest pitches are gone, but it was more than that.

Back in bed, damp with sweat and yet shivering with cold, I tried to understand who it might be and told myself old stories all over again. The fire of driftwood in the middle of the August darkness, the sound of the waves as I walked back along the beach alone from the place where I had left her standing at the water's edge. Soon enough they were gone, all of them. Very late in the night, I remembered that I had mentioned to you these mysterious calls, oh not that many really, over the years, but they go on. It was then I realized that it must be a cruel prank, created by someone who has been sitting here listening to me. Now I look at every face staring toward me and wonder who it was.

To business. You will of course remember from our first hour J. W. Morrice living on the Left Bank, painting and drinking. It appears that in the 1890s he was in touch with a number of American artists, Maurice Prendergast, Robert Henri, William Glackens, and for a short while, there was among the group another Canadian artist. Probably you will know the name, though it is now more obscure than in the days of my boyhood. A man who was, among other things, the founder of the American Boy Scouts.

There is an astonishing story about this man's youth. He had a plan for what he wished to do with his life, and his father dismissed it, saying, No, become something important. Become an artist. That in Toronto in the late nineteenth century. It sounds unlikely enough, doesn't it? The father appears to have been an unlikely character.

The man who was there in Paris, though he was out of place and knew it, was Ernest Thompson Seton. One of the studies tells us that he was still calling himself Thompson at this time, but I think that is wrong. Thompson was of course his name. Ernest Thompson, born and brought up under that name, but his father, an Englishman who emigrated to Canada to fail at just about everything, liked to brag of their family's connection to the noble Scottish Setons, and eventually, his son took that name, and it was under that name he became known as a naturalist who wrote stories about animals and illustrated them with his own drawings and paintings. As a boy I collected his books, and my copies, some of them very early editions, are now in your library here. Unless they have been stamped LIBRARY DISCARD and tossed out. I didn't check.

When he introduced me two days ago, your president mentioned my little book, *The Carol of the Birds*, and I don't intend to repeat here all the things I said in that book about the specialized artists following Audubon. The great Audubon, who did portraits in order to make a living and find the time for his first love, the painting of birds. I once aspired to own an early edition of his book, but I never got beyond the Book-of-the-Month Club reproductions. I still have a couple of them framed on the wall of my apartment. The snowy owl is a favorite since it takes me back to a great moment of my boyhood. A lovely memory.

My dog was named Jim—I can't remember why—and this is a story of a boy and his dog. I wonder whether boys still have dogs, and whether they still attend Boy Scout meetings in church basements and learn to tie knots. It seems unlikely, but that is the world I grew up in, and I used to take my dog Jim for walks in the fields and woods on the edge of town, and we would chase rabbits and set grouse into noisy flight among the trees. In the summer, we went fishing.

When I moved here, after my years in the big cities, I began to watch birds more systematically, keeping a checklist, spending hours on the beach observing waterfowl and shorebirds. Anne was used to my habit, and it was always easy to pick up the binoculars and announce that I was driving down to the water. The pastime of a summer day, and an easy lie to tell when I began to need one.

The print of the snowy owl hangs over the desk where I work or try to work, as it has for years, as it did in the months when I was working on *The Carol of the Birds,* slides arriving, books on interlibrary loan. It wasn't an academically respectable pursuit—wildlife art is thought of as the art of the department store—but it had its roots in my early life, and it helped to assuage my loneliness in the years when I was alone in the big frame house.

Jim and I had come through a patch of woods that afternoon and through a small valley where Jim had chased a rabbit and barked at a noisy red squirrel, and on the far side of the valley was an empty field, one that was not farmed, for some reason, just long grass growing wild, with a few hawthorns here and there. Jim was far ahead of me, but I knew that when we came to the next road, we would meet up. I can't remember the season of the year, and it's not clear to me why the owl should have been there, late going north, early coming south, but suddenly and silently there it was, a large white bird, not pure white but flecked with traces of gray like shadows on snow, and it lifted itself into the air just in front of me, and I stopped, astonished and breathless. I swear there wasn't a sound as it came up in front of me, so that it was like a spectre, close to me, then gone, over the grass, into the trees and vanished.

That is a story that I tell myself, about a world where I once lived. When I got home I tried to draw a picture of the owl, but I couldn't get it right, and I'm not sure that I have got it right now, describing it to you. The very rhythm and contrivance of any sentence or paragraph is misleading. When I was young, I admired the animal stories of Ernest Thompson Seton, but if I try to read them now, they appear to me mannered and false. As an artist he is neither Morrice nor Audubon, and yet there is something touching about his survival in the face of an unpleasant and unhelpful father who lived in a world of boastful falsity, about the way he endured an unhappy marriage until his daughter was away from home.

When he was in Paris, he spent his time at the zoo, studying the animals there, those that had been bought to replace the former stock, all eaten during the siege of 1870 when the Germans blockaded the city and there was no food. *The only reasonable thing to do with our feathered friends is to eat them.* That was Tarrington's comment in a review he wrote of *The Carol of the Birds.* We were not otherwise in touch in those days, and the review was an act of malice.

It was back in those years, just after a graduation ceremony, that one of our former students appeared in my office door, one of Tarrington's regulars from his nights in the barroom. We spoke of nothing much, and then the conversation turned around and I found that he was telling me how Tarrington had paid him to keep an eye on Madeleine when hubby was away. While D.T. was in Paris screwing whatever he could get, this student played detective with the abandoned wife lest anyone else discover the silky texture and pearly iridescence of her skin. One of the questions I was never able to answer about Madeleine is how much of what she was developed from her own nature and how much from what Tarrington had done to her. After that conversation in my office, I knew a little more about how it had all happened, now it was too late to make anything of the knowledge. The enduring question: was it always too late? The artist's blindness makes possible the artist's vision.

Seton, who once was Thompson, is not in anyone's eyes an important artist, but just as the convex mirrors are an image of one moment of Flemish art, so his animal pictures, along with the stories they illustrate, embody a moment in the developing culture of North America. He did some fine bird studies, but his illustrations have all the annoying false drama of their kind, and in fact they are demeaning to the animals. The most impressive things, in many ways, are the incidental drawings, the illuminated title pages. In the introductions, Seton gave credit to his wife for her design of the books. He is eager to tell us that she suggested to him what to illustrate. Though there was some deep incompatibility between him and this young American woman that he met on the boat on his way to Paris, he struggled to be a devoted husband. That saddest of struggles.

Imagine a mirror not merely convex but spherical, catching everything at once. We were in a nursery where Anne wanted to look for black currant bushes. It was that last summer. Anne was just back from her extended visit to her aunt, and we had met Madeleine in a supermarket. She didn't drive, and when Anne chose to offer her a ride home, she accepted and invited us to stay for dinner. On the way, we stopped at the nursery, and while Anne looked for her black currants, Madeleine and I affected to ignore each other and wandered aimlessly. The nursery sold not only plants but garden decorations, and one of them was a little stand with a spherical mirror on top. I suppose it was intended to go in a pool or amid the flowers to catch the bright colors and reflect them back.

I stood at one side and looked at the shining sphere, and I noticed how it showed Madeleine's figure, some distance off on the other side, reflected it back to me only a little distorted, and as I watched, she turned and looked at me intently, and as she was studying me, the mirror showed Anne, who appeared from the door of a greenhouse and stopped to watch Madeleine watching me. Madeleine was wearing a very short dress that day and those Indian sandals—water buffalo, weren't they?—and her pretty legs were bare. Tarrington was still absent. The three of us were about to go to her house for dinner, and the moment hovered over those three figures, caught in a shining globe. The mirror focused all these things to a point in my brain, and I half understood the meaning of it. What I thought I understood was what I thought was freedom.

I would like to forget that telephone call last night, that voice. This morning, wanting to discuss it with someone, I tried to call Annabelle, but she was unavailable or refuses to speak to me.

He heard voices, you know, Ernest Thompson Seton. One voice, mainly. It gave him instructions about how to live his life, and he called it his Buffalo Wind. Well, he had to call it something. If I put it to you as a question, if I put it to you, Mr. President, still here loyally listening, whether it seems likely that the man who founded the American Boy Scouts heard voices speaking to him—before I had told you this story, of course—I doubt that you would have expected it. That may simply go to show that we expect too little. It was also a period when many people were fascinated by these things. Spiritualism answered some need. It never dies, I suppose, that longing. There's nothing new about the New Age. Charles G. D. Roberts, who was a professional acquaintance of Seton's—they both wrote animal stories—liked to play with ESP and horoscopes and was once visited by the ghost of a little girl.

Who had committed suicide. Some choose to return, others don't. Some bodies are never found.

In the next few years, I hope to return to the magic of my childhood, to write more about the use of animals in art, from the religious allegories of the medieval period to the work of our time, scientific in its details, escapist in its meaning. It is only as we have begun to wipe out the animal world that we have chosen to put it on our walls. We can see the meaning of anything only when we are threatened with its loss. Animal art has gone from a reflection of a new scientific taxonomy, to an expression of the earliest conservationist ideals, to sheer nostalgia, and will go beyond, soon enough, to the hysterical fear and hatred of the animal rights activists.

As I was telling you that story about Jim and the snowy owl, I reflected on how that boy became a university professor and found himself here in front of you. All accident, really, but representative. I am at one with history. My father was in charge of purchasing for a large store in a middle-sized city set among fertile farms. It would never have occurred to him or his brothers to attend a university, but by the time I completed high school, it was becoming a common thing, and so off I went. Too lazy to work, I suppose, and I did a master's degree instead and got a fellowship to go somewhere else and begin a doctorate. As the universities went on expanding, jobs fell into my lap. Tarrington was able to exploit all this, to become an adjunct to the new ruling class, while I was prepared to settle for a quiet life. I remember that when John Kennedy was elected president of the United States, Tarrington noticed that Harvard was moving to Washington and began to show an interest in all things American. His mother was American, of course, so he had one foot in the apple pie.

My favorite recipe: mixed metaphors on toast. Tarrington is toast. D.T. is a Library Discard. It was a couple of months ago and I was idly pressing the button on my remote and watching pictures appear and disappear when I recognized his face. It was one of those pretentious cable channels, and Denman

Tarrington was generously offering his views of just about everything. A new book was being written, it appeared, about his heart attack. This was clearly a lie as Tarrington had no heart. There was a direct wire from his brain—a capable one I admit—to his penis, which, as he made clear to the deep-browed man conducting the interview, was still in a flourishing state. The book was to be called *Heart Murmurs* and was to encompass all the great themes of his oeuvre. He actually said that, and the man actually listened to him. As I watched I kept hoping that he would have another coronary infarction right there on the air, but of course, for all the fake spontaneity, the interview was taped and edited and Old D.T. was alive or dead somewhere else. He was about to appear, we were told, to deliver the opening public lecture at an important conference in New York. They announced the date.

Some of the problems in Seton's marriage were inherent in who each of them was. She was a city girl; he was a country boy. His earliest days were on a pioneer farm in southern Ontario, and when his father moved them to a poor area of Toronto, the small, innocent, cross-eyed boy was miserable. Birds and animals were always his greatest love, and he built himself a little cabin in the Don Valley to escape. So of course he married a woman who loved city life, and when they moved to the country imagined that their house was haunted. The ghost of a murdered musician was the story.

Anne never succeeded in meeting the ghost in our house at the edge of the country, much as she wished it. Perhaps no one had been murdered there. When we arrived, the house was still bloodless. It was, I feel sure, something less than mere chance, that when I moved out of that house, my daughter Sylvia got back in touch with me. At last she felt free to do it, and I met my grandchildren, the little Greens. She had stories to tell about the years between, about Anne's hard fate, and as I watched Tarrington's heavy, confident face smiling at the world, famous on television, I willed the clogged arteries of his heart to contract, and his body to fall from the chair to the studio floor, the producers cutting quickly to some other image. We all need someone to blame. Recall the rage of mad old Maugham.

Be patient. I will get to the point. I'm sure I will. Last night, as I lay awake after that phone call, the mind racing, as if everything in my life had to be accommodated, put in order, comprehended and forgiven in the next five minutes, I recalled that in my first lecture I had not mentioned Morrice's war paintings. Lord Beaverbrook was responsible for getting him commissioned. It wasn't his kind of subject, but he worked steadfastly enough at it. Met Augustus John, I believe, who was doing the same things. Under conscription. We all know that experience, from time to time, of being under orders from another place. We hear the orders of a voice, even if we don't call it Buffalo Farts.

Art began with animals. You have all seen versions of those cave paintings from France and North Africa. Men and women hiding in holes in the earth, suddenly felt a need to mix up red mud with water or urine or the sap of a tree and to make the world's first steps at interior decoration. If we don't count the bower bird, and that is not quite the same thing—though for all we know the man in the cave was doing it to persuade a woman huddled in a corner that he was a clever geezer, much smarter than Ugh who lived in the cave next door and was making eyes at her. It's difficult not to make jokes about people who live in caves. I grew up with a cartoon called, if I remember, Alley Oop, in which the characters were oddly shaped figures dressed in hanks of fur.

I'm not sure if they had fire in the caves, or if the drawings were done in darkness or by a little glimmer of distant daylight. A blank, unmediated life, and scholars try to understand what was in the mind of the person who felt the need to record the shape of bison and antelopes. A way to control them, magic to put the prey in their power—that's one of the standard explanations, but I've heard it suggested that it was something more detached, an impulse of awe and wonder, the impulse behind all art. Not to eat it, but to know it.

Yesterday, before your president kindly took me out to dinner, I had a few minutes free and I spent them in your library, glancing at a few books on animals in art to prepare myself for today's effort. I was startled to find, on the same shelf as all the beasts, a book called *Woman as Sex Object.* I suppose the cataloguer was working in categories like Art, Subject Matter Of, and women and birds went to the same place. English slang, 1960s. And Jerome Bosch gave us lots of feathered friends in his sexy garden of earthly delights.

Everything is connected to everything else. The falcon god of the Egyptians prefigures the hawks I saw hunting over the marsh behind the Summer House. From the window where I stood at the end of that long night, watching the pale gray light that comes before dawn, when the luminescence comes up out of the ground, slowly, slowly, while in another room, my daughter was sleeping, and far off the tongue of water was luminous as pearl, the sky was empty, no hawk, and for the moment the birds were silent. I had passed the night—from the coming of darkness through standing by Madeleine watching the distant fire, to more darkness, and driving from street to street searching for Anne, finding nothing. And nothing here when I returned. Everyone was gone, and I knew it would all be changed, but I couldn't see how, not yet. Though I stood in a well-built house, I might as well have stood in a cave or on the bare desert earth worshipping animal gods, eminent and careless. Alone, we are as bare as critters huddled in a cave, making lines on the rock face.

Ernest Thompson Seton lived to be a very old man, settled in New Mexico, married to a second wife. He sired a child when he was somewhat older than I am now. A terrifying thought and not entirely credible. You can't, I'm certain, imagine me the father of a red little thing, screaming out for the comfort of its mother's breast. I am a grandfather, after all, a retired professor.

There is an entertaining story about Seton in Paris, trying to get rid of the carcass of a dog he had been dissecting. You know the sort of thing. Police searching for a murderer who may be throwing pieces of his wife's body into the Seine. Seton is trying to do the same with the body of the dissected dog. Perhaps he made it all up. Perhaps it was a dark dream. You must see what I mean.

Since animals can't be paid to hold a pose, animal art depended, at least until the invention of the camera, on the infinite patience of dead models. Audubon would wire freshly killed birds to a grid in order to produce a lifelike rendering. The illustrators of bird books all too often had to work from skins and stuffed birds in museum collections, and the colors, especially of the unfeathered areas were not always perfect. Audubon worked on a large scale and with great precision and of course always put his birds and animals in a suitable landscape, but there is a strange mock eternity to his portrayal, something of the magic stillness that catches us in naive art. His landscapes have all the ghostly precision of Henri Rousseau.

Art stops things dead. The truth shall make you free, but the facts shall make you nervous.

Over the doorway of Victoria College at the University of Toronto, it says "The Truth Shall Make You Free." I noticed it when I stopped in there many years ago to visit an old friend. I had been just up the street at the Royal Ontario Museum where there was a show called "Animals in Art." It was during the days that I was working on my little book, and the trip to Toronto was enlightening. It was a surprise to discover how many artists from how many countries were painting birds and beasts.

That trip was also the only occasion in my life when I found myself in intimate circumstances with a complete stranger, a cheerful young woman I met on the train. It's hardly a matter to be discussing from a public platform, but Victoria College says the truth shall make you free, and I've always wanted to express my gratitude. Auburn hair. Thank you, my dear. You see life doesn't end when we believe it must. It is only art that brings everything to a standstill, the fox unmoving in the snowy landscape, as if he might be that charming stuffed dog in the Victorian exhibit at the museum. When the dog passes to his reward, have him done by a taxidermist, and set him up next to your favorite chair, send him to the dry cleaners now and then.

When I was young, popular magazines offered courses in taxidermy, something you could take by mail, the ads right next to those for Charles Atlas who guaranteed to produce muscles by dynamic tension. I wonder how many young men were haunted by the fear of being the skinny goof who had sand kicked in his face by a bully, the one who would never get the girl.

You might have had Tarrington stuffed, you know, and added him to the material in the archives. The corpse would have been fresh enough, kept damp by all that warm steam from the shower. A remark in poor taste, perhaps, but it would have been in the spirit of his best work. He was after all the man who called a book *Geographies of Standing Flesh.*

He was missing from that image in the spherical mirror at the garden centre, still off in Paris, doing research. The three of us are small in that gleaming reflective surface, round as the earth, and the curve of the mirror makes the sky above look like a whirlpool of cloud spinning downward, a bright flash to one side the suddenly revealed sun. The clouds are flying by, but we are motionless as models posed for the artist to catch and record. *Johannes de Eyck fuit hic.* Kilroy was here. Tarrington was in Paris. Somewhere behind a tree, his student, the spy, watches it all, like the eye of God. Madeleine had caught him at his spying one day that summer, he told me in our later interview, and invited him into the house, and one way and another, she got the truth out of him. When I came back from Paris, I knew that something about her had changed, but I didn't know what it was. It led her to demand an account from me of Tarrington's activities in Paris. Thinking that I had my reasons, I told her.

We keep returning to Paris. When I was in New York, something strange happened to me. I had flown into Newark, and now I was in a cab, going from the Port Authority bus terminal to my hotel, and I discovered that I was speaking to the cab driver in French. Natural enough I suppose, since I had flown from Montreal, but I believe that I thought I was in Paris, though the cities don't resemble each other in the slightest, and the cab, which appeared to be falling apart and had a thick grille and glass separating me from the driver, was a dead giveaway. I spoke to the driver in competent French, he replied in what I took to be demotic Spanish and we lapsed into an appropriate silence until I reached my destination.

Nobility, perhaps ersatz nobility, is one of the features of animal art. *The Monarch of the Glen.* We portray them as noble creatures, the horses, lions, dying stags, though in one period animals got into art mostly when they lay Dutch and dead, a heap of game ready for the pot, piles of ducks and hares which must have stunk to high heaven before the artist was finished with his delicate and perfect rendering of the fur and feathers. A kind of still life, which in French is, appropriately, *nature morte.* Dead nature indeed. Still, the ospreys, nearly wiped out by D.D.T., are coming back. My last day here, before I moved to Montreal, I drove down to the river mouth, and then walked over the rocks to the high point that you all know, and I saw an osprey hovering there, and watched him plunge into the water and then lift himself into the air again, and of course I saw nobility in the creature's eagerness and power.

He got the job, you know, the man in the room next door to Tarrington's corpse, and that was some small consolation for the loss of his wife and children.

When he picked up that ringing phone, the voice on the other end was not the office secretary, but the chief accountant himself, asking him if he was free to come back for another talk that very afternoon, and he said that he was free, and as they made the arrangements, he thought what a good thing it was that he had told them from the first interview about his marijuana conviction. They had accepted it, with a joke about all the ones who didn't get nabbed, glances from one to the other, all knowing that some of them had smoked up and probably indulged in other recreational drugs, and they were not going to punish him because he had the bad luck to get pinched. The conviction, after all, was for simple possession. Perhaps they considered that his first-hand experience of a correctional facility would give him insight into the criminal mind.

I wonder if there is such a thing as the criminal mind. The inability to postpone gratification: that's the sociologists' phrase for it. The middle class gets to where it's going by waiting to have children, by saving for a house. I am tempted to say that Tarrington never postponed a gratification in his life, but that can't be true, can it? He wrote those books when he might have been drinking or chasing women, and I have wondered from time to time if his relentless appetite wasn't a pose, tough talk from a good hard-working Canadian boy. Perhaps he lied to me in Paris. He might have been spending all his time at the Bibliothèque Nationale, and I passed on the lie to Madeleine, and she opened the vodka bottle and prepared herself for revenge. The truth shall make you free.

There is a terrible animal painting by George Stubbs, terrible in the old sense, instinct with terror. *Lion Devouring a Horse,* it's called, and it's found in the Tate Gallery. The lion is on the horse's back, its teeth and claws sunk into the flesh, and the horse, a powerful creature, white, with a pure white mane and tail, twists its neck in desperation, its big teeth trying to reach toward the cat that is destroying it. The scene, of course, comes not from anything seen—though there are rumors that Stubbs observed such an unlikely event in Italy—but from artistic precedents and the mind of the painter. Stubbs was a painter both workmanlike and brilliant who started out as a student of anatomy and lectured on the subject to medical students and made his living as a painter of horse portraits for the aristocracy. Stubborn and self-assured, a North Country workman, yet he must have had terrible dreams. Perhaps it was the love of horses that made him wish to see one in such a moment of extremity, the throat strained, the mouth open, the eyes wide. Such things occur in the imagination of every man.

My young friends in the second row are back—all but one—and they are questioning that last word. I said man and meant man. I cannot imagine that a woman would paint such things, though perhaps you have your own vision of *terribilità*. I have caught glimpses, but it is not the same, or not yet. Perhaps men and women will come to share the same nightmares. I look down at all the faces that watch my performance, and I have no idea what lies behind them. Setting out the menu for dinner. Making plans to write a book review already overdue. Wishing I would finish so you can get to the nearest toilet. Wondering what your lover is up to at this moment. At least no one is sleeping today. The dozy have departed, gone to nap elsewhere.

In my first lecture, you will remember, I reflected on the flavor of the Edwardian world and the figures who populated it, not quite Victorian, not quite modern, and Ernest Thompson Seton was another of them. A decent upright man, no doubt, who thought that woodcraft could keep boys out of trouble, and idealized his picture of the Indian brave. He proved to his wife that the ghost in their isolated house in the country was only the sound of wind through broken glass—that was the song of the murdered musician. He went for long walks in the country, and the sickly boy who heard voices lived on into his eighties and sired a child not long before the end. Yet he liked to draw wolves, was drawn to the ferocity of predators, the sharp teeth and the snarling over the bare bones of what they devour. The natural world lives on flesh, and the hawks I watched crossing the marsh were hunting for what they could kill. There is something a little theatrical about the wildness of his wild creatures.

Anne and I stood in the yard with that marsh beyond us and beyond that the sea. We stood on the lawn that was full of dandelions and small clover flowers and swatted the badminton bird back and forth, pretending there was a net. We had been to the beach that day, and Anne's legs—her pale pink skin very sensitive to the sun—were reddened with a sunburn that would keep her awake during the night, and in the dark, I would get up and find a bottle of baby oil and rub it tenderly into the burnt skin, my fingers noticing the gentle curve of the flesh, the whiteness of the round belly. Pink roses and the white.

Whiteness, the white horse being devoured by a lion, the white swan, the captive unicorn in a field of flowers. When Anne looked in the mirror in our bedroom, hoping to draw what she observed, she couldn't see herself. The mirror was empty. It was fastened on the inside of the closet door, and when I sold the house I left it, but it has no mind to remember what it saw.

I sip water and reconsider. There are medieval manuscripts with accurate drawings of birds, and the illuminations in many of them show what appears to be accurate observation of the natural world. The commonplace would have it that the world was entirely symbolic in those days, an allegory of faith, every creature in the bestiary a myth complete with inaccurate biology, the phoenix, the pelican wounding its breast to feed its young, and yet in the middle of this, some monk had looked at a chaffinch and knew what it was like, so that the little bird in the corner of a manuscript is as lively as any on a branch in the woods. Pisanello and his circle produced birds in the same loving detail as Audubon. Observation preceded taxonomy and curiosity is always with us. Seton raised young prairie chickens and found that the dance they do was innate, hard-wired as we would say now. "The Hard-Wired Prairie Chicken Dance." Sometimes I have thought that Tarrington's essays began as titles and he then had to invent material to go along.

In New York recently, I stood in the Metropolitan Museum and looked at a remarkable horse painting by Rosa Bonheur, purchased in 1887 for a goodly sum by Cornelius Vanderbilt. Yes, I will come back to Rose Happiness.

I had intended to mention that the earliest known work by George Stubbs is eighteen plates illustrating a book on a new system of midwifery, the artist intruding on the privacies of parturition. He was always fascinated by anatomy, having that earnest application to fact and enquiry that came along in his time and brought us the spinning jenny and Josiah Wedgwood. Stubbs produced figures for Wedgwood, and in spite of all his seriousness and hard work, he ended his life in want. I have not seen those plates of women torn open to give birth. Nowadays every father observes the thing he put in there being expelled into real life, but I didn't. I was presented with Sylvia when she had been licked into shape. The bestiary again.

Applied Anatomy: The History of Sexual Advice. You will all have read that one, I'm certain. That one got him on the television to boast about his own sexual prowess. I tried to avoid hearing about it, but for a few weeks, Tarrington was ubiquitous, and I was forced to imagine what he did and who he did it to. Lies, all lies, as likely as not, or so I persuaded myself. All the business about tantric yoga and female submission.

I have a plan for the money I am being paid for giving these lectures—yes, I am being paid, and handsomely too, I must confess, though I suspect they sliced a little off the original offer made to the Great and Famous. You needn't look embarrassed, Mr. President, it's only to be expected. Save a little from this year's share of the endowment and next year you can go to the very top. My plan is to go to Paris and to spend my days in the Louvre, to document, for my own purposes, every picture of possible use to me. The horse paintings of Delacroix, for example. It is some time since I have been to Paris, and I understand that the city is plagued by an epidemic of upscale boutiques. You might as well be in Toronto, people say, but I'm sure the river is still there, and the trees and the gold stone of the old buildings. I will sit by the Medici fountain and watch the lovers. I am too old to postpone gratification.

My voice is growing a little hoarse, as you can hear. Three days of shouting in the acoustic horror that is Madden Hall. I remember when concerts were held here, but the musicians objected and finally they were transferred to St. Paul's, just down the block. There the musicians complained about the smell of incense. Musicians are chronic complainers. Men and women are chronic complainers. Things are never what they were or what they could be. A kind of vision, I suppose, to be stricken by possibility, an appetite for life expressed in dissatisfaction, a No which is a Yes, and better to be articulated, set out in vivid words than stifled into a mere energyless silence, though every complaint is beside the point, is only the approximate notation of what is missing.

Notation: it's been pointed out that every artist has a way of painting an eye, a nose, a mouth, his own shorthand of strokes. Stubbs painted his horses on a large scale, with a careful sense of the musculature, that love of anatomy and the ways things work. The man I began with, J. W. Morrice, saw horses as working creatures, part of the city, whether Montreal or Paris, and he had a quick, accurate way of painting a horse, a few strokes and the shape was there among the other shapes, a colored object among the other colored objects. He drank, perhaps because the effect of alcohol was to make the sheen of the surfaces more intense; meaning and expectation gone, and what was left was pure notation, the love of paint. A kind of ontology, pure present. That's the reason that music is only music in fragments, set free from time.

Have I made clear how very thin those pieces of wood are, on which Morrice did his sketches? Fragile, and sometimes very dark, as if the picture were half a secret. The little portrait of Léa Cadoret in the shade of trees, all shadowy greens: he would tell and not tell. Each time I leave the Musée des Beaux Arts after examining those small mysterious things, I climb on the homeward bus, number 24, and I am taken west along Sherbrooke Street. At certain times of day, the bus passes a number of schools, and adolescent boys and girls stand by the edge of the road and some come aboard. There was a day when I sat by the window, and looking out, I saw two girls in school uniforms, short kilt, long socks, white blouse, one of them tall and a little gangly, the other short, almost plump. Their faces were turned away from me, but I knew if they turned I would know them, Anne and Madeleine come back to haunt me, starting life again at the place on the great wheel marked Youth while I am trapped in the seat marked Age.

Say that with a long sweeping stroke I have lifted the bird so high over the court that it is hard to make out whether it is a shuttlecock or a chickadee flying from tree to tree. Watch its slow eternal descent.

Living here, you will all have watched the tide coming in, the moment-by-moment encroachment across the beach, or the slow rise over the rocks. The whole ocean is tilting toward you, with all the power of those tons of water, and you know that nothing can stop its arrival, nothing can hold it back. Far along the beach, we can see the fire of driftwood, and the shapes of men and women close by moving out of darkness and into darkness. Annabelle Disney was there somewhere, but today she is not available to give her testimony. She is an absent witness, if a witness at all. She was one of those figures far off by the fire as we stood by the edge of the water. *She was never seen again.* The night smelled of salt, and as we stood among the dunes, I felt the eyes watching us, turned away and walked back toward the burning driftwood.

I expect that the striped ties will return for the end of the last lecture, since they were here for the beginning of the first. Their pattern of presence and departure is unreadable, but all truth is unreadable until it is the heap of dead facts we call history. Sometimes I have flattered myself with the thought that all the best of Tarrington's essays, the ones that made him famous, grew out of our conversations, and when I have that thought, I have to admit that I would never myself have written them. The ideas would have vanished into time. There was a balance of forces in the days when we were here, like one of those very close games of badminton when the bird sailed to every corner of the court, and as I stood off the back corner and drove it down the line, I could see Anne in front of me, leaning forward on her toes, her tidy sweet body all on the alert, Madeleine, her eyes wide, watchful, breakable, and Tarrington's bearded face and simian arms coiled into a ball of ferocity ready to strike out. In later years, his essays were excessive, full of empty gestures as he went on from woman to woman searching for death or the perfect American orgasm.

North America is many things, none of them comfortable. Though Ernest Thompson Seton idealized life in the wilds, it was nearly the death of him when he was a boy. His health had collapsed and he was sent to spend the summer with a farmer near Fenelon Falls. The whole family came down with malaria, and in a state of hallucination he imagined giant snakes coming after him. Odd how these invalid boys live almost forever. He survived to become one of the important figures in the discovery of Nature with a capital N. It was in those years that the great parks were being created, Banff and Jasper, Yellowstone and Yosemite, imaginary wilderness preserved as the continent gave in to civilization.

Now the surface of the moon is covered with garbage. Every little picture store has prints of foxes and geese, perhaps an eagle or even a wolf. It has something to do with the nature of sentimentality, how we adulate what we destroy, like Ugh-the-caveman's jealous neighbor scratching out an antelope in red ochre and then setting off to bring one down.

It was probably an attempt to escape any taint of sentimentality that led Audubon to draw birds at exactly life size, big big, small small. He had the scientist's regard for accuracy, and this may be the source of the haunted quality of his work. His birds symbolize nothing, and they are both alive and dead.

Corpses posing as living birds, as if Denman Tarrington had been stuffed and set up on the stage here in a chair to listen to my remarks about him.

Water, water.

To begin again. Strange stories cling to the reputations of the famous, and scholarship has the job, pleasing to the puritan, of scrubbing off the encrustations of myth. Audubon had the habit of inventing new biographies, especially the stories of his early life, not the first or the last artist to do it, for they all grow confused over what happened as opposed to what ought to have happened. Surrounded by memories as I stand here, I have given you gratuitous and probably tiresome glimpses of my own past life, and not being an artist, I have been limited to the events, but I might have invented a larger story, opaque and splendid, myself as hero or antihero. Concerning Audubon, somehow the tale got about that he was the lost Dauphin, Louis XVII, the King of France in disguise paddling down all the rivers of North America looking for rare birds.

There were a few Audubon prints in my now lost collection of slides. They used to be very popular. As I said, my copies came from the Book-of-the-Month Club—my mother belonged—but they have been replaced in public favor by more contemporary animal pictures, slick, silent things.

My slides are still, I suppose, lying on the floor of a cab somewhere in Montreal. When I return there, if I can remember the name of the cab company, I will phone and try to reclaim them, though what earthly use they will be, I can't think. I doubt that I will receive another such invitation. There will not be another sudden death. Surely not. When the phone in my apartment rings, it will be the ophthalmologist's secretary reminding me to come in for another test, or it will be someone who wishes to do a survey of my shopping habits or a young man speaking elegant French who wishes to sell me a subscription to *Le Devoir.* Or it will be another of the silent caller's silent calls.

Last night was surely a prank or a delusion. Perhaps it was a dream. After all these years of waiting for a voice to speak, the obsession has gone deep and returns as a nightmare. There are periods of months and years when nothing occurs but the usual wrong numbers. It is possible to achieve a small moment of enlightenment from a wrong number. The Thérèse or Raymond who is being sought has a momentary being, something known, and it is not altogether unlike the moment—watch carefully now as I shuffle the cards—when I was in your library looking at a small shelf of books on animals in art and found myself looking at something called *Woman as Sex Object*. Of course you may take this, especially my friends in the second row—and I can't help wondering why your other colleague isn't here, whether she is the most easily offended, the most easily bored, or whether she has some personal tragedy to accommodate—you will take this as a typical inappropriate joke from an old sexist. Well, so it may be, but the book was there, and whatever we legislate about the connection of man and woman, it is true that the cataloguer—another sexist perhaps—contrived to place the book on that shelf, and it is also true that artists have stared at women and noted each detail, that they have liked nothing better than to undress female persons and record the texture of flesh, not beauty but the pure phenomenon. Tarrington observes in one of his essays that Delacroix's *Lion Hunt* and Rubens' *Rape of the Daughters of Leucippus* show a similar frenzy, a similar tormenting of the posed or imagined bodies. A note on historical iconography: in the movies I see these days, the act is mostly performed with the woman on top. Make what you will of that. The spirit of the time expresses itself in a myriad of odd ways. Who is not its master becomes its slave. Madeleine was ahead of her time.

We are coming toward an end. The usual signal, my dry mouth, the glass too often emptied and refilled. A lurching gait. I am watching for the appearance of a striped tie, which will be a signal. He takes the clip-on out of his pocket, bends as if to cough and fastens it on. That will be enough. The end will come. Some of you have been with me for all three hours, not just your president who must as a part of his official duties. I'll set you free, dear Mr. P. Tomorrow you will be on your own, and so will I. After the lecture, I will return to the motel room, where Delirium Tremens would have stayed if he had survived to give this series of talks. Perhaps he would have taken back with him a fresh young thing he'd picked up in the course of his time here. Myself, I will return there along the snowy road, and I will look in the mirror and fail to see, as always, the meaning of what has happened. It will be the same face, the face I deserve, as Orwell put it. In the unicorn tapestries at the Musée de Cluny, the young lady shows the unicorn his face in the mirror and he appears to accept it with a certain self-satisfaction. The unicorn may or may not belong in a consideration of animal art. Less animal, more symbol. Tidy, white and one-horned. I saw the horn of a unicorn once, in an English cathedral, part of the collection of wonders.

When I get back to Montreal, the check will go to the bank, and I will phone and make reservations for a flight to Paris. Where we began, Tarrington and I at one café, Morrice and Ernest Thompson Seton at another, or perhaps not, perhaps it was the same one, the mirror at the back catching both moments with its perfect equanimity. There ought to be a riddle about the mirror which sees everything and knows nothing. Maybe there is.

That young woman I overheard in the library may by now have made the decision about the tattoo her lover wants. Roses on her butt. The skin reddened from the piercing, as if from a sunburn. I understand that tattoos can be painful, but I suppose that is the point; the marks left by suffering have an extra meaning. That and the permanence; you can't change your mind and get a divorce from a tattoo. Sign for a tattoo parlor: Flowers That Won't Die Till You Do—Something More Permanent Than Love. I never saw the young woman's face, but I imagine her in a certain way, and when I do I think how very young she is. At that age I was still preoccupied by the death of my dog Jim, though I didn't admit that to my undergraduate friends. We were all learning to be witty and untouched.

I hear the slow humming of the universe expanding all around us. I can posit, as everyone does now, an alternative universe in which I looked in a convex mirror and saw, close up, distorted, my own young face, and behind me at an oblique angle, just caught in the corner, someone else, a pale figure almost too small to make out, and seeing this, I understood it. A very different universe.

When he retired from the YMCA he took up gardening. He would work there in the little yard even on rainy spring days, coming in full of aches and pains, but consoled by the richness of the earth, by the way things grew where he planted them. It wasn't a fancy garden, a couple of roses, flowering annuals—just like those the robbers used to stifle Uncle Pumblechook—irises and peonies and delphiniums, the usual old-fashioned things along with a few green onions and radishes for salads. He often thinks of the son who died at Dieppe, though the thoughts are momentary, stray memories, an awareness of a boy he once knew, a boy standing by a bicycle with a cigarette in his mouth, his eyes half closed against the smoke.

Back in Montreal, when I have rushed to deposit the check lest you change your minds and stop payment, I will hurry down to the Musée des Beaux Arts on Sherbrooke to make my homage to the Morrice collection, to reassure myself that the paintings are unchanged, untouched by my words. They will be on display and just as before, but there is always the worm of doubt, the possibility that commentary has altered them for the worse, made them flatter, more obvious.

I said I would return to the horses of Rosa Bonheur. Rose Happiness kept a lion, wore trousers and smoked cigarettes. It all sounds like George Sand as played by Merle Oberon in that movie about Chopin. I was young when I saw that, and was quite smitten by her for a while. Trying to decide what a woman should be like, and here was a new version. Rose Happiness kept a lion. When I was in New York, just before I left, I stopped at the Metropolitan Museum, almost as if I knew I would be called on to come here and speak to you. I looked at a few things, and the last of all was her great horse painting. Eight feet tall it is and twice as long. Creating it must have been like painting the side of a house with a half-inch brush.

The story is that she visited abattoirs to see the bodies of her subjects flayed, and her love of horses and knowledge of them comes out in the painting on Fifth Avenue, the tremendous musculature of the shoulders and thighs, the wild eyes of the white one in the middle of the herd that is being directed into a paddock by a handful of men, the power of the beasts under their control. Rose Happiness sees their splendor but she is not maddened by it. Perhaps she knows why women and animals are on the same shelf. She kept a lion and her specialty was the painting of wild creatures.

Look, there it is, the first of the ties has returned. Time to stop. One more glance at the vast canvas of Rose Happiness, that vision of great and mastered horses, and I leave the museum.

A PRAYER TO THE ABSENT

CARMAN DESHANE put his suitcase on top of the small chest of drawers and went back out to the car. There was a four-lane highway in front of the motel, and behind it a bit of scrubby bush with a creek running through. At the back of his unit was a trailer park. Just along the road, he'd noticed a sign for a planned subdivision. Deshane opened the trunk. Inside was the microwave, an electric kettle, boxes, one with a few dishes and some cutlery. He listened to the sound of a tractor-trailer from the highway. There was a shout from the other side of the square of units. Two guys with an electrician's van, drinking beer, out-of-town tradesmen here for a construction job. He picked up the microwave and walked slowly up the concrete steps from the parking lot and into the motel room. By the time he got to the table next to the front window, he was dizzy, his chest was tight and he was having trouble getting his breath. He put down the shiny black microwave and went and sat on the edge of the bed.

Maybe he should have got someone else to carry it in for him, but he hated to admit to himself that he was that badly off. He imagined his heart, a flabby, weak thing struggling ineffectually to move blood through his body. On the table beside the bed was a bottle of rye. He reached over, took off the cap and took a small swallow. He had pills somewhere in the suitcase, a small pharmacy, the four a day, the two a day, the others, but this was closer.

He put the cap back on the bottle, sat there with it in his hands. First time in his life he'd ever been able to sit still. Now he was too tired to do anything else a lot of the time. His restlessness always drove Audrey crazy. Can't you just sit down for a minute? she'd say, and he couldn't. They'd get in the car and drive somewhere for a coffee, or to a bowling alley in a suburb on the other side of the city, places where he felt like a stranger. Over the years he'd worked most parts of Toronto, and as long as he thought somebody might recognize him as a cop, he couldn't relax. That was why they'd moved to Scarborough, and then farther out after that. Not that it did much good.

When he was working, Deshane liked to be recognized as a cop. They knew who you were, and it kept the shit to a minimum, but it was like a suit of clothes you could never take off. Then he retired and found that without that suit of clothes, he wasn't there at all. His daughter Carol was always suggesting hobbies for him, wood carving or photography. She told him he should write his memoirs. When he first got out of the hospital after the heart attack—six months after Audrey died, six months to the day—he sat down and wrote five pages about joining the navy and going to sea on his first ship, and he carried those pages around with him, though he couldn't have said why, but he knew he was never going to write any more of it.

The day after Audrey's funeral he started to drink, and he stayed drunk for most of a week. When he didn't answer the phone, Carol came and found him, surrounded by mess and empty bottles. He told her he was all right, that he'd get sober and clean it up, and he did. When he had the house back in order, he took a bunch of the old photograph albums round to Carol and Grant, so she could see that he was sober and clean and shaved, and then he went to a real estate agent and put the house on the market.

For almost two years after that he lived in a high-rise apartment, and he hated every day of it. One day he started packing things into the car, dishes, the electric kettle, his winter boots. He didn't know why he was doing it, but it made him feel better. He drove round to see Rolly Menard, his old partner, and they had a drink, a couple of drinks, and just as he was leaving, he asked Rolly if he ever felt as if he wanted to move on, not even knowing where he was going to? Rolly just looked at him and said he was always a weird sucker and clapped him on the back.

After he left Rolly's, he got on Highway 400 and started driving north, and he spent the night in a motel near Huntsville, and he was able to sit with a bottle of rye and watch television without wanting to pitch the bottle through the screen. Now and then he'd go to the front window and see the cars passing. The next morning he drove a few miles along the road and had breakfast in a place with stuffed fish on the walls and old-fashioned wooden booths. He liked that. He stayed three days, and when he got back to the apartment he hated, he decided to move out.

The pain in his chest was better now, and he could breathe more easily. He put the bottle on the bedside table and went back to the car. It was almost dark, and up the hill on the east side of the motel, he could see the lights in a little group of stores. When the stuff was unpacked, he went up to the office at the front. He'd paid a deposit last week when he found the place, and he'd pay a month in advance now while he had the money in his pocket. He'd cashed a pension check this morning.

There was a covered walkway that led from the parking lot out to the front of the motel. On one side of the walkway was a door into the office. Inside, there was a young couple renting a room. The man wore a bomber jacket. He had blond hair with a bald spot at the back and short sideburns, a round face that looked hot and red. The girl with him was wearing jeans and a black silk jacket. Her blue eyes—so wide they looked as if she had no eyelids—were glancing around the room trying not to settle on anything while she waited. They'd both been drinking, and the sexual hunger came off the two of them like a smell. The man got the key in his hand, and the two of them were out the door. Behind the counter, the guy who ran the motel was putting away the cash in his wallet. He was slim, good-looking like an old movie star, straight nose, dark eyes, a good mouth, but the skin on his face was slack. He looked over the counter and smiled.

"What can I do for you?"

"I'll pay you the month."

The man opened a drawer and took out a copy of the receipt for the deposit. He put it on the counter and turned it around.

"Did I ask you your name?"

"Doug," the man said.

"There you go, Doug." He put the cash on the counter. There was a sound of laughter from the television set that was playing in Doug's apartment behind the motel office.

"I'll see you later."

Outside he went back down the walkway and along the path that led to his unit. It was dark now. The couple he'd seen was in one of the units nearby, her legs in the air.

A few minutes later, he was sitting in an imitation English pub, run by a real Englishman. A television set, with the sound off, showed a soccer game. At the bar of the imitation pub sat an imitation cowboy. He wore tight jeans and tooled brown boots, a suede jacket over a denim shirt and a big cowboy hat, and he sat on one of the bar stools with a pint of beer in front of him. He was talking to the bartender, and his voice sounded as if it was produced by something broken. His hands didn't have the look of a man who'd done a lot of hard work with them. Years ago, Audrey took him to a movie about a guy in New York who dressed like that, Jon Voight it was, but he looked to have more fun with the outfit than this guy. Whatever it was this cowboy was waiting for, it was going to be a long wait. Maybe this place was busy on the weekend, but today there were only four people here, Carman, the cowboy and a couple at the table nearest the bar, a pretty redhead and a bulky guy with a moustache. He had thick hands and heavy shoulders, a domed head, balding at the front. His eyes were bloodshot, as if he'd been drinking all day.

The real Englishman came down to his table and Deshane ordered a pint of Guinness. The man dropped a menu in front of him. The guy with the moustache was boasting about how much money he was making from a pyramid sales scheme, and the girl was talking about an agent who might be finding her work in a commercial for Labatt's.

"I have the look they want," she said.

"Last week," the cowboy said, "I was talking to a guy who's looking for extras for a shoot up in Kleinburg."

Everybody wanted to be in the movies. Even his daughter Carol, who was mostly a sensible girl, got it in her head in high school that she was going to be a model and spent a lot of money on courses for it. The people who made the money were the ones giving the courses. He looked at the cowboy, the awkward face with uneven skin. Instead of getting the train west, you bought the clothes. Soon enough there wouldn't be any trains west, just the little suburban lines taking people from the subdivisions into the city.

"You do have a look," the cowboy was saying to the redhead. "A certain kind of thing. A style." He smiled, hoping to charm, but the smile was awkward on his face.

The redhead smiled back. The man with the moustache had a record—theft, fraud, maybe assault on a woman—he'd bet on it. Deshane looked at the thick hands that lay on the table. He would have liked to go outside and find the man's car—it wouldn't be hard to guess which was his—and put the license number into the police computer. The redhead looked toward Deshane. He was sure she'd take some rough treatment from the man she was with, but maybe she was happy with that. People got what they wanted. The guy would never have big money to spend on her. For all his talk. Deshane would have liked to put him in jail.

Deshane stood in the open doorway of the motel room and looked at the night sky. Then he got in his car and started to drive. Thousands of headlights moved through the darkness, cars in long lines on their way somewhere. He drove without thinking, found he was on the Don Valley, dodging from lane to lane, and then he was downtown, turning up Parliament then west towards Yonge.

The girl standing at the curb had long shapely legs; the little shorts and high heels showed them off. It was almost a pretty face, toothy and thin. He pulled the car up in front of her, opened the passenger door and waved to her to get in. There was a guy, familiar somehow, in a doorway shouting something at her, but she got into the seat and pulled the door shut behind her.

"You want a blow job?" she said. "Sixty bucks."

"I don't know what I want," he said, but he reached into his wallet as they sat at a red light and took out three twenties and gave them to her. "Can we take a ride?"

"Are you a cop?" she said.

"Why'd you ask?"

"That guy, Joey, was shouting at me not to go with you, that you were a cop."

"He your pimp?"

"Thinks he is. Are you a cop?"

"Used to be. I'm retired."

"You want to fuck me?"

"I don't know. Let's take a ride."

"You paid. I guess we can do what you want. For a while."

They were back on the Don Valley, going north.

"Where are we going?"

"Up where I'm staying."

"You're not, you know, some kind of a ping pong ball, are you?"

"A ping pong ball?"

"Like weird."

"No. Not about girls anyway."

"You mean you do boys?"

"I mean I never hurt a woman in my life."

He wondered if that was true. As the fast lines of cars moved in and out of each other's headlights, he remembered a detective who made a deal with a whore, that he'd let her off on some charge or other if she'd come to his apartment for a little party, just lie there in the bedroom and take on all comers. Deshane had been at the party, and he'd had a couple of drinks and then gone home. It didn't appeal to him. Mostly he'd been faithful to Audrey. When he hadn't, it was once or twice when he was out of town.

The girl in the seat beside him was quiet for a while, then she started to fidget.

"I got to get back to the street, you know."

"I paid you."

"How long's it take to give a blow job? We're going to the fucking north pole."

"A holiday. I'll give you another sixty when we get there."

"Then I blow you?"

"We'll see."

"You're taking me to the fucking burbs. I hate the burbs. Fucking Scarberia."

"That where you come from?"

"Fuck, no!"

They drove in silence. He turned off the Don Valley onto the 401.

"What is this? We going to Montreal?"

He didn't bother answering. Why couldn't she just shut up and come along? He'd paid. He'd driven downtown without any plan, and picked her up on impulse, but now, for some reason, he wanted to take her back to the motel. He was stubbornly determined that he was going to do that.

"You got a cigarette?"

"I quit. I got a bad heart."

"You going to die if you fuck me?"

"I don't know. Maybe. Hell of a way to go."

"It'd be shit for the girl. Fucking corpse lying on top of you."

They were pulling into the motel. He drove along the front and turned down the lane that led to the large grassy square at the back, then drove along the edge till he came to his unit. Now that he was here, he was ready to regret the whole thing. It was a stupid idea.

"Come in and have a drink and I'll take you back downtown."

She got out of the car without saying anything and her high heels banged up the steps and across to the door. He opened it, switched on the light and they walked in. Most of the things he'd brought here were still in boxes and the suitcase. He hadn't bothered to unpack.

"You live here?"

"I'm just moving in."

"You got a toilet?"

He pointed to the door.

"I'm ready to piss myself."

She went off to the bathroom on her high heels, her little ass tilting from side to side under the shorts. He reached into a box, found two glasses and poured some rye into each one. He put hers on the table by the bed and sat down in the chair. He was restless and tired, and his stomach hurt. The girl came back out of the bathroom pulling her shorts straight. He pointed to the glass.

"What's that?"

"Whisky."

"I don't drink whisky."

"So leave it."

But she picked up the glass and took a swallow.

"You going to ask how a nice girl like me got to be a whore?"

"Because you're too lazy and stupid to do anything else."

"Fucking cheap shot."

She drank more whisky.

"You want to see my tits?"

"Sure."

The shirt she was wearing was pink, with a pattern of silver sequins. She pulled it up and he looked at her breasts, small and young and raw, one bigger than the other.

"You don't have a wife?" she said as she put the shirt back down.

"She's dead."

"You fucked anybody since then?"

"No."

"Think you still can?"

He didn't answer. He could feel the pressure in his shoulders and back, and the beginning of the pain. He got up and went to the suitcase, got out a pill and put it under his tongue, felt the burning sensation against the membrane. Then he went back to the chair.

"Listen, if you're going to die or something. I'm getting the fuck out of here, and you still owe me some money."

He took his wallet out of his jacket pocket and held some bills out to her. She took them and put them in the pocket of her shorts.

"You want me to do something?"

"I'll be OK in a minute."

He listened to the sound of his own breathing, a car starting up in the parking lot, the hum of traffic on the highway, the sound of the girl tapping her fingernails against the glass of whisky. He breathed slowly. The girl's face was tense and ugly, the lips drawn back over the teeth as if she might start to bite and scratch.

It was taking a long time for the pain and pressure in his chest to ease. He might need another pill. He closed his eyes and waited, concentrating on sounds, on the hum of cars on the highway.

"I got to get out of here," the girl said.

He couldn't open his eyes. All he could do was to concentrate on breathing, on staying alive. He thought he heard the sound of the door. He waited, and very slowly he started to feel a little better.

When he opened his eyes, the girl was gone. He went to the door to see if she was waiting for him by the car, but there was no sign of her. Well, she had enough of his money. He locked the door behind him, got undressed and got into the bed.

Norma was imagining elevators. Her legs had been bad for a couple of days, and getting back and forth between the store and her apartment above wasn't easy. Sitting in her rocking chair, she was reflecting on the wonderful small elevator that could be installed to carry her like some stage divinity from earth to the realms above. She couldn't afford such a thing, of course, and would not be able to between now and the final apotheosis (or mere dropping dead), but there was a certain pleasure in looking across the store and seeing the imaginary elevator rising, like a vast dumb waiter, herself seated in it, a complacent smile on her face.

Norma was surrounded by things for sale that mostly no one bought, or so it seemed. She tried to calculate whether business was altogether bad or if this was a mood. Moods, the weather of heart and soul. She was ready to face the blizzards, the hurricanes and snowstorms, but not days of cloud. Cloud today. No blaming the menopause, which was safely past.

She needed to do something. No point sitting here being A Victim of Circumstance. This was what she had chosen, and now she must go on choosing it. Vacationers were arriving at the nearby lakes, and some of the things for sale would actually be sold.

By the back stairs, on a bedside table painted purple, was a portable tape player along with an assortment of tapes she'd picked up from a couple who wanted to sell a garage full of stuff when they moved. They put the damnedest things on tape nowadays. She got up, went to it, and put on her favorite, the one of tropical bird calls, and there she was among exotic trees, green air, green earth and warmth that went all the way into her sore bones. A foreign land with a foreign sun, deep comfort to the soul and body.

She was at the back of the store, where it hung over the ravine, looking always a little in danger of tumbling in, and she could see the sun in the leaves of one of the large maples that also hung over the rock cliff. At her feet was the narrow wooden staircase that led down to a small storage room with one tiny window and cracks in the floor opening into empty space. There was a trap door over the stairwell, and she kept it closed in winter; to be in the little room was as cold as being outside. Its side walls appeared to be hanging from a few nails in the floor joists, which were cantilevered over the ravine.

The tape ended with a loud click. She went down the stairs, which were steep, and as she went, she held on to things, floor, wall, to balance herself. On the darkest days she imagined coming down here, pulling the trap door shut behind her and waiting for death or some other revelation to visit her. If she was alone, let her be alone. Once there was a husband. Once. Company. A vain, foolish man, but weren't they all? Open their zippers and their brains fall out. She couldn't remember if she'd heard that or made it up, but she'd used it a lot. And her tough story about going to see Steven and his bimbo, crashing into the house and pulling the sheet off the poor bare creature. It made a good story, and at first she had thought it was funny, when she was wild and crazed and out of control, but for years afterward she remembered the girl's body, the patch of pubic hair bigger and longer and thicker than hers had ever been, a forest where things happened that gave them joy, while Norma lay alone and chilled.

She didn't know where they were any more, or if they were together, and when she saw her son Arthur she didn't ask. Arthur found her eccentric and tried to avoid her.

Norma turned in a circle. Why? Because. Why was she down here? Because. She turned again. There was some child's game where you turned like that. Or they spun you to make you dizzy. She turned once more, then three more times. Norma has turned six times in a circle, now what will she see? A little dizzy, she leaned against the wall beside the window. To the right was the trunk of a maple tree, rising at an angle from the soil at the side of her neighbors' house. It looked as if the roots went under the house and might lift the foundation if the tree should fall, and they talked of having it cut down. Imagine it tilting into the ravine, the corner of the house lifting, cracking. Sometimes she liked visions of disaster, the floorboards cracking beneath her, her fat old body plunging down onto the rocks.

She listened to the waterfall. In the ravine, sunlight glittered on the racing water. Short-sighted, her glasses left upstairs, she could see no details, only a pattern of gray and silver and green and black, and those flashes of light, and then another moment of dizziness spun her brain, and she had to lean back and close her eyes.

When she opened them again, she was staring at the stone wall that made one side of the little room and supported the framework of the building above. Against it were piled two or three boxes of books left here until she had time to sort and price them. Beside them an old school desk, the writing surface missing. Her business was rescue, of the abandoned, the fragmentary, the useless; her business was faith in unlikely possibilities. She was like the therapists, all those lullaby boys, who found the little fragments of strength and hope, and listened, their listening a song of comfort, those miners of darkness, those lullaby boys, but her work of salvage had its own dignity. Who would ever find a place for that broken school desk, stitch it back into the fabric of life? Not without its comic nobility, this garbage-picking business of hers. Save us all, Norma, the broken things cry out. Oh save us from the landfill site, from burial and rot, for we have the beauty of manufacture upon us. We were produced by the willful brain and would not return to being mere atoms. Save us, Norma, save us.

She turned herself around in a circle once more, she couldn't resist it, and she promised all the lost objects of the world that she would do her best to save them.

And then she was sitting on the floor of the little storeroom and she was cold. It must have been all that foolish spinning that brought her down, and now she was wakening from some kind of doze, and chilled through. Cool air rose from the earth and rocks through the gaps in the floorboards. Even the sound of the waterfall was cold. She wondered if she could summon the strength to stand up; there were whole days now when weakness took her in this powerful impersonal way, and she was only aware of her incapacity in its grip.

She tried to get up, had to turn round on hands and knees, sunlight there below on gray and green shapes, something blue. Got hold of an old board nailed across the studs and heaved herself up, on her feet now, leaning against the wall and panting. Down here so long, there must be something to be found, some message. She walked slowly across the room to a pile of cartons. On top of one was a small cigar box. Norma couldn't remember ever seeing it; it must have arrived with a truckload. She lifted the lid.

Even in the dim corner of the room there was a glint of light, and when she took the box toward the window, a reflection of full daylight fell on the shards of pale shining gold, with patches of darker color, sharp lines of fracture on the surface. She reached into the box and took one of the shiny pieces of material in her fingers. It was light as a sheet of paper. A tiny fragment broke off, split into even thinner sheets.

It was years since she had walked through the woods to one of the old mica mines. They were derelict now, dangerous water-filled holes surrounded by second growth bush. In the early days of settlement, farmers hauled wagonloads of the golden ore into the larger towns to sell, a cash crop that could be harvested in winter.

A thin layer of mica slid loose under the pressure of her fingers. Clear as glass or the water in a forest pool, the pale brown of water over fallen leaves. She held it to the light and saw the world golden beyond it.

He woke in the dark, and he felt a great happiness, and then he knew that he had been dreaming of Audrey, that in the dream she was alive and they were together, but the dream was over, and the room was black and cold, and he wanted to be asleep again, but he knew that he would lie awake now, listening to his heart beat. He tried to remember the dream, as if that might bring some comfort, but every second it was farther from him, and the memory was a taunting of his solitude.

He pulled himself up in bed and turned on the light on the bedside table. There was a book open there, a science fiction paperback he'd bought at the milk store when he went there to get instant coffee. It was one of those stories about the development of dangerous new germs, and it kept him reading. Beside it stood the bottle of rye and a small glass. He poured just a little of the amber whisky into the glass, picked up the book, and started to read, taking a little sip now and then. It was better than lying in the dark hoping for sleep to come.

This was how you passed the night. He looked up from the book and examined the room. The wall facing him was made of concrete blocks, heavily painted. One course of blocks and beyond that there was another identical room, empty, or with a stranger lying asleep. It was very quiet. If he listened carefully, he might hear a car or truck passing on the highway. The curtains that he'd drawn over the window had a pattern of running deer. Over the foot of the bed was a cheap blue blanket with a lot of the color worn out of it.

It reminded him of a motel room that he and Audrey had rented in Florida, near Fort Myers. How they spent hours walking on the beach and always tracked sand into the room. The salt fishy stink of the shells Audrey collected and brought back to the room was all around them as they lay close together on the bed. It was an ordinary sort of place, but it was their best holiday, one of the times he'd forgotten about Toronto.

Even as he sat there, perfectly still in bed, he could feel the chaos in his chest as the ruined heart labored to do its work. The doctor would listen to the heart and test his blood pressure and find more pills to prescribe to keep him alive for a few more days, a few more weeks. He already had the blue ones, the yellow ones, and the black and yellow capsules to put under the tongue. Not much point to it all, but something in you didn't let you quit.

It was hard to live without work. What you did. How you spent your life. You complained about it, but there was nothing else really. He hadn't been trained for this emptiness. Starting in the navy, tossing around in a corvette in the North Atlantic, there were jobs to be done. The decks awash in rough weather, other ships, friendly and hostile invisible in the rain and fog, and in the worst of it you slept where and when you could and woke for your watch and hoped to survive. Now you were useless. It was unfair of Audrey to have died.

To have left him like this. Mostly women lived longer, and they were better at it, somehow, just living.

He took another sip of whisky and tried to go back to reading about the killer germs attacking the city. It was how you passed the night.

Sometimes Norma gave up on sleep. She would get up and read or wander around the store, or even go out for a walk, and after an hour or so, go back to bed. It was easier to sleep once it began to be light. Tonight, she'd lain awake for an hour, and now she was making her way, a little laboriously, down the steps to the store. She would sit there in her rocking chair for a while and stare out into the night, as if she were thinking. Or maybe she would be thinking. Sometimes she wasn't altogether sure what thinking was; apparently there were those who could do it in a step-by-step sequential way, whose brains set up and solved equations with no irrelevant interference from daydreams and bodily needs and scraps of old memories.

Maybe she didn't have anything large enough to think about. She went step by step down to the store, a dressing gown over her cotton pajamas, silly childish things like those track suits that people wore to go bouncing by her windows. Norma remembered a time when it would have been inconceivable for respectable men and even more for respectable women to run up and down the streets in odd collections of clothing. That was something to think about, as she sat there in her rocking chair, why all that had changed.

Why do things change? Now there was a subject for meditation. She could have a good long rock over that one. She reached the bottom of the stairs, twisted her hip the wrong way, flinched from pain, and went to the front window. To survey the empty night street. There were streetlights on this part of the main street, though it wasn't clear why. No one walked out there at this hour.

Except someone was.

A child standing in the street, looking toward the old hotel which stood empty and ominous a few feet away on the other bank of the narrow river. She unlocked the door and went out to the sidewalk. The small figure looked in her direction, interested but also unconcerned. It was the boy from the cottage she rented out, son of the young woman from Virginia who'd turned up a few days ago.

"I'm Luke," he said.

"What are you doing out in the middle of the night?"

"Exploring."

"Shouldn't you be in bed?"

"I don't know."

"Of course you know. And you should. Your T-shirt's on backwards."

"It was dark when I was gettin' dressed."

Norma liked his Virginia accent. He looked perfectly self-possessed as he stood there in the street, but she couldn't just leave him, not at this hour.

"Do you want to come in here?" she said.

"No. I want to go in there." He was pointing to the hotel.

"Why?"

"I don't know."

"At night?"

"Sure."

"Aren't you scared?"

"I wouldn't be if you came with me."

That shut her up. Here she was in her pajamas and nightgown, at some unknown hour of the morning, on the main street of the village, talking to a small child, who was, in his innocent way, propositioning her.

"Come in before we wake up the whole neighborhood," she said.

They entered the store, and Norma closed the door behind them.

"Actually I need to pee," he said.

"Children always need to pee," she said. "It's one of the things I remember about children. They always need to pee but especially when you're in a car on a busy highway."

"Do you have children?"

"I have one boy, grown up. His name is Arthur."

Unseen for some time now. Probably as a result of her own foolishness, which was endless.

"Why didn't you pee on the side of the road in the bushes? People do that in the country."

"I forgot."

"Well, the toilet's upstairs. I'll show you." She started back up the stairs, weary by the time she was halfway, but trying not to show it.

"Does it hurt you to climb up the stairs?"

"How did you know that?"

"I don't know."

"An old cripple eh?"

He didn't say anything. He was too young for polite reassurance, probably didn't know it was being asked for. Upstairs she turned on lights, wondering if the boy saw the place as a mess. Or maybe he was used to such things. She pointed out the toilet, and while he was in there, she went to her bedroom and pulled on pants and a shirt over her pajamas, put on a pair of sandals. When she came back out, the boy was standing in the kitchen.

"You got dressed," he said.

"Well, you're dressed. Did I put my shirt on backwards?"

"I can't tell."

"Neither can I."

"Are we going to see that place?"

"You mean the hotel?"

"Is that what it is?"

"It's what it used to be."

"It doesn't look like a hotel."

"Not like a hotel in a big city. This is just a small village and that's an old-fashioned hotel, but that's what it is."

"I stayed in a hotel once when I was little."

"Where was that?"

"New York. My mom's boyfriend took us there. Matt. He used to be her boyfriend. He used to make her cry."

The boy's face was sweet and blank. What did he see in hers?

"So you want to look at the hotel," she said.

"I thought it was a haunted house."

"Have you ever seen a ghost?"

"No."

She opened a closet where she thought there was a large flashlight.

"We'll go and take a look," she said, "if I can find the flashlight. I don't think we better go inside tonight. It would be too dangerous. We could fall through a hole in the floor or the stairs might collapse."

"That would be neat."

"No, it wouldn't. We'd get hurt. But we can have a look around, and if you stay a while, I'll try and get hold of the people that own it and see if I can show you inside some day. I'll tell them you want to buy it."

"I don't have enough money."

"I won't tell them that. And don't you tell them that either."

"OK."

"Do you know my name?" She couldn't find the flashlight, was opening drawers now.

"No."

"Norma."

"OK."

"That's OK is it?"

"Sure."

She had finally found the flashlight, in the cupboard under the sink. Like as not the batteries would be dead. She pressed the button forward and the light came on.

"Good," the boy said, with that placid male sense that his approval mattered. There were worse ways to be, she supposed, than feeling that the world was significantly the better for your satisfaction with it.

"And after we look at the hotel, you'll go back to the cottage and get to bed?"

He nodded, and they started down the stairs. The hotel was one indication of the generally lousy state of property values in the village. The last Norma heard, it was owned by a family in Toronto who had inherited it from the son of the last man to run it, and they were waiting for the price to go up before they tried to sell it. Standing there by the river through winter wind and summer sun, the paint was peeling, and the wood, good old white pine as it was, deteriorating.

The day would come when there was nothing to do but tear it down.

She and the boy stood in the street and looked at the frame building. There were two small balconies on the second floor, one overlooking the street, and one built over the ravine, looking toward the brick wall of Norma's store, the wall with the faded advertisement for boot polish, ghostly now, old-fashioned type, old-fashioned words.

Sometimes at night she thought she heard voices from that balcony, voices singing.

The windows in the front were boarded up, and there was a sheet of plywood over the front door, but she remembered that there was a window along the far side that they could peek in. She led the boy down that side.

"Be careful," she said. "You could break your leg."

"So could you," he said.

"I know."

She played the light on the ground in front of her, ground which was full of weeds and stones and tough springy Manitoba maples. She pushed past a couple of them, whipped by twigs, and looked back to see how Luke was doing. He slid neatly through and stood close to her. The window was a few feet ahead. It wasn't boarded, but the earth sloped down so it was just above her head.

"The window's too high to see in," she said.

"You could lift me."

"Could I?"

"Sure."

Ahead of them to the left and a little below, she could see a light through a black lace of leaves. A window in one of the houses along the river. Earlier there had been a bit of wind, but now it was still. There was something. In the distance.

"Listen," she said.

They listened. A breath of air, the rattle of old leaves and then the almost silence. A sound, faint and far off.

"What is it?" he said.

"Wolves," she said. "Wolves howling. But a long way from here."

"Really wolves?"

"Really."

They listened again. The sound drifted away. You thought you heard it, but you knew now you were probably imagining it.

"There are really wolves here?" he said.

"Near here."

"I didn't know that," he said, appreciative.

Norma stood closer to the window. She shone her light up into the room and saw the grooves of a wooden ceiling. This old place could be quite something, with a few thousand dollars and a little imagination. Well, quite a few thousand dollars and a lot of imagination.

"Are you going to lift me?" he said.

"I'll try. Then that's it for tonight. You go home to bed."

He came over close to the window. She gave him the flashlight and tried to decide how to lift, bent her knees and put her arms around his legs and did her best to stand up. She gasped. There were pains all up and down her back, but she got him up to where his head was even with the glass of the window. He put his arms up to shine the flashlight in the window and looked intently.

"What's it like?"

"It's empty, but it's funny. It's like a picture in a book."

"I can't hold you any longer."

Trying to bend to put him down, she lost her footing, tumbled, and found herself lying on the ground, with a sore hip where she'd fallen against the edge of a rock. The boy stood with the flashlight in his hand, waiting for her to get up. She managed to do it, not gracefully, but she was on her pins again, though a bit dizzy and wobbly.

"Well, this is quite an adventure."

"Yes, it is," he said.

He handed her the flashlight, and they made their way back to the front of the hotel. She half expected to meet police or a suspicious neighbor, but the street was empty up to the curve both ways. There was a little puff of wind against her face, and the waterfall went on with its endless idiotic roar.

Carman Deshane had no idea where he was. Yesterday he started to drive north then east. Last night he'd found a motel on Highway 7, and in the morning he started out again, taking back roads, making turns on impulse, and now he was in the middle of nowhere. The road he'd been following had come out of a stretch of woods and past a small house, not much more than a shack, that stood helplessly on the rock that cropped up everywhere here, and then the road ended where it met another at right angles. So he turned right on the new road and it was leading him through a marsh, the water lapping against the sides, coming almost over the roadway itself. At low points, the ruts were full of water and he couldn't see past the thick growth of reeds. Water splashed up and he half expected the engine to stall, the car to coast to a slow stop.

He wondered how many miles it was back to the little frame house. There had been a skinny old man in black rubber boots standing in the yard, staring at his car as it passed by. A pile of split wood beside him and a rickety sawbuck beside that. The wreck of a car rusting away at the edge of the woods behind the house. Then it was gone and he'd found himself on this dirt road that looked as if it might vanish into the long reaches of the marsh. Ahead of him the road dipped and was completely covered by water. It wasn't clear how deep the water was, and he could see the car going in, sinking down, vanishing. Miles of country out here without a single human being in it. It had been settled and logged a long time ago, and now most of those who had settled it had abandoned it for an easier life.

Water sprayed up the sides of the car, but he came out the other side and the road began to bend to the right and he saw a small hill where it vanished into another patch of woodland. As he drove up the slope into the trees, he noticed that there wasn't much gas left in the car. If he saw a sign anywhere for a town, he'd better follow it. Otherwise he'd find himself out of gas at the side of one of these meaningless old roads. He didn't have it in him to walk for miles, and he had no idea how long it would be before another car appeared.

It was a cloudy day. The depths of the woods were secretive and still. He could stop the car, wander off into the trees, lie down to die like an old dog, curled in a hollow among the fragrant piles of leaf-mould.

A few miles further on, there was a crossroads and a little sign with the name of a town, and beyond that, he began to see the flash of a lake between the trees, then a sign for a little park. He turned and drove down the narrow road to a parking lot at the edge of the water, stopped the car and got out. There was a flatbed truck there and beside it a man unloading picnic tables. When Deshane got out of his car, the man nodded to him, but he didn't speak. He was tall with reddish hair and skin coarsened by the sun. He had long arms with tight ropy muscles and covered with blond hair, and he was unloading the truck alone. When the last of the tables was off, he got into the truck and drove away.

Deshane stood by the edge of the lake and looked out over the shining surface to the hills and islands beyond. Far out he thought he saw a boat and someone fishing. He looked over the surface of the lake, smooth and bright as mercury.

Norma stared out the front window of the store to where the street bridged the river, just above the waterfall. She studied The Fisherman. He'd been here every day for a week, on the concrete abutment by the river, with his folding chair, the tackle and bait. He sat there, a small thick figure with a round bald head, hunched on the chair, his rod in his hand, waiting, his fishing line vanishing in the slow deep water above the dam, thinking his thoughts or not thinking them. A stringer fastened to the leg of his chair hung down into the water beside the abutment, and it was impossible to tell if there were fish on the stringer, pickerel and perch, maybe even a big pike with its long jaw and malicious grin. Perhaps at the end of the day, he took them off and threw them back into the water that was the color of clear coffee, and never took anything home, or maybe he took them home, all of them, every time, and gutted them and put them away in a freezer. If there were fish on the stringer. Did he catch any? She had never been sure. All day he sat there, and the sun brought out the freckles on his bald head, and his line was heavily enough weighted that it stayed still in the water. The current made a V shape around it, one branch of the V on each side of the line, and even when the cars went over the bridge, he didn't look up, just stared down into the brown clear water as if he could see the fish and as if his look were drawing them toward him. It was always when she wasn't watching that he arrived or left. When she looked he was there, or not there.

Right now, he was there, still, waiting. Norma was waiting too, for someone to come to her hook. The bait had just been dropped in the water. A sign hung in the front window of the store. COTTAGE FOR RENT. The young woman from Virginia, whose son took Norma out exploring in the middle of the night, had left and re-entered the Other Realm; people Norma knew nothing about, which was most of the world. Norma had an ad about to come out in the Kingston newspaper, but in the meantime, perhaps the sign in the window would draw someone. Most people who came here had their own places on the back lakes, or if they were traveling, they kept to the main roads, but she did see strangers about from time to time, and the cottage, which was on the other side of the main street, the first of a series of small places along the east bank of the river above the falls, had a broken-down dock that could be used for fishing or swimming or putting a boat in the water, so long as you did any of these things carefully. The dock ought to be repaired or replaced, but to build something that wouldn't be taken out by the ice in the spring would cost more money than Norma had. As things stood, the dock had posts on the bank and projected over the water, and she took over a hammer and nails from time to time and bashed on a new board here and there. That had been her system with the cottage, an occasional visit with a hammer and a lot of nails, and she was aware that the whole establishment lacked elegance. The pump wasn't very efficient and the storage tank wasn't very large, so you had to use water with discretion or the pump lost its prime and priming it could be a messy business, with water flying around. Damn cold when first done in the spring. A reminder that it was probably time to have the Shit Man come and pump out the holding tank. More money. She bought the cottage once when she was flush, thinking that property was always a good investment. Safe as houses. Never live by old sayings.

Last summer she did well enough. Even in September there was that sad and pretty little thing came out from the city looking for a place to recover from something mysterious, Bad Sex of one sort or another by the sounds of it, and she paid her rent and took invigorating swims in the river, seen once or twice running shivering through the cooling air back to the cottage. Miss Virginia, recently vanished, was charmed by the place at first, but she'd promised for a week and stayed only that.

Norma rocked in her favorite chair and looked through the sales book. Not a bad month now that she did the figures, if you kept in mind that there was never going to be a good month, and there were other things about life here, like waking in the night to hear the waterfall. She was, as they said, her own boss, though she was a discontented employee all the same, tempted to join a union and stick it to the management whenever possible. Demand a new contract. In a few months, she would get the old age pension, and that would help, her reward for hanging on all these years. Sell up and move to a little apartment in the city. Maybe.

She plugged in the electric kettle to make tea, and while it was heating went to the front window to check on The Fisherman. Nothing there. He was gone, and when she studied her watch, she discovered it was later than you think. Across the road on the shoulder just before the bend, there was a car parked, a big-old-fashioned-one, and beside it stood a man, also a big-old-fashioned-one, in a worn tweed jacket, tight in the shoulders, his hair combed straight back over his balding head, tossing his car keys in his hand, impatient and irritable, as if he'd been kept waiting for a hell of a time by some foolish woman. He was staring at her window. COTTAGE FOR RENT. Norma wondered if he could see her behind the glass, observing him, and wondered if seeing her would drive him away, and prudently slid out of sight, returned to the rocker. What will be will be. Maybe his wife was at the grocery store, and he was staring in the window while he waited for her to come back. She rocked some.

Carman opened the door of the shop and walked in. It was one big room, with a ceiling of pressed tin in ornate patterns painted over with white paint, walls with breaks in the plaster where old partitions had been torn down, and it was crowded with junk—China, magazines, books, furniture with more furniture piled on top. On the wall, an old fashioned photograph of a nude staring over her shoulder and beside it an ad for Royal Crown Cola. Some dresses and army uniforms hung on a rack, looking as if they might be full of fleas.

Near the back a woman sat in a rocking chair and stared at him. She didn't speak, only fixed her eyes on him as if waiting for him to tell her his business, and he thought he should get out before he started knocking things down and breaking them. You couldn't turn around without hitting a vase or a pile of plates. There was a strange noise in the background, birds, and he looked around to see if she kept exotic creatures in cages. There was an old metal cage hanging on a metal stand near the back, but there was no bird in it. A click and the sound ended.

"That's the end of the tape," the woman said. "If you stand still you can hear the waterfall." She was heavy, and she sank down into the chair as if she had no intention of getting up. She was wearing a black suit jacket over a black turtleneck sweater, and the sweater emphasized her jowls.

"I know," she said, as if she'd read his mind, "I'm a fat old woman and that's about all. You looking for something in particular or driven by random curiosity?"

She was still staring at him.

"I saw the sign," he said.

"You want to rent the cottage?"

For the first time, she showed a little interest and began to get out of the chair. Straightened up with a tiny groan.

"It's on the river," she said. "The other side of the road."

"I just stopped to look around," he said.

"The best decisions are made in obedience to a sudden impulse."

Carman didn't answer. He still felt as if there might be bugs crawling out of things and touching him. The woman was walking down the shop toward him, studying him as if trying to decide whether to reach out and touch him, perhaps to push him out the door.

"Shall we go and have a look?" she said.

"I didn't plan to rent it."

"You just thought you'd come in and bother me for nothing."

"The store's open, isn't it?"

"It's business hours," she said.

She was close to him now, and he was aware of her big stomach, bisected by the line of the belt on her black slacks. Audrey had always kept herself thin.

"Are you going to look at the cottage?"

"Yes."

She pointed to the front door, and once they were outside, she turned the sign from Open to Closed and locked the door.

"The Fisherman's gone," she said. "First he's there, and then he's not."

Carman didn't answer. It didn't seem to have anything to do with him. They crossed the road, went along a hundred feet to a side road and turned left over the gravel where the unpaved road joined the pavement, then down a slope. The side road was shaded by a row of old maples. Down by the river, flat and dark and smooth with little ripples of current, there were a couple of willows growing. The cottage sat above the ground on concrete blocks and heavy pieces of squared timber, and underneath it, chained to one of the concrete blocks, was an old rowboat painted green. Once, when he and Audrey were first married, they rented a cottage for a couple of weeks with a boat like that. They fell out of it one night while they were trying to make love on one of the wooden seats.

The woman was going up the stairs to the back door.

"Watch your step," she said.

There were broken boards on the steps and on the porch.

"You'd want to get that fixed," he said.

"Would I?"

"You could fall through."

"One of these days."

She led him inside the cottage. It was furnished, more or less, and it looked clean. From the back door where they'd come in, you could look through the kitchen past the small living room and out a wide front window to see the willows and the river, the old dock.

"How much are you asking?" he said.

"How long are you staying?"

"Depends how much you're asking."

"Depends how long you're staying."

She was staring at him again. He didn't like it.

"Why are you staring at me?"

"Am I?"

"Yes."

"Tough tittie," she said.

"All right," he said. "Let's forget the whole thing."

"You're a bad-tempered man."

Carman was beginning to feel a pressure in his chest and wondered if he should take a pill. He wasn't going to do it in front of this woman. He started for the door.

"You thinking about a week?" she said. "Two weeks?"

"I'm not planning on anything."

"Take it for the rest of the summer; I'll give you a good price."

He stopped and looked back at her. Over her shoulder, he saw the three chairs and a small table that were the furniture in the living room, and beyond that the window, the grass, the river flowing darkly past the gray dock. A bird flew low over the water, blue and quick, a kingfisher, sunlight on its wings.

"All right," he said. "I'll take it."

"For how long?"

"The summer if the price is right."

She named a price, until Labor Day. Cheaper than the motel, and she offered to throw in sheets and towels.

"But you wash them yourself," she said. "I'm nobody's washerwoman."

She was staring at him again.

"You got a Laundromat here?"

"Nope. Down the road another ten miles."

It was hard to get used to the fact that these things mattered now, where you washed your clothes, bought groceries. Audrey had sheltered him from all that. The fat woman stared. Abruptly she held out her hand.

"Norma," she said.

He didn't want to shake her hand, but he had no choice. It was warm in his, and her grip was firm.

"Carman Deshane," he said.

"You moving in right away?"

"I'll stay the night," he said, "then I have to go and pick up some stuff. I'll give you a check for a month."

"Come back to the store, and I'll get you the sheets and towels."

He'd started the day miles from here, with no thought that anything like this would happen. Now he'd rented a cottage from a woman he didn't like. When they got back to the store, he wrote a check. The woman had mumbled something and left him standing while she disappeared through a doorway and thumped up the stairs. He waited a long time. She was taking forever, and he stood helpless and irritable, looking over all the rubbish she was selling and wondering who would put out money for any of it. Beside the front door were two electric stoves with stains on the enamel, and above them on the wall hung some sort of banner from an Orange Lodge. An oak filing cabinet with little drawers, the kind you'd find in an old library. The Queen smiled down three times from the wall above. Across from her, Royal Crown Cola and the photograph of the nude, her hair long and wavy, her head back and looking over her shoulder and into the air, her body shapely but not the current fashion, the proportions too big and classic. The woman appeared at the bottom of the stairs and noticed him staring at the photograph.

"Good-looking girl," she said. "We all were, once upon a time."

She had a heavy-footed walk, and she came toward him as if she might barge past and knock him down, but stopped and put the piles of towels and bedding in his arms. He thanked her and turned to leave.

"Wait a minute," she said, and pushed between two tables and took down the photograph of the nude. "I'll throw this in as part of the deal. Long-term loan, to cheer the place up a little."

"I don't want that goddam thing," he said.

"Why not?"

"I just don't want it." He wouldn't have her making fun of him.

"A pretty girl," she said. "Not quite art, but nice all the same. You imagine some photographer in 1952 admiring that pretty body and getting her to come to his studio and show herself. Daring thing in those days. When I look at that I wonder where she is now, getting older, husband with Alzheimer's, thinking about how long it will all go on. You wonder if she still has that picture of herself, her big perfect body."

"I've got no use for the goddam thing."

She was staring at him again, as if she knew something but wouldn't say it.

"I guess you're not interested," she said.

He didn't answer, just turned and walked out. He couldn't help it, and he blamed her for making him do that. He wanted the cottage, but he wanted her to leave him alone. Crazy old bitch. He called her that and worse all the way along the road and down to the cottage, feeling like a fool with the pile of bedding in his arms. After he made the bed, he went to the trunk of the car and got out his box of papers and photographs, never unpacked at the motel, and he put the picture of Audrey on the table by the front window.

The next day, Carman drove to Toronto through the busy summer traffic of Highway 401, went to the motel and packed up his possessions. He'd been there less than a week, and Doug refunded him part of what he'd paid. Carman hadn't expected anything, but the man was quick to make the offer, an odd look on his handsome ruined face as if he was frightened, a look Carman had often seen when he was a cop, but he couldn't understand why he was seeing it now. Still, he took the money.

When he got everything into the car, he was exhausted, so he lay down on the bed and slept for an hour, then decided to explore the bit of bush behind the motel before getting back on the road. All along the creek bed, there was an earth wall that had been built to hold back the water when the stream flooded in the spring. The motel had been built on the floodplain, and it wouldn't take much to inundate it. The dike was covered with grass and the sides were steep, but here and there a path led up to the top and down the other side. Then there was a path that led along the creek, a place for people to get a bit of air or walk their dogs. There wasn't a lot of water in the creek now, but here and there you saw deep holes.

The bush was mostly scrub. Manitoba maples, sometimes a big bent willow hanging over the water, bushes that he couldn't identify growing in clumps. Where the banks narrowed, you could hear the babble of water. He stood there by one of these riffles and listened, aware that behind the chattering of the water, he could still hear the cars on the highway. That steady hum, like a hive of bees.

The water was shallow here, the bottom sandy with an occasional round rock. Then, as he watched, a huge fish appeared, like some water monster, so big that it had to force its way through the shallows, its back out of water, the tail flapping wildly to drive it forward over the sand, and it was gone into the deeper pool on the other side.

He couldn't believe what he'd seen, a fish that size in this little creek. The creek emptied into Lake Ontario not many miles away, and the fish must have made its way up from the lake, a huge carp, or one of the salmon that they'd planted since the lampreys were under control and the lake a little less polluted. Whatever it was, he decided to walk upstream and see if it came into sight again in the next shallows. It must mean something, that great fish. He followed the path, but ahead of him, the path turned away from the stream and went round a section of thick undergrowth beneath two willows. He was sweating as he pushed his way through the bushes, but he wanted to stay close to the bank of the stream, watching for the thick dark form of the fish. A branch had fallen into the water here, and other pieces of wood floating down had caught on it, creating a kind of dam and the water rippled noisily over it.

As he stared down into the water looking for his sea monster, he saw something waving in the water like a weed, like a small white human hand. Then it was gone. He looked at the light in the riffles of water, the slick surface and brown depths, a Styrofoam cup on the sand of the low bank on the other side. The air was thin and resonant, and he had the crazy feeling that a murder had taken place somewhere in this bit of abandoned land. The body thrown into the creek. Then it was as if he might be the murderer but had forgotten it all, and they were coming for him. He had to get out of here. Always, over the sound of the stream, he could hear the cars and trucks on the highway. He could feel the hard beating of his heart, and all of his life was coming toward him, to find him here. Or was it his death? He looked back toward the water, searching for the white waving hand, but he saw only a tangle of branches, current pulling weeds. He made his way back along the stream to the motel where he washed up, splashed cold water on his face, took his pills. It was time to go. He'd find somewhere for lunch and then get away from the city and drive back to the cottage he'd rented.

Late that night, Carman stood by the other river, the one that ran past the cottage and listened to night noises, frogs crying out whatever it was frogs cried out, a sound of water running among reeds, wind, the waterfall. Around all these sounds there was something bigger, a silence around the noise in the way that around the glittering stars there was darkness. Something clean and terrible. Earlier in the evening he'd sat by the back window with the pages he'd once written about his first days on the corvette, and read over the words. What he'd written didn't really tell what it had been like, the metallic edge to all the sounds, the way the whole boat vibrated with the power of the engine that drove it through the water. How close and narrow every passage was, the low doorways. The smell of the sea air and the bitter smoke from the funnels. He hadn't said those things, but when he read the bare narrative, he could remember them, and he didn't need to write them down. The first officer named McCann, ill-humored and with an exceptionally foul mouth even among young and rough-spoken sailors. There was the satisfaction of having your whole world close at hand, and the knowledge that out there in the fog there were other ships, and perhaps a storm looking for you.

That was what he recalled, or thought he did. It was a long time ago now, and there was a lot that you didn't remember, as if, for days on end, you hadn't lived at all. It was gone. Carman brushed away a mosquito, turned from the river and walked through the darkness back toward the house, and as he did, he looked toward the next-door cottage and saw through the window the young woman who lived there, as she stood in the lighted kitchen, washing dishes. She had two small girls; he'd seen them in the yard when he got back. She had come over to say hello when she saw him unpacking the car. Amy. After she had introduced herself, she stood smiling at him as if waiting for him to tell her his story or to ask for hers. Carman thought that she wanted to tell him more than he cared to know. She was tall, slim, dressed in shorts, her legs pale and thin, but she had large breasts that seemed flagrant and misplaced on her slender body. There was no sign of a man at the cottage. The place was built on a mortared block foundation and had aluminum windows, as if they lived there all year.

Carman watched her through his wide window and wondered whether he would get to know her. There was something uneasy, discontented, about her face, the way she moved.

Norma unplugged the whistling kettle and poured boiling water into the filter over the three tablespoons of coffee. It was a good smell, and she turned the stove to simmer and went to the table to eat her shredded wheat. Which was good for her as the coffee wasn't. There were more and more things that weren't good for you, and odd things that were. From time to time, she liked to get dried fruit and nuts from a health food store in the city, and while she was there, she would stare in astonishment at the bottles of magic pills. If she went to the right kind of practitioner, she would be told to choke down some of these things. Pills made from roots and weeds and dirt. Eat dirt and you won't hurt. Unfortunately, she didn't believe it. There was a new pain in the back of her head this morning, also in her legs. The headbone's connected. Days you'd wish it disconnected.

One cup of coffee done, she took the second to the bedroom and began to get herself dressed. There was a mirror on the door of the closet and mostly she avoided it. Her shape grew more and more that of an egg. An egg with a leg and another leg. She had to sit down to pull on her pants and socks, and she worked away at it all, panting now and then, and soon enough she was kitted up for the day, all in green like one of Robin Hood's merry men. Somewhere in the closet was an old green hat with a feather that would complete the effect, and she poked through dead things until she found it and set it on her head. Raffish. That was a kind word for how she must look, but it did her heart good to be absurd. In celebration, she would do dishes and make the bed.

It was an hour or so later, as she was going down the stairs to open the shop, that she remembered once again that her cottage was rented for the rest of the summer. Hooray for the bucks. Ill-tempered son of a bitch, though, with a murderous look in his eyes. Maybe hiding out from the law and she would learn that he had a string of bloody killings to his credit. Still, he paid. Unless the check bounced. Yesterday he'd gone off to get his possessions: say, guns, knives, instruments of torture. What did a thumbscrew look like?

Norma had brought the pot of coffee downstairs with her, and she put it on the hotplate at the back of the shop and popped a tape into the player and got something nebulous and soothing. Not as good as the birds. The sun was shining in the back window and making a pattern on the set of kitchen chairs, shapes of light falling on the red paint. Beautiful, you said, and then wondered how a thing got to be beautiful. Norma checked her watch and decided it was too early to make the phone calls on her list, which were anyway people wanting to sell and what she needed was people wanting to buy. Upstairs she had some very early copies of the *Saturday Evening Post,* and there was a dealer in Toronto who might take them if she offered to pack them up and put them in the mail. She went to the front door, unfastened the lock and turned the sign round. Now she was open for business. She tried to see whether her tenant had left the cottage, but the driveway was hidden behind a clump of elders. While it was morning and her joints still loose from a hot bath, she should bring up some of the books from the basement, price them and get them on shelves. It was so much easier to do nothing. Shut off the tape, which was so soothing it made her furious, and turned on the radio. Talk or music: she chose music and found CBC Stereo was playing something lively and pleasant. She couldn't tell one composer from another, but she knew what she didn't like. Heavy stuff, that's what she didn't like.

On the way down the back stairs, she caught the long pheasant feather of her hat on the edge of the trap door, and the hat flipped off, but when she got to the bottom of the stairs, she put it firmly back on, collected a cardboard box of books and labored up the stairs with them, a lot of puffing but she got there, and when she did rewarded herself with a cup of coffee and a little sit in the rocking chair. It creaked when she sat down, a tribute to her fatness, and that made her talk back a little, but then she sipped coffee and rocked contentedly, and closed her eyes, and thinking she might fall asleep, she set the coffee aside and let the hypnagogic images that were lurking at the edges of her eyes come out to play.

The bell on the door woke her, but by the time she had her eyes open, the man was standing close to her, watching. A thin beard and a greasy cap pulled down on his forehead, pants tucked into rubber boots. His thin chest dropped in a long curve to the sag of a pot belly, and he had long arms that hung loosely at his sides, fingernails that looked like the claws of an animal. Out of the back country to the north.

"Well?" she said.

There was a honking noise, and it took her a second to realize that it was his speech. He had a cleft palate. These things could be repaired now, but where he lived, the news hadn't arrived. Norma got her wits together, got herself up from the chair, but the man didn't move to give her space, just stayed where he was. She wanted to push him away.

"I was asleep," she said. "You startled me." She hoped he'd repeat himself without being asked. He did, and it became clear that he wanted to show her something on his truck, and when she had agreed to that, he turned and walked to the door, his rubber boots scuffing against the floor as he moved. He threw open the door when he reached it, and she caught it on the way back and let herself through to where his small truck was parked, right in front of the store. He pointed to the back and honked. Norma went to look.

Ten glass eyes looked at her. Sunlight on fur. Five of them in life-like postures that exaggerated their deadness. A raccoon, a weasel, a mink, a squirrel and a wolf, stuffed and mounted. Creative taxidermy: the squirrel was climbing a branch, the raccoon stood by the stump of a small tree, the others were posed on varnished pine. They were old, and the fur had a dusty look, but there was no obvious damage. Though she was used to dealing with the world's abandoned things, the sight of these animals gave Norma a chill, and she wondered where the man had found them. Maybe he'd stuffed them himself in earlier years, had read an ad in a magazine and sent away for the course in do-it-yourself taxidermy then gone about the woods killing things.

"How much do you want?"

"Twenty." Or that's what it sounded like.

"For the lot?"

He looked as if that wasn't what he had in mind, but then he nodded. Norma reached into her pocket where she kept a small stash of bills and took out two tens and handed them over. He put them in his shirt pocket and reached into the truck to begin unloading. Took the wolf first thing. Norma had just picked up the squirrel on its branch when she was aware of car doors opening and saw, a few steps in front of the truck, a man coming toward her, a man with a familiar face. Oh. Oh God. It was her son, Arthur, and there was an unknown young woman with him.

"Don't just stand about," she said. "Pick up a creature and come in."

The man in the rubber boots had walked to the back of the store and set the wolf on top of a round oak dining table. Norma set the squirrel beside it and turned to go back. The narrow aisle between the pieces of furniture was crowded by the man with the cleft palate, Arthur holding the raccoon and its stump and his girl carrying the mink and the weasel. She was maybe thirty, and she was smiling. There was a little dance, and the two of them came toward her, as the rubber boots of her other visitor scuffed their way to the door. Norma took the raccoon from Arthur and put it beside the other two animals. She'd have to get a hairbrush to get some of the dust out of the fur of these new arrivals. As she stood there in her Robin Hood costume—Lincoln green, wasn't that what they wore, those cute thieves?—she was aware that Arthur and his new squeeze—must be that—were trying not to stare at her hat with its long draggled feather reaching out toward them. She could have taken it off, but wouldn't.

"Mother," Arthur said, "this is my friend Julie."

Norma took the mink from the woman and put it on her desk among the disorderly pile of receipts and phone numbers and unpaid bills. The girl wasn't pretty, though some might have called her handsome, square bony sort of body, short hair, slightly crooked face with sharp hazel eyes. Norma offered a hand, which was taken and crushed. She must be one of those weightlifters.

"What happened to your wife?" she said to Arthur.

"I told you we'd split up, last year."

"You did no such thing."

"I did."

"Never heard a word of it."

"I remember perfectly well."

"You're making it all up."

"I phoned you one night." He was starting to get angry. She always made him angry, and she sometimes enjoyed it. "When I phoned you were . . ." He stopped.

"Drunk may be the word you're looking for."

Julie was looking around the place.

"Not on the booze any more," Norma said to her. "For a while I was treating my aches and pains with large doses of vodka and forgetting things. After a bit I decided I was feeling more worse than better."

"Have you tried acupuncture?" Julie said eagerly.

"No. Foolish business."

Looked offended. Gave a glance at the hat.

"How old are you?" Norma said. Compounding the offense and enjoying it.

"Twenty-nine."

"Arthur must be getting on for forty by now, aren't you, Arthur?"

"You must know how old I am."

"It's all a blur, those years before Steven took flight with his bimbo. I was thinking about Steven the other day. Is he still with that girl?"

It was a long time ago, but not long enough.

"No, he's not."

"I hope she left him for some young stud."

"I'm not sure."

"Yes you are, but you're being loyal."

She turned to Julie who was standing with her head drawn in a little, like a boxer ready to feint and counterpunch.

"Are you and Arthur planning to stay together or is he just dipping his wick?"

The young woman burst out laughing.

"I've never heard that expression before," she said. "It's very colorful."

"I'm full of colorful expressions," Norma said. "I'm sure that's why Arthur brought you to see me."

"We came because I insisted."

"Why would you do that?"

"I wanted to meet you."

"Why? Because he said I was a terrible old bitch, and you thought it was a challenge."

"Of course not."

"Now that I think of it," Norma said, "I do remember getting a call. It was from Margaret. She said you'd found a bimbo too."

Margaret was the abandoned wife. Norma had been in her cups when the woman called, dutiful or weepy, it was all pretty vague, but if she remembered right, she hadn't been able to do much but suggest that Margaret hire someone to cut the balls off her erring son. Nobody had said anything in response to her last sally, so she went right on.

"So he left Margaret for your sweet ways?" she said to the young woman.

"No, we met just last month at a party."

"What is it you see in him?"

"You're his mother, you must know."

Norma looked at her son, and for a moment she did, and then she didn't.

"Somebody go lock the front door and we'll go upstairs and I'll make some fresh coffee."

No, they weren't going to do that, it appeared, were on their way to Toronto in a rush and had only dropped in for a quick look at the old monster. Norma said a few more objectionable things and stuck out her tongue at them as they left. Arthur was a stick, and not even this bright young thing would make him anything more than that. All her fault, no doubt; she'd been a respectable person while he was little and had liked his nice-little-boy manners. Ugh. Not long after they drove away, Amy Martyrdom from the cottage down the way came in to talk, her big breasts hanging disconsolately inside a white T-shirt, and while her two little girls checked out the stuffed animals and then wandered around breaking things, she admired Norma's foolish hat, drank stale coffee and chattered about masturbation and whether the lesbian option was right for her. Norma liked Amy Martyrdom, though she couldn't have said why, and she listened patiently to all this, thinking again what a strange world it was that this not unattractive young woman was dying of loneliness and couldn't manage to get a leg thrown over her from time to time. Once upon a time, couples stayed together and kept off the beast that way.

Carman had slept well, and this morning he had walked along the short main street past the deserted hotel to the side road that led down to the river below the falls; now he stood on the concrete wall above the thickly twined, rushing water of the millrace, surrounded by the noise, and looked upward to the buildings at the top of the ravine. Trees cut him off from the sky, and light was reflected off water and granite and hanging green weed. As he looked up from his vantage point at the edge of the falling water, he could see the back of the buildings above. Something fateful and dangerous about standing here, as if the houses might suddenly tumble down the hill toward him. He turned and looked downriver from his green cave of leaves, into a huge sunlit space, sky and fields. Below the falls, where the river grew wider, was a field of tangled grasses and weeds, wild barley, daisies, buttercups, the red branches and pale leaves of flowering dogwood, and over the fields, the wild canaries rose and dipped in their characteristic flight, never far above the safety of the earth, yellow as the buttercups, black as coal.

He looked back up the stream toward the waterfall and thought he saw something moving at the edge of the water, a bird or animal, but it was gone again. The sound went on, unchanging, and the water ran close to him, and he took deep breaths of the wet air. It was all new to him; he'd never been in this place before. The world was full of things you've never seen. Once Audrey got him a subscription to *National Geographic* for Christmas, and now and then on a weekend, he'd sit down with the magazine and look at the pictures of other countries, read about them, but at the end of the year, he told her not to renew the subscription. He didn't want to spend his life reading about places he'd never get to. He knew there were men who went on for years living that way. It took all kinds. Being a cop you saw that. A few years back, Carman took things for granted, but now, retired, knowing that he was in bad shape, he looked back, and everything in his life was unlikely and strange. Would Audrey have understood that if he'd tried to tell her? Maybe. He had too much time on his hands now, too much time to think. Carol was right; he should have a hobby, but it was too late, and he didn't know what a hobby might be for a man like him. Not working with his hands: he could change a washer if necessary, put weather stripping on a door, but those were things you did in order to have them done, not for their own sake. He looked back up at the waterfall. For centuries, perhaps millennia, there had been a waterfall here where the slow river, draining the land above, had made a path that led it over a granite cliff and then rapidly among rocks for the next hundred yards until once again it began to flow tranquilly through flat land and wide patches of marsh. The years told their story over and over, an old sleepy song of long winters, the earth buried in heavy drifts of snow, and then in spring the rapid melting, rivers high and dangerous, the waterfall heavy, brown with mud, loud in the cool nights, then in the long dry summer, the water coming with less urgent power, and clear as it made its way between the boulders at the foot of the little cataract.

Settlers arrived, and on every river someone built a mill, as they had just where he stood, where the situation was perfect, a good drop, a kind of plateau halfway down the hill for the building, only a small dam needed to direct the water into the millrace. Maybe the first mill burned down, as mills so often did, and was rebuilt. A village grew around it. Now the mill was gone, derelict for a long time and finally torn down, only the foundations left, the millrace. The hotel, built for travelers in the good days, was a ruin.

He turned away from the river and started along the path that would lead him back up to the street, thinking about his father, how he would set out in the dark on cold winter mornings to go to work in the Halifax shipyards, and Carman would say to himself that he wasn't going to end up like that, rising obediently every day and doing what he was told. What he'd done wasn't much different after all, a few years in the navy, then he went to Toronto and pounded a beat and met Audrey and started to work in plain clothes and now it was over. You dropped in your ticket and rode the streetcar to the end of the line, or maybe you took a transfer, another one, but the cars only ran so far.

Carman walked up the narrow road to the main street very slowly, and when he got there he wasn't too short of breath. There was an old man on a chair fishing from the concrete abutment at the edge of the bridge, and as Carman walked down the side road toward the cottage, the two little girls from the cottage next door were splashing around in the water at the edge of the river, naked in the sunlight. Their mother sat on a folding chair nearby.

Norma was grooming her wolf when the tenant arrived. She had bought a cheap hairbrush from the grocery store and she was brushing the hair of her new stuffed wolf, getting a lot of dust and dirt out of him. The creature was starting to look quite handsome, glass eyes wiped with spit and Kleenex and now very bright. She looked toward her tenant, the putative murderer, who was coming toward her. She could tell he was mad from the way he opened the door.

"What's wrong now?" she said.

"The water," he said.

"You ran it too long. Lost the prime on the pump."

"All I did was take a shower."

"You shouldn't do that."

"What am I supposed to do?"

"You've got a whole river at your back door."

"I don't know what kind of an outfit it is if you can't even use the shower."

"You can if you don't stay in too long. It wasn't made for you to stand around in hot water playing with yourself."

His eyes went hard. Norma was afraid of him at that moment, but there didn't appear to be anything to do but wait. He looked away, took a deep breath, gathered himself together.

"Do you get it fixed?" he said. "Or do I just do without water."

"I'll show you how to prime it," she said. "Then next time you can fix it for yourself."

At the back of the store, she kept a little canvas bag of tools. She went and got it and met him at the front door. Her back and legs were stiff today, and she had to work hard to keep herself chugging along at a normal rate and looking like a real human being. The man didn't speak.

"You're retired," she said.

"Mmm."

"What did you do when you were still alive?"

"Cop."

They were going down the slope of the gravel road and Norma was afraid she might fall.

"Are they all as bad-tempered as you?"

"No."

Norma didn't say anything more, partly because she was a little out of breath from the walk, which had gone too fast for her. When they got up to the side of the cottage, she led the way to the corner where the plastic pipe came in from the river.

"Which one of us is going underneath?" she said.

"You have to crawl underneath?"

"That's the pump in there." She pointed to where the small blue pump sat bolted to a board that was wired to a couple of concrete blocks. It was a jerry-built arrangement, but it worked.

"We need some water," she said and set off down to the river with an old pot that was left hanging on a block of wood that held up the corner of the cottage. The edge was weedy but the dock was high out of the water, and she wasn't sure which was the more dangerous to her in her crippled state. When she got close, she saw a big stone among the reeds, and she managed to get a foot on that without falling in and got the pan half full of water. Getting her foot back off the stone was harder than it appeared, and a toe was dampened a little. The man stood by the side of the building waiting for her. A cop. Imagine that. At a distance, his face was all dark lines, eyebrows, thinning hair, mouth, a hard jaw. Mr. Law and Order. She crossed the grass to where he waited.

"I'll go underneath," he said, "if you tell me what to do."

She handed him a set of vise-grips, then she took a metal cup out of her bag and gave him that and the pot.

"There's a metal plug on the top that screws in and out," she said. "You take that out and fill the chamber underneath with water. Then I'll turn it on from the reset button over there and we hope for the best."

He put the vise-grips in his pocket and crawled on his hands and knees the few feet to the pump, pushing the pot of water along beside him.

"Is this it?" he said, pointing to the hexagonal nut on the top.

"That's it."

He unscrewed the nut and began pouring cups of water into the chamber.

"How much?" he said.

"Till it looks full."

He poured in some more water, then looked back toward her. Norma went to the switch under the edge of the cottage, beside the nail where she hung the pot. She turned on the pump which whirred a little, bubbled, and then shot up a geyser of water. What didn't catch him on the way up splashed back down on him from the floorboards.

"Jesus Christ!"

He looked darker, sodden, more murderous, and Norma felt a certain perverse pleasure in his discomfiture. He wouldn't be taking any more long showers. But she knew better than to laugh out loud.

"Keep pouring in water."

He filled the cup and poured it into the small hole. The pump was bubbling out air.

"Keep pouring in a little at a time as the air bubbles out. When you hear it starting to suck water put the nut back in."

The man crouched under the building and Norma sat on the grass to watch him. In a minute or so, she could hear the water coming up.

"There," she said.

The man crawled out, wiped his face with a handkerchief then stood, brushed off his trousers, dumped the water back out of the pot and hung it in its place. He handed the vise-grips to her.

"Thank you," he said.

Well, she thought, at least he isn't a whiner.

"If you spelt vise-grips with a c, it would make a new name for the police," she said. "The Vice-grips."

He looked at her as if she were a crazy woman. Maybe she was.

"Why don't you have the pump out here where you could get at it?"

"I don't know. It was under there when I bought the cottage, and I've just never moved it."

"I'll see you later," he said, and without another word went to the back porch of the cottage and up the broken stairs. As Norma watched him go in, she reflected that she really should get this and that repaired. This and that and the other. Someday. She started back up the road. Her dead animals were waiting for her.

The great blue heron he'd been watching as it stood in the shallow water by the dock flew away and night fell on the river. As the days passed, all these things grew familiar. Now it was dark, he could go to bed, or read a book, or turn on the little television set he'd bought and see what he could pick up with the built-in aerial, or he could just sit here in a comfortable chair beside the window looking from darkness into darkness as minutes went by, as the river flowed past, a light down by the bridge reflected on the surface. If you looked upriver, you knew that the water was there in the night but you couldn't see it. Off through the trees, light in a window, small and far off. Someone else's life.

A pale ghost crossing the grass toward the river. The long white body of his neighbor gone skinny-dipping after the children were asleep. Her pale dim shape was almost invisible now as she walked into the water, only a hint of something in the darkness, then she dived in and he could see nothing. He picked up the glass of rye and sipped from it, waited for her to come out. A peeping Tom now. But he hadn't sought her out. Or so he might say, though he had known as he sat here that she would appear. You knew things without knowing how. Rolly joked about that, Carman's magic powers. Carman the Mentalist, he called him. It was true that if they walked into a place where someone on the staff was stealing, Carman would know pretty quickly who it was, whether or not he could prove it. Nothing magic about it, just had to pay attention. He could smell it, he used to say. You knew more than you knew. He had walked by that stream behind the motel, and he'd known that once, however long ago, a death had happened there. Just as he'd known that tonight his young neighbor would go naked across the yard to swim in the river. In a certain kind of book, she would come to his door instead of returning to her own house, and he would welcome her in and take her to bed. Things that happened in books. He took another sip of whisky and watched the river. Something moved. She was climbing out of the water. As she came closer, he could almost make out the shape of her big breasts against the long slender body, and he drew back from the window into his chair, lest she see him there observing. Just before she disappeared from his view, she looked toward him. Yet he swore that she couldn't see him here in the dark. She imagined him here, watching, was pleased to be seen, looked toward him so he would know.

She was gone, but he sat perfectly still, waiting for the knock on the door. Time was passing again, in rapid heartbeats now. He was a sick old man and she would have no interest, and yet when she came across to introduce herself, there was a hunger in her eyes, she flirted a little, a hint of craziness, or maybe just being too lonely. Carman picked up the glass of rye and tasted it in his mouth and down his throat and thought about what it would be like to have a woman in his bed. A stranger. They said human contact helped to keep you alive. Or any kind of contact. For a while Carol had tried to convince him he should get a dog or a cat. She had a couple of kittens when she was little, and watching them, Carman had concluded that cats were a lot like some of the criminals he pursued, all nerve and driven to destroy, the big kitten eyes staring out of the narrow head as it raced about looking for something to kill.

He heard the knock almost without knowing it. What he had imagined. Had she waited out there all this time? He turned on a light as he went to the door, his heart beating fast. Opened the door and found Norma standing there, her head sunk into her shoulders, eyes fixed on him with that hard stare.

"Keys to unlock the boat," she said, and reached out. "Forgot them before."

He took the keys, and she turned away and started down the steps.

"Watch your step," he said.

"I know," she said. "The goddam porch needs fixing. I'll get to it."

She was vanishing into the darkness.

"One of these days I'll do it," he shouted after her. "You can pay for the wood."

"Don't bother your little head about it," she said.

Carman closed the door behind her and stood for a minute with the keys in his hand. The boat. Not sure he'd ever bother to take it out. He tossed the keys on the kitchen table. Well, the knock at the door had come, hadn't it? Now he'd go and take a pill and get into bed to finish that paperback about the destruction of the world by new kinds of germs.

Norma was trying to think about things, to be orderly and systematic and reach a conclusion. She'd gone through all this before, it was one of her techniques on nights when she couldn't sleep. Trying to figure out what thinking was and do it. It was better than TV. She lay in her bed, aching in this part and that, and wondered if she could have a few smart thoughts about pain. A stimulation of the nerves that warned you of damage being done, or damage that had been done. It was possible that the night was full of people who were not experiencing pain, though there might be those whose pain was worse, whose pain was excruciating. Excruciating: whatever that meant. If she didn't fall asleep soon, maybe she'd get up and look up excruciating in the Shorter Oxford. From (fire up the high school Latin) *crux*, cross? Like the pain of being on a cross? Now it was getting all theological. Was God responsible for pain and why would God invent such a thing?

This wasn't thinking, not what she had in mind at all. Pain exists. Next step in the syllogism was what? One, two, ergo three. *Quod erat demonstrandum*. Always liked the arrogant certainty of that old tag, not that she'd ever thought anything was proved by formal logic. What was proved was that if you dropped a man out a window, he would hit the ground. Proved enough, though there was always the possible day when the sun didn't rise and bodies floated upward into the air. Wasn't there? And was this thinking? Ruminating, which, as she remembered was what a cow did with its food. Another word to look up, but by the time she gave up on sleep, she would have forgotten all these linguistic duties.

Excruciating. Crucifixion had got all tangled up with Christ and martyrs, but it was a common punishment, the Romans were at it all the time, malefactors (always liked that word) artistically draped over their wooden frames on every hilltop. Make them suffer. How did the pain of crucifixion compare with what her body went through on a bad day? Well, the exacerbation of the nerves didn't kill her, though on the very worst days, she wished it would. All right, Norma, enough of that. That's not thinking, it's whining. Change the subject. To what? The Vice-grip in her cottage. She liked her joke even though he hadn't the wit to appreciate it. She could design a whole new TV series. The Vice-grips. She had taken a certain delight is seeing him crawling sodden out from under the cabin, trying to resurrect his dignity. Sad critters, men, so delicate and touchy, of limited use for fetching and carrying and screwing. As she walked along the dark road to the cottage a few nights ago, going to give him the boat keys, she'd caught a glimpse of Amy Martyrdom strolling naked across the lawn after a skinnydip in the river. The lights were off in Carman The Vice-grip's cottage when she arrived; he must have been watching Amy running around in the buff. Now there was a phrase that needed looking up. One of those antiquated things she'd picked up from her mother. That impossible woman that she grew more and more to resemble.

She should keep a pad and pencil by her bed to make notes of all the things she wanted to look up. One of the advantages of her business was that she got good books for a song, and over the years she had made herself a very satisfying reference library. She'd always hoped to get the complete Oxford in all its many volumes, but never had. The Book-of-the-Month Club version with the magnifying glass had turned up, but she couldn't read it even with the big lens. Then there was the dictionary of classical Greek that she'd been unable to resist even though she didn't know the Greek alphabet. Elegant mysterious shapes, sinuous and oriental. That was a project, she'd once thought, for her old age, but now she was well on her way to old age with no sign of Greek being learned today or tomorrow. Or even the day after tomorrow. In the long cold winter nights perhaps.

She turned and felt a new stab of crucifixion. They said you felt all this in your brain, but it sure seemed like the hips and legs to her. It's all in your head, my dear. Also in her head was a growing desire for a cup of cocoa. She rolled over, got an arm under her and pushed herself up to a sitting position, then with another push, got standing and went for her dressing gown. Back in the kitchen, she opened the inside door. A mosquito hung on the screen and beyond was the sound of the waterfall. Sometimes at night like this, she heard voices singing, a woman and a man on the balcony of the old hotel lining out Victorian ballads, pretty tunes in lovely harmony, but she could never quite get the words. Or it was angels who sang without words, only strange sounds, or the words that might be formed by those sinuous Greek letters in the old lexicon? Yes, everyone knew that angels sang in Greek. *Kyrie, kyrie, kyrie.* The earth in robes of melody, the words from the oldest of old times. The angels of night and summer sang, incomprehensible and sweet. She would drink her cup of cocoa and listen to their mystic adorations.

The days went by. He watched the flowing river, the birds. They were good days, though he knew his heart was failing, the end waiting close by. Now once again the light was going, and Carman was about ready for bed. He pulled open the drawer where he kept his clothes to find pajamas. He'd thrown everything in one drawer when he arrived, and now it was time enough to sort things. Not that he had many clothes, but he took out some polo shirts and opened the bottom drawer to put them in. From the bottom of the empty drawer, a photograph of his own face looked up at him. What kind of joke was this? He took out the old newspaper and threw it on the bed, put away the shirts and then picked it up again. The *Toronto Star,* six years ago. Detectives Deshane and Menard arresting a suspect in the murder of little Melanie Ovett, his own face hard and blank as the camera clicked away and he and Rolly, one holding each arm, took the creep into the station. They'd been the ones to find the little girl too, her body stuffed behind a ventilation shaft in the basement of the apartment building. Carman remembered when he found her, he started to cry—he couldn't help it, but he got hold of himself, Rolly never saw it—and that was when he began to think about retiring. You saw bad things and heard about worse, but when he saw that pile of rubbish that was a kid, could have been his daughter once, he wanted to find the man who did that and beat him to death with his own hands. Wasn't hard to find the guy, he was living with the mother, and after he confessed, he told them that he couldn't help it, the little girl was always coming on to him. Shut up now, Carman had told him, shut up now or I'll kill you. Rolly took over, and they got him out, and the photographers were waiting when their car pulled up. Detectives Deshane and Menard arresting a suspect. He folded up the newspaper and put it back in one of the drawers, then got into bed.

He read for a while, a book about a plan to blow up an airliner, then turned out the light. It was late, but he didn't go to sleep. It was a warm night, the window open, a small screen in the gap. A car stopped. Voices. Carman lay listening to the night noises, the endless songs of frogs, high and low, the cry of a bird, a car far off, farther, a door opening, a hint of breeze, a barking dog, soft voices somewhere, a splash at the edge of the river, and behind it, faintly, the sound of the waterfall. The frogs went on and on. Did one stop and another begin, or was it the same ones, singing the whole night? Then among all these soft sounds, somewhere close by a woman cried out, and he was about to get up, to go and help, when he realized what he was hearing was a cry of pleasure. What sounded at first like suffering. Another and another. It didn't stop, little rhythmic details of articulation crossed the dark, throat music, panting breath. They must be out there on the lawn, next door, between his window and the river. If he went to the back window, he might be able to see them. It was what men and women did, and Amy had found herself a partner for the old song and dance. They didn't care if they were heard or seen. Or wanted to be. At the back window, he had watched her naked crossing the lawn, the long body and heavy breasts, and she had looked at him watching. Now her noise went on and on, and it worked in his nerves. Let them goddam keep it to themselves. The woman's moans and growls continued. Carman had never heard a woman go on like that. His failing, perhaps, that he had never brought a woman to such a protracted desperate extremity. It didn't stop as the minutes passed, and he put the pillow over his head not to hear it, though it made him feel he might suffocate.

And yet he soon slept, unconsciousness welling up to take him, and when he woke in the morning, the pale white curtains were full of sunlight, and far off a dog was barking. A car started and drove away. Carman climbed from bed, emptied his bladder and walked to the back window. Upstream, sunlight was glittering on the surface of the river, and even where the trees shaded the water, it had a sheen of light. Just to one side among the brilliant green spears of the grass, he saw a young rabbit, perfectly still, the soft quick ears almost translucent in the summer brightness. So nervous, so quick: all its safety was in the instantaneous snap of nerves. It had big dark frightened eyes. A sound or a movement startled it, and it was gone.

Norma on the nature of time: it passes. A time for this and a time for that. *Et cetera.* And so onward was how we assumed it went and would go. Once upon a time. Which time? The other time, the time of old stories. Once upon a time, a small child, she had climbed the stairs of her grandmother's house, a brick house on Victoria Street—every town had a Victoria Street—and she had walked into the room where her Aunt Sadie had died many years before, and as she stood in the room, she had felt the presence of her aunt, a thin nervous woman she had never liked, and the sense of that presence was so strong that for a long time, she could not draw herself away from it to go back down the stairs, and that night when they were sitting on the porch, watching the moths that flapped helplessly around the streetlight, she had tried to tell her grandmother, who thought she was talking about ghosts and didn't approve, but it wasn't ghosts, not altogether, but the inability to understand how a person could exist and then not exist. Years went on and more and more of them did it, started not existing, but she wasn't sure she understood that any better. Five years ago her friend Moira started not existing, and Norma still missed her. No one to argue with. One day Moira had been there, and the next, it seemed, she had never been there at all. Not that quick really, of course, but painful and protracted, and yet when you looked back, it was sudden and shocking. You could hear the voice in your head, but the phone wouldn't ring. It was no wonder they invented heaven and hell, easier to imagine that than the nothingness of nothing.

Norma remarked that this meditation on time was becoming a meditation on death. She closed her eyes and tried to listen to the flow of time. What she heard was the waterfall, time's interpreter, and the voices of boys shouting somewhere down by the river. Boys who would soon be men. On her lap lay a copy of *The Mill on the Floss,* which she had fished out to reread. She did that at least once a decade, read slowly through those wonderful pages where time was like time and yet without the sharp edges of unease. Like the Tullivers' mill, her house stood above the river, though here the mill itself was gone, the power of time no longer harnessed to active life. The river ran only because rivers ran. The cycle of rain and river and ocean and cloud went round and round. Then the river came into flood and Maggie died in her brother's arms, went back to a childhood before time was. Except she didn't go back except to nowhere, as if to the time before she existed. Into the pages of a book where time passed word by word and line by line, but you could look back and reconsider and so time never passed. Memory could look back across life, but couldn't reconsider, no, not really; the turned pages were turned. There were those who remembered an abduction by flying saucers and the strange beings who did things to them.

Time, you old gypsy man. Norma opened her eyes, stood up, belched mightily, farted daintily and decided to close the store for the day. A woman a few miles east wanted her to come and look at some things. She'd call and see if they could arrange to drive her out. If she bought anything, she'd hire Egan McBride to pick it up. She ought to have a car or a truck, but last year when her van crawled away to die, she didn't have the money to replace it, and she was trying to do without.

Carman found himself at the door of Norma's store, not wanting to be there, but there was no phone in the cottage, and he'd promised he'd get Carol a phone number in case she ever needed to know he was still alive. It was good of her to worry about him. He'd planned to ask Amy if he could give Carol her number, but then yesterday morning he'd seen her loading suitcases in the car, and she'd waved and shouted that she was moving. To live with a man. Well, judging by the noise he heard that night the man must be quite something. Why not go to him?

Now the cottage was empty, and he preferred it that way. In the dark he'd wakened suddenly and with the thought that there was someone near him or in the cottage next door, and for a moment he'd believed that it was Audrey, a confusion from his dreams. The mind, unattached to real things, got lost among the unreal ones. As a cop, you'd go to the door of an apartment high up in a building and an old woman would answer, and every question you asked made the eyes change, hide, go out of focus, and you knew that every question was an assault from a world that had been lost, that memory and television had carried the woman away so far that she couldn't come back to talk about whether she might have heard screams, whether she might have been looking out her window on the night in question, might have seen the events in the parking lot. You would have sworn that she had never known there was a parking lot, that there was nothing beyond the windows. She had gone inside and wouldn't come out. Trips to the grocery store were made with her eyes turned down to the pavement, not to see anything, to be safe. You asked her questions as carefully and as gently as you could, with the thought that perhaps just once she had looked out the window and remembered, but nothing came, and you thanked her and closed the door.

Norma was sitting in her usual place, the rocking chair near the back. The tape of birds was playing, and afternoon sunlight came in the back window and fell on the stuffed wolf which stood beside her chair, on guard. As usual she stared at him and didn't speak. Carman told himself that he wasn't going to get angry.

"I have to ask you a favor," he said.

"You need your back scratched, like my friend here." She reached out and put her fingers in the wolf's hair and drew them back and forth.

Carman could feel the anger start, but he held it in check.

"I have a daughter in Toronto," he said.

"What happened to your wife?" she said. "You leave her for a sweet young thing?"

"She died."

"I thought it was universal, taking off with a bimbo. My husband did it and now my son. Maybe it just runs in the family. Did she die recently?"

"A year and a half ago."

She nodded, watched. He wished she'd stop staring at him like that, not saying anything.

"You shouldn't stare at people," he said.

"Is that why you're so mad at the world, because she died?" she said.

"Could be."

"A man who liked his wife," she said. "Put him in a museum. Last specimen extant. We should find who did my wolfy friend here and get you stuffed."

He didn't tell her she was a crazy old bat; he had a favor to ask.

"My daughter wants a phone number. In case anything happens. I thought I could give her yours, if that's OK?"

"So she can phone every two days and send me down to see if you've had a stroke yet."

"She won't likely phone. I keep in touch."

She was staring again.

"I don't suppose I can say no to that. Filial piety and all. My son mostly tries to avoid me, though that's my own damn fault. I'm always rude to him."

"Why's that?"

"Because he deserves it."

"You're rude to everybody so far as I can see."

"They all deserve it."

Carman took out a pencil and paper.

"You'd better give me that number."

She recited the seven digits, and he put them down.

"So Amy Martyrdom's moved out," she said.

"Is that her name?"

"It's what I always called her. Suited."

"She went this morning."

"Finally found a man. I thought she'd probably have you in there before long."

"A little old for her."

"I don't know. What man could turn down tits like that? The way she told me, she was open to offers.

"She talked to you about that?"

"Couldn't stop her."

Carman put the pen and paper in his shirt pocket. Tonight he'd go to the pay phone by the garage and call Carol.

"About the phone," he said. "Thank you."

She patted the wolf.

"What do you think I should ask for this?" she said.

"Damned if I know."

"I'm getting attached to it. When I talk to it, it always looks interested. Can't say that for most."

"Maybe you talk nicer to it."

"That's true."

A bell rang as the door of the shop opened and two men came in. They both had moustaches, short hair, shiny clean skin. Carman let himself out and walked down to the cottage.

At first she had no idea. She looked at the postcard in her hand, a picture of two buxom superheroes, one male and one female, on a background of exploding stars. On the back in careful printing, it said, *Did you buy the hotel? I saw one like it on a cowboy video. Love Luke.* It had an American stamp and was addressed to her with only her name, the town and the province, but it had arrived. The Post Office had its moods, and sometimes was unpredictably efficient. Luke. The boy in the middle of the night. Miss Virginia's son. She wondered if she ought to recognize the two unnatural figures that were bursting out of the sky, all tits and thighs. Male superheroes all had tits now—pectorals they were called.

The boy's printing was clear and almost elegant. She wondered where Miss Virginia had taken him now. She looked like a woman who knew too much, pretty, but everything strapped in place and lacquered. Even when she revealed her perfect body by sitting on the back dock in her bikini, it gave the impression of flesh that was under orders. The boy was polite and intelligent, even charming. The woman must be doing something right. Norma would have written a response to the card, but she had no address. The boy was gone, not to be seen again. A case of neverness.

She'd bought a bag of groceries at the general store which was at the top of the hill near the mailboxes. As she'd struggled up the steep street to the store, she'd wondered again what would become of her when she could no longer manage the climb. The Overholts, who owned it, were friendly enough people, and they might make a delivery now and then, but probably, once she couldn't make the climb, it would be time to move into town, to an apartment. Sit all day and watch television with the rest of the Golden Age Club.

A red sports car with the top open, what must be a vintage car by now, drove up the hill. Through the branches of the big maple that grew halfway down the hill overhanging the road, she watched the glitter of the upper river. When she was halfway down the hill she could see past the leaves and along the gravel road, and there was her tenant, The Vice-grip, doing something to the back steps of the cottage. Wood lay on the grass, and he was pounding nails. Fixing the back steps of the cottage. She'd never told him he could do that, or if she had she didn't remember, which amounted to the same thing. In fact she'd told him not to bother. Of course it was time it was done, but she was annoyed at his presumption. He should have asked politely, preferably hat in hand, and she might, with regal condescension, have given him permission to repair her property. Now he'd expect her to pay some vast sum for the wood. She knew the price of wood these days. He should mind his own damn business, but what man ever did?

Instead of taking her groceries home, she crossed the road. Shook her fist at a small truck that tried to kill her on the way across. When she got close to the cottage, she looked at the neat piles of wood, the new framework with the first boards nailed across. It was cleanly done, but dammit he should have asked. He looked up and saw her but said nothing. He was wearing his criminal-on-the-run look, perhaps a result of cutting things up and pounding nails through them. She had herself noticed that driving in a nail could make one satisfyingly savage. Her ears rang as he drove one in.

"I suppose you're going to hand me a bill for this," she said.

"No." Bang, bang, bang.

"What?"

"I'm enjoying myself. But I wouldn't want to do too much of it."

"But you want me to pay for the wood."

"Don't bother. It wasn't all that much. I'm as glad to know I won't be breaking my leg."

"It wasn't that bad," she said.

He put another board in place and took nails from a small brown paper bag.

"Am I some kind of charity case?" she said. "You think I can't pay my way."

He didn't answer. The nerve of a barge horse, as her grandmother used to say. He pounded a nail. Bang, bang, bang.

"I don't need any favors," she said, loudly over the noise of his hammering.

Bang, bang, bang. He ignored her.

"You never asked me if you could do this."

"I said I'd fix it sometime."

"And I said don't bother."

"Is it better if I break my leg?"

He was hammering again.

"It's my cottage. If I want it repaired, I'll say so."

"You're too late, and the stairs were dangerous."

"How much did the wood cost?"

"It doesn't matter."

"It damn well does matter."

"I said I'd pay for it, didn't I?"

"And I said you wouldn't."

He had the hammer raised over another nail.

"All right," he said. "I've got the receipt in my jacket pocket. I'll bring it over to the store."

"You might as well give it to me right now."

He stood up, the hammer still in his hand, and for a moment, Norma thought he might strike her down with it, but he put it down on the unfinished stairs, walked over to his car, took the jacket from the front seat, and pulled a piece of paper from the pocket. He came and gave it to her, and she was shocked at the total.

"You bought tools," she said. "You expect me to pay for those tools?" By now she was being completely unreasonable, and it pleased her.

"Deduct the tools," he said. "I'm sure you can do the arithmetic."

Now he was being patient and long-suffering. It was a lucky thing she didn't have the hammer in her hand. She put the piece of paper into her shopping bag and turned to walk away. The pounding started again. By the time she got home and up the stairs to the kitchen, she was out of breath. No sooner had she sat down than the phone rang, and it proved to be the man's daughter wanting to leave him a message. Norma wasn't polite, but she wrote the message down. Maybe she could find someone to deliver it.

They'd finished dinner, and now they were sitting around the living room. The television was on, but nobody was watching. Carol was flipping through *Vanity Fair,* just looking at the pictures, and Grant had the *Globe and Mail Report on Business* and was going through the stock-market quotations with a pen, checking something off now and then. Grant had big ideas about money, but Carman didn't think he had the brains and the nerve to go with them. He'd always treated Carol well, and Carman liked him for that, but there was something about him that was soft and sad. Maybe if they had kids he'd grow into himself. The two of them did well enough. They got by. Grant managed a paint and wallpaper outlet, but he wasn't given a lot of freedom by the people who owned the chain. Carol was a receptionist in a big company office. It was one of those old-fashioned jobs for a woman, not the kind they were supposed to be getting these days. Sometimes she thought they might promote her to something better, but it didn't seem very likely.

They had car loans and a heavy mortgage on their little house near Dufferin and Bloor, a mortgage taken out when rates were high, and there wasn't a lot of slack in their budget. Carman wished he had more to help them out. When he sold the house, he gave them a piece of the cash. Carol said he shouldn't, but he told her she might as well have it now, not wait around for him to die. They'd done some repairs, paid off a big credit card bill, bought a dishwasher. When his heart finally blew up, there'd be some insurance money. That was about all he could do.

"Gold," Grant said. "Gold is always a good investment. Has been for thousands of years. You just have to get the right stock before everyone else."

"I never followed the market," Carman said. "Never had the brains for it."

He did what he could to discourage Grant, though probably nothing but losing money would do that. He only hoped it wouldn't be too much.

"Hasn't she got an incredibly beautiful face?" Carol said. She was holding up the picture of some actress. He knew he should recognize her, but he didn't.

"A lot of it's done by the photographer." He said that, but there was something about the face that was naked and riveting. A world of beautiful women promising perfection, but nobody ever brought it home. What happened was something different. Sometimes he thought that being a cop had ruined him.

You always got called when people were at their worst. The things they hid from the world, the cops got to see. Most of what you heard was lies. You saw blood and rage and the way people could convince themselves that whatever they did was right. Someone took away the bodies, and you tried to make sure that your notebook was accurate and complete so that you didn't have a lawyer make a fool of you in court. If necessary, you lied. The old system was to grab the most likely suspect and beat a confession out of him, and it worked. If you didn't do it yourself, you knew others who did. You said it didn't bother you, and you were afraid that might be true. At the end you got a pension.

"I've been reading up on some of these technology stocks," Grant said. "There's money to be made in them. The new economy."

Carman wanted to go over and shake him a few times, to wake him up, shout at him that he wasn't a bright guy and he should catch on to that. He got up from his chair. Carol was still looking at the photograph of that hauntingly beautiful face as if by staring at it, she could find herself looking like that. She wasn't a bad-looking girl. A photographer like that could make something of her too. What she'd always wanted. To be a model. To be someone the camera loved.

"Time for me to go," he said.

"Don't rush off," Carol said. "Stay and watch *Seinfeld*."

"You know me," he said. "I get restless. I'll come back another time. Or you can come and visit me."

"Is that place all right? The cottage?"

"Yeah. You should come out sometime. I'll take you fishing."

Carman had bought himself a cheap rod and some worms from the general store and had fished a little from the dock and caught a couple of perch. He was planning to take the boat out when he got back the next day.

"I don't know why you didn't keep the apartment," Carol said.

"I didn't like it. Ten floors up, locked in a little box. Not for me."

Carol hugged him, and Grant shook his hand, and he left. When he got in the car, he took a few deep breaths and checked his pulse, just to prove he was still alive. Then he started back. The long summer daylight hung in the sky over the city as he drove across Dundas toward the Don Valley Parkway. There was a crowd outside the Eaton Centre watching a busker juggling. A young guy with the exaggerated arms and shoulders of a bodybuilder stood on the next corner, dressed in tight jeans and a tank top, advertising himself; he was watching a well-dressed woman in a pale fawn suit and carrying a briefcase as she walked by him. Carman caught a red light at Church, and while he was waiting he saw a girl get out of a low black car. It was the young hooker he'd taken out to the motel. She was wearing the same shorts and sequined T-shirt. Working clothes. She looked around her, as if she was searching for someone, walked a few steps, turned and walked back. Meeting a friend, a pimp, a john. She couldn't stand still. The light changed. Carman looked at the young pretty legs as he moved away into the traffic, toward the highway, and as he drove through the oncoming darkness, he could remember the little breasts she'd shown him, her edginess, the way she moved on high heels. She had brought off dozens of men since that night, in parked cars down an alleyway or rented rooms, a trail of used condoms left behind her. Maybe one day she'd walk away from the life, or maybe not. If you thought about it, she was a beautiful girl, but she'd never have the brains to see it.

As a young cop on the beat, he'd wondered about hookers, what they thought about while some man was using them for a toilet, but then you saw a hundred more of them, and you stopped wondering. They were as impersonal as cab drivers; they got the customer where he wanted to go then picked up another fare.

The lights of the car reached out along the night highway. Carman kept his foot down. Somewhere in the night, a young animal might run into the glare of the lights and go under the wheels. Staring into the darkness, the opposing headlights flashing into his eyes, he thought he saw that young girl, thin and naked, caught in his headlights, her mouth open trying to say something to him. Carman shook his head to rouse himself and opened the window to let the cool night air roar over him. There was a headache starting behind his eyes.

By the time he got to the village, driving past Norma's store, which had a light on in one of the upstairs windows, turning down the gravel road and into the driveway, he was so tired that at first he couldn't get out of the car, and for several minutes he sat there, unable to move, his legs and back aching, feet swollen and tight inside his shoes, his head pounding, but he knew he must get himself inside, and he opened the car door, stood for a minute holding on, listening to the frogs, the waterfall, some distant music, then he got himself up the back stairs and into the house. He sat on the edge of the bed to pull off his shoes and trousers and shirt, then rolled in and pulled the covers over him.

It was early when he woke, and from the bed he could see an irregular patch of sunlight falling on the kitchen floor, shimmering with a pattern of blown leaves. He was still tired, but he wanted to be out on the river, and he got himself up and took a quick shower, drank a glass of juice, and picked up the oars, the fishing pole and the box of worms from under the cottage. One afternoon he'd dragged the boat down to the water, and now it was tied to the dock front and back, the nose into the weeds at the edge of the river. He laid rod and worms on the dock and climbed down into the boat, which rocked heavily, then reached down the pole and oars, set the oars in place, untied the two ropes and pushed off, the boat floating quickly out from his last push and starting to drift in the current as he took his place and took the first pull on the oars. He rowed easily, not pushing himself, just using slow strokes to propel himself upstream past the other cottages. At the last cottage, a woman was cutting the lawn with an old hand mower, and she waved to him. She'd introduced herself one day, but he couldn't remember her name. He waved to her and dipped the oars. With a look over his shoulder, he checked the slight bend in the river and turned the bow of the boat to follow it. Ahead he could see the old railway bridge. Sometimes on weekends, kids played on the bridge, jumping from it into the deep water below. Halfway to the bridge there was a thick branch of an old willow leaning close to the water, and he planned to tie the boat there.

Beside him, a large dragonfly hovered over the shining surface of the water on its transparent wings, then flew upward and out of sight. The sun was shining on his back, and he liked the sensation of warmth. He felt the bow of the boat bump against the willow branch, and he turned, caught some of the leaves, then the branch itself, and shifted on the seat to reach the rope and tie it. He should get some kind of anchor for the boat. Then he could drop anchor and fish anywhere on the river.

There was a small silver spinner on the line, and he fastened a worm on the hook behind it and cast the lure downriver, let it sink through the water, then began to reel it in, very slowly, feeling the pull of the current again the line. The river reflected the blue sky and in the shallows the round green leaves of the water lilies floated on the surface, two white flowers floating among them, but the depths of the river were a deep brown like clear coffee. Somewhere down there, the fish moved in their cold place. Within the skeleton they had an extra sense to read the movements of the current, and the muscles of the long thin bodies made them quick and efficient through the flowing water. They hunted and slept in the filtered light of day and in the shapely fluid darkness, quick and simple and persistent.

He lifted the lure from the water and cast again, the weight of it pulling the line evenly off the reel, dropping with a small slap into the water as he turned the handle of the reel once to engage the drag, then waited as the lure sank glittering into the invisible depth of the river and finally began to draw it back. A patient kind of suspense, the fingers attentive for a change in the action of the line. Audrey might be back at the cottage, expecting him. Wasn't. The boat floated in the middle of a great emptiness. Sunlight. Birdsong. The trains no longer arrived here. The hotel was boarded up. He cast and retrieved.

When the sudden tug on the line came he was astonished, as if he'd forgotten there was any point to this activity except the waiting. He snapped the rod up and began to reel in the line. The rod bent and the tight line ran through the water as the fish tried to escape, then it came upward, and the fish jumped into the light, then dropped again, and he drew it in, saw it at the side of the boat and lifted it carefully aboard. A bass, green and fierce-looking, the tail flapping against the bottom of the boat. It was long and thick-bodied, and he decided that he would keep it and eat it for dinner. A lot of the fish were full of chemicals these days. Carcinogens. He laughed out loud at the thought. He wouldn't be around for the cancer to get him. He unhooked the fish, broke its neck and left it in the bottom of the boat as he baited the hook again. Anything more he caught he'd put back.

He watched the sunlight catch ripples made by the current as it ran against the side of the boat, little folds of water reflecting the light. The air was full of quiet sounds that made you feel the silence behind them.

Norma had decided to be good the next time she saw Carman Deshane, though she had to admit he brought out the worst in her. Well, bad temper, whether that was the worst or not. Maybe it was the best. It kept her going. She'd been an old bitch over the porch stairs, she knew that, but she didn't like surprises, and she didn't like men taking things over without telling her. She'd worked out what she owed him for the wood and had it sitting in an envelope, and someday when she was feeling good she'd take a walk down to the cottage and deliver it to him. She was supposed to be taking a look at Amy Martyrdom's place as well, just to see if it was all right. Amy had called her from the city to ask her to do that and had mailed her the key. She was still paying the rent, not trusting her new happiness too far. Smarter than she looked. When she called she wanted to tell Norma everything about her sex life, but after a couple of minutes Norma cut her off. Put A into B, fold C over D etc. People did get worked up about it, she had herself now and then, but hearing someone boast about her orgasms over the telephone was nobody's idea of a good time.

Sometimes Norma was tempted to call Aeldred, who was her last lover and was probably available, his most recent wife gone they said, but she held a grudge and besides she mostly felt too lousy.

As if summoned up by her thoughts of him, The Retired Vice-grip pulled up in front, got out of his car and approached the door of the shop. She reached into the desk drawer for the envelope of money, and by the time he came in, she was on her way to meet him. She held it out.

"For the wood," she said.

He held the envelope in his hand for a second, as if he was thinking something, but she couldn't read his face. Then he put the envelope in his pocket. Warm as it was outside, he was wearing a tweed jacket.

"You have any scrap metal?" he said.

"Now that's not a question I was expecting."

"Do you?"

"If I get any, it mostly goes to Spare Parts."

"Where's that?"

"A sculptor. Josef Ancil is his name, but he has a big sign on his studio from an old garage. Says Spare Parts, so most of us call him that."

"What's he want with scrap metal?"

"Builds things out of it. Very nice, some of them. I've got a little one upstairs. Made out of the blade of an old plow welded together with some bolts and a couple of other things."

He ignored that as something of no interest.

"I'm looking for an anchor for the boat. I thought you might have something around I could buy from you, something heavy and not too big."

"Why do you need an anchor?"

"Fishing."

"You always been a fisherman?"

"Not for years."

"Catch anything?"

"Yes. A few bass, a pike. Surprised me."

"Josef would likely have something, if you feel like a drive."

"All right." She'd expected that he'd hum and haw and say no. Surprise.

"Don't suppose it's good business to take off whenever I feel the need, but I enjoy it."

At the front door, she turned the sign. Closed. A firm satisfying word.

In the car, she turned down the window and laid her arm on the edge to give the sun a chance to start a little cancer. She hadn't been to see Spare Parts for a long time, and she was looking forward to the long shed full of odd assemblages of old metal, and a few of wood. Most of the wood was roughed out with an adze but now and then he'd get hold of hardwood and turn out a piece with a high polish. The metal piece in her living room was something she'd got in trade for some ancient squared walnut that she'd picked up a few years back. Spare Parts had taken one look and decided that he must have it, and after a lot of negotiation, she'd made the trade. She was out of pocket, but the sculpture had given her enough pleasure to justify that.

The road ran down a hill, and close to a lake, and in the distance she saw a boat on the water, and then it disappeared behind a stand of spruce. You could imagine so many things taking place behind those trees. A few miles further, they came to the turnoff and drove along a gravel county road that twisted between snake fences and patches of bush. There was almost no soil over the rock here, and the fields were full of wild grasses with patches of blue burr and purple vetch, yellow butter-and-eggs close to the ground, daisies and black-eyed Susans. A thousand flowers. Millefleur. The tapestry of waste land, logged and abandoned. They went around a turn, and she saw the big sign in old-fashioned lettering. Spare Parts. The house was a low nineteenth-century limestone with white trim, mullioned windows six over six, well kept up. Josef was usually to be found in the workshop, a tidy frame building attached to the long log shed where he stored wood and metal and some of the completed pieces that hadn't sold.

In front of the shed was a big garden, neatly planted, a few rows of tall corn, tomatoes that hung, round and pale green, among the dark green leaves, hills of squash and cucumbers, rows of beets and beans. Spare Parts had a girlfriend in town who came out for a weekend now and then and helped him with the garden, but he was a bugger to work and probably would have kept everything perfect even without her. Looking at his sturdy muscular body, watching the slow steady way he worked, it made you understand why God had troubled to invent the male.

Carman was parking the car at the end of the lane. Spare Parts, his welding mask pushed up from his face, came out of the door of the workshop and stood under the big sign, staring at the car to see who was arriving. Norma waved to him. He nodded, almost smiled.

"My friend here is looking for an anchor for his boat, Josef. I said you had the best collection of scrap metal in Eastern Ontario."

He nodded and pointed to a pile of junk just inside the door of the log shed. Carman walked over to it, looked down for a minute and took out a piece that looked like a large flat doughnut. He hefted it to check the weight.

"How much do you want for that?" he said.

Spare Parts, not a great one for talk, held up five fingers. He had short heavy hands that looked as if they'd have no skill at all, but he could do anything with them. Norma watched him as the other man found his wallet and took out a bill. Josef had a tight, almost mean-looking face, very concentrated and closed, but if you got him to speak, he was bright and even funny. He took the bill and shoved it in his pocket.

"All right if we look around the shed?"

He nodded and went back into the workshop. Norma made her way to the wide shed doorway while Carman put his anchor away in the truck. She stood in the centre of the floor and looked around her. A couple of pieces were oddly unbalanced and wrong. Maybe they weren't finished, or maybe she just didn't understand them. Another used the curving teeth of an old harrow to make something that looked at if it might fly, an organic, insect look to it. A pile of steel T-bars lay against a wooden box, and behind them was a geometric form like a crazed jungle gym. When Arthur was little they'd had something like that in the yard, but all symmetrical and with none of the delight of this.

"You like this junk?"

She turned to look at him, didn't like the look on his face any better than what he'd said.

"Yes."

"You call this sculpture?"

"I do."

"If I fastened a lot of junk together, would that be sculpture?"

"Depends how well you did it."

"How could you tell?"

"How can you tell Donatello from Canova?"

"Never heard of either one."

"So what the hell do you know about it?"

"Not a lot."

"Then don't advertise your ignorance."

She could see the face grow still, the life withdraw from the eyes, and she looked at the pile of steel T-bars behind him and knew that he was very close to breaking her head with one of them. Not to encourage him, she turned and walked away. The window of the workshop was bright with the blue glare of Josef's arc-welding torch, joining metals by the transforming anger of electricity, Josef behind a mask to keep his eyes safe from the brilliance at the point of fusion.

She heard footsteps behind her and waited for the steel bar to come down and break her skull, but they went toward the door of the shed and away. Maybe he'd drive off in the car and leave her here. If so she'd beg Spare Parts for a ride.

Damn fool deserved everything she'd said to him and more. She wouldn't tolerate stupidity. No doubt one of the reasons that Steven had left, having found some adoring little thing who'd tell him he was a genius and had the biggest dick she'd ever seen. Stupidity was endless.

In the corner of the shed was a mobile made from thin curled pieces of metal, painted white and dark red. She went toward it to study it more closely, as Carman took his murderous look back to the car. The mobile was a beautiful thing. Calder's idea, of course, that such a thing might be. Spare Parts was good, but not a giant. Would you know if you met a giant? A sign on the forehead, Genius at Work. Sorry but I'm busy creating *The Rite of Spring.* New things, unheard-of until now; the modern is very up to date. Norma wasn't. She went missing somewhere just west of Mark Rothko. Assuming The Vice-grip waited for her, she could tell him about color field paintings on the way back. He'd be sure to enjoy that. Idiot. No doubt the wife had been the same, TV and recipes clipped from magazines. She couldn't even imagine the daughter. Whereas her son Arthur could be boasted of as one of the supreme bores of our time. Now that was an accomplishment.

She looked toward the car. He was sitting in the driver's seat, waiting. Well, he'd got his anchor, hadn't he? And he should be used to her temper by now. If he didn't want to make her mad, he shouldn't behave stupidly.

Carman lay in bed and listened to the sound of rain on the roof. He'd planned to go out fishing this morning, but when he woke, he heard the rain and changed his mind. Fishing was supposed to be good in the rain, but he wasn't going to bother. So he lay in bed and heard the soft reiterating sound over his head and dozed and thought about things. Lately he'd taken to remembering men he'd met on the streets. That junkyard reminded him of Billy McTeer. Billy had a store that sold a bit of everything, including stolen goods. On one side of it, appliances, on the other car parts, and in between some furniture. Jewelry in the back counter. After a few months of playing games, threats, promises, hints, Billy became Carman's best informant, and it was a long time before Carman realized that he didn't do it because he had to or because he was scared of the police; he liked turning people in. Enjoyed the act of betrayal. Every time he gave Carman information, his long face would take on a funny smile, and he'd give Carman a big wink. Then one day Billy didn't open the store, and nobody ever heard from him again. He'd talked once too often. Nobody spent a lot of time worrying about who had got rid of him. It was one of the hazards of what he did. Carman missed him, but not much.

Carman couldn't do this before, lie in bed in the morning, lazy and useless, his thoughts drifting. It must be the river close by that calmed him. When he got up, he'd make coffee and sit by the window to watch the pattern of raindrops on the surface, then he'd have toast and watch some more. Later on he'd go up to the pay phone to call Carol and invite them out for a weekend. The cottage was small, but they had a tent, and if the weather was good they could put it up in the yard. He'd get a little barbecue and some charcoal and they could cook some steaks. Carol would like that. She enjoyed those storybook things. Since Amy left, the yard was always quiet and private, a cedar hedge on one side, an empty yard on the other.

If the rain stopped, he'd walk up to the general store for some groceries. He liked the two teenage kids who worked there, a brother and sister, niece and nephew of the Overholts, smart and pleasant both of them, same body shape with short heavy legs, same perfect teeth. At first he wondered if they were twins, but the boy was older.

When he woke this morning he'd been dreaming about Audrey. In the dream he knew that she was supposed to be dead, and there was something about her skin, gray and porous, that suggested the skin of a corpse. Every day when he sat by the back window, her eyes in the picture watching him, he struggled to understand what death was, how she could have been here, looking just like that picture, but now was gone. Amy, his neighbor, was gone, but he could find her. Norma talked to her on the phone sometimes. A car might pull up and she would climb out, her big breasts in front of her; she might even move back into the cottage, slip out through the darkness to swim, but Audrey wasn't at the end of any electronic circuit, and she wouldn't come back. They used to believe that the dead were in some other world, that we could die and join them; you could understand how people wanted to believe all that.

A gust of wind blew rain against the bedroom window, and it began to fall more noisily on the roof, the drumming faster. On the back lawn there would be a robin searching for worms. Tomorrow the hot sun would draw back the water that had fallen, taking water vapour high into the air to form new clouds, which would be carried around the world, and in some other country, rain would fall.

The Day of the Bad Habit. Putting It into Words. Her Kind of Foolishness.

Some days her mind did tricks like that; everything turned into the title of an imaginary book. The Chapters of Common Life. The Table and Chair Suite. Other People's Kitchens. The Business of Failure. Waiting for Cash. Sun of the Summer Mornings. The Day after Insomnia. The Closed and Open Shop. Cars That Pass, Cars That Stop. Life on the Radio. Dances for Aging Bones. The Long Comfort of Chairs. Double Entry Bookkeeping for Amateurs. The Book of Numbers. How to Repair China. Tacks, Taxes and Taxidermy. The Age of Antiques. Antiquity Unsung.

Unsuitable Activities for Unstable Seniors.

The Weasel's Little Teeth.

Quandaries for the Quaint.

Xenophon on the Xylophone.

How Dumb Can You Get.

The Long Comfort of Chairs. Riversound. The Taste of Morning Coffee. Cars That Pass, Cars That Stop. The Day after Insomnia. Sun of the Summer Mornings. The Suddenly Coming Customer. You Just Never Know.

Lost Mica Mines. The Tourist's Question and Other Disappointments. Doing Your Best Anyway. Forced Smiles. Mother Taught Me Manners.

Giving Directions. The Short Goodbye. The Kindly Chairseat. The River That Runs Forever. Just Another Day. The Tenant Passeth By. Retired Vicegrips and Other Questions of Conscience. The Rented Cottage and the Empty Cottage. Exodus. Martyrdom Wins Out. Amy in the Rough Arms of Love.

The Waterfall Goes On and On. Summer Days and Winter Nights. Thoughts of Lunch. The Common Sandwich. The Gospel According to Mustard. Hypnagogic Dancers. Goodbye, Hello, I'm Here. Cars That Stop, Cars That Pass. The Long Summer Afternoon. Small Sales and Making Change. A Book to Read, a Book to Sell. The Question of Traffic. A Walk to the Post. The Epistle of Arthur. Motherhood for Crabby Dames. The Waterfall Goes On and On. Toward the Close of Day. The Open and Closed Shop. Symptoms of Living. The Food We Eat. Mosquito Harvest. Lessons for Nightfall. A Prayer to the Absent. Last Words.

The water was black, heavy and shining like oil as he moved the boat toward the shore, which fell away from him as he propelled the boat with long strokes of the oars. Then he was moving ahead, and he knew that the dock was close by, and the boat slithered into the mud at the edge of the black water, embedding its prow in the weeds and slop, and he knew that he would sink into the mud as he tried to climb ashore, but the dock was almost in reach, so he stretched his arm and caught hold of a corner of it and pulled the boat near enough that he could clamber up. He knew that he should tie the boat, but it was taking all his strength to get to the dock. He would have to abandon the boat. Once on the dock, he had to step carefully down to the lawn, and it took a long time to cross toward the house. It was hard to lift his feet. A light was on in the house, and he could see someone reading by the window, thought that it must be Audrey waiting for him, but as he came a little closer, forcing his legs to bear him, he saw that at the cottage next door, the back door was wide open, though it was almost dark inside, only a hint of something like candlelight. She had left the door open for him, and he knew that she was waiting. He stopped pushing his way through the long grass and studied the open door, the gaping darkness, and then turned and struggled toward it. He could no longer see Audrey reading by the window.

Once he was inside the cottage, he spoke, called out her name, but there was no answer, and he was aware that the long hall led to a number of rooms, and he could see that in each room a candle was burning, but when he looked inside, no one was there, until he came to the last room, which had no candle, only a little light that seeped in through the doorway, but when he reached the door, something was blocking the light and he could hardly see. Amy was lying on the floor, her long thin legs spread to show a dark bush of hair. He knew that he had come too late, and that she was dead. She had been waiting for him, but it had taken too long for him to row the boat to shore and to cross the lawn. Now he didn't know what to do. He could feel the hot pressure of his desire for her, but you couldn't do that to a dead woman, but still he found himself releasing his clothes and lying on her, and as he did he saw her face form a smile and the eyes opened, and then he was on his knees looking at her, and she was covered with blood.

He woke, shaken by the dream, the taint of blood lingering in the mind. Outside, the sun was shining brightly, and he heard voices. Carol and Grant were already awake and down at the river. He could hear them splashing in the water. Last night Carol insisted that she was going to get him in the water today. He told her he had no bathing suit, and she said they'd drive into Kingston and get him one. In fact he had a pair of old Bermuda shorts that Audrey once bought him that he could wear to swim, but he didn't think he would.

Once up and washed, he took the bottle of drinking water out of the fridge and filled the kettle. Apparently some of the people in the cottages drank the river water, but he wasn't going to. He watched from the window as Carol dived off the dock. The water was too shallow to dive, and he nearly went to the door and shouted at her. Hard to remember that she was grown up. Probably she didn't mind him fussing a little. She knew it was a sign of affection. She knew that he'd be lost if anything happened to her; she was the last thing left to him. They'd only had the one child. Audrey had a hard time of it in childbirth, and there wasn't a lot of money, so they postponed having a child for a few years, and then tried for a year without success, and by then it seemed too late. They had Carol, and they both loved her, and that was enough. Every time a report came into the station about a kid missing, Carman found himself phoning home to make sure that Carol was all right. It was superstitious, but he had to do it. He saw too much of how uncertain things were, kids lost, kids run over.

Carol had bought a new bathing suit, yellow and bright green. It made her skin look pale. She said that this afternoon she was going to lie on the dock and get a tan, and Grant reminded her about skin cancer. Carman wanted to scoff, but he knew that Grant was right. Or thought he knew. If the scientists knew what they were talking about. They sometimes did. What a world, when the sun had grown dangerous.

When the kettle boiled, he made a pot of coffee and got out the sweet buns he'd bought at a bakery a few miles away. He'd got those and a little hibachi and charcoal, steaks and a couple of bottles of wine. They drank the first one last night after they arrived. Carol insisted that today they were going to see Norma's store. She was sure she'd find something valuable on sale cheap, though he'd warned her that Norma would just stare at her and be rude. Maybe she wouldn't. Maybe it was Carman set her off.

They'd sat out on the lawn last night, drinking wine until the mosquitoes drove them in, and Carman had whittled away at a piece of the pine left over from the stairs, making himself a float to use fishing in the deep water above the dam. He wasn't sure it would work, but he was going to try it.

Carol had looked across at him as he carved the wood.

"I've never seen you do anything like that before," she said.

"Never had so much time on my hands."

"You going to catch fish to feed us?"

"Maybe. I'm not sure they're not full of chemicals. All right for me, but you still have years ahead of you.

"All that pollution," Grant said. "You'd think they'd do something about it."

"Not much to be done by now," Carman said.

They sat in silence drinking their wine, and soon the mosquitoes came.

Now Carman went out the back door and shouted to them that he had coffee made, and they picked up their towels and rubbed themselves dry. As he turned to go back in, he looked at the empty cottage next door and remembered the dream, the naked bleeding body. The brain so full of strange things. He poured himself a glass of juice and took two pills. Last night before dinner, his chest had been bad, and he'd had to put two of the nitroglycerin capsules under his tongue before it eased, but he'd managed to do it without Carol noticing. No point worrying her.

Now he put the plate of buns on the table, two wineglasses full of juice, and three mugs for coffee. Carol and Grant came in the back door, both with T-shirts pulled on over their bathing suits. Grant's shirt had SUPERSALESMAN written on the front. Carol's was long, almost as long as a mini-dress.

"This is such a great place," Carol said. "How did you find it?"

"Accident. I was wandering around back roads and I ended up here. Saw the sign in the store window."

"When you told us about it, it sounded crazy, but I can see why you wanted it."

"I like the river."

"Are you going to go swimming with us?"

"We'll see."

"You're a good swimmer, aren't you?"

"No. Your mother was. I can stay afloat."

"Didn't she once win medals for swimming?"

"That's right."

"I bet the land around here's a good investment," Grant said.

"Why?"

"It's a nice place. One of these days it will get developed."

"Could be."

Carol was pouring coffee for them all.

"Shall we tell him?" she said to Grant. A kid with a secret.

"Sure."

Carol looked at him.

"We decided last night not to wait any longer. To have a baby."

Carman walked away from the table. Sudden tears in his eyes at the thought of this baby, the memory of how Audrey had wanted grandchildren, and at the same time, he knew in some terrible way that he wouldn't be around to see it. He knew it, though he wanted not to. By the time he'd got the milk out of the fridge and put the bottle on the table, he had control of himself.

"That sounds like a pretty good idea."

"Is that all you have to say?"

"It's a great idea, but if it's a boy, don't name it after me. I never liked the name Carman."

"I never much liked my own name either," Grant said. "I wonder who does?"

"I like mine just fine," Carol said.

"When you were a kid, you always wanted some fancier name," Carman said. "Candace was one you liked."

"I don't remember that."

"We would have called you Candy," Grant said.

"Two for a nickel," Carol said. "Look, what's that, that blue bird?"

"A kingfisher. I see them all the time."

"It moves so fast."

"The field down below the waterfall is full of goldfinches."

"What are they like?"

"Wild canaries. Yellow and black."

Carol stood by the window with her cup of coffee, staring down at the river.

"I always thought I was a city girl, and I never thought I'd like a summer cottage, but I see why people have them."

"We had cottages in the summer a couple of times."

"All I remember is being bored. For me the best holiday was when we went to New York."

"Drove me nuts. Crazy drivers. Crazy people. Dirt on the streets."

"We thought we might go to New York for Christmas this year," Grant said.

"You're welcome to it."

Carman poured himself a second cup of coffee, though he knew he shouldn't. They were young, planning ahead, while he was always startled to wake in the morning and find he was still alive. The way it was, must be, should be perhaps, if you thought all this hodgepodge of living had a meaning and necessity. He had spent years enforcing the laws, and that was right, though maybe hopeless. You put one kid in jail, and the next was in a corner of the schoolyard kicking the shit out of someone smaller than he was, getting ready for the next step. The world was as it was. The cops kept a closer eye on a factory if the owner handed out bottles of rum at Christmas time. You never thought of that as corruption, just good manners.

Carol turned from the window and looked at him, and for a second he thought that she knew what he was thinking.

"Can we come back some other weekend?"

"Whenever you want."

Grant was at the table glancing through an out-of-date newspaper.

"If you want to go fishing," Carman said, "we could get a couple of cheap poles at the general store."

"You two go," Carol said. "I'll amuse myself."

When the young woman walked into the shop, Norma didn't know who she was. The friendly smile on her face made it clear that Norma was supposed to recognize her, and an attempt was made, futile at first and then, just before the girl was going to have to introduce herself Norma recognized the face, and still unable to come up with the name, indicated that she wasn't entirely at sea by asking if Arthur was parking the car and was then perfectly astonished to find that the woman was on her own. "I just thought I'd come and see you" was the line.

She stood there, bold as you please, smiling. Norma finally remembered her name. Julie. There was nothing for it but to be friendly, so Norma sent her back to the door to lock it and put up the Closed sign, and the two of them went upstairs, Norma doing her best to be spry and light-footed and disguise the pains in her back and legs. When it became obvious that she was being watched, she told the girl about her imaginary dumb waiter, and the girl made a show of amusement. Possibly was amused.

Upstairs, Norma boiled water, dug out stale biscuits, set them on the table beside the old cigar box full of sheets of mica, which for some reason she'd dragged up here a couple of weeks ago. Left on the table because she didn't know what else to do with it.

"How's Arthur?" she said, for lack of anything better to say.

"He's worried about his father."

"Why's that?"

"Steven's had a couple of mild strokes recently. Once when he was having dinner with us, he couldn't talk for ten minutes. He went to lie down for a while, and then he was OK. Another time he fell and the doctor said it was probably another stroke. He's taking medication, but there could be another one any time."

Norma thought about it, Steven silent and helpless. Felt nothing much except the awareness of general mortality that dogged her days and would. She set the tea on the table.

"Is that why you're here?" she said.

"I guess so. I wanted to talk to you again, and I thought it was something you might like to know."

"Why?"

"You were together for quite a while. You had a child together."

"Where's the bimbo?"

"She moved to Vancouver a few years ago. She was offered a good job out there."

"Steven's on his own."

"Yes."

"And you expect me to go running back and help him through a difficult old age, wipe his ass when he gets incontinent and hold his hand while he's dying?"

"No. Nothing like that. I've been mad at a man who betrayed me. I know you don't get over it. But I thought you might want to write or give him a call. Mostly I thought you'd like to know."

Norma poured tea.

"Yes, I suppose I do like to know, though I couldn't honestly say I care a lot."

The younger woman met her eyes, and Norma realized that she'd been staring. It was a bad habit and got worse. Privilege of age, to indulge your bad habits freely. For a while they were silent, drinking tea, crunching dry biscuits. Country hospitality, more or less. Norma could feel her stomach growling. Other growls to come close behind.

"Does all this mean that you're serious about Arthur?"

"Yes."

"Lucky Arthur. Don't you find him a little . . . heavy?"

The eyes met hers, surprised.

"I mean mentally. Humorless."

"He has quite a nice sense of humor when he's relaxed."

"I don't suppose he's ever relaxed around here."

"Parents and children. They set each other off."

Norma finished her tea. She was mostly annoyed by this attempt at friendliness. The girl was trying to remind Norma of a time before she was a bear rumbling in its cave, sharp claws, querulous temper, as if there was such a time, before the pelt was matted and torn, the old bear fat and slow from too many grubs and berries. As if there was such a time. Christmas-card scenes, the three of them sitting by the fire, Norma and Steven watching over Arthur as he builds complicated machines with an old-fashioned Meccano set inherited from his loving father. Norma has made cookies and the parents drink their tea and eat macaroons while they admire the talents of their son, and outside the cold snow falls, but they are safe from it. It must have happened, things like that. They were a family once, and Arthur had been a bright and loving boy. Norma sat on the edge of the bed and read him books, something about a duck. As if there was such a time. The bear shifted its heavy shoulders, sniffed the dark.

Norma looked at the younger woman who sat across from her. She looked proud of herself, the dark eyes shining in the square blunt face. A few months in Arthur's bed and she thought she had the right to poke the old bear with a stick and rouse it, drive it down the road, make it dance, would be shocked if she found bleeding claw marks on her face. She thought that what she was doing was love, correctness, a helping hand. Incorrigibly stupid like all her race.

"If you ever wanted to see him, I could drive you."

"That's all gone by. Steven made his bed. Made mine too. Time was I wept to have him back, while he was pumping the bimbo into seventh heaven. I can't even remember him now."

She had no idea whether or not that was true. She had a momentary image of the dark curling hair on his chest, his red mouth, but that was a young man, not an old one. What terrible hungry sentimentality had driven this girl to come to Norma when she might have stayed away? What evil corruption of the imagination that she would have called love? Norma would have no more of that. She would be preserved from the well-meaning.

"You're probably right," the woman said. "I shouldn't have interfered."

Norma looked toward her, and there was a candor in her look, and something subtle and real. Needing a response, having none, she took the box of mica that lay on the table in front of her and pushed it toward the girl.

"Take this," she said. "It's not worth anything."

"What is it?"

"Mica, from one of the old mines."

The girl opened the box, and her small thick fingers took out a small sheet of the mineral and held it up. The light caught it and shone silver and gold. One of the thin sheets slid off the top of the piece and broke. She swept it up with her fingers and put it back in the box.

"Are you giving this to me?"

"I found it in my storage room. I can't remember where it came from. They used to mine it near here."

"What for?"

"Electrical insulators. Some of it was used in stoves. Or they ground it up to make industrial fillers."

Julie took another piece and sat with it in the palm of her hand.

"You go back to Arthur and make him happy," Norma said. "You've done your best."

When Julie looked at her now, she was different, older, as if everything up until this moment had been a performance, a pretence of youth and innocence. Now her face was that of a woman of no particular age, who knew what there was to know, the earth smell of the bear's den where Norma passed the long winter, the itch of ticks, the anger at being poked and prodded. They were simple female animals, watching.

Julie took up the box, turned away from the table and walked down the stairs without saying a word.

A couple of days of rain, and now the heavy August heat. By the river there was some freshness, but if he walked as far as the store, Carman was bathed in sweat, found it running into his eyes, and he would keep trying to wipe it away with his arm, but the arm was damp with sweat as well. He'd bought some iced-tea mix at the store, and he mostly sat in the shady part of the yard with a glass of iced tea. Even in the middle of the day, he sometimes found he was dozing off, though at night he'd lie in bed with one sheet over him, trying to keep the dark thoughts away. You'd hear a single mosquito in the dark and wait for it to come close enough that you could swat it. He'd swat his arm or shoulder where he felt the tingling presence, and the tiny noise would start up again, letting him know that he'd missed the insect and wondering whether to turn on the light and get up to find and kill it.

That was one good thing about the high apartment in the city. The bugs never got up that high. Maybe the only good thing. If it cooled a little in the evening, he thought he might take the boat out and fish for a while. It had been too hot for the last week, but now and then a breeze would come up in the evening. He thought of the fish in their sunken world where the heat of the sun was filtered by tons of water, and it was always deep and cold, though if he stepped in the shallows by the dock to cool himself, he was aware that even the river water was warmer than when he came here. He remembered once, years before, he and Audrey had gone away to Wasaga Beach for a weekend in September, and how the water was warmer than the air.

In spite of the heat, there was a little patch of red leaves on one of the big maples. The dryness, someone said, though he'd read somewhere else that it was the change in light that caused the leaves to change color. He was having trouble finding things to read, almost wished he had those old copies of *National Geographic*, to see the mountains of Tibet, with smiling Tibetans drinking yak's milk, tribes of Pygmies in the jungles of Africa. What ever happened to the Pygmies? In all the reports of wars and disaster in Africa, there was never any mention of them. As if they never existed at all. One of the tall tales that travelers came back with. Men with heads below their shoulders.

How would he find out if the Pygmies were still there? He wanted to know, supposed that he could drive to Kingston and look them up in the public library, some day when it wasn't so hot. Maybe he should offer Norma a drive to town, though it didn't work out too well the last time he drove her somewhere. Spare

Parts. Junk. Carol and Grant had gone up to her store when they were here, and Carol reported that she wasn't rude at all, almost friendly, and when Carman went to the store a few days later to give her a month's rent, she'd pleased him by saying that his daughter was a pretty girl. There might be a library closer than Kingston that would have an encyclopedia. He'd ask her about that.

A day like this, it wasn't hard to imagine the heat of the African jungle, the tiny dark men invisible among the trees. Now there were helicopters overhead, bombs dropping. He put the helicopters out of his mind, thought of the quietness under the high trees, the closeness of the air. Carman closed his eyes and knew that he'd soon be asleep.

Norma was astonished when The Vice-grip arrived at the store offering her a drive to Kingston. A payoff for saying a few days ago that he had a pretty daughter. Well, he did, and the girl had been well-behaved, and Norma had managed for once to be pleasant to him. It emerged that he wanted to go to the library to consult an encyclopedia. Norma offered him a deal. All he had to do was go to the shelves at the back of the shop, and a recent Britannica waited for him. In exchange he could drive her to Aeldred's place. She had some business she wanted to do, and, if the truth be known, and why not, she wanted to look at the old animal, see how he was faring. A vile curiosity.

He wanted to learn about Pygmies, it appeared. Why Pygmies? she said, and he said he just happened to think about them, people will think about the oddest things. So he went to the shelves and took things down and frowned over the books, which told him half of what he wanted to know. Were they still there among the starving millions, and how were they managing? Well, she'd never thought to wonder about that, herself, but she could see it might be of interest to some. Anyway, he found out the names of the tribes and something about their history, and was happy enough to give her a lift. When he asked who Aeldred was, she gave him the purely professional description.

Late in the afternoon, he came back in his big car, and they set out through the baked countryside. It was a little cooler today, but not much. A day to think about the perils of winter. Temperate climate: too hot in the summer, too cold in the winter. Norma remembered the trip to see Spare Parts and speculated on her own ability to sustain a modest level of good manners. When they reached Aeldred's, Carman took a look at the pile of old railway ties, wagon wheels and broken furniture and decided to wait for her where he was, behind the wheel. As she walked up the slope toward the barn, the hot humid air of late afternoon pressed down on her, and she felt her clothes damp with sweat and glued to her skin. She walked out of the bright sunlight and through the wide doors of the barn. The shade of the big building cooled her a little. Old furniture was piled in rows, one thing on top of another, and chairs hung from the ceiling. She looked along a row of chests and into a dark corner where the door of an old tack room stood open, and after a few seconds her eyes adjusted to the darkness and she could see Aeldred sitting on his old bus seat against the stone wall. As she walked toward him, one of his cats, black with a couple of white spots, came out to greet her, the tail straight in the air, the eyes watching her as if assessing how much of her might be edible. Aeldred had a book in his hand, his glasses down on the end of his nose so he could read over the top of them, thighs spread, one hand tucked into the waistband of his trousers. Aeldred could usually be found touching himself somewhere; he liked the feel of flesh, his own if there was nothing else close by. A marmalade cat lay in his lap, a gray one sat on the window sill, and on a pile of straw in the corner, another slept in a heap of kittens. On a table with a broken leg she saw the remains of a meal with flies on it and a bag of shortbread cookies.

"Haven't seen you for a while," Aeldred said, then looked back at his book, an old one in a dark blue cloth binding. He began to read aloud. "Mrs. Berry is an exceedingly white and lean person. She has thick eyebrows which meet rather dangerously over her nose, which is Grecian, and a small mouth with no lips—a sort of feeble pucker in the face. Under her eyebrows are a pair of enormous eyes, which she is in the habit of turning constantly ceiling-wards."

"Who wrote all that?"

"Thackeray. From something called *Men's Wives.*

"Was he an expert?"

"Come here and let me look at you."

The book was set down on the table, and he held out his arms. What he meant was not look but feel, and Norma wasn't at all sure that she was so minded, but she'd always had a weakness for Aeldred, and now she went toward him and he tossed the marmalade cat aside, put his arms around her hips and rubbed his gray beard against her belly and mumbled a little. A smell of cat came from his clothes. A few years back they had the habit of getting together now and then. It had ended when one of Aeldred's women succeeded in getting him to marry her and insisted on fidelity. Norma could have told her that this was a mistake, but she wasn't asked. The marriage didn't last long, but long enough that she got out of the habit of Aeldred and hadn't wanted to start in again. There was something both hypnotic and repulsive about the way his hands were stroking her. Carman had said firmly that he'd stay in the car, but if he were to change his mind and come in, he would be shocked. He looked like a man who might be easily shocked, in spite of all the dark things the police observed.

Norma decided she'd had enough and moved away, and the marmalade cat came back and began to wind around Aeldred's feet, rubbing against his ankles and purring loudly. Aeldred picked it up.

"Someone said you'd sold your van," he said.

"The knacker's yard, unhappily."

"What are you driving?"

"Not. I got a ride with a neighbor."

She looked at Aeldred's face, the way the thin gray whiskers came out in patches on his cheeks, grew thickly around the mouth, the dark circles around his eyes, and the heavy bags beneath them, the deep wrinkles in his forehead, the gray hair still growing well forward. Ontological Man, he liked to call himself, Pure Being, meaning he was too lazy to get about much, preferred to sit and eat, maybe think a thought now and then, or not, liking to have something warm close by, all in all an indolent fat man without vanity.

"Think I'd cut up satisfactorily," he said.

"What?"

"You were studying me as if you were planning to sell me to the slaughterhouse."

"No."

"Does this neighbor rattle your bones."

"None of your damned business. Don't presume."

He shrugged.

"I have no secrets," he said.

"Do you have any money?" she said.

"Not much."

"I've got two wood stoves, an old cookstove, and an airtight."

Aeldred made something of a specialty of wood-burning stoves and Quebec heaters. The drive shed beside the barn was full of them. Aeldred looked toward her, then rubbed the back of his neck for a while, pushed his fingers over his face, breathed in and heaved a long sigh.

"You want to sell or trade?"

"I could use an infusion of cash."

"Did I ever tell you that I was once going to be a dentist?"

"No."

"I usually tell that story."

"Is it true?"

"It's a good story."

Norma said nothing, wanting to force him to reply. She'd got the two stoves for a good price, even with the cost of having Egan McBride and his son-in-law haul them in. Carman's rent was paying for her groceries, but there was a house full of stuff coming up for sale, and she'd like to have the cash on hand to make a prompt offer before the heirs began to have second thoughts.

"What kind of price are we talking about?"

She named a figure. Aeldred stroked the cat, as if trying to feel the shape of its bones. The one in the window jumped to the floor to wind itself around his legs. Aeldred reached down and rubbed it with his hands, moving its loosely hung bones in his grip.

"And I'd have to pick them up, I suppose."

The cat was stretching itself with pleasure in his hands, but Aeldred's eyes were on Norma, looking her over carefully as if to assess how much weight she'd put on since he'd last lain on top of her and what the effect of the new weight would be. He set the cat aside and reached out for the package of cookies.

"Like a shortbread?"

"No thanks, Aeldred. Never liked them. They have a salty taste."

"That's the butter," he said, taking a large bite from one and licking a crumb off his lips with the thick dark red tongue.

"I should never have married that woman," he said.

"We're talking about money here."

"You are."

"You want to think it over, give me a call?" she said.

"I could make you dinner sometime."

Was it flattering that Aeldred was still interested? Probably more than could be said for that sour old bugger who was sitting waiting in the car, at least as far as she could tell. He looked at her as if she might be a dead fish. A man who'd loved his wife. That's what he was. She was aware that he would be impatient sitting out there in the car, unable to keep still, turning the radio from one station to another then shutting it off.

"I'm going now. You think it over."

"The price is a little high, but I'll come round and take a look. We might manage something. You could look around while you're here. Maybe we could arrange a trade."

"I'm looking for cash," she said. "You come and check them out." She turned away, put a foot wrong and hurt her back but tried not to show it. Her face was hot and there was a tingling in her hands and feet. Time to get back to the rocker and close her eyes.

"I should never have married that woman," Aeldred shouted after her. She stopped and turned in her tracks.

"It was the smartest thing you ever did," she said. No reason, just bad temper. The shade of the barn failed to cool her now; her clothes were soaked through, and she thought she might faint, but she made the effort, turned back and walked out into the blinding sunlight and got to the car. Carman's dark look was turned toward her as she struggled to get into the seat, used the last of her energy to pull the door shut and put her head back, her eyes closed.

"You all right?" he said.

"It's too damn hot. Too damn hot to live."

He was starting the car. She kept her eyes closed, running away from it all, though she couldn't have said what that was. The past, perhaps, the smell of Aeldred, the ease with which he'd left her behind for the short-lived marriage, the ease with which he was inviting her back. That was Aeldred: open the package of cookies and eat till they're gone then open another package. All of it together, the heat, the exhaustion, the grim aging appetites, left her empty, unable to even speak. There was nothing to be done.

"You should come down and sit by the water for a while. It's cooler there."

"Climb in and drown myself. That'd be cold enough."

He didn't say anything more. She'd been a rude bitch again. Norma knew she should open her eyes, make conversation, but she couldn't do it. Even to open her eyes would take more energy than she possessed, and with them closed she was in her own keeping, untouchable, in a private place as safe as sleep and dreams. The air from the open window blew against her face, and the noise of it against her ears helped. If she could go far enough away, she would find her way to some great joke. The Great Joke of Being. Ontological Man indeed. Consider the lilies of the field was all well enough, but by now he was not much better than a bum, old Aeldred. Sitting in a corner of a barn full of junk, playing with himself. A biological accident that he happened to smell sweet. If he still did. She'd never know. Consider the lilies of the field. Take no thought for the morrow. Be hungry and cold. She could put a sign in the front window of the shop: Spirituality For Sale, Cheap.

She opened her eyes. They were going past one of those bleak hopeless farms built on limestone with a few bare inches of soil over it. By now the owners would have jobs in the city and keep a few cattle as a hobby.

"Damn hard land here," she said.

"You're alive."

"Barely."

"Did you sell him the stoves?"

"What's it to you?"

"I guess you didn't."

"He's going to come and see them. He'll make me an offer."

"Will it be good enough?"

"Depends how I'm feeling that day."

She looked across at him. He gripped the wheel tightly, as if he was strangling it.

"When you were a cop, did you knock people around?"

"Not usually. Didn't need to."

"Why's that?"

"Most criminals aren't too bright. Even the smart ones screw up eventually."

They turned at the next crossroads. On the left was a field of hay and on the right was a large woodland, the leaves dark and thick, a wall of green shutting you out.

"There's an old mica mine back in those woods," she said.

"Mica?"

"All kinds of uses. They used to dig it out of the ground and haul it into town. It was a way of making a few dollars in the winter."

"Is it all shut down now?"

"Not exactly shut down, just abandoned. Holes in the ground. I have this idea that there must be something to be done with them. Tourists or some damn thing."

"Some day you should show me."

"Why?"

"I can be your first tourist. Try it out on me."

"Then you can start work on the theme park."

Norma closed her eyes again. She started this trip thinking she liked Aeldred, looking forward to seeing him, but now she hated him, though she had no good reason, no legitimate excuse. He was what he had always been. They turned another corner, and she opened her eyes to find the sun, which was toward setting, was shining straight into them. August heat, but the days were getting shorter already. She looked across the seat at the bulky body of the man with his straight thin hair as he leaned over the wheel.

"When I get home I want to have a little nap," she said, "but if you came over later, I'd make a couple of sandwiches."

"Shall I bring the bottle of rye?"

"You could do that." What a stupid idea that was, she thought to herself. She had enough trouble feeding herself.

Carman stood at the edge of the road and listened to the sound of the waterfall, looked at the moths fluttering around the streetlight, and felt the evening air cool on his bare arms. Ghosts watched from the empty hotel. He was a little astonished, pleased with himself, unsettled. He and Norma had drunk too much of the bottle of rye that he'd brought with him, and she had invited him into her bed and he had accepted, not sure whether anything would come of it or whether it would kill him, but they'd managed well enough, and here he was alive and feeling good about it. A bat flew by into the street, a sudden black shape that vanished into the darkness.

She'd made no bones about throwing him out afterward. There had been a little spell of sweetness, but within five minutes of the event, she was starting to get bossy and irritable. He turned his leg the wrong way and got a cramp in the calf and had to parade back and forth naked from one end of her bedroom to the other to try to walk it off, while she dragged a dressing gown off the back of a chair and put it round her. Once the cramp was gone, she handed him his clothes and announced that she didn't want him keeping her up all night, then tromped out of the room and left him to reassemble himself, which he did, looking at the rumpled bed, the pile of books and dirty cups on the table beside it, the jars full of buttons on the chest of drawers, with an old circus poster on the wall behind, clothes hung over chairs and the bedposts. As he got his socks and shoes on, he heard her banging pots and pans in the kitchen, talking aloud. Dressed, he went down the hall and stood in the doorway while she threw things around. When he'd first walked into the apartment, he was shocked at the state of the place, the sink full of dishes, more on the counter and the kitchen table, and Norma had pushed them aside only far enough to make room to slice bread and make a couple of sandwiches. He was just as glad she'd told him to leave. He wouldn't have wanted to see all that in daylight.

As Carman walked back toward the cottage, he realized that he was still a bit drunk. He couldn't remember how much rye they'd gone through. He'd left the bottle on the floor of the living room beside the piece of welded cast iron she called a sculpture. A little breeze came up, shook the leaves over his head, then everything was still. The darkness breathed, and he breathed with it. Alive. Astonishing really. That fat old woman, that crackpot. Pictures on the walls that looked like some mess a kid had made. Dirt in all the corners. He'd gone to use the bathroom once, and the tub was greasy and caked with dirt. There was a metal bar on the wall that helped her get in and out. Bad back. When he was hobbling about with the leg cramp, wincing, she told him to be quiet, that he was in no more pain than she was most of the time. Men were all crybabies. Maybe she was right.

Carman was laughing. The two of them must have been a sight. Himself, he'd grown thick in the middle, lumps over the kidneys, having to slip a pill in his mouth before the act to keep him alive through it all, and she was just this side of obese, and neither of them moved around too gracefully, but they got themselves together and did the job. Carman felt as if he wanted to tell someone, but there was no one to tell. He could imagine Rolly Menard if he got him out of bed in the middle of the night to say he'd just got laid for the first time in years. Too bad Amy Martyrdom had moved. Norma said she liked to talk about these things.

Not that she'd be impressed. What they'd achieved was nothing like the grand opera he'd overheard from the back lawn, but was a very good thing all the same. When he got to the cottage, he walked down toward the river, remembered the pale shadow of Amy's bare body moving through the night. He could think about that without embarrassment now. He'd like to see her there again.

A mosquito flew round his ears, and he slapped at it, without effect. He decided to take the boat out. In the darkness, he missed his footing and got one shoe soaked while he was trying to get the boat untied, but he managed to push it off, and he rowed out into the river and up the first wide section, where he threw the anchor overboard. Its splash was loud in the quietness. When he felt it hit the bottom, he tied it off, and settled himself. By the shore, he could see the dim transient gleam of fireflies. He looked upward, and the dark sky was full of stars. As he sat there, feeling the current of the river pulling his boat against the drag of the anchor, he thought how one night or morning, it would all end. The heart would stop. Sooner or later, and why not? What started must finish.

As he sat there in the night, aching a little, but lightened, wondering what it would be like to have a cigarette again, he thought of all the women in the world.

The skinny little hooker with her tight shorts. Amy Martyrdom's big breasts. Back in the cottage, his picture of Audrey sat on the table by the window, impassive and unchanging. Just down the river, beside the waterfall, Norma was settled in the mess of her apartment. He wondered to himself what she was thinking about. He couldn't imagine. Women were different. He doubted that she was thinking how that one act made death a less fearful thing. Right now at least, it did, but he was a little drunk and very surprised and there was no saying what morning would be like.

Somewhere in the night he heard an owl, a sound like a dog barking, and at the edge of the river, the fireflies moved.

Clean the mirrors, Norma. See what you are. No, rather not. Only time is to blame for time. I didn't choose to be old and fat. Not old at least, and it's not clear about the other. A life spent dieting is its own vulgarity. Like Jehovah I am what I am. Should have said no. Most certainly should.

Carman had come by on his way to the grocery store and invited her to come to his cottage where he would barbecue steaks, and she had said yes, and now was in a dither about it, and wondering if she would end up in bed with the man once again, and how much they would need to drink before going at it. That other night, she'd brought it on herself of course, pissed enough to dare and he pissed enough to take the dare, but that was in the past, and the world had spun on its axis a few times since then, sunset, sunrise, the millions at their business. Arteries closed off. Rivers in flood. What she most wanted now was some woman to talk to, wished that Moira would come back from the dead or that Amy Martyrdom was still around, or even that Arthur's Julie would step in the door. Not that she'd tell them about the little adventure, Moira perhaps but not the others, but just to have a woman there would make her less trapped by it. Right? No, not quite that. Hell, she had it wrong, but she had it right as well.

A thing she wanted, and a surprise at that, was to talk to Julie again. Maybe only because Julie had the nerve to come and poke the old bear and take her chances with the teeth and claws. Norma found herself hoping that Arthur stayed with the woman. She might make a human being of him. Well, then, Norma wanted to talk to her, she could pick up the phone, but not so simple, she had no number, didn't even know if she and Arthur lived together, and couldn't find out without asking her son, and she wasn't ready for that. Nothing was what you wanted. After the little adventure with Detective Deshane, she had been unable not to wonder what might come next, and now she'd got what she deserved for wondering, a barbecue by the river and then, and then, and then, and she didn't know if that was what she wanted or what she most didn't want. Nobody deserved to be born to all this. The unborn were safe and holy. It was easier being dead.

A moralizing voice responded, calling for courage. Stuff it, moralizing voice. Enough is enough. Besides he makes me mad, and I'm almost certain to say something rude and bring the evening to an end in disarray. He was another person and other people were too damn much to bear, just being there, just not being you. Notable quotations number 86. Food, though, there would be food, thick red steaks, burnt from the barbecue, bad for the health in every way, nice conventional summer grub, and then they could go out in the boat and watch the moonlight on the water and sing old songs.

She sat down in the rocking chair and gave a couple of good kicks. Now that she'd invited him and he'd invited her, it would be her turn again. Well, he wasn't coming back to the apartment. From what she'd seen, he probably kept the cottage clean, damn him, and next thing he'd be wiping his finger over her tables like a mother-in-law. Censorious. His face was full of disapproval. It was a permanent part of his expression. Men were like that, even Aeldred, who, being dirty, could stand the dirt, would tell her she didn't read widely enough. Widely enough. Blah. She never opened a book any more. Great reader once. Now she stared at the wall, waiting for a crack to open and Entities to flow in from the other side of time. No, Detective Carman Deshane wasn't getting back up the stairs. As a sop to duty, one day, she'd take him off into the woods to see the old mica mines. He'd shown an interest. The bugs in the woods wouldn't be as bad now, after a mostly dry summer. Maybe he'd have a bright idea about what could be done with the old mines. There must be something.

Red meat and rye whisky. The police force at play. Oh mother, dear mother, come home to us now. Blah. Don't play bingo tonight, mother. Stay home with daddy and me. Blah. Oh hell, bumbling around with whiskied widower was better than being A Victim of Circumstance. Or was it that very thing? How did you know? Deep philosophical questions. The Queen looked down three times from the wall and waited for Norma to answer. The Woman with No Clothes looked back over her shoulder thinking about the answers to all the hard questions and knowing that the perfect health of her big perfect body was the final and eventual answer to all things. At that age being beautiful was a career. At that age Norma didn't look bad. She should have had herself stuffed, like her friend the wolf, whose glass eyes observed her with all the detachment and clarity of a taxidermical god. Two of the smaller animals had sold, to a dusty blonde woman who was a teacher in a free school—an unlikely story, that, Norma thought, as if there still were free schools. However that was, the raccoon and the weasel had gone off to a new life in the big city, and the dusty woman had hankered after the wolf, but Norma, not wanting to lose him, had put the price too high, and now she was tempted to take him upstairs and declare that he was Part of the Establishment.

What she should be doing tonight, instead of going off to some kind of social occasion was getting out her Greek dictionary and learning a little. Become a scholar. Once, she thought she remembered, she had aspired to that, or something like it. She was Good in School. Had a degree, in fact, one of those General B.A. degrees that could be considered a ladylike accomplishment. Then she took a trip, came back, married Steven, did a little part-time teaching, furnished the house with old furniture that she refinished herself, eventually got knocked up and produced Arthur. As Time Goes By. Remembrance of Things Past. The Recipe for Cookies. How Dumb Can You Get?

As she sat here rocking, little explosions were taking place in the arteries of the brain of the man who once was her husband. She imagined him sitting at dinner, unable to speak, the panic on his face, Arthur watching him, confused. A transient ischemic attack. She'd read that phrase in a magazine somewhere. She didn't buy magazines, but they came to hand, and she studied things like prostate cancer, preferring the conditions she thought herself least likely to get. What she'd got didn't bear studying, a shapeless set of bad experiences to which they gave one name or another name, the consolation being that it wouldn't kill you. We could just call it old age, she said to the doctor, and had to endure a humorless little lecture on the wonders of medicine in drawing distinctions among the various ways of going down.

She rocked the chair. Aeldred was coming tomorrow to look at the stoves. She had an appointment on the weekend to look at the furniture in the uninhabited house of a dear departed. Intuition told her there would be something good. Aeldred would buy the stoves, she would reinvest the cash and come into possession of good things. Business would boom. Boom. Boom. Boom. Once, for a short spell, she had a bass drum in her stock of rare things.

One thing to be decided was whether to wash herself, at least the smellier bits, and then what to wear. Whatever she wore, she'd probably spill her dinner on it. She was unsettled to realize how much she was looking forward to the first glass of rye. Perhaps the two of them could end up as a pair of muddled and affectionate old topers. No, she didn't want to be one of a pair of anything. As she was thinking about that, the telephone rang.

The great blue heron in the evening twilight. The beak an extension of the thin head and long neck, a sudden and formidable weapon. The body changes shape as the neck unfolds and then extends, the heron still on its long legs, in water that catches the sky's deep blue. A snake armed with a sword. Timeless the world of animals, the predator's patience, stillness going on and on, and then the head plunges into the water and comes out with a fish, turns it, swallows it down, then again the stylized grotesque stillness of the long body in silhouette against the dark mirror, the head like a knife at the end of a whip, the ominous slender potent neck.

Carman watched from his window, fascinated by the bird's perfect concentration as it stood in the shallows on the far side of the river and waited and killed. The light was gradually vanishing into the west, the darkness pouring down over everything, a thick blackness coming out of the east and then in a few hours, morning would come that way again, light creeping over the edge of the world, a gray pallor, then a band of green and gold and pink striking the clouds, and the sun would appear once more.

A boy walking across Camp Hill cemetery in Halifax and then through the Public Gardens, the grass wet with dew, the leaves thick, the air smelling of the sea and of the harbor. What he could remember. That he crossed the Public Gardens and walked past the Lord Nelson Hotel and down Spring Garden Road. While his parents, his older sister, slept. More than once, he got up before anyone in the family, but the summer sun was ahead of him, and the day was bright, the streets still empty except for a milkman and his horse, the wagon stopped at the side of the street, the horse with its tail up, dropping round balls of dung into a steaming heap as it stood waiting, and when the milkman returned and shook the reins, the wagon moved off, the wheels rolling over the fresh turds brown with their speckles of undigested chaff, and once the wagon was gone, sparrows would come to pick it over for something edible. A memory or blend of memories. You knew you must have seen just such a thing, one morning, but you couldn't be certain how many such mornings there were when the boy set off from the little house to walk down to the harbor, where dead fish and driftwood and used safes floated in the water that slopped against the wharves, and there was the big dark shape of an oil tanker on the blue water.

The heron lifted its wings and rose into the darkness and vanished behind the willows. Night and morning, and the seasons passed, and in winter, the river would run through fields covered with snow, black and shining among the white fields. He wondered if it would ever freeze over. The current was strong. When he sat in the boat fishing, he could feel it pulling against the anchor. It would be interesting to know if the river froze. He didn't know what he was going to do in the fall. He could stay on here for a month or so after Labor Day, but the place would be too cold after that. It had no foundation and wasn't winterized like the cottage next door. Which was still empty. Norma said Amy had a lease for another six months.

Norma was in Toronto for a funeral. It was just before she came down to the cottage for steaks that she heard her former husband had died of a stroke. She didn't mention it to Carman until after she'd had a couple of drinks. He could have said she was in a strange state of mind that night, except she always was, so far as he could see. Here's to the night, she kept saying as she drank. Here's to the night and the darkness. He thought perhaps she wouldn't want to go to bed with him, but she was eager, in a defiant kind of way; then he'd hardly caught his breath when she was back up on her feet, dressing in the dark, vanishing out the door.

That boy walked through Halifax on a summer morning, making his way down to the harbor to dream of ships. Time was he went to sea and saw a war. Came back and joined the police. Even then the world was simple. They pursued and entrapped queers, hanged murderers. Criminals knew what they were and expected what they got. Gradually it got to be something else, until it wasn't clear who was on your side and who wasn't, and then suddenly you woke in the morning with aches and pains. One morning in the cemetery he saw a couple asleep under one of the bushes, their arms round each other, their faces empty, and he thought that they must have been there all night, and he was frightened for a second that they might be dead. He looked at them, the woman's round face, the man's sandpapery whiskers, wondered where they would go when they woke up, and then he walked on, and at the corner of Barrington Street there was an old woman staring up into one of the trees, as if she might find a great bird or an angel waiting for her, bringing her a message.

Norma sat in her rocking chair, and the universe went on about its business. Summer at its peak, ready to end. In Antarctica, it was the dead of winter, and the wind howled over the mountains and the endless expanses of ice. It was the coldest place in the world and its seasons were upside down. So they said. Yesterday, she had sold several pieces of furniture to a couple who were furnishing a cottage, and had got a good price for a mahogany sideboard picked up the week before. Last night as she lay in bed, a breeze touched her, and she thought it was the first hint of fall.

Steven was still dead. Dutiful for once, she had gone to Toronto to stand up and bear witness with the man's only son, at a brief and awkward moment in the funeral home, everything in the charge of some non-denominational cleric who was a friend of somebody's friend. The bimbo sent flowers. God, it was all so awful. Norma did her best to be a good conventional person, not to embarrass Arthur by farting or tripping or saying something rotten, and perhaps she'd succeeded, trying to think kind thoughts about Steven. To imagine that the years they'd spent together were good, and maybe they were, some of them. She remembered their marriage ceremony. That was awful too. He was a good fuck most of the time. He earned a living. What else was there to marriage?

What did the Antarctic penguins do in winter? Did they still parade around in their comical fashion or did they swim north to someplace a little warmer? Life was full of large questions. If you are an Antarctic penguin, how cold is too cold? Why are penguins funny? Do they see the joke? Oh Coldest Antarctica. The Mountains of the South Pole. The End of the Known World. Like Carman pursuing his Pygmies, she could look it up.

When it was over, they all went back to Arthur's apartment near Davisville and Mount Pleasant. Julie, it appeared, had a place of her own, farther east. Norma took herself for a walk a little way down Mount Pleasant, looking in the windows of restaurants and florists and furniture stores, all very pleasant, Mount Pleasant, and she wept a few tears, for herself most likely, maybe for Steven, long gone as he was, and then she went back to the apartment, looked out the windows at the lights of the endless city, let Arthur and Julie take her out to dinner at an expensive restaurant all done in black and silver and selling fish things and strange vegetables, and after a sleepless night on a bed unfolded from a couch, she got into Julie's car and was driven back. They talked a little during the trip, not much, and when they arrived, the river was still running, the waterfall still falling. As she climbed out of the car, Norma saw a boat on the water, Carman fishing. Norma offered to have Julie overnight, and meant the invitation, wanted her to stay, but she said she had to be at work early the next morning and left.

She could understand the people who had a dozen children. Never any peace, but life was compelled, and surely there were not these moments when the rocking chair refused to rock, and it was hard to remember why. She kicked out her legs. One decision had been made. She was going to buy a car, some kind of efficient little thing. Cash her RRSP and to hell with old age. Mobility was needed, at least until she settled in her little seniors' apartment with the cable TV and gave her soul to the airwaves.

She tried to remember Steven's face and wasn't sure she could. Served him right. She could remember his private parts, what he was proudest of, after all, like most men. She wondered what the bimbo brought to mind from her youthful adventure. One dick among many. After Norma bought her car, she would drive to Kingston and look at all the places she had lived, mostly places that she and Steven had lived together. That was the last thought he'd get from her. In fact, until Arthur turned up with his new girl she had largely succeeded in putting him out of her mind. That was harder with the dead. The living were moving on, and you could never imagine what they might be up to so you ignored them. The dead had nothing but their past, and so they were complete and persisted in being what they were. Gone, they were harder to forget. Even stupidity took on a certain mute perfection.

Norma was thinking. Sitting and rocking and thinking. Though of a highly variable temperament, she was at the moment in the grip of a certain serenity. Or was it inertia? Through the front window of the store, she could see two couples in holiday garb, examining her things and engaging in discussion. They opened the door. One of the women had the look of someone who has already made up her mind.

Carman tripped over a small outcropping of rock and nearly went sprawling. Norma stopped, stared at him with a look on her face that made him want to knock her down.

"You'd want to watch where you're going."

"I'll do that."

If he said anything more he'd find he was getting mad, and if he got mad, he'd get madder. All the way along the road since they'd left her store she'd picked at his driving, like a child picking at a sore, as if she was determined to start a fight over something. A mosquito landed on his neck. He started to walk faster. Her breath came heavily from just behind him.

"What's your damn hurry?"

"The woods are full of bugs."

"I haven't seen any."

"I have."

"They must be attracted to your sweetness."

He didn't answer. The whole outing was ridiculous. He didn't care about the damned old mica mines, however determined she was to get there. She should get a car of her own instead of expecting him to drive her all over the countryside. He watched where he was walking to avoid tripping again. They were following some sort of old road, a logging road maybe, that wound through the rock of the Shield and the second-growth bush—maple and beech and a few birches, here and there a tall spruce. It wasn't a hot day, but he was sweating from the exercise, and Norma was puffing more heavily behind him. He didn't look back. A hundred years before, men had come in here and logged it. Had the road been cut to take the mica out? A truck or tractor must drive in now and then or it would have been completely overgrown.

Something was waiting for you in the woods, though you never knew what it was. Even that little bush behind the motel. The fish, the memory of an old crime in the air. Here it was the hard men leading hard lives, who had given themselves to this cold rocky place and broken or not broken. Everyone broke eventually. He felt the pocket of his jacket to make sure he had the nitroglycerin pills. Magic against sudden death.

Norma spoke from behind him.

"I don't know if you're trying to kill yourself or me," she said, "but either way, slow down."

Her voice was hoarse because she was short of breath. He stopped and looked back. Her face was pale.

"Is it much farther?"

"I can't quite remember. I'll recognize it when I get there. Remains of an old shed by the road and a path off to the left."

"You want to sit down and rest?"

"I'm not such a damn cripple as that."

He started walking again. A red squirrel chattered at them. A jay screamed.

The old hard lives whispered behind the trees, invisible among leaves and branches.

"There's the shed just up there."

It wasn't a shed any more but a pile of old gray boards rotting away. Carman doggedly put one foot in front of the other. He thought he remembered saying he wanted to come here, but right now he couldn't think why he'd had such an idea. They reached the shed and Norma said that just beyond it they should go to the left, and when they did they were in a bit of a clearing, with a slope down at the far side, and a couple of piles of rock. The ground was uneven, and under his feet the earth was soft and slippery, he saw that the ground was covered with glittering fragments of mica. Norma was going on ahead of him and he bent and picked up a couple of pieces of the odd substance.

She was talking, more to herself than to him. There was a scrabbling noise, a gasp, and she was gone. He stared, as if this might be some kind of childish trick and in a moment he would see her peeking at him from behind a tree. The woods were silent except for the wind in the leaves and the sound of a jay, and already he was moving carefully to where he had last seen her. The edges of the deep hole were thick with fallen leaves, and when he looked down, he saw her in the water, below steep sides of rock and earth. The edges were slippery with fragments of mica. The water must have flowed into the open pit where the mica had been dug. He looked around him again, as if there might be someone to help. He was a city cop. You always had a radio, a phone. If you went into the burning building, you knew that help was on its way.

By now he was sitting on the edge of the pit. It was perhaps eight feet down to where she was, and if he slipped into the water, he'd never get out. He eased his body over the edge, his legs out to catch the sides and slow his descent as he slid down. The rocks scraped him and he could feel his hands being torn, but by lying flat against the slope, he used the drag of his body and clothes against gravity and managed to stop himself at the edge of the water. One leg went in, but his right foot was on a small rock ledge, and he anchored his weight there. He could see her body in the dark water just under the surface where three yellow leaves floated, and there was a shimmer of reflection of the sky. He reached in and got hold of something and pulled. He realized that he was holding her by the hair, but he didn't dare change his grip or he'd drop her. He had her face out of the water. There was a nasty wound on one side of her head, a little blood, and she must have been knocked unconscious as she fell. As far as he could tell, she was breathing, but it didn't seem possible to get her out of here.

His heart was pounding, and he could feel the familiar pain and tightness in his chest. They could both die down here. He looked up, to see how far he had to lift her, and at the edges of the hole he could see little glittering fragments of the mica. He was holding Norma out of the water with his left arm, and it was starting to ache. He got his right hand into the pocket of his jacket, managed to get out two pills and put them under his tongue. A little magic to help him along. Beside him, there was a place where the slope of the old excavation was a little less steep, and he reached down, got his other hand on a piece of her clothing and leaned toward that side. It took all his strength, but he got her head and shoulders out of the water; he knew if he let go, she'd slide back in. For a moment, he stayed still, bent over the round face with its roll of fat beneath the chin, but she was breathing slowly, blood spreading from the wound, the eyes closed, for once not staring at him.

"You really are a pain in the ass, Norma," he said.

He tried to think, to make a plan. He couldn't lift her out of the hole. Even young and healthy he couldn't have done that. The only hope was to get out himself, which would be hard enough, and to pull her out. With what? Bent over, he put one knee on her shoulder and pressed down, to hold the inert body in place against the slope, and with his hands free, he took off his belt. Then, pushing her about unrespectfully, manhandling her heavy breasts, he managed to work the belt around the body and under her arms and to buckle it. It gave him a kind of handle, and using it to move her, he managed to get himself a few inches higher and get her body a little further out of the water. Her hips were on the ledge, with the legs dangling, but now he could let her lie there for a second and rest his arms. Once more he examined the old digging. A little above him a tree root as thick as his wrist grew out of the earth. He reached up and took hold of it. It looked solid, and he reached up, took it with his right hand and pulled. He let his weight drag on it, and it held. That might be enough to get him back out, but he didn't dare leave her. Awkwardly, nearly losing his balance and falling into the water himself, he took off his trousers. He put the wallet and keys in his jacket pocket, then tied one leg of the trousers around the belt he'd strapped below Norma's arms. He pulled on it, hard and dragged her a little further away from the water, then he reached up and tied the other end round the piece of root. If she came to and struggled, would she plunge herself back into the water? He didn't know, but he knew that he was never going to get her out of here on his own.

He stood for thirty seconds and breathed as slowly and calmly as he could.

"Norma," he said loudly and touched her face.

The eyes in their pouches of skin opened for a second.

"You fell into an old mine," he said. "I can't get you out, but you're tied so you can't slip in again. You'll have to wait here while I go for help. Do you understand?"

Her eyes opened and then closed and she lay inert, but she was still breathing, and when he checked the pulse in her neck, it was steady. He looked up and wondered if he could get himself out. Best to go very slowly. The root would hold his weight, if he could get his foot on it, and then he might be able to reach out of the hole. He saw a couple of soft spots just above his feet, where the ground was soft and full of bits of mica, and he tried kicking his toes into one of them, and he managed to get a toe hold in one, then in the other. Within a few minutes, he was standing on the root. There was pain in his chest, and he was having trouble getting his breath now, and for a long time he stood there and gathered his strength. He heard Norma moaning a little and he spoke to her, repeating his reassurances, telling her to wait. If he could just stay alive long enough to get to the road, it would be all right. Someone would come.

His fingers were searching just over the edge of the hole for something he could hold to pull himself out. He tore at grass, but it came loose and dirt fell into his face. There was nothing. Once more he kicked into the dirt until he had a toehold, and he found a rock just above his head where his fingers got a little purchase. He levered himself up, though he hated to step away from the stability of the thick root, but now he got his left hand farther out and found a bush he could grip, and it held his weight while he scrabbled up and got an elbow over the edge. He was kicking dirt back down onto the woman below, but there was no help for it. Awkwardly he dragged himself over the top, then lay on the ground panting until he could get to his feet and start back through the woods, the way they'd come. Close to his face, he saw an ant holding something in its mandibles as its thin legs carried it over a dead leaf. He pushed himself up.

Dirty-faced, his shirt-tails hanging over his underpants, he started to walk as fast as he dared through the woods. Sunlight in the leaves made it look like a scene from a calendar. Great outcroppings of rock were covered with lichen. He was still breathing hard, and his whole body was aching. He thought he'd never been so tired. He got out a couple more pills and took them. As he walked, he checked the pockets of his jacket. The cars keys were still there; if need be, he'd drive to a neighbor's house. He thought of Norma coming to consciousness and discovering herself trussed in a belt and tied to a root with a pair of trousers. She wasn't a stupid woman. She'd figure it out and wait. So he hoped. Or she'd kill herself out of sheer bad temper.

He was in the grass of the overgrown field that led to the road, and through the bushes at the edge of the road, he could see his car. He tried to remember where they'd passed the nearest house, couldn't, but when he got to the road, he heard a car engine, and aware that he looked ridiculous, standing in his underpants, wet and ruinous, he summoned up his old police dignity, stepped into the middle of the road and held up his hand to stop whatever was coming. Well, Norma, he said to himself, when he saw the vehicle approaching, you were born with a horseshoe up your ass. It was two men in a four-by-four. The driver had a funny look on his face as Carman came up to the door, but before he'd heard half the story, he had his friend out opening the wire gate that led to the road through the woods, and in a minute, Carman was in the back seat, and they were bouncing through the woods to the place he'd left Norma.

Carman just sat leaning against a tree and watched them while they got her up. Even with the two of them, the vehicle, and chains, it wasn't easy, and she got bumped a little, but within fifteen minutes she was out. Carman just sat, exhausted. One man was tall and one was short and they moved around with a certain frantic efficiency. Carman watched as if it made sense, but he was helpless and a long way off. The men put her in the four-by-four, and the two of them were about to set off to drive her to the hospital in town. They assumed Carman was coming with them, that he'd want to stay with her, but Carman had rescued his trousers, what was left of them, and all he wanted was for them to drop him off at his car, even though he wasn't sure whether he could drive. He was no help to anyone now. The driver—his name was Larry or Harry or Garry—offered to drive Carman home after they got Norma seen to, but he refused. He'd had enough. When he saw them drive away, he opened the door to drive himself home but he was starting to shiver, and he didn't think he could drive yet, so he got in the back seat and curled up there, pulled a blanket over himself and waited for the shivering to go away. He wasn't sure that he shouldn't check himself into the hospital as well, but he wasn't going to do that. That would kill him for sure. His chest hurt, and he felt in his pocket for a pill, wondered if he'd taken too many. After a while, the shaking eased a little, and he fell asleep, and by the time he woke up, the afternoon sun bright in his eyes, he felt as if he could drive back to the cottage and get himself cleaned up, take his ration of pills and pour a good-sized shot of rye.

Norma tried to move in the narrow hospital bed, but the weight of the cast kept her still. She lay in the darkness of her room and watched as Doctor Life and Doctor Death went softly past along the hallway. She'd asked the nurses to leave the door open for the night, terrified of being trapped in here. About as mobile as a beached whale with this cast on and her back half useless. In the other bed, her roommate, a woman who'd fallen off a roof, snored softly. She hadn't explained to Norma how she got on the roof to begin with. Now and then Nurse Pain would go by in one direction, Nurse Grief in the other. A machine beeped, or an announcement would be heard on the hospital P.A. Once she had been told the code for a cardiac emergency. Code 99, was that it? The sudden drama beloved of television. Danger and resurrection. Most of the time Doctor Life and Doctor Death went about their slow business of postponement. Medicine was the science of postponement.

Norma's broken head ached, as did her deteriorated back and broken leg, but she wouldn't call for Nurse Pain and ask for something. Tomorrow she would be home and could take an occasional aspirin from her little stock of medicaments. Mostly her medicine cupboard was full of the soap and toiletries that Moira used to give her for Christmas and which she never used up. That and two cans of baked beans. She had no idea how the baked beans had got there. One day she looked, and there they were, and she couldn't bring herself to take them out. Surely baked beans could cure something.

Her last visit to The Vice-grip at her cottage, she'd taken a look in his medicine cabinet after using the toilet. He had all colors and shapes of prescription drugs. Must be in terrible shape. She didn't want him dying on her hands. She supposed she ought to feel gratitude to him for dragging her out of that hole, but it came hard. She'd never have fallen in if he hadn't made her so mad that she was blinded by irritation. Driving like a maniac, getting in a snit when she mentioned it, then trying to defeat her by walking so fast and whining about the bugs. No wonder his wife had died. Only way to get away from him. He'd been to see her this afternoon and offered to pick her up when she was released in the morning. She'd agreed to that though she didn't want to. What she should have done was get Aeldred to come for her in the truck. Set her up in the back of it in an old stuffed chair. Better than building up a debt of gratitude. Aeldred had given her the eye the day he'd come to get the stoves. Easier to deal with him, lazy and disreputable as he was. Tried to cheat her on the stoves, but she didn't let him.

She hadn't told Arthur she was in here. In fact there was no need for them to keep her once they'd bandaged her head and put a cast on her leg and probed and pinched a few places to make sure she was alive. They wanted her to stay for observation, but she didn't think anyone had observed much. Check vital signs, offer bad food, say good night. When she got home she'd write Arthur a letter and tell him about the adventure. Not that she could remember much. Falling, cold, being trussed up, The Vice-grip talking to her, then those two yahoos—Garry and Paul, why did she remember their names?—hauling her out, a lot of shouting and grinding of motors, chains. Attached a chain to her and just let the little truck drag her to the surface, was that it? Maybe not. It seemed to her that one of them was down the hole with her. By then she was aware she was soaking wet, and the cold went all the way through her bones. As they drove to town, they kept her wrapped in a blanket and Paul told jokes to encourage her. They were bad jokes. Country jokes.

Apparently she'd been underwater when Carman got hold of her. She couldn't remember any of that. Feet in the water maybe. A wonder she hadn't caught pneumonia, but apart from the bangs and bruises she was in working order. Doctor Life and Doctor Death passed by in white coats. What were they doing here in the middle of the night? Was someone dying? Steven had died. And Moira. Funny thing to be dead. It was her belief that anger would keep her going for some while yet. Rage will keep you forever young. Acting youthful too: she'd been performing the act of generation, though nothing would be generated, and a damn good thing too. It was too late for the dozen children now. She had what she was going to get.

If she ever got out of this cast and mobile she might be tempted to do it again, a pleasant thing, but she wouldn't have him around in the morning to hear her moans and groans, to see the laborious struggle to get her out of bed and standing. A little passing warmth was enough. A night act done in the night.

One of the nurses had got her clothes washed and dried so she'd have something to go home in. Something else to be grateful about. Norma had been as unctuous as she could manage. It was a kindness, but she preferred not to need kindnesses. Never need anything. Only possible if you were richer than she'd ever be.

One of the doctors passed the door on his soft silent shoes. Was it Doctor Life or Doctor Death? She wasn't sure she could tell them apart.

At ten o'clock, he drove up to the front of the hospital, and saw the nurse push the wheelchair through the automatic doors. Norma's leg in its heavy cast stuck out in front of the chair, and the bandage on her forehead, the black eye and bruising down one side of her face made her look like two people, one whole, one damaged. She was staring aggressively at the cars, but when he pulled up, she looked away. He got out and waved to the nurse who pushed the wheelchair over while he opened the passenger door.

"Stupid business," Norma said, "pushing me out here in a wheelchair like some kind of cripple."

"It's a hospital rule," the nurse said. "Once I put you in the car, you're on your own."

"Give Carman another chance to kill me. It was him knocked me down the mine shaft, you know. Terrible bad temper."

Carman ignored that. The nurse, who was a small woman, from the Philippines he would have guessed, looked at him as if assessing whether that might be true.

"You're Norma's husband," she said.

"He certainly is not," Norma said.

"A neighbor," Carman said.

"Tenant. On a temporary basis."

The nurse had Norma on her feet, and was about to help her into the car.

"I think the back seat would be better," she said. "More room for the cast."

"Yes," Norma said. "Make it that much harder for Carman to finish me off."

Carman closed the passenger door and opened the other one, and the two women got Norma in, sitting sideways, with the cast stretched across the seat. Norma gave a royal wave to the nurse who closed the door, smiled at Carman and pushed the wheelchair back into the building. Carman got into the driver's seat.

"Let's get the old girl out of here," Norma said.

Carman pulled out of the driveway and drove down to the lakeshore.

"Why are you going this way?"

"Because it's the way I want to go."

"It's the longest way."

"It's the way I want to go."

Norma leaned over so she could see herself in the rear-view mirror.

"What a mess," she said. "I look even worse than usual."

Two sailboats moved over the smooth water of the lake, the white curve of their sails outlined against the blue water and blue sky. Closer to shore, a figure in a wetsuit was skimming across the water on a sailboard.

"Are the customers lined up at the door?" she said.

"Weren't when I left this morning."

"No, I guess not."

The road turned away from the water, and the sailboats disappeared.

"I suppose I should thank you," Norma said. "For saving my life."

"You're welcome. But don't do it again."

"Why not? A bit of excitement. Adventure."

"It damned near killed me getting you out of that water."

"Such a fat woman."

"That's all right so long as I don't have to haul you out of any more holes."

"How did you do it?"

"I'm not sure I remember. Ask me after I've had a couple of drinks."

The car moved through traffic, going toward the highway that would take them back out into the country.

"You're going to have trouble with the stairs," he said. "With that cast on."

"I have trouble with the stairs without the cast."

"We can get you up there, but you'll never get back down."

"I suppose I could close the place."

"I'll come over and run the shop if you like. Sit in the rocking chair for a few hours. That's all you do, isn't it?"

"I think a lot. It's the thinking that's the hard part."

"You can do that upstairs. If anyone comes in, I can likely find something rude to say. It will be just the same as if you were there."

"I'm never rude to customers."

"You were rude to me."

"That's you. You looked like a murderer."

"Well, I'm not."

"Anyway, it's Labor Day next week."

"I thought I might stay on."

Norma looked at herself in the rear-view mirror again, made a face and slumped back in the seat.

"So you're going to be around for a while yet," she said.

"A while."

"What are you going to do when it gets cold?"

"I called Amy and arranged to sublet the other cottage for a few months. It's winterized."

"You did that?"

"Yes."

Norma said nothing. Then she made some noises as if she were talking, but not opening her mouth. Then silence. They drove through the last of the suburbs and into the countryside. The grass was dry, full of wildflowers. Carman felt a little dizzy and was having trouble concentrating on the road. He'd be glad when the trip was over.

"So you're going to spend the winter down there by the river."

"Looks like it."

"I expect you'll regret it."

"I might or I might not."

"Why are you staying?"

"Same reason I drove along the lakeshore. Because I want to."

"Damn willful man."

"Yes."

A NOTE ON THE TYPE

The text was set in 12 point Centaur with a leading of 16 points space. Originally designed by Bruce Rogers for the Metropolitan Museum in 1914, Centaur was released by Monotype in 1929. Modeled on letters cut by the fifteenth-century printer Nicolas Jenson, Centaur has a beauty of line and proportion that has been widely acclaimed since its release. The italic type, originally named Arrighi, was designed by Frederic Warde in 1925. He modeled his letters on those of Ludovico degli Arrighi, a Renaissance scribe whose lettering work is among the finest of the chancery cursives. Arrighi was produced by Monotype as the companion for Centaur in 1929.

Book composition by Jean Carbain
New York, New York

Printed and bound by in the U.S.A.